THE COMMUNIST COOKBOOK

SHARMISHTHA ROY CHOWDHURY

PENGUIN BOOKS

An imprint of Penguin Random House

PENGUIN BOOKS

USA | Canada | UK | Ireland | Australia
New Zealand | India | South Africa | China | Singapore

Penguin Books is part of the Penguin Random House group of companies
whose addresses can be found at global.penguinrandomhouse.com

Published by Penguin Random House India Pvt. Ltd
4th Floor, Capital Tower 1, MG Road,
Gurugram 122 002, Haryana, India

Penguin
Random House
India

First published by Penguin Books India 2013

ISBN 9780143415596

Typeset in Adobe Caslon Pro by SÜRYA, New Delhi

Printed at Repro India Limited

www.penguin.co.in

MIX
Paper from
responsible sources
FSC® C047271

This is a legitimate digitally printed version of the book and therefore might not
have certain extra finishing on the cover.

PENGUIN BOOKS

THE COMMUNIST COOKBOOK

Sharmishtha Roy Chowdhury teaches History at Emerson College, Boston. She lives in Connecticut. *The Communist Cookbook* is her first novel.

For Sunil and Mili,
who never tire of my army brat tales

ONE

When George could no longer stand the gloomy interior of the room, he walked out to observe the early-morning barracks scene unfolding in the square below. Through the lush bougainvillea, the sun's rays cast trellised shadows on the golden-milky liquor of his tea. Sipping the steaming liquid, he watched as below him squads of men formed up and jogged their way in dusty clouds to morning drill. 'Good luck, George!' some of his former mates shouted at the slim young man in pressed jungle greens. George smiled and waved his travel papers back at them, clasping the documents tightly. These were his papers to the train, and to the Officer Training School at Mhow in central India. If he passed the rigours of reading, writing and the physicals at the OTS, he would in some months' time be commissioned as Second-Lieutenant George Clark. Age twenty-five. Regiment unknown. Future unknown.

In the cool morning of a north Indian December, George found himself remarkably clear-headed. He was one of the lucky ones, out of the fifty or so enlisted men who had gone before the Selection Board in May to be put through various tests: physical fitness, psychological aptitude and so on. George had been one of the few deemed qualified to proceed for officer training at Mhow, a garrison town in the Central Provinces.

It was George's battlefield performance that had earned him a

Selection Board nomination from his Commanding Officer in Burma. In June 1943, he had been part of a long-range penetration patrol in northern Burma. His group had been part of a larger detachment that included a patrol group of the Seaforth Highlanders, a battle-hardened unit of Scotsmen. They had attacked a Japanese base and in the battle that followed, George had earned his citation by fighting hard, covering his men as they retreated and, above all, by refusing to leave behind the body of Rifleman Michael Briggs on the battlefield. For this act, George had been wounded, hospitalized in Calcutta, promoted to Sergeant, shortlisted for the officer's Selection Board, but in one of those inexplicable twists of military logic had then been posted, not back to Burma as he thought he might be but to a new unit in Pithampur, a small, princely state in the eastern Punjab.

Here, among the waving green wheat fields, a contingent of British forces—two battalions resting after the Burma campaign—helped the old Raja keep an uneasy peace between himself and his people, as Indian National Congress activists, Communist agitators, war reversals and economic turbulence chipped away at the prestige and the power of the British Empire. George had served his year with the 7/13 Yorkshire Rifles in Pithampur in aching boredom. There had been no spectacular uprisings here, just daily grumblings of rebellion that were squelched by the heavy hand of the Pithampur police. Still, the inactivity had had one positive effect: over time the nightmares about Burma had faded from George's consciousness, even the vivid recurring one about the skirmish that had earned him his OTS entry.

In the dream, George found himself inching forward with the others in his long-range penetration patrol, through the grass then into the jungle, leaves brushing against his sweating face. To his right, Rifleman Mike Briggs breathed heavily, so heavily that George hissed at him to be quieter. Morale in the group was average to low. Everyone knew that this operation was about to end. The Chindits campaign, dreamed up by Col. Orde Wingate, the eccentric British Army officer so beloved of the higher authorities and so despised by lower-level commanders, was supposed to harass the Japanese forces behind the enemy's lines. Although the Chindits succeeded in troubling the Japanese, by early 1943 most of the special units had retreated into India, and the campaign had boiled down to the occasional hit-and-run attack by local units that were able to organize it. George's section was one such group.

Around the advancing men, small animals scurried away. George saw a slim shape writhing away from them into the denser undergrowth. He slowed down immediately—if anyone was bitten by a snake then that was it for him, there were no evacuation procedures for long-range patrols in this war. All the men had painted their guns dull black, and sweat further darkened the jungle green of their uniforms. The straps of his pack were cutting into George's sweaty back—he knew that the skin was going to be raw and bloody at the end of this operation. Sweat was already dripping from his forehead into his eyes, and he had to keep wiping his eyelashes with a handkerchief. In front of him he saw the whiplash-thin figure of Sergeant Bill Bowers scratching his itching groin. Rashes, conjunctivitis, athlete's foot—these were the least of the illnesses that struck down soldiers in this theatre of war. Gentian violet was the only medicine prescribed by the Medical Officer attached to the unit.

George saw a slight rustle in the undergrowth and dropped to the ground. Instinctively, he pulled his grenade and lobbed it at the living, breathing body he knew was crawling through the shrubbery. The dream always ended at this point, leaving him sweating and yet cold in the humid dark.

The reality in Burma had been just as disorganized as his remembrance of those events. There had been a suppressed shout from the front of the line, somebody staggered into him, all followed by a semi-orderly taking up of positions amid a rattle of guns and whining of bullets that struck and ricocheted off trees, creating explosions of bark and leaves. George was half-smothered by the weight of Briggs whose foot was resting on his shoulder, throwing his aim off, and who, despite the cursing, would not move. Suddenly, the firing ceased.

'We have to get out of here,' was the general sentiment articulated by the sergeant leading the platoon, and as George tried to rise to his feet, he discovered that Briggs's weight on him was in fact that of a dead man. Michael Briggs, twenty-one years old, lay sprawled in the dense undergrowth, his lifeless face creased and frozen in the last pangs of pain. The sergeant cursed softly, and, as if on cue, a concerted attack by at least three Japanese machine guns began on their position. In the melée, everyone scattered, George dragging Briggs, then hauling his body across his shoulders in a fireman's lift and lurching in the general direction of safety. Briggs's dead hands dragged behind him and caught on tree branches and shrubs, slowing George down. A rushing noise filled his ears and his eyes dimmed from time to time. It was later that he discovered that he too had been shot three times in the leg, but in the mad scamper to safety the injury had not registered in his brain. Later, collapsing into the sergeant's arms he drifted into unconsciousness, dimly aware of being lifted onto a makeshift litter. There had been a lot of walking, he recalled, then a murmur of voices, some trucks, a field hospital and finally Calcutta, hot and humid but strangely restful after the madness of the jungle.

'A luv'ly sight, ain't it, mate?' The nasal East London accents of Nate Mason cut sharply into George's reverie. The composition of the 7/13 Yorkshire Rifles had been turned topsy-turvy by the war, so that the traditionally North-Eastern English unit now had men from all over the country to make up any which way for manpower shortage. Nate, the Londoner who had never set eyes on the rolling hills of Yorkshire for which his unit was named, grinned down at his barracks-mates all booted up and being led away by snarling NCOs. Now the East London man shook George's hand for the last time and added as he walked away. 'And the RSM wants to see you double quick, Clark.' George had never been 'Nobbie' or 'Nobs' to any of his fellow soldiers.

George raced down the stairs, at the foot of which Regimental Sergeant-Major Tom Barrett waited. You did not keep an RSM waiting, even if you were soon going to be several notches above him in the hierarchy. RSM Barrett—'Sir' to all cowering recruits—was a soldier of the old school, the most feared person in the battalion after the Colonel. George stiffened to attention in front of the older man.

'All ready then, are you, son?' said the RSM, breaking the solemnity of the moment with a grin. Before George could respond, the RSM added quickly, 'Captain Keeler wants a word with you afore you leave.' The formal way he said those words made George remember Watsby and the imperious Miss Todd who would enter Alice's kitchen to order the household meals. But Alice was far away and the dusty Pithampur barracks were not Richford House.

'Yes, sir.' George saluted the old tyrant. The RSM, all six feet of crustiness, turned away and moved on in search of his next victim. George unlocked his bicycle and rode towards the officers' quarters. So many things to think about on this, his last day as a soldier in the seventh battalion of His Majesty's Own 13 Yorkshire Rifles.

If the war had not broken out, George reflected, he and Alice would by now have been married. He would have taken her away from her endless series of indifferent jobs as live-in cook at various London and country houses. The two of them would have made their house in Watsby, Buckinghamshire, where he would be an eminent veterinary surgeon. Their first home would be ... At this point George's daydream usually broke into shards of uncertainty.

First, he would have to tackle the problem of veterinary college. It would have to be St John's in faraway Edinburgh, the only place that his father could afford. Old Mr Clark was a respected farmer in Watsby, but not one of the wealthiest. Then, George would have to cram like hell to get through the entrance exam. And there was, of course, the whole age business. With the Red Army chasing the Germans out of Eastern Europe, it was clear that the war was at last going the Allies' way in Europe but who knew when demobilization would actually happen? Would George be too old for such a demanding programme of studies? Could he hold out on a student stipend, while his classmates in the reserves settled quicker, made homes and drew grander pay? And then there was Alice, with her laugh and her love of gazing into shop windows. Would she like the country life?

For, Alice was a London girl with a love of the streets and sounds of the city. When George had met her, she was a cook at Richford House, the country seat of Sir Charles Darrow who had made his money clothing the unfortunate draftees of the

First War, many of whom still lay mouldering in the fields of northern France and Belgium. George often visited Richford House with old Mr Farthers, the local veterinarian, as he dogged his footsteps, hoping to learn some skills through an unofficial apprenticeship. Coming out of Richford House's slippery stables one cold spring morning, where he and Mr Farthers had battled unsuccessfully to save a colic-stricken horse, George had walked, sweaty and dirty, to wash at the tap behind the kitchen. The ice-cold of the water matched his mood, despondent at the loss of the horse, a fine, dark thoroughbred that now lay still on the wet stable hay.

'Hullo!' A pretty, dark-haired girl looked at him from the kitchen doorway. 'I was just sending Agnes out with the pail of hot water.'

'Thank you, miss.' He smiled tiredly at her. She seemed too young to be the cook, but the starched white apron gave her away. That and her unmistakable air of authority over Agnes, the scullery maid, who trotted out and placed the bucket of hot water near him. He scooped some into his palms and felt sensation return to his aching arms. The tall girl had disappeared, but through the half-open door, the aroma of eggs and sausage drifted in the sharp air.

Farthers, the chief veterinary surgeon, walked up at this time but declined the cook's offer of tea and breakfast. 'I'm heading back to the office, George,' he said, his face creased with disappointment. 'I'll telephone Sir Charles from there. You can stay and have some breakfast.'

So, Agnes seated George at the large kitchen table. He looked around at the big flagstoned country kitchen with its two big fireplaces and two stoves. Around the forbidding old stove, there hung a gleaming wreath of copper pots and pans. There was another newer gas stove and around this the tall cook, introduced to him only as Mrs Robbins, darted, throwing sausages into frying pans and yelling at Agnes to fetch various things.

'It's good of you to give me breakfast,' said George, appreciating how hard-pressed for time she was. He was not about to give up the invitation, though. The morning was still too cold and he had worked hard on an empty stomach.

'Oh, nah,' she said, not rudely, but in a friendly way. 'Would you like tea?'

'I would love some,' he said gratefully.

She placed a mug in front of him, following it up with a steaming plate of eggs, mushrooms, haddock and grilled tomatoes. Mrs Robbins winked. 'It's what Sir Charles will eat soon. So you can't say it's not good enough.'

The next time he met Alice was in front of the depressing little shop in the village that sold, it seemed, everything. There were dresses and shoes, gloves and hats, and scissors and cotton wool. As George came up behind her, she smiled at his reflection in the window.

'Afternoon, Mrs Robbins.'

'It's Alice,' she said. 'And I am Miss Robbins, but everyone in the kitchen calls me "Mrs". Don't ask me why. Must be a country thing.'

She accepted his invitation into the little tea shop nearby where the elderly Mrs Maple looked disapprovingly at this breach of class and social protocol. George was the son of old Mr Clark, upright yeoman farmer, owner of a fairly large farm with several cottages on it, and deserved better than a mere cook, even if Alice was Sir Charles's cook, up at Richford House.

'Old cow,' Alice muttered as Mrs Maple banged down a plate of cream buns and plum cake on the table, then clattered away, her stooped back conveying all the disapproval she could muster. Then the two of them set upon the sweets, talking and eating at the same time.

'Ah, but this is just a bit of fun for me, see,' she said as George helped her into her coat an hour later. 'I'm only here because my cousin Becky, Sir Charles's cook, is having a baby and I'm helping her out. She'll be back in July, she says.' She invited him to drop in any time at the kitchen for tea.

'Won't Sir Charles mind?'

'No. He's hardly ever here and if he doesn't see it, he can't mind, can he? But that fool, Barton—the butler—sometimes gets all snippy when my friends come calling. He and Ma Todd—she's the housekeeper—they should've run a galley ship, they should. Work us like slaves, they do. "Mrs Robbins— there's too much salt in the sauce today," Mrs Robbins—the trifle feels too heavy."' Alice's mimicking of Mrs Todd's affected posh accent was spot on. They both laughed, which made Mrs Maple behind the counter scowl even more.

George returned to Alice's kitchen two days later at teatime. And went there every day he could spare thereafter. War was in the air, though, in those warm, summer months. In November George's visits to Richford House ended abruptly when he was called up.

Cycling through the cantonment grounds in Pithampur, George could see that there was change afoot. It was time, yet again, to paint, clean and scrub, to keep the soldiers busy so that they didn't get into trouble. The whitewashed buildings of the officers' houses were being painted. Behind the tall walls of the Commanding Officer's house, George could see the heads of a squad of men in vests and khaki shorts, carrying ladders and paint brushes. The CO whose house was being repainted was a grand and awe-inspiring figure, always seen crisply attired in olive green and dazzling with silver and gold medals. In a battalion test, young private Ernie, semi-literate and starving until the war had drawn him into the army, had put the CO's name down in response to the question, 'Who is Great Britain's Prime Minister?'

Taking a sharp left turn around the CO's house, George raced down to the large roundabout in the middle of which was set flowering bushes, and behind the bushes, most incongruously, the Officers' Club. Nobody knew why it had been built in the middle like that. Legend had it that when the current Pithampur ruler's grandfather was forced to accept a British supervisor's command over his political and military affairs, he decided to get back at the imperial class with this piece of architecture. Officers who wished to enter the club had to cross the road in the middle of this roundabout, putting their lives at risk in the face of any oncoming horse squadron, or nowadays, motorcars and motorcycles.

North of the club, and directly behind the CO's house, seven bungalows set one behind the other, marked the beginning of the Officer's Quarters. George stiffened and straightened his back at various officers, on their way to drill. Like their men, they wore shorts, but their half-sleeved shirts gave away their higher status. That and of course, their nonchalant gait, the carelessly confident stride of authority.

Captain Edward Keeler, the battalion adjutant, lived in a warm, yellow-painted house. The Keelers' garden was full of flowers; it was winter, the season of particular abundance in South Asia.

'George, George!' Nigel, Captain Keeler's seven-year-old son came rushing out at him, bursting with energy. He was one of the lucky children, allowed to be with his father, as wartime travel restrictions had gradually eased. He was followed by his mother, Nancy, who nodded at George in reply to his greeting. Her thin mouth had set itself in a permanent oval of disapproval. Out of this pinched circle came only sharp little phrases, almost always beginning with 'Don't'. Not that Edward Keeler—'Daft Teddy' in the men's private conversation in the barracks—was personable, either. He followed his wife and son out onto the veranda and scowled at George.

'Ah, Clark!' Daft Teddy's Sandhurst drawl always grated on George's nerves. 'So, you're off to the OCTU, eh? What time do you leave?'

'The truck to Ambala leaves at four, sir.' Ambala was the rail junction for several lines on the northern railway, and was a two-hour drive from Pithampur. Passing through Ambala's crowded town and railway station was almost de rigueur for any armed forces personnel travelling in north India.

'Well, then look here, would you mind seeing Miss Sunderland before you leave? She was asking about you—something about recipes?

George blushed. 'Yes, sir.'

The recipes had started off as a gift for Alice the first Christmas of his mobilization, when he had been billeted in a large barracks near London, originally belonging to the East Surrey Regiment. Here, during the high noon of the Phoney War from 1939–1940—when the Germans would not attack, and neither would the French and the British—the camp's French-trained chef, Ned Allen, mobilized against his will from a smart London restaurant, had turned the shabby barracks kitchen into a culinary temple. No amount of turn-outs at the crack of a winter dawn, no amount of washing trestle tables in cold water, no amount of lung-bursting runs around the park, could dent the cheer in Alpha Squadron's new recruits. There was Ned and his warm brick-lined cookhouse to come back to.

His first morning as conscript had been the worst for George. 'Gaddup! Gaddup! Gaddup!' a monster shrieked in his ear. It was dark and the Sergeant's silhouette in the doorway did indeed look monstrous and primitive, blocking whatever light there was with his menacing, lumpy body. All around George the barracks room came to wailing, groaning life. Shivering, the young recruits were led away to wash and clean and dress up for their morning physical training. Two hours later, they returned, dazed and trembling with exhaustion.

'Oh, Sarge!' Fat Harry wailed, his big belly wobbling in anguish. 'I'm going to die! Oh yes, I am!'

'Sharrup!' the Sergeant silenced him with the wave of a huge finger. The same finger indicated to them the general direction of breakfast. 'Half-hour, no more, got it?'

Down they went, all twenty-five of them, not a man over twenty-one, to the other side of the stadium and into a long, warmly-lit room. Heaven must surely be this feeling, thought George as his tired lungs grasped gratefully at the wondrous aroma of the warm, peaceful room. The fragrant silence of Ned's kitchen filtered out the voices of noisy, shouting strangers and the smell of their sweat. In the room, the squad now moved forward eagerly, clutching their enamelled plates and mugs, drawn irresistibly to the table at the end where Ned smiled his large benevolent smile at the newcomers. George could scarcely believe his eyes as Ned and his three assistants heaped coddled egg, sardines, kedgeree and toast on his plate and filled up his mug with strong, sweet tea.

'This ain't 'alf bad,' breathed Alf Miller joyfully as he launched into his meal. Alf slept on the bed next to George, and the two had struck up a guarded, whispered friendship in the dark, after the lights had been turned out.

The two men got to know Ned even better when, after the first month, they were put on kitchen duty. This chore, usually despised by others and therefore the object of much avoidance, came as an unexpected boon to Alf and George, as Ned's kitchen was no drudge's nightmare, but rather a refuge from the jostling, sweaty cacophony of army training. Ned, tall and blond with a slow, wide smile, began his days early. An insomniac, he rose eagerly each morning at four, to start cutting and peeling and chopping pounds of onions, potatoes, turnips and carrots. His two assistants came in at five to help him light the huge stove in the kitchen. As they stumbled in sleepily, Ned greeted them with big mugs of coffee—he never drank tea—and piles of buttered toast. "'This is as good as heaven,'" George wrote to his younger brother, Tim, who read out his letters to their mother. "'Today, Alf and I ate fried fish, lamb stew and fruit salad after the men had had their bangers and mash. Ned tells me that his friend is trying to sell a new style of modern furniture to the Langham Hotel, but they aren't going for it.'"

'He writes different now,' observed his mother, darning socks by the fire. 'And it's always about food. Did I starve him then? And what's wrong with our cooking, eh?'

When George wrote to Alice with pretty much the same news, he received a prompt demand for recipes.

'I won't be able to go to those fancy French cooking schools,' she wrote. 'So, you have to send me the recipes so I can teach myself. Can you believe that I am still here? Becky says that she isn't coming back after all—the baby is keeping her that busy. And old Ma Todd wants me to stay till they find someone else.

It's taking them a long time, I can tell you that. Everybody's busy with the war.' That Christmas, he had Tomkins, the Commandant's clerk type out forty recipes on the special paper he bought at Marks and Spencer. He bound them in green and red ribbon and gave them to Alice, on Christmas Eve. He couldn't decide which was better—her whoop of delight, or her warm kiss.

Alice left Richford House shortly after George was ordered to India. 'Well, you have to get me some recipes of how they cook out there in India,' she told him firmly after crying at the news. 'That will give you something to write to me about.' At a later point in the war, she wrote to let George know that she had found employment with a famous Hollywood star, Richard Clarke, of English origin, in London for the war, living in Mayfair with his very American film-star wife. They had been impressed with her cooking during a brief stay at Richford House and had hired her when she left Sir Charles Darrow's employment. She requested George to send her interesting recipes that would make her skills valuable to her new employers. 'Otherwise, it will be off to the wretched NAAFI canteen for me, or something miserable like that,' said Alice, referring to the canteens run by the navy, army and air force institutes, where enlisted men bought their refreshments. Too old to be drafted, Richard Clarke had volunteered his skills to entertain soldiers and officers outward-bound to the major theatres of war.

In the battlefields of the east, George had had little time to act on his culinary promise to Alice. His year in Pithampur, though, opened a surprising gateway into Indian kitchens through his contact with Miss Deborah Sunderland. She, unmarried and fifty-ish, lived in the crowded city—the native part—of Pithampur. This was out of bounds for the British contingent except with permission which was often refused. When the Congress agitation spread to Pithampur in 1942, however, and the local reformist Sikhs began to demonstrate against the autocratic old Raja, the then resident British Commanding Officer had begun to send over to her place three or four soldiers weekly to clip her hedges and mow her lawn, keeping an eye on her. Two years later, George's CO simply continued the tradition. Miss Sunderland always wrote polite notes every Christmas to the CO, thanking him for the men's work and followed this up with a crate of oranges from her little orchard to be distributed in the barracks.

George was chosen for this weekly task of visiting Deborah Sunderland, to the indifference of his barracks-mates, all of whom said that they would rather go out of their minds with boredom or attend cycle parades in the still summer of north India than clip hedges for a middle-aged English lady. So, every Friday, George, Nate Mason and Mike Knowles got onto their bicycles, their revolvers in their holsters, and rode past the silent sentry at the northern gate of the cantonment. A small, smelly pond on the left and a huge open ground on the right marked the beginning of the civilian section of town.

The three men were always met at the cantonment gate by a silent white-turbaned Sikh, all intense eyes and lean face. Even though his services were not required after the first few times, he still showed up each week to lead the three soldiers to Miss Sunderland's home. On that first excursion, on a hot June afternoon, George was all eyes for the two-storey houses that almost choked off the narrow streets with their shadows. Sometimes, he saw an inner courtyard through the occasional open door. In these courtyards there appeared to be nothing more remarkable than bronze pots and pans and sometimes a sleeping goat. There were some shops open, but in these too the shopkeepers dozed on thin white sheets spread on the stone floors. They seemed to sell mainly cloth and oil and spices, all the things that farmers could not produce for themselves. Wherever the people were awake, they came out to stare at them, never having seen Englishmen up close. What struck George was the silence of the whole business, as people appeared, still in a daze after the afternoon sleep, to watch the unusual business of three cursing, sweating British soldiers making their way through Pithampur.

In this way, twenty-five minutes later, the three soldiers arrived at Deborah Sunderland's house in a little alley. An old man in a white tunic and loose trousers opened the small door set into the high wall. George felt like he was entering a fortress, so high was the wall.

Inside, a peaceful garden sloped up sharply to a small, white house. The garden had an abundance of mango and blackberry trees and a wild overgrowth of flowering shrubs. At the entrance to the house, an Ashoka tree coloured the place green with its long-fingered leaves. The whole effect was cool and hot at the same time, and all the three soldiers were struck silent at the beauty of the place. A middle-aged woman opened the door and beamed at them from behind horn-rimmed glasses. Her dark blonde hair was done up in a bun and she wore a cool, printed cotton dress with some lace at the collar and the sleeves.

'Good afternoon!' she smiled. 'Do come in.'

As they sat, rustling and shuffling, in her cool drawing room, full of pictures of relatives and friends, and with an ancient stove that was redundant in the summer heat, Miss Sunderland went off to get refreshments. Among the Victorian clutter, a large framed picture of a strikingly beautiful girl in the belle époque fashion of Paris, cast a gentle glow over the room. Miss Sunderland returned with a tray piled high with rock cakes, potato scones, jam and sandwiches. The old gatekeeper, who also seemed to be the odd-job man, shuffled in with a large pot of tea, some cups and a plate of cone-shaped patties. George bit into one and was transported into a world of flavour he had never experienced. By their expressions, he could see that his two mates felt the same.

'Samosas,' explained Miss Sunderland. 'Potato and spices stuffed in a pastry case and fried. The green herb there is coriander or Chinese parsley.' George asked for paper and pen, and wrote the recipe down carefully, to the amusement of his companions. But Miss Sunderland nodded when he explained about Alice. 'I once used to be a great collector of recipes, too. For myself, though.' After that, she wrote out the recipes of everything she offered the men and gave it to George at the end of each visit. Her handwriting was neat and round and Edwardian. He in turn posted it to Alice to add to her collection.

The three young soldiers spent all their allotted time, sipping tea, eating and chatting with Miss Sunderland. She twinkled at them from behind the teapot and waved away their suggestion that they should clip her trees or hedges. 'Oh, no, the garden is just fine, thank you, boys. Although, I suppose you could trim some branches, just to please the Colonel. Such a nice man. A scone, Mr Knowles?'

'How did you come to Pithampur, Miss Sunderland?' George asked one day, rather daringly. It was their fourth visit and they had just feasted on a variety of cakes and sandwiches. The high point of the meal this time had been a patty with potato and fish filling, flavoured with cumin and green chillies.

Nate and Mike looked at George sharply, silently scolding

him for his improper query. But Deborah just smiled at him and told them that she had arrived in Pithampur nearly two decades ago and had stayed on. Deborah pointed out the picture that George had admired on their first visit. 'That was I,' she said quietly and suddenly; in a great coalescing of observation, George saw that the high cheekbones of the young girl were indeed Deborah's and the eyes, though lined, still had the same light. Clearly, she had been a beauty in her youth. But Deborah Sunderland's portrait gave no hint of the story of her dramatic past.

TWO

What Deborah Sunderland did not tell the young soldiers was that it had been autumn, cold and bracing, in 1908 when she had boarded the *SS Clarion* in Liverpool with her mother, headed for Bombay. Her father, Philip Sunderland, an old India hand, held the exalted but mysterious position of Political Agent, with a special mission to the kingdom of Bhutan. Nearly eighteen, Deborah was excited to be out of England. The following year, she and her mother would return to London, where her aunt Nancy was to arrange a debut of sorts. 'And until you return, my dear,' Nancy had confided to Elizabeth Sunderland, her youngest and well-beloved sister, 'consider this year as an opportunity—the possibilities of India. So many fine young men.'

Deborah's rare and delicate beauty had already caught the eye of numerous young men of good standing, some of uncertain means but romantic inclinations, and several overweight, rich old widowers. But Elizabeth wanted a dashing army officer for her Debbie, preferably one in the Guards, and with a fair amount of private money tucked away in the family estate. So far, their residence in quiet Weatherby, in the depths of Wiltshire, had brought few such prizes to their doorstep. So, Elizabeth had decided that if young men were not to come to her, then she would have to go find them for her Debbie, so beautiful and so eminently suitable for more than what the village vicar and his blushing poverty could offer. She and Deborah spent six months in London, a moderate allowance from her brother helping nicely to make up for what Philip's modest remittances were unable to cover.

But, Deborah stubbornly refused to fall in love with any of the young men who visited her cousin Hettie. Elizabeth then decided to take the drastic step of spending a year with Philip in India. He was elated at the suggestion that Elizabeth and Deborah join him after Christmas, and immediately set about arranging matters. He asked for and received a temporary posting to Calcutta. Here, he employed a small army of servants and set them to cleaning a large house that he had found in the vicinity of Alipore, a posh locality in the European part of town. Everything seemed set for an idyllic family life for the Sunderlands. Neither Philip nor Elizabeth Sunderland, however, had counted on scandal.

When the *SS Clarion* steamed into Bombay harbour in early December, her stately anterooms reeked of shame. Young Miss Sunderland, so beautiful, so divinely English in her rose-printed tea dresses and dainty shoes, was the talk of the ship's society and the absolute despair of her mother. In Alexandria, she had declared her intention before at least five people of eloping to America with Neville Shaw, the brooding young actor who was part of the vaudeville troupe on board. The couple had been spotted walking the deck, Deborah completely unchaperoned by her desperately outwitted mama. They had also been caught kissing behind the curtained partition that separated the haves from the have-nots, the upper and the lower decks. In the privacy of her cabin, Elizabeth Sunderland lay down as often as she could, stunned by the wantonness of her daughter. 'Oh, my dear! The utter depravity of the boy!' she confessed tearfully to plump Mrs Adams who promptly conveyed this to a shocked and delighted bridge foursome.

Deborah remained defiantly in love until the second last day of the voyage. That afternoon she had stepped eagerly through the forbidden door to the steerage, her green dress fluttering in the Arabian Sea breeze, a few minutes early for her rendezvous with Neville. From the darkened interior, she heard him laugh. But this laugh had a dreadful, coarse sneer about it, and the words that followed stunned her into silence.

'That's all right, mate. Adie's the one for me. Debbie's posh, but I don't much care for her, see? I've seen enough of her, if you know what I mean.' Coarse guffaws followed this insinuation. Neville's breath was sharp and audible as Deborah froze in the doorway. She stepped back into the glare of sunlight and went away without a word. In the anteroom that evening she danced as if her life depended on it with old Colonel Masters, half-deaf, ancient and therefore the only man who would agree to be her partner. Neville sent her a note through one of the younger stewards, which she tore and threw away without a second glance. At half-past three the next day, the ship docked in Bombay.

Her father waited on the dock, his kindly face creased with happiness and a secret anxiety. When, at last, his wife and daughter descended the gangway, he waved and went forward eagerly. Betty and Debbie, his world was complete. But Elizabeth looked tired and Debbie curiously frozen. His wife's embrace was glad, almost fervent; his daughter's lips on his cheek were cold, like the tone of her voice.

'Debbie, child . . .' His words trailed off in embarrassment. He was not generally effusive.

Elizabeth was beginning to look tired again. Hailing a porter,

Philip hurried his little family away to the nearest Inspection Bungalow in an enclosed carriage, both his women silent. Debbie looked out and saw Bombay slip by, streets full of noisy people, women clothed in jewel-like colours that she had never imagined existed. This kaleidoscopic world vanished abruptly the minute they turned into the British quarters. The long driveway of the Inspection Bungalow deposited them at a pretty whitewashed bungalow, built to look out over the Arabian Sea.

The sea glinted with a steely light not unlike her father's eyes when Elizabeth confessed to him in exhausted little sobs the high drama of their passage. In Bombay, they were invited to a few homes, and everywhere, Philip Sunderland saw to it that Debbie came into contact with no men of undesirable background. Unlike those of dukes and earls, the Sunderland name was not resilient or secure enough to withstand scandal. Deborah must make her selection of mates from among her social equals or higher.

Deborah noticed her father's careful moves, but did not object. She was really quite cross with Neville. He had been so much fun but now here she was, more or less a prisoner, because it had turned out so badly with him. It was as if there were two people within her: one watching the other go through the tedium of visits to English families resident in Bombay; dressing in a yellow silk gown for the Governor's reception; sipping tea with her mother on the porch; while the other Deborah felt her senses stir and rise with the aromatic odours from the kitchens, the greasy ones from the faraway hellhole in the Inspection Bungalow, the spicy ones from the workers' quarters behind the stables, the smoked ones from the gardeners' lunch.

At the Parkers' tea, one afternoon, she asked for the recipe of the delicious fried dumpling. Mrs Parker looked at her worriedly, as if the iced cake she had served might have caused this strange insanity.

'I don't know, my dear, the *khansamah* did it. They are rather good, aren't they?' To the consternation of all present, Deborah asked for a piece of paper to note down the recipe from the aged khansamah, the old Muslim cook who could hardly see for glaucoma. The cook could not be called into the dainty drawing room, so he and Deborah were both sent into the little room off the hall, where, with the help of young Emily Parker's good-humoured translation, the recipe found its way into Deborah's notebook.

'It's all too dreadful, Philip,' Elizabeth sobbed to her husband later that night. 'She has changed so much before my eyes in just these last few months. She seems so bored with all that I thought she might find so exciting—the dances, the picnics, the parties.' Philip's response was another carefully crafted political move. The three of them would leave in two weeks' time for Calcutta and then, in May, would go up north to the hills, maybe even to Bhutan, the mountain kingdom to the north-east of India. At the end of the year, all three would head back to England for his long leave, this sordid year forgotten.

Deborah Sunderland's culinary marvels were to one day delight three young soldiers in Pithampur, many years later. After the third month of her acquaintanceship with them, she would begin to provide them high tea. Deborah remembered the first time Nate Mason sighed audibly in contentment at the lamb pot roast that appeared, garnished with fried rings of onions. The meat was tender and exquisitely flavoured. A cool mint and yogurt sauce complemented it perfectly. It became George's favourite lamb dish as well. And it was in the unlikely kitchens of the Inspection Bungalow at Bombay that this dish was born.

The two weeks in December 1908 before the Sunderland family left for Calcutta were very trying ones for Elizabeth Sunderland. She could only watch as Debbie demanded to meet the cook in the evenings and to go over his recipes. One of the Bombay sub-division clerks attached temporarily to Philip's service provided uneven translation services. One day, Debbie and the cook surprised them with a leg of lamb, roasted, not boiled, fragrant with cumin and coriander, and garnished with onion rings and coriander leaves. The steamed pudding that followed had raisins and was coloured orange with saffron. At the back, the servants made their meal off the leftovers, delighted to be able to eat more than dull, boiled mutton.

A three-day train ride across dusty central India deposited the Sunderlands, bone-tired and grouchy, in Calcutta. Deborah could hardly believe her eyes at the multitudes that thronged the station. She also noticed that Philip Sunderland was already getting into his stride, waving briskly at porters, skinny fellows who never appeared to collapse under the weight of the boxes they carried. Philip's assistant, Martin Rogers, had hired a coach for the Sunderlands and another for the vast amount of trunks and boxes that Elizabeth had insisted upon bringing from England.

As they rattled along through Calcutta, Debbie tried to make sense of the world around her. Here, the roads were narrow and long and the people in the streets seemed nervous and watchful. She remarked on this, and Martin Rogers replied with a grim nod.

'Yes, there's trouble brewing. Ever since Bengal was divided in 1905, we have had nothing but trouble. Even though

Congress—the main nationalist party—has split between its moderate and extremist factions, the young men in Bengal are turning to revolutionary violence.'

'There's no rest,' Philip Sunderland chimed in, looking worn under the burden of both his personal and official cares. 'You try to manage the Turks in the Balkans and then suddenly, it's the Bengalis in India. But not to worry, my dear,' he added hurriedly, noticing his wife's alarmed look, 'our house is secure against the ruffians. You'll never get to see a single one, I promise you.'

And, indeed, all the four months that they stayed in Calcutta, Deborah never came across any Indians except the servants. She spent her time running the house and organizing the meals with her mother. To Elizabeth's alarmed bewilderment, Deborah moved the cook out of the bawarchikhana, a mysterious sooty cavern situated some distance away from the main house, and into the pantry inside the house. Rafi, the cook, was not pleased with the new arrangements. In the faraway bawarchikhana, Rafi had presided like a grimy conductor over an orchestra of black coal stoves that belched soot and smoke into the Calcutta air. Under the new dispensation, Rafi presented himself in the reading room each morning around nine. By this time, Philip had been dispatched to office, his stomach tight with breakfast, the only meal that Rafi was allowed to prepare in the bawarchikhana. In his desperate attempts to convince the family of the superior ways of the bawarchikhana, Rafi's breakfasts began to take on dreamlike qualities—toast, eggs, even the hated bacon (which one of the non-Muslim boys prepared) accompanied with kedgeree, fried betki fish, aludum and greenpea kachhoris. Then, one of Philip's many office clerks would come over to help Deborah order the day's meal, translating blushingly from English into Bengali for Rafi. In a jumbled mixture of Bengali and English, the day's menu was decided.

'Ah, but you should not put cloves in the end, ma'am, you should put it in the beginning,' he said one day.

'Why not?' Deborah asked. She vaguely knew that the boy's name started with an H. The cook scowled at the interloper who seemed to double his workload with every gibberish-sounding English word.

'This I have heard my mother instruct my wife,' said the boy, hesitantly.

At this point, the bearer brought a note on a tray to Elizabeth. She read it. 'Your father wants Hrishikeshbabu back at the office immediately.' She stumbled over the long name.

'If it is not too inconvenient, Hrishikeshbabu,' said Deborah. 'From time to time, I would like you to translate some of your mother's and wife's recipes for me.' The young clerk smiled and promised.

Hrishikeshbabu spent mornings translating for Deborah, bringing carefully written recipes from his mother and wife for the young girl. Deborah and young Mrs Hrishikesh (she never did find out their family name) struck up an indirect and strictly culinary relationship that lasted until the Sunderlands left Calcutta. Over a few weeks, Elizabeth was conscious of a change in the servants' attitudes. It seemed that the more un-memsahib-like interest that Deborah took in the preparation of the meals, the more respect she acquired in the domestics' eyes. Casting aside his initial resentment at Deborah's intrusion into his domain, Rafi revealed a hitherto-undisplayed desire to please the Sunderland palate. Through Hrishikeshbabu's translations, he suggested, he vetoed, and he presented new recipes.

The Sunderland dinner party in January had a culinary success beyond Philip's and Elizabeth's wildest expectations. 'This chicken is so-o delicious! I must have a second helping,' cooed silly Mrs Evans, delving deep into a golden, luscious dish. Pieces of tender chicken floated in a sauce full of rings of caramelized onions, thickened with almond paste and garnished with finely chopped mint leaves. Happy guests nodded and smiled at each other over mushroom and spinach soufflé seasoned delicately with mace; collars of lamb stuffed with cottage cheese and green peppers; fish baked in a rich yogurt sauce that shocked people's taste buds into life with its subtle flavours of cloves and cinnamon; carrots and peas served plain to balance all the other dishes; and potatoes, steamed in a rich broth of chicken stock, parsley and other herbs. Earlier, they had all exclaimed over the hors d'oeuvres, thick almond soup, celery soup and fried hilsa fillets, accompanied by naan bread, cut into dainty squares, topped with wilted cucumber rounds and a spot of Bengali mustard sauce, a wicked but delicious parody of an English teatime classic.

Deborah had had to fight tooth and nail with her mother to gain control over the kitchen and to allow the cook to prepare these daring meals for their very English guests. 'They all seemed to like it, Mother,' she told her mother after each soirée had concluded. Friends and neighbours invited them over to their homes almost constantly in the next few months. Invited back, they were treated to more of Deborah's innovations.

'I wish I had your khansamah, Mrs Sunderland,' sighed Penelope Harris one day, the visiting wife of a tea estate manager, biting contentedly into a large cheese puff on a morning visit. No ordinary cheese, this home-made paneer was seasoned with fresh basil. If only she knew, thought Elizabeth bitterly, that my only khan-whatever is my daughter!

The days were already misting over with heat, a prelude to the summer. Meals were getting lighter and less complicated. Clear soups and light fish entrées, followed by fruit for dessert.

'We will go up to the hills in May,' Philip announced a little later in the week. 'I need to visit Bhutan again.' His wife frowned; she was getting used to Calcutta and English society here, although it was so much more uptight than London and so less forgiving of lapses in social manners. She was determined to go home with Debbie in a few months. But she cheered up when Philip suggested that she prepare a large, going-away party.

Deborah, too, looked forward to the hills. She had heard much about them, especially from young Hugh Trevers, subaltern with a battalion of the Devonshire Rifles, shortly to be sent to Baluchistan. In Deborah's cool, reserved company, Hugh Trevers found himself talking of Darjeeling and the little kingdom of Bhutan. He described the Buddhist monasteries perched on the bleak Himalayan hillsides, their prayer flags waving in the cold mountain breezes, and he told her about the Tibetans who travelled down from Lhasa to sell their colourful wares in the street below the Mall in Darjeeling. When Deborah asked him to describe the food, Hugh sat up.

'I don't really know,' he said, puzzled. 'I've never eaten any Tibetan food.'

'What a pity!' she replied. 'It sounds so interesting.'

At the end of May, a full month after the European quarter in Calcutta had emptied itself of women, children and high officials, the Sunderlands travelled north to Darjeeling. In the days before they left, time flew by in a whirl of packing, gowns, hats, flannel sheets, and sturdy shoes for walking in the hills. At the station, Martin Rogers, the assistant, waited patiently, and handed the women into the carriage with a deftness born of long practice with such tasks. Then, the train pulled away as the sky turned golden red and the grimy city skyline yielded to the lush green of the countryside. Deborah marvelled at the new India that spread itself before her eyes. Here, there were no smelly, grey streets, no shouting merchants or shopkeepers, no soot-blackened slums. Here, in the clean, rain-washed fields she saw wiry men and women driving ox-drawn ploughs around their lands, their simple huts appearing like dots on the horizon. Small children, sometimes stark naked, cheered as the train passed. Their mothers spread brightly coloured cloth on the edges of little ponds, ringed by coconut trees. But the people looked extremely poor.

'Why are they so poor, Papa?'

Philip shook his head. Some ten years ago, on the urging of one of his colleagues—whom Philip suspected of harbouring Liberal sympathies—he had read the tract written by the venerable old Congressman, Dadabhai Naoroji, on how British rule itself was responsible for the 'Drain of Wealth', the process by which India was impoverished to Britain's advantage. Philip could not argue with the numbers presented by Naoroji but he had rejected indignantly there and then the idea that he or his colleagues were the root of the problem. Why, if we left, he argued, this whole place would just fall apart. It was only the Crown—Victoria still reigned at the time—and the British administrators who could keep peace among the mess of sects and races that was India. Remembering those talks now, Philip tried clumsily to present them to his daughter, but there was something muddled in his own head about these matters. In the end, he simply asserted the inherent benevolence of British rule and left it at that. That was the firm belief of his circle, and he had no desire to complicate his own thoughts on the matter.

The Sunderlands had a family compartment to themselves. In the compartment next to theirs, two young English women were travelling together to meet up with their husbands in Darjeeling. Elizabeth and Deborah went over to talk to them. The talk soon turned to Calcutta society and the tiresomeness of hierarchy in official circles. Elizabeth Sunderland laughed with the other ladies although she was upper class enough to ignore the painstaking attention to etiquette exhibited by British women in India. They were probably—poor things—the daughters of modest accountants at home, struggling now to act as aristocratic as the Viceroy in Calcutta. So much of these poor women's status lay in trying to forget where they came from and who they had been.

No, Elizabeth Sunderland's grouse against civilian society in Calcutta was not its fussy rituals of rank but its complete barrenness of suitable young men. The young men in Fort William were mainly from the Indian Army, and Elizabeth was absolutely sure that life in India was not for Deborah. She would marry, if all went according to plan, a dashing young man from the Brigade of the Guards or a suitable cavalry regiment, and make her way up perhaps to a general's mansion, retiring in old age and a plenitude of grandchildren, to a country retreat full of dogs and horses. Oh, now if only the girl would stop taking this peculiar interest in cooking. But the silly girl had not even bothered to engage the attention of that nice young Hugh Trevers. He was just the right sort, and his regiment was due back in England in a year's time.

'Do you think, Mother, that I could learn some Tibetan cooking while we are in Darjeeling?'

That cooking again! Elizabeth, generally sweet-natured and accommodating, shot her daughter a stern look.

'Come, Debbie, we must return. Your father must be wondering where we are. *Good* day, Mrs Rodney, Mrs Thomas. It's been *such* a pleasure! I'm *sure* we'll meet again in Darjeeling. *Goodbye.*'

The next morning, the train deposited them in Siliguri station, where the Darjeeling line met with the main line. Some hours later, the Sunderlands were on the Toy Train, truly a tiny miniature of the belching beast that had brought them from Calcutta. On this, they chugged away and up to Darjeeling. Looking out at the green hillside that rose on one side and the steep drop on the other, Deborah and her mother gazed enchanted at the cool majesty of the Himalayan countryside.

'How completely different it all is from Calcutta, Papa.' Deborah leaned out of the window as the train wound through pine forests with thick fern undergrowth. Sudden low expanses of tea estates broke up the forested hillside. Mist fell upon the mountain slopes like a blanket of white gauze. And then, a long circular movement, a charming temple, and they were in Darjeeling, the engine puffing like an exhausted horse after a long day at work.

That evening, they stayed at the dak bungalow, a low, red-tiled government guesthouse, set up in the hillside among the pine trees.

'If we are to visit Sikkim and Bhutan, then I need to get permission for the two of you,' Philip broke the news to his wife. 'That may be difficult. Things are a bit tense hereabouts.'

Elizabeth looked alarmed but her husband laughed comfortingly.

'It's all right, my dear. Haven't we been safe enough these past few months even in Calcutta? But there is some trouble brewing between the Chinese and the Tibetans. I would expect a war soon. In any case, we need to patrol the region quite closely these days.'

As it turned out, Philip was unable to get permission for his family to visit Bhutan, and had to leave alone for his two-month tour. Arrangements were made to lodge the two Sunderland women in Kalimpong, a town not too far from Darjeeling, where the views of Kanchenjunga were just as spectacular. In the two weeks that remained before Philip's departure, the three of them busied themselves with sightseeing. Once again, Deborah took the dak bungalow cooks in hand, so that all the summer guests at the crowded guest house showered praise on them for their clear golden soup on which floated herbed croutons; roast chicken rubbed with lemon juice and garam masala; mutton stew fragrant with cinnamon; and vegetables steamed in a spicy broth. 'The best cooks I have ever seen in all of India!' declared a pompous old District Collector, who was on his last visit to the hills before he retired from the Civil Service.

In the afternoons, they all went for walks. While their menfolk indulged in deeply involved talk of government and policy, the women in the transient summer community walked along the Mall, where Indians were not allowed, eventually joining up with the men for tea at the Planters' Club. Deborah smiled at her tea companions. They smiled back. She dreamed of the food that would accompany this divine tea—sandwiches, scones, little cheese puffs.

Pithampur as a place had come up repeatedly in the worried conversations of the men over their port and cigars after dinner. The Raja of Pithampur, old Mahavir Singh, had just asked for the recall of the British Political Adviser on the grounds that he was not vigorous enough. The Raja had followed this up with a wholesale repression of dissident activities. 'Not vigorous enough, the old rascal! It's too bad he's under the direct protection of Simla, otherwise we would have shown him something about vigour,' sneered young John Niven, District Collector in Bastar, and a grateful summer refugee in Darjeeling. The men had just rejoined the women in the lounge and John smiled at Deborah, hoping for some encouraging response to his vocal masculinity. At the District Collector's house the next day, the conversation was entirely trivial as the Collector's sparrow-like wife chattered animatedly with her visitors, eyeing Deborah's London-tailored dress rapidly, memorizing the pattern for her own tailor. Darjeeling was so gay, was it not, in summer? When were they to leave for Kalimpong? In two days? Oh, they must get in touch with the good Reverend Graham there, doing his charitable works for the orphans of the hills: And so on, in the dull, meandering way of teatime chatter.

Two days later, the Sunderland women left for Kalimpong. They travelled in a group with several women, the District Collector from Chapra district being their male escort and protector. First, the group journeyed down the mountain by the small, chugging train to the edge of the boiling Teesta River, then they mounted sturdy mountain ponies or settled down in small gharries for a fairly long trek up to Kalimpong. Deborah rode a tiny pony and stayed close to her mother's gharry. The road wound round and around the hills; there were huts with crops drying on the roofs. Women and children were busily at work in the terraced fields in the timeless routines of farming.

Before the main town came up, the group took to a little path that wound tightly up the hillside. At the top, their guide Sonam, a brawny Tibetan, opened the gate to a wonderfully English garden, all wild and careless colour, behind which was the most charming cottage that Deborah had ever seen. On the porch stood two ancient ladies, one supporting the other. These were Rachel and Sarah Burton, spinster Anglo-Indian sisters who now ran a lodge for summer visitors.

They all slept well and soundly that first night in Kalimpong. Deborah awoke in the bright Himalayan morning and went to open her lace-curtained window. The faraway peak of Kanchenjunga turned from white to crimson as the sun rose in an explosion of colour. A few moments later, a girl in two thick pigtails brought her a pink porcelain cup of tea, and bread and butter. There was still an hour to breakfast, so Deborah beckoned to the maid and went out into the garden.

At the end of the strip of lawn, sown thickly with croquet hoops, there was an orchard. Still exploring, Deborah entered the orchard, followed uncertainly by the maid. After a while, the girl came to a complete halt and let Deborah proceed. Deborah walked briskly among the trees, their thick branches interlocking over her head and blocking the sunlight. Soon, she had left the cottage quite far behind and the path sloped steeply downward. The walk back would be harder, all uphill. To her right, a rustling sound brought the first hint of danger. Her breath caught in her throat as she remembered all the warnings about revolutionaries and terrorists that her father and numerous other people had given her. In the middle distance, she thought she saw some movement, a flash of colour. Turning sharply, she called out, 'Who's there?'

Within the dark shadows of the fruit trees, a darker shadow moved towards her. A few minutes later, a young, slightly built Sikh man emerged, looking at her solemnly. He seemed about twenty-five or twenty-six, maybe even a bit older.

'You have no reason to fear, miss,' he said, in perfect English. He seemed completely assured, his confidence at odds with the situation. Didn't he know that he could be arrested for being here? She had merely to raise an alarm and this man would be put away for many months in a dark, unlit Indian prison, the kind invoked by nannies to scare children into good behaviour. His word would count for nothing against hers. But this man simply nodded at her curtly before he disappeared again into the trees. He came out again, this time carrying some paints and an easel.

'The Misses Burton allow me to use the grounds so that I can paint Mount Kanchenjunga. The view from here is magnificent.' He gestured to a clearing.

'You are an *artist*!' In an exhalation of relief, Deborah stressed the last word.

'We Sikhs can't all be simple soldiers.' Sarcasm hung heavily on his words. 'So, yes, some of us are artists.'

'Well, Mr . . . er.' Deborah tried to recover some wit. 'I really don't care what you do in life.' They both laughed, the ice broken for now.

If only Deborah could have guessed that out of such disjointed phrases would grow the love of her life.

'Ah, yes, Satinder,' said the elder Miss Burton, when Deborah mentioned her little morning adventure. The breakfast company waited for more information. Deborah learned that Satinder was the son of Sardar Rajinder Singh Silonia, the Prime Minister of Pithampur, a tiny princely state in faraway Punjab. Pithampur *again*, she thought. Wasn't that the place the men had been discussing in Darjeeling? Sardar Rajinder Singh, wise man, had sent his eldest son to England for studies and Satinder had even trained briefly in law. But, inexplicably, when he returned, he did not settle down to the predictable life of a high official in princely Pithampur. Instead, as his father pored over yet another incomprehensible telegraph message from Calcutta, Satinder announced that he was leaving for Simla, and he did not know when he would return. And no, he would not join the army as an alternative career or even retire quietly to the family farm to manage the tenants. He was going to . . . paint!

'We are the Silonias of Silonia!' Prime Minister Rajinder Singh shouted, shocked at what he thought was a demented announcement. 'What will our people say? That my son, who we sent to England with so many hopes, is throwing away success for,' his voice cracked with emotion, 'for some colours and brushes?' Satinder listened to his father in silence, but the Prime Minister could see that the boy was lost to reason. The following month, Sardar Rajinder Singh and his wife travelled to Simla along with Satinder and a retinue of servants to set up a home for the family artist. After all, if the boy wanted to paint, then he had to have a lifestyle suitable to the family's status until he returned to his senses. However, within two months, Satinder was fed up of such an existence. On a grey, dark dawn in July, he packed his paints and some clothes into a bag, took some money from his mother's box and left. A note informed his tearful parents not to worry about him. A train brought him to Siliguri. From there, he walked up to Kalimpong, and turned up one day at the Misses Burtons' doorstep, offering his services as night watchman in exchange for the freedom to paint during the day. He had been with the Burton sisters for about four months.

On a dazzling, clear morning, Deborah asked Satinder about his decision to leave his career and his family. 'Miss Sarah Burton does so like to tell my story,' he smiled and continued to paint—not brilliantly, but with an eye for colour and detail. His beard and turban were surprisingly neat for an artist, Deborah noticed. Then, he looked at faraway Kanchenjunga, its snowy slopes burning with the bright colours of sunrise. 'It's not as romantic as she likes to believe. In fact, it is rather sad.

'One day I was at the royal durbar, the court, when the Raja refused to pardon a young widowed woman the tax she owed the government. In fact, the Raja could not, because his own position depends on timely tax collection. If the revenues fell short, then the king might have been demoted from an eight-gun salute to a six-gun salute. Or something like that. And I stood there, reading out the telegram from Calcutta to His Majesty. And this woman, who had lost her husband, and who had been pregnant at the time of harvest and so could not collect the crops and pay the tax, she was going to lose her land and her meagre possessions—because Calcutta would not yield even a little bit. So for the sake of an eight-gun salute, this woman and her child were turned out into the streets of Pithampur to beg for a living.' He stared into the distance. 'I have not told Miss Burton this story,' he added softly, adding a detail to his canvas, where Mount Kanchenjunga was slowly taking shape.

The sun came up and away from behind the great mountain. Its slopes were now a blush pink, like Deborah's face. 'I think,' said the bane of the Sunderland family. 'I think that I am in love with you.' Satinder was silent for so long that she thought that he had not heard her.

'I think that you had better go now, Miss Sunderland.' Satinder picked up his brushes and paints, and began putting them away. 'You are young,' he continued. 'And I have to live here.'

'You're young, too!' she shot back. But Satinder merely smiled and shook his head. He did not escort her back to the edge of the orchard as was his usual habit. That evening, over dinner—a good meal of tender mutton and *petit pois*—Deborah heard from the elder Miss Burton that Satinder had left on a month's leave.

'Oh, is that so?' Deborah pretended to be admiring the cutlery very closely, while she fought off bleakness. 'And where does the lawyer-artist go on holiday?'

'Oh, who knows?' said Miss Burton. 'But this time, he is going to Darjeeling. His parents are visiting there, and he is going to meet them. In any case, it is rather annoying, as it is sudden. But he has been so reliable these past months that I could not refuse him his request.' Deborah's heart was cold and heavy at the loss. First Neville, now Satinder. She must be really unlucky in love. None of the men she loved seemed to love her back, at least not as ardently.

'Miss Burton,' Deborah put down her glass on the fine Belgian lace tablecloth.

'Yes, my dear?'

'Would you show me how you run your kitchen? I would, if you would allow it . . . I could stay back here and live and work here. I—I love it here already.'

⌒

George peddled hard and furiously through the narrow lanes of Pithampur. It was already half past nine. What recipes *could* they be that Miss Sunderland wanted to give him so urgently? A sharp left around the crossroads and then he was there, in front of the little door in the wall.

'Good morning, Miss Sunderland!' George called out to Deborah, who had appeared at the door of the house. She looked fresh and rested. 'I'm sorry for coming so early, but I leave today for Mhow, for the OTS, the Officer Training School.' He couldn't help adding proudly.

'Thank you for stopping by, Mr Clark.' Deborah led him into the drawing room, now sunny and bright as the curtains had been opened to let in the light. 'I wrote to Captain Keeler, asking for you as I wished to give you something small by which to remember me and Pithampur. Unfortunately, Maninder, the man who brought you here each week, was not allowed into the cantonment yesterday, so he brought the package back.'

She held out a brown paper parcel. It was flat, hard but bendable. Felt like paper.

'You can open it if you like, Mr Clark.'

So he unwrapped the package, feeling the coarse jute strings slide through his fingers. It was a book, a handmade one, a portfolio. He opened the cover and was astonished. It was a collection of recipes, all in beautiful calligraphy. But it was the borders of the book that were truly spectacular. They were hand-painted, all of them, in stunning colours and great artistry. Deborah Sunderland had gone to extraordinary lengths to get this work of beauty for him.

'Why, you shouldn't have, ma'am!' George was delighted and touched.

'The pictures are all done by friends of mine here in Pithampur, they are all artists. I hope your friend in England, Alice, will be happy with these recipes,' Miss Sunderland twinkled at him.

Deborah insisted he stay for a quick cup of tea; they chatted about England, the war, the Soviet victories, and the situation in India.

'Well, now Miss Sunderland,' said George playfully, as he stood up to leave, 'you never did tell us. What brought you to Pithampur?'

Deborah looked at him a long moment and then answered briefly. 'The same thing that keeps me here. It is a man in the Pithampur prison. A man I would like to marry should he ever be released.'

In the stillness of the silence that followed, a raucous bird screamed down harshly at the world. Then George bent over and, quite forgetting propriety, hugged Deborah Sunderland.

'You take care of yourself, Miss Sunderland. I'm sure everything will be all right.' It was inadequate, but all he could muster.

As she watched the young soldier walk down the path to the gate, Deborah Sunderland thought: Who would have known in that long-ago summer in Kalimpong that I would spend my later years in remote Pithampur, waiting for the release from prison of a lawyer-turned-artist turned anti-imperialist and anti-monarchical agitator?

At the end of September 1909 when her father returned from his travels in Bhutan and Sikkim, Deborah had a frank discussion with her parents.

'I know, Papa, that you will be angry. But I do not wish to return either to Calcutta or to England. I would like to stay here in Kalimpong. I have asked the Misses Burton if I can stay with them and help them take care of the lodge. I will also give lessons to the children in Reverend Graham's mission.'

Stunned by their daughter's decision, Elizabeth and Philip Sunderland held each other, worried and talked late into the night.

'Oh Philip, Philip,' sobbed Elizabeth in an exhausted monotone, looking out of the window at the huge moon rising in the sky. 'How will I ever . . .? How shall we . . .?'

It was then that the good yeoman stock in Philip Sunderland rose. Since Debbie would not be persuaded to change her decision, the next best thing would be for all of them to stay here with her. He would ask to be posted back from Calcutta to Bhutan, and Elizabeth could stay here in Kalimpong with Deborah. In any case, Kalimpong was as pretty as a picture and it was a perfect place for his family while he did his job in Bhutan, as an agent of the British government in India. Philip Sunderland had no idea then just how completely Deborah would break with his carefully planned future for his family.

THREE

By early March, Mhow was already warm and dusty. The central Indian plateau on which Mhow stood was a rolling vista of swelling hillocks, clumps of small trees, and the occasional furtive movements of startled, small animals. George's horse, a chocolate mare called Jalebi, plodded determinedly up the steep slope towards Abdul Khan's tomb. Slightly behind him, Tom Davis and Martin Marks coaxed their horses up the hill. In front of him rode Roy Coulson, a taciturn cadet who was a bit of a loner but spent his free time with the three.

Tom, Martin and George had become friends from the first day that they had run into each other the previous December. At the Indore railway station, meeting amidst a great, seething mass of people, the young men had eyed each other warily until a uniformed Railway Transport Officer herded them into a truck to continue their journey to the Officer Training School in Mhow.

'What I just don't get is,' complained Martin on the long and bumpy road to Mhow, 'why this place? I mean there are others, aren't there? What about Bombay?' He scratched his neck and adjusted his cap.

'Think we can get some decent grub in this place we are going to?' piped up Tom. 'I'm starving. Damn train, the food was bloody awful. Who runs those ghastly dining rooms in the stations anyway?' There was no answer to that, so the three of them smoked cigarettes and watched the countryside outside.

The truck roared in high gear over flat, parched land. Sometimes the odd temple would catch George's eye, brick dome brooding over a quiet pond. In three hours the young cadets were deposited in Mhow, which seemed to be mostly flat, dry scrubland with an occasional stretch of rolling hills, all dotted with villages and bristling with banyan trees, jackals and snakes. It was here in the Central Provinces that the British Indian Army had established its Officer Training School, one of several that sprang up in wartime India.

Breaking into George's reflections, Jalebi neighed and reached out to bite the rump of the horse in front of her. It reared up while its rider, Roy Coulson, turned around and cursed her. 'Stop that, girl!' George turned Jalebi's head sharply off to the right. Martin and Tom laughed and jeered good-naturedly.

On George's first morning out among the low stables of the riding school, the syce had brought the high-stepping, liquid-eyed Jalebi to him. Her name, said the syce, was an English one that he could neither pronounce nor remember. But he called her Jalebi because the mare was so sweet-tempered. George had barely mounted when Jalebi tossed her head and tried to back into the bushes. 'She is also very playful,' said the syce, fondly.

This ride and the picnic breakfast out at Abdul Khan's tomb was part of a socialization process—of getting the cadets acquainted with the culture of the officer class.

'Being an officer is not about running longer or faster than the men you will command,' Major Ronalds, their officer-in-charge, told them that first morning out in the dazzling sunshine in front of the plain stone building of their instruction room. 'Most of you are in as good a shape as the men. And they will respect you all the more for having come up through the ranks.'

In his pale blue eyes, they could all see a faint glimmer of pride. He himself had come up the hard way. If the war had not broken out, Major Ronalds would probably have retired, gratefully, as a Captain. But now, with the Burma front experience behind him, he would shortly be leaving for the European front, promoted to Lieutenant-Colonel. And who knew to what further glory in this topsy-turvy world where war and battles decided the fates of nations and rulers?

'Being an officer,' Ronalds continued in his clipped accent, 'also means learning to do certain things socially and doing them well. Has anybody here ever ridden? Or played tennis?' A dozen people put their hands up, George, Tom and Martin among them. George's experience as old Dr Farthers's unpaid apprentice came in handy when it was needed. The training routine for the cadets now consisted of an endless series of drill parades, dress parades, dinner nights, physical training, and classes in tactics. Different sporting activities filled in the rest of the time. This was the way officers lived. Hard work, hard play.

George quite liked the play and enjoyed his rides. Few women crossed their lives in the first few weeks of training, though sometimes they saw slim, lonely figures on bicycles, some dressed in Auxiliary Territorial Service uniform, snobbish daughters of senior officers, who tossed their heads at them from a great, disdainful distance.

Each time he saw them, George remembered Alice with terrible and aching clarity. The war had changed life for Alice too. The cinema star Richard Clarke, her employer in London, had arranged it so that Alice's job as cook for his household counted as War Work, labour deemed essential to the war effort. Thanks to Richard's famous actress wife, Susan Clarke, Alice had access to plentiful supplies of American food and to even more plentiful Hollywood glamour, so it seemed.

'I wish you were back,' Alice had written in her most recent letter. 'We have had lots of blackouts, and butter and eggs are hard to get. Still, life here with the Clarkes is lots of fun. Yesterday, David Niven came for dinner. I could hardly cook, I was so excited. I made the chicken dish you sent me the recipe for—it was delicious.'

It was a typical Alice letter. And yet, from the tone of her letters George sensed that Alice was moving into another world, a world far removed from Mhow, Pithampur, and the hell of Burma. No common experience—not even war—could help make her understand where he had been for four years. And equally, she was moving in realms that he could only guess at. A world where movie stars—those beings whose adventure stories he had thrilled to in the only cinema at Watsby—were part of one's everyday life. They were growing apart, inevitably, as the war moved their worlds further and further away from each other, like drifting continents, but George felt at once too weak and too indecisive to break decisively with a relationship that he knew had outlived its time in his life and hers. This bloody war!

The first of the horses had already reached the top of the hill. Their dismounted riders looked down and yelled encouragement to the others still trudging up. George dismounted, and Jalebi bent her head to tug at the grass until a syce led her away to the makeshift stables at the back. The clutter of people began to resolve itself into a pattern. Swarms of waiters in spotless white uniforms rushed around with trays of large, steaming mugs of tea. George gulped appreciatively at the sweet, hot liquid and nodded to the other trainees. Tom and Martin came up to stand beside him as he took in the breathtaking view of Mhow spread out, dusty and dry, but ruggedly beautiful on this March morning, a blue haze hanging over the countryside.

Turning back to the warm smells of breakfast and a cheerful scene of camaraderie, George looked up at Abdul Khan's stone mausoleum. In the distance he saw a beaming Roy Coulson talking with an Indian man, scruffy and all creased in smiles himself.

'Let's eat, shall we?' Tom pointed to the table, around which men already buzzed like bees. A mountain of porridge, scrambled eggs, sausages, kedgeree, mutton and potato chops, baked beans, toast, plum jam disappeared in less than half an hour. Clearly, wartime rationing had not touched the refectory facilities of the British Army in Mhow.

George, Tom and Martin went over with Roy to see Abdul Khan's tomb.

'Now whose tomb was this again?' asked Tom as they descended the stairs into an underground burial place. Unexpectedly, it was Roy who answered. It turned out the man was a veritable fountain of knowledge about the region.

'I think Abdul Khan was a general for this old king, Shah Alam, who ruled here in the seventeenth century till some other Mughal general from the north came along and carved up the place. This was before the Holkars took over the Malwa region in the eighteenth century. I . . . er, read a lot about this place when I was in the hospital at Indore,' Roy added, suddenly self-conscious.

'Who's that?" muttered Martin as a shadow darkened the doorway.

'That chap there?' Roy pointed at a rather weather-beaten face peering anxiously at them from above, blocking the light sometimes with his movements. 'That's Ramu Chowkidar. He

first told me about this place. He's the watchman for this place.'
It was the same man George had noticed conversing with Roy
earlier.

'You speak Urdu?' Tom was interested. There was obviously
much more to Roy than they had imagined.

'Oh, just a little bit. I picked up some while I was in the
hospital in Indore. I had bad arthritis, you know,' Roy blurted
out, suddenly. 'It was pretty horrible. This fellow here, Ramu,
helped me with some herbs and things. He used to be in Indore
those days.'

'Herbs?' George was interested but slightly disbelieving. The
four men walked up and out of the underground tomb into
almost blinding sunlight. The watchman stood at a little distance,
wearing khaki trousers, a colourful shawl around his shoulders;
on his head sat a battered white cap. Roy said something to him
and he came over slowly, shuffling along in worn, white canvas
shoes, no doubt handed down from a British soldier.

'Where does he get his herbs from?' George wanted to know.
Roy rattled off something to which the man replied animatedly.
He grew his herbs on his own small plot of land in Mhow. Roy
filled them in on Ramu's story as he knew it.

Ramu Chowkidar was the caretaker of Abdul Khan's tomb,
employed by the government at the wage of twenty rupees a
month, a wage that he had had to accept to retain his government
job. And how did their precarious state come to pass, here in
Mhow? Well, ten years ago, when Ramu had been young and
strong, his wife, Indumati, had sent him from their native land
in Kolhapur, in western India, to find work in Indore, in central
India. This move had also put an end to Ramu's hobby in
Kolhapur, of growing different kinds of herbs that he then gave
to ailing friends and neighbours. Indumati had always liked the

smell of the herbs her husband grew; the smooth pastes that he made always cured her headaches, brought on by the smoky kitchen with its belching woodstove.

Indumati's cooking was renowned in her village near Kolhapur and her services were often enlisted during weddings. She routinely turned out samosas, burfi and petha for two hundred people at a time. She got little or no money for her efforts, though, as all this was the normal quid pro quo services of rural life. So off they went, parents and two sons, to Indore where Ramu Chowkidar found a better-paying job as one of the three watchmen in the old fort of Ahirabad. European tourists often came to look at the majesty of the fort and to marvel at the tale of Shivaji's exploits. It was here that Shivaji, the most famous rebel against the Mughals, had come to defend the fort against Delhi, and had supported his armies through the collection of taxes from the villagers. The warrior king lived in Ahirabad for two years, to the intense anger of Raja Vir Singh, the local ruler, who was overshadowed by his more charismatic rival. One morning, as mysteriously as he had arrived, Shivaji vanished, taking his fighting men, and leaving the fort open to the Mughal Army that quickly reclaimed the lands for the Mughal state. Vir Singh paid the price for defying the march of time—he was replaced by a Peshwa ruler who in turn gave way with ill grace to the encroaching British East India Company with their new armies and strange new laws of succession that did not recognize the rights of adopted children.

Ramu and Indumati spent peaceful years in Ahirabad. They knew nothing about Vir Singh or the East India Company. All they knew was that it was Ramu's job to keep the fort clear of trespassers and squatters and to close up the place at night. In return, Ramu got thirty rupees a month and was allowed to pitch a small hut near one of the western walls of the fort, at the crumbling ruins of the former royal pavilion.

Ramu's and, especially, Indumati's lack of appreciation of the history of the place would be their undoing. Indumati once told a European visitor—a scholar of Sanskrit and Persian, in fact, who had come up to speak to this charming example of Indian peasant womanhood—that she did not know anything about Aurangzeb or Vir Singh or the Mughals, but this fort wasn't much use to anyone now, was it? And look, what happened to all those kings and other powerful men? All dead and gone to heaven or hell or other lives. Could those men do anything now to stop her, Indumati, from lighting her woodstove in full view of their grand royal quarters? And now if the gentleman would allow her, could she carry on with the lighting of the stove? She stalked off, grumbling at the disruption to her routine.

The scholar was deeply shocked at her complete indifference—'may I say total *contempt*'—for this unique, *historical* place, and wrote a three-page letter of complaint to the Chief Archaeologist of Indore, expressing his sentiment of absolute *outrage*. His mood was not lightened when the following day in the Indore bazaar he heard a passing herd of British soldiers complaining about their route march to 'that heap of auld stones'. Hurrying away to Agra the next day, he soothed his offended sensibilities by taking in the wonders of the Taj Mahal by moonlight. His letter did not go unacknowledged though—in fact, a few days after receiving it, Ramu's supervisor suspended him from his duties. The order was promptly put on hold, however, because at the same time a large number of white people were jailed in Ahirabad, and Ramu became part of the manpower required to look after them, while making sure that they did not escape.

George raised an eyebrow at Roy.

'It was the Germans,' Roy explained. 'A lot of German civilians were locked up in Ahirabad when the war broke out. Although most of the German POWs were taken to the Purandar fort near Poona.'

For five years, Ramu and other chowkidars guarded the inner precincts of Ahirabad fort, while more serious-looking, uniformed men patrolled the outer perimeter. Indumati earned some extra money by washing the clothes of the internees—all in all, the arrangement was quite pleasant for everyone. The prisoners were all men; the memsahibs were either allowed to go away or imprisoned somewhere else, Ramu did not know. Among these interned sahibs was Karl, who often tried to talk to Ramu and the other chowkidars. He would even pay them small amounts of cash to help him with his beautiful garden, just behind the communal barracks.

There, in the dry winter months, Ramu helped Karl coax beautiful plants whose names he did not know, out of the black, volcanic soil. Here and there, Ramu planted mint and tulsi, which delighted Karl. The tall German brought out small bags of seeds and two great books to show Ramu, when the guards were not in sight.

One day, during the monsoons, Karl fell very ill, as people do during that season. The camp doctor prescribed some pills, and Indumati cooked him light meals. Solemn-faced, the internees gathered around Karl and whispered in low tones. Some of them even spoke harshly to Ramu, as if he had ordered them to be locked up, he grumbled to Indumati. On the seventh day when Karl's fever was still raging, he called Ramu to his bedside in a hoarse tone. Then, Karl had Ramu half drag him, half carry him to the garden. The Deccan air, usually so dry and clean, now smelt wet and heavy with rain, and the thick soil had turned green, the only time of the year when the craggy plateau's jagged edges were softened with luminous colour. With unsteady, shaking hands, Karl picked some herbs and gave them to Ramu, indicating to him in sign language that he was to wash them and mix them in a drink for Karl. But Ramu knew that Karl had missed an important ingredient. For a racking cough like his, one had to also add tulsi, sweet basil. He took some tulsi leaves off a plant and showed them to Karl. Karl looked doubtful but by then he was exhausted with his effort of walking outside and made no objection when Ramu brought back his half-Indian, half-European herbal drink.

After two days of drinking this potion, Karl still had a fever, but he knew now that he would survive. The ache in his joints had lessened somewhat and his throat was no longer as closed and inflamed as it had been. Within a week, he recovered almost completely and was walking short distances. Since Karl was not permitted to go to Ramu's hut and see his herb garden, Ramu would bring him, from time to time, some herbs to see and to smell. The German would examine them and then write notes in his journal.

Ramu and Karl's joint venture fell apart when the German civilians were either let go or relocated. On a still, warm October morning in 1944, Ramu found to his surprise that there was a bustle of khaki-clad soldiers. He saw Karl talking to a British officer who had a list in his hand.

'Do you have any clothes for that sahib?' he asked the dhobi who had just arrived with the dismal news that all the prisoner-sahibs were leaving, but he did not know where.

'Yes, there are these shirts and half-pants.' Ramu took them over to Karl, whose pale blue eyes lit up momentarily in a smile. He asked the British officer if he could take Ramu outside. The officer looked at his watch impatiently and told them to be back soon. He gestured and a British soldier strolled nonchalantly after Ramu and Karl, keeping one hand on his rifle, just in case. Outside, the predawn sky had just turned a light pink. In the herb garden, there were small sparrows and cocky, aggressive mynas who fluttered away as the two men approached. There, in German and sign language, Karl told Ramu that the plot was now his: 'Alles ist deine'. They stood together looking at the waving plants, a small, thin Maratha peasant and a tall, blond Bavarian, neither smiling. There were no farewell gestures between them, just an unspoken acknowledgment of parting, worlds separating after a brief union, never to meet again.

All that week, Ramu spent his spare time carefully transplanting the younger herb plants from Karl's garden to his own. After the prisoners left, life in Ahirabad slowed down considerably for Ramu and Indumati. And then in November, the bombshell fell. One day, Ramu's boss called him to the office and told him that the earlier crime—that long-ago crime of Indumati's scornful dismissal of the European scholar's sensitivities—had attracted severe punishment and he was to be dismissed immediately on grounds of neglecting his caretaking duties. Ramu pleaded with the man. The supervisor, a worried-looking man contemplating an India-less future, nodded in absent-minded sympathy. He had no particular grudges against Ramu, and the following week he called Ramu in again and handed him a letter.

'Go, talk to this sahib in Indore,' the supervisor told Ramu. 'There is a chowkidar's job in the military hospital. It is not a permanent job. But when things have settled down here somewhat, I can fit you into another permanent job in Mhow at the old tomb of Abdul Khan. And,' he concluded sternly, 'don't let your wife be talking nonsense to visitors again.'

Ramu nodded gloomily and five days later, the little family left Ahirabad for nearby Indore. Ramu carefully transplanted his herbs into terracotta pots and packed the seeds into individual bundles. Every morning, he left to patrol the wards, although most days there was nothing to do except chase away the fat hospital cats looking greedily for more food. It was on one such day, when Ramu sat outside the general ward, tapping his stick and listening to the faraway noises of the more boisterous outpatient department that he ran into Roy Coulson who was rubbing his arthritic hands and staring vacantly out into the distance from the veranda.

Ramu guessed the nature of the scowling soldier's ailment by the way he held his hands out gingerly and trod lightly on his feet. Even as he thought this, one of his recent patients, Shok Ram, appeared in the door of the ward.

'Is everything all right?' Ramu asked.

'Yes, so far, thanks to you,' replied Shok Ram, moving his fingers to show that they were free of pain.

'That sahib there,' Ramu pointed to Roy. 'He has the same ailment as you.'

'Why, my employer knows him,' said Shok Ram. 'I should tell him about you.' Shok Ram went inside to talk to someone and presently, a harassed-looking British officer with an arm in a sling emerged from the ward and went over to speak with Roy.

The officer with the injured arm was apologetic. 'Look, I don't mean to interfere,' he told Roy. 'But my servant tells me that this fellow here cured him of his arthritis. And he absolutely insists that I should tell you about it. I had to warn you. Looks quite a frightful quack, if you ask me.' When the officer returned to his bed, Roy looked at Ramu and then gestured to him to come over.

'I was desperate,' Roy recalled with a heavy sigh as the others looked at him incredulously. 'I had this course here to join. I didn't want to be low-medical category. And, well, I'm here, aren't I?'

After he felt Roy's inflamed hands and feet, Ramu retired to another ward to think of the herbs he would need. He rose early the next morning and woke Indumati too. While she got the stove going, he sat outside his little ramshackle quarters, chewing on a neem twig and rubbing his face. She peeled ginger and ground fresh turmeric on a stone slab. He ground cinnamon and cloves in a mortar. Separately, he made a paste of red chillies, his eyes watering from the hot fumes. Then, Ramu took his clay bowl and went into his little garden. He knew he should test the yellow flowers on Roy first before he made a poultice of it, as many people were allergic to it. There were also the purple-white flowers that helped relieve pain. Returning to the sun-splashed corner near his door, he resumed the work of grinding all these herbs, spices and flowers into a paste. By the time he finished this, his older son, Hari, was fully awake and began helping him. They tied the cloves, cinnamon, ginger and turmeric pastes into a muslin cloth and placed the small bundle along with Ramu's other concoctions on a brass plate.

A few days after drinking Ramu's infusions made with the purple-white flowers and undergoing applications of the rather scary-looking paste, Roy Coulson knew he was going to be cured.

'Ah, sahib,' Ramu sighed when Roy told him that he would be going to Mhow in January. 'I too have been sent there by the sahib in Ahirabad.'

'Oh well!' said Roy after he heard Ramu's story about Indumati, the scholar, and her irreverent attitude to history. 'It could have been worse, you know. Better a job in Mhow, my man, than no job at all.' He tried to be jolly for poor Ramu's sake.

And now, in the March sunlight, near the bat-infested tomb of a bygone Deccani general, Ramu and Roy had met up again.

That evening, George received another letter from Alice. Tired and aching from the long ride back to Mhow, George opened it and as he read her words, the ache became a dull pain in his head.

'I am moving to America,' she wrote. 'Richard Clarke is taking me with him as his cook. I don't know how he has managed a visa for me, it's ever so hard I'm told. Will you come too? I know we never talked much about things between us, but perhaps it's time. Poor George, I didn't want this to be one of those kind of letters, but do write and tell me what you think.' She had also sent a photo of Richard Clarke, signed by him— 'To George Clark, with regards'. In the picture, the film star, greying handsomely, looked to be in his late-fifties.

Outside, on the veranda, George could hear Tom and Martin approaching. It was nearly time to head over to the mess for evening drinks and dinner. In the perfect March night, the smell of jasmine hung heavy, the stars glittered in the steel-black sky. They took two tongas to the mess, paying off the half-asleep driver with small change. The usual collection of shields and lances, photographs and paintings hung on the mess walls. In the round circle of the inner lawn, George could hear people laughing and glasses tinkling gently.

'Where do you think they'll send us after this?' George asked the others, as they settled down with their drinks.

'I opted for the Seventh Highlander,' said Roy after a few minutes. 'I always wanted to go to a Highland regiment.'

'I want to go into Int,' Tom Davis piped up. He had always been fascinated with Intelligence work.

'Don't you have to go to a regular battalion first?' The others reminded him.

The senior dining mess member, a bewhiskered relic from the last war stumbled in at this point of the conversation, drunk as always and calling for the bearer. A fresh whisky sour was brought to him and after he had his first sip, he gestured to the four young officers-in-training to sit down.

'So your commissions are in soon, eh? Well, who knows how long the war will last? Just heard that the Russians are almost in Germany. Or they may ship you off to Malaya or something. Dreadful place, hotter than India, if you can believe it.'

George tried not to think about Malaya. He tried to think what Hollywood looked like but could think of nothing. Only the faces of famous actors came to mind. David Niven and Clark Gable smiled at him in black and white. What sort of towns did actors live in, really?

'Dear Alice,' he wrote that night, while his servant, Ram Prasad, pottered around, getting his uniform organized for the next day. 'Alice, I really am sorry that there have been so few recipes for you these few months. Now, about this other matter, here is my plan: you go ahead with Richard Clarke and I will try and come over after the war is over. I don't know when that will be, but one reads so much in the papers that it is going entirely our way in Europe. And then . . . who knows? So you go ahead and once the war is over and when my number's up for demob, I will try to follow you to America.'

It was altogether a cowardly, indecisive, unsuitable letter for the messy situation that his life was in, but it would have to do. George sat for a while, then took out the portfolio of recipes that Deborah Sunderland had gifted him. He looked at the booklet almost every night. The beauty of the pictures comforted him, as did Deborah's beautiful calligraphy. For some reason, George had never sent Alice a recipe from this portfolio. He felt that the recipes needed to go with the beautiful little collection of paintings, that they should never be separated from the jewellery of their setting. Getting into bed and carefully tucking the mosquito net around him, George fell quickly into a deep, dreamless sleep. The next day, Ram Prasad ran the letter over to the daftar for mailing.

The next few days were hectic ones for all the cadets. They got their signals regarding their future postings. Martin looked gloomy. He had been posted to the Burma front and was going into active combat almost immediately upon commission. Tom was off to the 6th battalion of the Somerset Rifles, currently in Sicily. Roy had got his desired Highland unit, but it was going to Burma. All three of George's preferences had been turned down. Instead, he was to report to the 126th battalion of the East Yorkshire Regiment, currently stationed in the northern town of Bajapur. To soften the blow, the army was also pleased to grant him two weeks' leave at the end of the course.

Things changed rather quickly after that. The news of the cadets' postings was soon overshadowed by more exciting news from Europe. That first week of May, the wireless announced that Hitler had committed suicide and that Soviet forces had more or less taken Berlin. Confirmation of the end of the war in Europe came a few days later. Cheers went up all over the lounge. Drinks were bought for each other, and the creased and careworn faces of the young men who had had to grow up very quickly became momentarily lighter and happier.

'Where will you go?' asked Roy of George. 'Do you want to come with me to Nainital? It will be cooler there and there will be lots of parties and women, and fresh, cool air.'

But George ultimately decided on Kashmir, with a break in Pithampur to pick up a box of books and clothes that he had forgotten to bring with him. His old battalion—the 7/13 Yorkshire Rifles—was moving out and they could no longer hold the box for him, wrote Nate Mason, his old friend who had good-naturedly kept his things for him. So a stop in Pithampur was imperative for George.

In mid-May, on a warm, dusty morning, they all went their own ways. A few days before that, George received another letter from Alice. It was slightly breathless, as if she was writing in between mixing drinks for a cocktail party. But her message was clear.

'I don't think putting off decisions for two or three years is a good idea,' she wrote. 'I think that we should leave each other free to go our own ways. Good luck with everything, George. I hope you get the regiment you want. I feel so sad but I think this is the right thing to do, at this time.'

So that was that, George thought as Ram Prasad loaded his trunk and bedding onto the truck taking him to the station. Here he was, starting out a whole new life without much thought, only a heavy feeling in his heart where once had been a warm memory of a tall London girl with a slight cockney accent. He carried Alice's last letter and Richard Clarke's photo in his carrybag. So many people had asked to see the picture that he kept it safe in a handy place.

Martin and Tom came to see George off at the station. The three newly commissioned subalterns waited on the platform at Indore station, where they had met five months before. Everyone was suddenly shy. As the train began to move, there was a rush of words.

'Good luck!'

'Give the buggers a good kick in Burma!'

'Write if you can!'

Then the train was out of the station, pulling through a row of slum houses; raggedy children shat on the tracks while their mothers washed pots and pans not too far away. The journey north seemed to take forever although it was only a day and a half. Getting off at Ambala station, the noise of the mynas roosting in the station rafters was almost deafening to George's ears. He took a tonga to the cantonment and later on in the day, hitched a ride with a 15-cwt truck heading out to Pithampur. Alone in the front with the driver, the flat Punjabi land spreading far into the distance, he suddenly felt awkward. The one star on each shoulder tab felt too shiny and conspicuous.

George's thoughts turned to Alice, his heart turning heavy again with the memory of the last letter. Their relationship would not survive being placed in limbo, and she had removed by swift surgery the unbearable pressures of uncertainty. Yet, he was human enough to also feel annoyed about his predicament. What right did she have to put him in this position? And in any case, wasn't it because of him and his hunting for recipes for her halfway across the world that she even got to be the kind of cook she was, working in the kitchens of movie stars and seeing all kinds of glamorous people every day. And in return for that, what did he get? A broken heart after three years of hell in Burma and India, meeting nobody worthwhile. Well, there were some nice people in India like old Miss Sunderland—her wonderful teas too—he conceded grudgingly.

On an impulse, George decided to go see Deborah Sunderland while he was here in Pithampur. Maybe she would even feed him like before. His gloom lifted a bit.

In the Pithampur lines there was nobody familiar. Nate and

the other fellows were nowhere to be seen, although the sounds and signs of everyday barracks life continued all around him—a sweeper dabbing listlessly at dust in a dark corner, a small boy collecting unwashed mugs, full of the dregs of tea.

He walked past the Quarter Guard, the armoury, and experienced his first thrill as an officer: being saluted with a crash of gleaming arms and polished boots. He then walked over to the Adjutant's office where a strange, red-faced officer greeted him cautiously. George explained his situation and the Adjutant became even more hesitant. 'Well, I really don't know. You can't just show up at the barracks. You can't . . . er, you know, fraternize with the men and all that,' he ended primly.

'I just wanted my books, sir,' George persisted politely.

'Well, I'll have them brought over to my office this afternoon, and you can pick them up later.'

'Yes, sir,' said George, meekly, trying to soften up the man for his next request. 'May I have permission to go into town this afternoon, sir?'

'Is it personal work?'

'Yes, sir, I would like to meet a friend. Perhaps, you know Miss Sunderland?'

The Adjutant's mouth tightened a little and his nostrils flared in discomfiture.

'I don't know, surely you know that she . . .' He licked his lips and looked away. 'Well, anyway, I'll have to ask the CO.'

The Adjutant picked up the phone, put it down and then left the room. When he returned ten minutes later, he was looking relieved.

'CO wants to see you. My NCO will take you. Purnell!'

A long-limbed man in his thirties, Purnell guided George across a neatly painted square of tarmac and into a low-roofed building with a number of offices. Heat waves danced off the square and at once George began to feel the familiar streams of sweat running down his back.

The CO's office in the middle of the hollow square was easily identifiable because of the two ceremonially dressed guards posted outside. Pithampur was quite definitely not at war, given the elaborate ceremonial regalia on display here. The CO's office was cool and dark, and George had to squint to focus after the glare outside. In the shadows he could make out a shape behind a large desk, which he saluted. Then he noticed somebody else sitting in a chair and he saluted that shape too, just to be on the safe side.

'Sit down, Mr Clark,' the CO growled in a low tone, acknowledging the young officer's salute with a nod of the head. George could hardly bring himself to look at the CO, the godlike figure that he had seen only once or twice in the pre-commission days.

'This is Captain James Ruffington,' said the CO, his whiskers shaking hugely with every word. 'He's in Intelligence, on deputation to the Pithampur administration.' George nodded, not sure what he was supposed to say.

'The Adjutant said you wanted to go into town to meet Miss Sunderland, Clark,' said Ruffington. Out of the gloom, his face emerged like an apparition. He had a pink, podgy face and short, plump legs. He looked like he did nothing more strenuous everyday than wake up and demand breakfast in bed.

'That's right, sir.' George tried to keep his tone even. 'Last year, we—some of the other boys and I—would go and see her every week. I just wanted to look in and see her since I was passing by.'

The CO and Ruffington exchanged looks and then the older man nodded to the intelligence officer.

'Well, look here, Clark, it's like this,' Ruffington began breezily. 'Miss Deborah Sunderland has gone and married a local agitator, Satinder Singh Silonia, after he was released from prison. He's not young, sixty or so. But he's always been a troublemaker, too close to the Congress and those Praja Mandals—the state's people's groups that are against the princes, you know. Of course, the old Raja is terribly angry. He expects that all English people should be helping him stay on the throne and not be working against him by marrying his opponents. So, it is a bit of a problem for us here.'

'I see,' George tried to fathom where the conversation was heading.

'So, this is what we would like you to do,' said Ruffington in the same cheerful way. 'You can go meet the lady, but could you do something for us as well? Oh, I don't mean steal their silver or go through their drawers or anything,' he added smoothly, seeing George's alarmed look. 'But just have a chat and get a feel of things. You know, just conversation.'

The CO pushed an envelope over the desk. 'That's your permit. Be back before seven o'clock. We'll have someone go over right away with a chit to let her know that you are here. Here, why don't you write her a note?' He pushed a clean pad of paper across the desk to George.

'Yes, sir.' George hastily scribbled a note on the piece of paper. He wished now that he had not given in to his impulse to visit Deborah Sunderland. But it was too late to retreat—there were too many other plans folded into his own by now.

FOUR

Across the neat little square, outside the Adjutant's office, the tall NCO who had shown George to the CO's office, stiffened to attention in his direction. George went off towards the mess, a white building set back in a placid green garden full of swinging, shady mango trees. In the lounge, a waiter brought a clattering tray over, a white napkin folded neatly under the teapot. George sighed and began to sip his tea. It was oppressively hot, he had a train to catch at night, and on top of that, there was now this rotten business of ferreting out information from Deborah Sunderland. Christ, he had practically been ordered to do it!

Out of the corner of his eye, he noticed some people coming into the lounge. It was Ruffington. With him was a taller officer, dressed in the unfamiliar brown uniform of the Crown Provincial Police. George sprang to his feet.

'Hot, isn't it?' asked Ruffington cheerfully as he drew up a chair near George, motioning the young man to sit down. The other man introduced himself as James Evans, officer on special duty in Pithampur. They ordered more tea.

After the bearer put the tray down, and padded away silently in white-shod feet, Ruffington began to talk.

'Look, Clark,' he said, all podgy briskness. 'I know you don't want to be dragged into this but it's for a good cause—*our* cause, if you like. It's not so much this old man Silonia that we are worried about—he's just the usual artist kind of person with dissident political opinions—but we are interested in some of his friends. You know that these Congress-types are up to no good, remember all that trouble three years ago? But things have just been getting worse and worse. And some of the Japanese Indian Forces are here too—the Indian National Army, who fought alongside the enemy in Burma. So I am now on deputation to the Resident, working out of his office, helping the chaps here to unravel all these connections between the Congress, the INA and the Praja Mandals.'

'And my job here,' said Evans, who had smoked nervously till then and had said nothing, 'is to make sure that Pithampur does not become a nest of sedition. I don't see much evidence of INA activity here though.' He shot a glance of cool dislike at Ruffington. 'And I really don't understand some of the links that Captain Ruffington is trying to establish. However, I do see it as my task to keep Pithampur relatively calm, given the rise in Sikh–Muslim tensions in the town.'

George was too close to it all to refuse the job; he understood that clearly. He had never examined his own politics seriously. He had pretty much wandered through life until the war happened and despite the terrible certainties that war and fighting had imposed on him, he was not sure if he had learned real, tangible lessons about anything other than physical life and death.

Oh, he had seen enough to know that things could not remain entirely the same, and he knew that he would vote Labour in the coming elections. In the heat of Burma and then later in the barracks of Pithampur, other soldiers had discussed the future with restrained enthusiasm, and had looked forward to getting rid of the old mess created by the 'toffs'. But George also realized now that as an officer, even a junior one, he was part of the system. He felt his acquiescence as a dull, cold ache of anxiety in his stomach.

'I don't really know how I am supposed to go about this, sir,' he said at last, trying to hide his irritation and his feeling of being trapped.

'Well, you don't really have to do much, you know,' Ruffington said amiably. 'All you have to do really is chat with Silonia, ask about the political temperature, nothing specific.' He stood up smoothly. 'And, we'll get you a lift in the evening to Ambala to your train.' He and Evans walked out into the blinding sunlight.

George gulped the last of his tea and then went out in search of a tonga. He took his carrybag with him, as it had all his papers, including the all-important Movement Order. At last a tonga appeared, its pony too weary in the summer heat to even toss its head, and they started off slowly, leaving behind the cantonment's neat, clipped lawns and its quiet streets.

It was early afternoon, and once more George found himself retracing the route of that first visit to Miss Sunderland's house with its sloped orchards. He directed the tonga driver from memory. They turned along the same old alleys. A skinny pye-dog uncurled itself to growl at the pony. Then they turned towards the house. George felt his pulse pick up even as sweat trickled down his neck. This would not be an ordinary courtesy call. Alighting, he gestured to the tonga driver to wait.

The old gatekeeper fumbled with the chain and let George in. There once again was the garden. The afternoon air was still, the mango trees were heavy and bent over with fruit while the jamun trees were dotted with flowers, with the promise of their ripe, dark fruit in June. Sleepy parrots squawked in annoyance at the nets protecting the mangoes. As he reached the door, it flew open and there stood Deborah Sunderland in a cool white dress. Behind her, a servant peered curiously before moving away inside.

'Welcome! It really is so good to see you again, Mr Clark!' she beamed at him.

The curtains of the drawing room were drawn tight against the sunlight outside. Around the sofas were scattered various small tables full of the assorted clutter that he recalled—photographs, Kashmiri boxes, a metal statue or two. A tiny kitten stretched its brown body under the sofa and yawned delicately.

'That one's new,' George remarked.

'Yes, my . . . er, my husband . . . yes, some things have changed while you've been away . . . well, his cat decided to have kittens. Very inconvenient to have so many. I couldn't bear to have them put down, so they are a bit thick on the ground right now. Now, how about some tea, Mr Clark? I see you've been commissioned since we last met. Goodness, things have changed for both of us.' She disappeared into the rooms beyond, to arrange for some tea and eats.

When Deborah returned, he probed gently into her marriage.

'Well, this is a surprise, you getting married. Nice surprise, though.'

'Yes, well, my husband is Indian, Sikh, in fact.'

'They did tell me that you had got married, back in the unit,' he admitted. 'Did you meet him here, then? You've been here many years, of course.'

'Well, I actually first met him in Darjeeling many, many years ago. Before the last war. It's a long story, Mr Clark; one day perhaps I shall have the chance to recount it to you.' Deborah gave him a brief summary of her meeting Satinder Silonia in the Himalayas.

'I suppose your CO or somebody must have also told you that Satinder has just come out of prison,' she said drily. 'I'm afraid he has a few unpopular opinions.'

George nodded. 'Is he for independence for India then?'

'Oh dear, it is more complicated than that. But, well, he can tell you about it when he comes. Ah, here is the tea.' A servant brought in sandwiches and patties, and a small, iced cake. In spite of his nervousness, George was hungry. He hadn't eaten a good tea in ages. Deborah saw him eyeing the cake and smiled as she poured the tea into pale green cups. She asked him about his life in Mhow, and he answered as fully as he could, wondering if he was giving away too much official information to a possible saboteur.

In the background, he was aware of the sun's fury slowly ebbing, the heat leaving the tired ground outside. An older man came in holding a mug of tea, and sat down. Deborah nodded at him.

'This is Mr Romesh Gupta. He is a friend of ours from Calcutta, staying with us a while.'

'How do you do?' Romesh Gupta brought back to George memories of Calcutta. In Calcutta, there had been only the cool stirring of the ceiling fans, and the brisk tones of the Auxiliary Territorial Service staff at the National Museum. No blood, no bandages, no screaming wounded lying on the Chindwin banks. And above all, no noisy, nerve-shattering light machine gun fire.

'Is this your first visit to Pithampur?' he asked Romesh Gupta.

'Oh, yes!' Gupta nearly shouted with laughter. 'But it's been a long visit. In fact, I have lived here for, let us see, fourteen years now. I am an artist, just like Deborah's husband, Satinder.'

George was interested in spite of himself. He had been told to watch out for Congress agitators and communist saboteurs, but what harm could artists do?

'So what sort of things do you do? Landscapes? Still life?'

'Oh, a little bit of everything. Why don't you come and see our work? That is if Deborah does not mind our trampling through the house?' Deborah smiled her assent and Gupta led George into a covered veranda at the back of the house.

The veranda had big glass windows, and screens to keep flies out. It looked out over another stunningly beautiful garden, full of trees and flowering shrubs. Six men sat around in various poses of concentration, bending over easels, their clothes smeared with paint. The room smelt of turpentine. George had expected complete quiet, but in fact the air was thick with chatter. Two of the men were at work on canvases, the rest were painting on cloth and paper, making deft, light strokes and colourful sweeps.

George had always imagined artists as solitary creatures, pursuing their calling in dimly lit garrets, wearing their isolation like cloaks. But here were these six people, engaged in individual work, but *together*. They were arranged around the room like pieces of statuary, except that these statues came to life every now and then in sudden moves. Conversation was continuous, with people joining and leaving the verbal trade as they wished. Sometimes a collective silence fell on the group, to be broken again by someone's outspoken thoughts.

'Where is Satinder?' Gupta asked of everybody in general.

"He said he would be back with more tea for us,' said one of the men, barely detaching himself from the general conversation which moved among English, Urdu and Bengali with fluent ease.

A slightly stooped Sikh man entered the room with a tray full of cups of rather strong-looking tea. Romesh Gupta introduced George to Satinder Singh Silonia. George got an impression of a pair of deep-set liquid eyes under a blue turban.

'So you are the young man who likes to cook?' Silonia's eyes crinkled in smiling acknowledgment.

'Well, more like collecting recipes really,' George had difficulty getting the last bit out, given the recently-changed circumstances between him and Alice. 'So, Miss Sunder . . . your wife told you about me.' And then, looking around him, it dawned on him that he was looking at those who had illustrated those beautiful pages that Deborah had gifted him six months ago.

'Did you . . .?' he began tentatively.

'We all did,' Silonia said. 'It was a pleasure. I hope you liked our work.'

'Though I wish that guard could have got hold of some better brushes. Remember when he . . .' began Romesh Gupta. The others joined in with their reminiscences of prison, captivity, and the guards.

'Your little project kept us going through those long days as state guests of His Highness in Pithampur prison, Mr Clark,' Silonia looked out at the garden, as he remembered.

They had all been in prison together, this gaggle of artists, accused of various crimes ranging from sedition to simply being artists. One day, the previous August, Deborah had come to visit Satinder, just as usual. She mentioned the weekly visits of the soldiers and talked about the young man who was collecting recipes for his girlfriend back in England.

'So, you see, I have decided to copy out some of my better recipes on some nice paper and give them to him as a present. Of course, he doesn't know this yet.'

'Well, I wish I had even that to do here,' said Satinder, somewhat sulkily. He had had diarrhoea a few days ago and was not yet feeling all right. It was then that the idea occurred, almost simultaneously, to both of them.

'I could get you paper each time I visit,' said Deborah, guessing that they had both hit on the same idea.

'And paints too,' said Satinder. 'We have nothing here. You realize that all of us will work on this.'

'Oh, that will be wonderful! It will make each page different and quite beautiful. Though I don't know about that Vishwa Sarkar. He is quite young and his style is not, not *quite* formed as yet. Oh well, I'm sure you will all work it out,' said Deborah, getting up to begin the hunt for art paper and paint, always hard in those days of rationing and sudden shortages.

For three months, the men had worked hard, passing the paints and brushes around from cell to cell. The criticism and input had to come before the piece had been completed, since the shortage of paper and paints limited the number of times one could start over. Luckily, the artists had all been packed into the same block, in different cells, divided by Congressmen, an informer and some communists. The informer, Manu, looked characteristically well fed. However, no one was sure how much he actually heard the others' conversation, as he spent the best part of the night singing sorrowful folk songs in a low, tuneless wail, songs that recalled long-lost villages and homelands never to be revisited. During the day, tired out by his night-long musical vigil, he slept.

He thus never noticed, or pretended not to see, the pieces of paper being passed from cell to cell. On each paper, different men designed borders in strokes sometimes bold, sometimes wistful and shy. The colours varied from dark blues and greens to tender pinks and yellows. Satinder drew on the images of his father's landholdings and the peasant women who worked the fields; Deborah used this as a frame for her sesame spinach recipe. Vishwa Sarkar's pastel pink-and-yellow-flowered border was more difficult; she finally decided to copy on this sheet her basil-and-fennel paneer recipe. Manjot Singh Sidhu, a timid, hawk-nosed man painted delightful scenes of deer hunts and campfires in the Mughal tradition. Within these borders Deborah carefully transcribed the recipes of coriander lamb roasts and yogurt potatoes she had learnt so long ago in Kalimpong. But the acknowledged genius of the lot was undoubtedly Romesh Gupta. He had come west with Satinder after their days at Santiniketan, had settled down in the decidedly more rugged lands of Pithampur, and had then proceeded to paint with a rare and unmatched productivity. Now, with Satinder and the others, he contributed the most dazzling pieces to Deborah's collection. His borders ranged from the abstract geometrical patterns of Bengali *alpana* to the graceful figure sketches he had learnt under the great master Nandalal Bose. Sometimes his efforts resembled those of his famous teacher—the vaguely Chinese-inspired rendering of women bent over cooking pots and fires, the dull golds and rich reds of their clothes and jewellery shimmering amid the incomparable greens of the foliage around their dwellings. On these brilliant sheets, Deborah copied out her best party recipes, something that would match the finery of the silk-clad women who toiled under their watercolour palm trees.

In the beginning of December, the imprisoned artists finally decided to wind up their efforts. The jail warden had become highly suspicious of their activities, coming down often and unexpectedly to ferret out trouble. He was a fat little man who wore round glasses very close to his eyes, giving him the vague look of a benevolent owl. But they had seen the bruises his cane had left on some fellow inmates. His mandate, as he saw it, was to kill those who came within his reach, either through severe beatings or starvation. These days the British authorities from the neighbouring Crown territories sent him their most troublesome prisoners: those who could not be hanged in British India and yet had to be eliminated. 'Transferred to Pithampur' written in many a man's dossier thus rid British District Magistrates of their problems without creating messy archival trails for future Commissions of Inquiry.

Balwinder Singh had arrived at Pithampur prison one evening, been hauled into a cell and left there for three days without food and water. The man groaned in agony for hours. Finally, Satinder bribed a guard to give the man some water and food once a day. The food restored the man to some strength, but then the warden came down to check on Balwinder's progress and was enraged to discover a weakened but alive prisoner. In pitch darkness one day, Satinder and the others heard the guards coming to get Balwinder. The next morning, a guard informed them that the man had been beaten to death and then dumped in the woods behind one of the Raja's palaces.

At Satinder's request, Deborah travelled to Ambala to meet with and protest to the District Magistrate about this incident. In his hot little office at Ambala, the DM wrinkled his nose in pretended distaste, in the timeless manner of imperial authorities up and down the hierarchy from Delhi to Dibrugarh, and said, 'Well, you know, Miss Sunderland, what these people are like. No sense of justice or fair play, you see. Pithampur is a native state, it isn't England, you know.' Afterwards, over drinks at the club, more appreciative civilians chuckled at his cleverness and the way that the issue had been resolved. 'After all,' said his colleague from the CID, winking genially, 'how is it our fault, if these princes are autonomous and we have no jurisdiction over their police?' They then moved into the dining room for a friendly dinner.

'The British upper classes are really quite a fascinating bunch, you know,' reflected Satinder while the other men returned to their work, the setting sun throwing a golden glow over the canvases and colours. 'In a disgusting way, they are. They are so involved in subterfuge and deceit, and so very pleased at their own skill at these. You know, until the last war, they were horribly condescending to their own middle class. But now, they have gathered, even if sneeringly, the English middle class into their bosom and are training *them* in the art of deception. And this is what one sees in all these little DMs and DSPs, not quite out of the top drawer, just ordinary boys for the most part, from solid middle-class stock. If the results were not so tragic it would be interesting to watch them being drawn into sinister games in the name of King and Empire.'

That was the first comment that anyone had made on the political situation during George's visit.

'Perhaps the middle class want to be absorbed?' he said, although Satinder's unexpected insight had summed up his own feelings on the issue as well. Deceitful toff, about summed up someone like James Ruffington.

'Well, yes, of course, Mr Clark. Sadly, the middle class is both the strongest and the weakest class in our times. The people from the middle class have many valuable and sound economic skills, but culturally, they carry a rather large chip on their shoulders, which is why they are always yearning to be absorbed upwards. This desire to be upwardly mobile will ultimately be the downfall of the middle class itself. A country where the middle class abandons its traditions of thrift and usefulness and hard work, and decides to adopt the sneering, slothful, credit-scrounging ways of the upper classes is headed towards decadence—and massive amounts of debt. Soon, unpaid tailors' bills will no longer be the prerogative of insolvent aristocrats. And when a whole society adopts those values of living beyond one's means, well, its downfall is not too far away. Maybe not in my lifetime, but certainly in yours. And by the way, these are not original thoughts. I believe Samuel Smiles said similar things about a hundred years ago. Have you ever read *Self-Help*?'

At this point, Deborah entered the room and ushered George back into the living room.

'So did you collect any more recipes during your last posting?' she asked smilingly.

George sighed and then unburdened himself of the news that he and Alice were no longer together, that she was no longer waiting for him.

'She became a cook to some movie stars during the war at home, Miss Sunderland—I mean, Mrs Silonia,' he reddened. 'And they want her to go to America with them. She wanted me to come too. But how can I say yes or no when I haven't been home for so long. I don't know what I am going to do next. My number for demobilization won't be up for a while.'

'Which film star does Alice work for?' Even Deborah Sunderland was not immune to the fascination of the movies.

'He's an old one, from before our times. His name is Richard Clarke. He's English but lives and works in America. Came back to do his duty during the war, though. Alice told me he was too old to sign up so they just had him doing some light Home Guard stuff, and some touring and radio.' Remembering that he had the signed photograph from Richard Clarke, he fished it out of his bag and showed it to Deborah. Her eyes widened as she took in the picture of the silver-haired man with big white teeth who smiled out at her from the photograph.

'Did you see any of his pictures?' George asked.

'Oh, no, my boy. But I met him very briefly many, many years ago, when he was very young.' She smiled now at the memory, no longer bitter, just fading.

'Really?' The idea of Deborah Sunderland knowing a famous American film star seemed improbable, given that she had lived in India since the age of seventeen or eighteen.

'Yes, he was a stage actor then. And he wasn't Richard Clarke in those days. His name was Neville Shaw. We met on the boat coming over to India. I sometimes wondered what became of him. It was such a long time ago.' Deborah smiled again—the old hurt had healed so well that she did not feel it at all. George left soon after, his immediate memory of Deborah's house framed by the hand-waving artists standing around the doorway.

FIVE

In the dead of night, the train groaned, shuddered and then screeched to a halt at Bajapur station. George had been awake and dressed for nearly an hour before the yawning ticket checker came to alert him that Bajapur was fast approaching. There was another officer in the compartment who had got in at Jammu, totally drunk, and had then cursed himself to sleep. He half-sat up now and snarled as George put his trunk and bedroll outside the door in the narrow corridor. George ignored him and stepped out into the warm night, stood uncertainly for a few minutes, and then walked briskly towards the Railway Traffic Officer's cell-like office. Behind him the train whistled and pulled away, screechily protesting its weight.

'You'll be heading up to New Bajapur, then, I see,' said the RTO whose job in this small, rather sleepy cantonment town was boring at the best of times. 'Well, if it hadn't been so late, you could have just taken a tonga; but there are a couple of lorries heading that way.' He chatted with George about the war and the situation in the East until his staff sergeant came to tell him that the truck was ready.

Outside the station, there was quite a bit of activity. The train stopped here only once a day, so passengers, their delighted relatives and friends, and numerous coolies all thronged around some rather ramshackle tongas. The RTO's sergeant showed him the lorry, its engine grumbling in the dark.

'You'll be for the 126th East Yorks, then, sir?' smiled the driver, his cheerfulness making up for a rather sloppy salute.

'That's right.' Ordinarily, George would have sat in the cabin next to the driver. But the front seat was packed with all sorts of crates and bags. He settled himself on a hard, wooden bench at the back of the truck. The driver latched the tailboard, threw some sacks of provisions over the top of it and went round to the front. They drove off with a jerky change of gears that nearly threw George off the bench. One of the sacks had burst open and tins of sardines and other food rattled around the floor. These tins of sardines no doubt belonged to some batch of foodstuff bound for Burma or some other combat zone; the driver had carefully pinched some of them for his own use. He wondered how the driver would dispose of these tins. Usually, soldiers ate whatever food they stole. Occasionally, one of them would set up a thriving little black market barter racket, padding his uncomfortable military life with a few luxuries such as better boots and razors, clothes and socks, cigarettes and soap. As a private, George had watched these antics with detached amusement. As an officer he would have to deal with these issues differently, he supposed.

He knew little about the regiment he was setting out to join. All he had been told was that the 126th East Yorkshire Regiment was a new battalion, crafted by welding two Burma-depleted units, the 33rd King's Own Royal Regiment and the 23rd East Yorkshire Regiment. The Commanding Officer was Col. Richard Holmes, a survivor from the 23rd East Yorks, and the first CO from one of the founding units of the battalion. The previous two COs had been posted in from other formations and had left after unenthusiastic and rather brief tenures.

The truck jolted along in the dark, and then with another jerk and a wrench and a great rolling and crashing of loose tins, it halted outside a gate. The driver and the sentry bantered good-naturedly about passwords; then the driver swung the vehicle around a curved path and deposited George in front of a grimly silent and dark mess building.

'Here you go, sir,' said the man as he took George's luggage down.

'Thanks.' George wondered who was going to let him into the building that hulked low and unfriendly in the darkness. He tested one of the doors. To his surprise, it opened; emboldened by this success, he stepped in and shouted for the bearer. A sleepy, tousled figure detached itself from the shadows and came towards him, saluting feebly.

'Ram-Ram, sahib.' The bearer then growled at somebody, and another slight figure, then another, came out of the dark, and all began to pull and tug at George's trunks. Finally, they made their way in a small, stumbling procession to a silent set of rooms at the back of the mess. The bearer lit a hurricane lantern; the other two men put their burdens down and all three inspected George curiously.

'What time would you like chhota-hazri, saab?'

'Half past five.' There was no point being late on his very first day. The bearer nodded and asked George for his uniform and shoes. Too tired to ask where they were going with his stuff, George undressed and then fell into the hard, musty bed, his mind wiped clean of all thought until the bugle blew at daybreak.

In the morning, a confusion of noises woke him up. First, there was the penetrating and slightly off-key reveille, succeeded by the lighter notes of faraway commands and of boots crashing. Then, there was a clatter and crash outside his door, followed by whispered curses and scoldings in Hindustani. Moments later, a young boy, his new servant, brought in his morning mug of tea inclined at an alarming angle and slopping into the tray. George hurriedly sat up and took the mug from the boy, who promptly left. Another man entered and hung up George's uniform on the knob of the closet door. George was startled. Who were these people? When had they found the time this early in the day to polish the brass buttons on his shirt to a gleaming finish? The man also put down a shining pair of shoes that George barely recognized as his own. He smiled. He was going to like regimental life, he decided, especially as an officer.

'What is the boy's name?' he asked the man, in his faltering Hindustani.

'Lal Ram, saab.'

'There is someone outside who wants to see you, sir,' Lal Ram came in again, speaking in slow but fairly good English. George was so surprised that he forgot to ask who the visitor was.

'How do you know English?'

'I worked for Miss Williams, who runs the mission school here in Bajapur. She taught me some English.' Lal Ram indicated again that there were people waiting. George slipped into a pair of shorts and his crumpled shirt from the previous night, and went out into the veranda. To his absolute astonishment, standing on the steps were Ramu Chowkidar—wearing his usual uniform of assorted, faded hand-me-downs from British soldiers, and Karl's white cap—and a woman he introduced as his wife, Indumati.

'Namaste, sahib,' said Ramu, handing him a sealed envelope.

George ripped it open and read the contents, fighting to keep the dismay he felt from showing on his face. It was from Roy Coulson, now on his way to Burma. Abdul Khan's tomb near Mhow had been decommissioned by the Archaeology

Department as in wartime the funds simply would not stretch so far to cover every minor monument. He asked George if he could help Ramu and Indumati find a job in his new location, preferably with a school or hospital or with the army. Coulson had somehow managed to put them on a troop train headed north, which was indeed a convenient conveyance for Ramu as he had a large collection of potted plants without which he would not leave.

'If you could just try on their behalf, Clark, it would be ever such a kindness,' Coulson ended his note. 'They really have nowhere to go, except back to their village which is a godforsaken place where everyone starves.'

'Oh bloody hell!' thought George. He hadn't even started his new career yet and already he was being burdened with camp followers. Through Lal Ram's translations he conveyed to the desperate couple that they should wait a few days while he settled in. Then, remembering that they were strangers in a strange land, just like he was, he gave them ten rupees. Lal Ram led them away to find temporary accommodation, Indumati's sari a vivid blur against the hot blue horizon.

Later, when faces and names had separated into clear identities, he learned that Lal Ram was an orphan from the hills near Nahan. The boy had wandered his way westward to Bajapur and had been working temporarily in the local mission school where the head, an American lady, found him useful as a jack of all trades. The taciturn man, Ratan Singh, was a long-time employee of the barracks, serving whichever military unit passed through those faded brick buildings. Recently, the movement of officers into and out of the barracks had increased sufficiently for him to hire Lal Ram.

But that first morning, after the first surprise of unexpected visitors from Mhow, every face, brown or white, was just a confused blur. There were important things to do such as report to the Adjutant and meet the other officers, and the men. Dressed in his new uniform, George hurried to the mess for breakfast. In the daylight the mess looked inviting, a low, stone building with a faded red-tile roof.

George entered the dark, cool interior of the mess gratefully and headed towards the dining room where he could already see four officers tucking into a substantial meal. He took in the decor with particular attention; this was now his new home, and in the army it would be his last. He saw that against the wood-panelled walls and dark, polished furniture, so dear to British military taste in India, the regimental silver seemed impossibly delicate. The sideboards creaked with bowls and vases acquired as booty from various battles across the world, as well as with trophies from Shanghai where the 33rd King's Own unit had chased the Boxer rebels. One wall housed sombre pieces from the Sudan. There was also more conventional military bric-a-brac—glass cases full of medals, and portraits of heavy-browed gentlemen in gold-braided uniforms who were looking down disapprovingly at the latest generation of dining officers.

In a quick appraisal as he approached the dining table, George observed that all four of his companions in the dining room were lieutenants, with two pips on their shoulders. A heavy silence presided over the small gathering, although one red-haired officer was trying to dispel the gloom with determined chatter.

'You must be Clark?' said the redhead cheerfully. 'We were to fetch you but John Lewis, the Adjutant, didn't tell us till twenty minutes before the train came in. I'm Ralph Barrington, temporary Lieutenant and Senior Subaltern.' The other three greeted him offhandedly and introduced themselves; the only other friendly face belonged to John Bacon. Then everyone became very serious as a major came into the dining room, followed by a padre, whose left arm was in a sling. There was a chorus of 'Good Morning, sirs' and someone mumbled an introduction to George.

The Major had a rather red nose, and waved George to his seat. 'Do sit down, sit down. Have some breakfast. Help yourself; there are no bearers at breakfast. You found your way then?'

'Yes, sir.' George helped himself firmly to scrambled eggs and sausage and toast. It seemed all very disorganized but it was going to be a long day and he didn't want to start it off on an empty stomach. The food tasted horrible—the eggs were rubbery, the sausage smelled and tasted suspicious, and the toast looked and tasted burnt. His reflections were interrupted by a grating animal sound, which was familiar and yet unthinkable in an army cantonment. It couldn't be, could it?

'Are those . . .?' he ventured timidly.

Barrington and John Bacon roared with laughter. The other officers smiled.

'Welcome to Bajapur, you've arrived just in time for the twice-weekly donkey fair,' Barrington explained. 'The donkeys gather every Tuesday and Thursday, and are traded and sold every Wednesday and Friday. The whole sordid affair takes place right against the cantonment walls, in the field outside. Nothing, not even wartime regulations, can drive away those bloody animals and their blasted owners. So, basically, we have to live with the damn thing the whole week.'

'Still, it makes you appreciate the quiet on the three remaining days of the week,' Bacon added, wiping up his eggs with toast. 'Monday is almost heavenly, till the donkeys come in again on Tuesday afternoon.'

'And so here we all are,' continued Barrington, laughing again. 'Stuck with bloody donkeys and with Rajinder Singh's atrocious cooking. Good thing I'm the Senior Subaltern, Clark, I'll lead you through the wonderland that is Bajapur and the 126th East Yorks. That's my job, you know, as Senior Subaltern. Have to make sure that you know how to use your fish knife and how to dress for dinner night, and all that.'

'There is also, er, a rather belligerent cow in the cantonment,' said the padre, whose statement triggered another wave of chuckles around the table.

'A cow?' George was incredulous.

'A cow, Mr Clark,' said the padre gloomily, pointing to his sling. 'She belongs to the pandit of one of the Indian units here and she simply charges at anyone who crosses her path. I complained severely to the Brigade Headquarters people when she knocked me down yesterday.'

'You're in for it here in Bajapur, Clark. Donkey fairs and charging cows,' said Barrington, merrily.

'The pandit has assured the Brigade that he will take preventive steps,' the padre said primly, regarding his tepid breakfast with fading enthusiasm.

After breakfast, George reported to the Adjutant, Captain John Lewis, who walked with a pronounced limp.

'So, you've arrived,' said Lewis, redundantly. 'Regimental kit—yes, I see you're presentable to the CO. Well, let's have a look here. All right, you can go to A Company. They are lucky, have two lieutenants already. Here, Rumkins, go and fetch CSM Billings from A Company.' At this point, a thin lance corporal detached himself from the shadows in the office and went away, grumbling audibly about the heat. Lewis went on without a pause, 'Well, let's see . . . oh dear, I sent for the Company

Sergeant-Major. But you really want to meet the officers first, don't you? Weller, can you give this note to Major Rudolph?' Another surly lance corporal ambled out into the glare of the sunlight.

As it turned out, both the Company Commander and the Company Sergeant-Major landed up together at the Adjutant's office. 'Whatever do you mean, Lewis?' harrumphed Major Rudolph, wiping sweat off his brow. 'Why didn't you just send the youngster to my office with everyone else?' It was obvious from Lewis's face that he had not thought about that. 'Well, sir,' he began weakly. Evidently, the unit was used to this because Rudolph and CSM Billings took George away without much further talk, walking him to a set of barracks built, like all its counterparts in India, around a patch of hard, dry grass.

It was the most incredible relief to step out of the blazing May sun into the shade. Most of the rooms were square and unremarkable, and full of men moving either bits of paper or bits of equipment. A painted wooden board outside a room proclaimed it to be the A Company office. Once inside, Major Rudolph waved George into a hard, wooden chair. Then he hastily slid into a drawer a novel and some loose sheaves of paper that had been lying on the trestle table, and began to interview the youngster.

'Well, let's see here, Clark. You've already seen action, good, good, so the men won't try and pull a fast one on you. Did that to Bacon, you know. Poor chap didn't know whether he was the leader of his platoon or its juniormost private.' So John Bacon was in the same Company, thought George. That would be good.

'Well, let's see now. Billings, Mr Clark goes to No. 3 Platoon?'

'You said No. 1, sir.' The Company Sergeant-Major had a quiet manner.

'Indeed, so I did. All right, No. 1 Platoon it is. Billings, send for Sergeant Hopper.'

'Sir.' The CSM disappeared.

'Well, as you can see, Clark, the whole unit's really busy. We are all moving soon, I do hope it is back to Europe. Except not to bloody Germany. It's in absolute ruins, I've heard. Not that Jerry doesn't deserve the thrashing. I say, did you see how nice the mess is looking? All the silver and everything have finally started catching up with us. The CO insisted that all the regimental property of the 33rd King's and the 23rd East Yorks' be given priority coming over from the depots back home. Need that stuff. Builds morale to have the mess looking good. Thank God, they aren't sending us back to Burma. That just wouldn't be fair to us, would it? You were there too, weren't you? With the Berks? Or was it the Yorks? Who knows when Burma will end? Do you play tennis?'

Major Rudolph jumped from topic to topic without pause, often without even waiting for a reply.

'Lunch is at the mess for you, isn't it? Food any good today? Usually, that damn fool of a cook comes up with all sorts of unspeakable rubbish. Drinks too much and cooks horrible messes all the time. Honestly, the food in Burma was better.' At this point the CSM returned with the Platoon Sergeant.

'Ah, Hopper. This is Mr Clark. Take him around, will you?' He waved everyone out of his office. As he left, George saw Rudolph turning the pages of the novel that he had pulled out of the drawer again. He had also pulled out some handwritten papers—notes, a novel of his own, who knew what? Major Rudolph had a look of relief on his face, the expression of a man who was finally being allowed to do some real work.

Sergeant Hopper was a tough, short little man, with a

pronounced cockney accent. Most of the men were in the barracks, he explained, except those away on guard duties and on cookhouse fatigues. Hopper led George to a set of rooms opening onto a shaded veranda. A stencilled sign indicated No. 1 Platoon's living quarters. They entered and soon George was busy trying to absorb the whirling sights and sounds in the room as Hopper changed from an affable little man into a heaving, yelling pink mass. In a sense, it was all familiar, except for George's new role. He had been on the other side not too long ago, and had participated in scenes like this quite a few times. This was a well-worn routine where the men were verbally cuffed and knocked into some sort of discipline when a new officer was presented.

As the shuffling and racing men settled down, George saw that there were about thirty soldiers who now stood in rows between two neat lines of beds. They were a mixed bag, some older, some younger, but physical exertion and tough warfare had etched themselves into lines on the face of even the youngest soldier, a soft-cheeked lad of nineteen. Many of them had yellow faces, classic signs of malaria, while others were clearly struggling with jaundice. Some of them might survive into old age, George thought, especially now that the war in Europe was over, but Burma had marked them forever.

They stood now, his platoon, in front of him, all of them staring fixedly at points other than his face. George put them at ease and then talked to them, briefly.

'Like all of you, I was in Burma, fighting the enemy,' George began, at first self-conscious, then warming to his theme. He went on to tell them that he was aware of the nature of their duties, having himself been several times on guard duty, cookhouse fatigues, and so on.

When he left to go to lunch, the atmosphere in the barracks room had become palpably more respectful.

George's self-confidence ebbed away, though, as he approached the mess. He darted into the lounge through a side door of the veranda and looked apprehensively at the scene. There were about fifteen other officers present. John Bacon and Ralph Barrington and a couple of younger officers, both captains, nodded to him. The more senior officers ignored him. The incompetent Adjutant, John Lewis, was huddled at one end of the room with Richard Brassey and another major, a red-faced weather-beaten sort of man. What was it with these majors? They all looked like they had been put through the wringer, with their leathery, sunburnt faces and bulbous noses.

After a while, an English mess corporal came in and announced in mournful tones that lunch was served. The officers filed out, lieutenants and subalterns last, and took their seats at the gleaming wooden table in the long dining room. George found himself between Bacon and Barrington, facing a sour-faced captain who pointedly ignored all of them. Two Indian bearers in white mess jackets began to dart around with trays, tureens and platters, and a dreary sort of luncheon got underway. Barrington and Bacon were both pleased as punch that George was going to be with them in A Company.

'I say, Clark!' Captain Lewis boomed cheerfully from across the table, 'you have to come over to the CO's office this afternoon. You were supposed to do that this morning, but oh well . . .' Everyone else grinned.

'If he doesn't send someone to fetch you, just wander across anyway, around three,' Barrington whispered to George. 'The Old Man goes to the office first before he heads off for the stables. There's this ATS, you know.' George was shocked. As an Other Rank, his CO had been a grand and majestic figure, as distant as the King from George's everyday life. He had never thought of the CO as a human being, far less had he thought of the CO in the role of Casanova with beery breath and groping hands, chasing Women's Auxiliary Territorial Service girls in India, the women who supported the military in non-combatant roles. But Barrington's behaviour was obviously crossing the line, because the captain on the other side curtly ordered him to watch what he was saying. 'And you, too,' he said, glaring at George, then turning his head away to ignore him again for the rest of the meal.

'That's the 33rd for you,' muttered Barrington under his breath. 'That's Dennis Middles, Captain, also from A Company.'

'Have to go. Orderly Room beckons. See you at tea,' Bacon said as he left. The Orderly Room was the administrative nerve centre of the battalion. 'Don't forget to see the Old Man now.'

As it was already pushing on to three o'clock, George decided to stop by the Commanding Officer's office right away. But Lewis was not there; perhaps he had forgotten that the CO was due at the office any moment? George decided to wait in Lewis's office, and, after a while, the sound of an approaching vehicle told him that the CO was nearing the office.

A tall, rather mournful-looking man unfolded himself from a car and walked up the short flight of steps to his office, connected to the Adjutant's by a curtained doorway. Through this, George heard him remark to the office orderly to send for the Adjutant. The office orderly replied that Captain Lewis was not yet in.

'What nonsense, Corporal! I distinctly saw someone in there as I was coming in.'

'That be Mr Clark, sir.'

'Mr Who? Oh, dammit, send him in this very minute.'

George marched in, snapped off a perfect salute, gazing warily at his new CO, Colonel Richard Holmes. The CO waved a finger gloomily at George.

'Well, Clark, welcome aboard.' At this point, a flustered Lewis entered the office and saluted hastily.

'Is it absolutely too much to ask you to be here on time?' The CO's sorrowful tone was edged with ice.

'Sorry, sir.'

'Now about Clark here. Didn't you send him to A Company? When does A Company go to Delhi?'

'A Company, sir? Oh, two weeks from next Thursday, sir. I mean, June 14, sir.'

'And it's May 25 already. Do you know what to take with you, Clark?'

'Er . . .'

'I'll take care of it, sir,' Lewis said firmly, clearly having overlooked informing both A Company and George of the impending travel plans. Maj. Rudolph, the Company Commander, would die of a fit, thought George, when he heard this.

'Now about . . . er . . . Thursday, Clark,' Lewis began as they left the CO's office and entered the Adjutant's, his limp even more pronounced than usual. 'You, Bacon and, let's see, Barrington and is it Parry? Oh, Parry's already in Delhi. I'll have to send him a signal to stay there. Well, anyway, all of you are to take your platoons to Delhi on Thursday, June 14. Security duty for the Viceroy before he returns to Simla. Maj. Rudolph, the Company Commander, will also go with all of you.'

'That's in about three weeks, sir?'

'Yes, look here, don't 'sir' me. You can call me John.'

'Yes, well, do we take . . .?'

'Oh, ask Bacon or Barrington, they'll tell you what to do and how to dress and all the rest of it.'

Oh, splendid, thought George. How on earth did the battalion function with such an inefficient Adjutant?

A pretty woman in ATS uniform entered Lewis's office unannounced. Her hazel eyes slid over George with perfect indifference and turned impatiently to the Adjutant. She flopped down elegantly in a padded chair without being asked to do so by Lewis, technically her superior officer, and sat in silence tapping her nails on the armrest of her chair. This was probably the CO's popsy that Bacon had joked about. George tried to get an impression of her without staring.

'Could you get Muriel to please come *out* of that office next door?' Her voice was loud enough to carry into the CO's room and, almost in response to her hectoring, another girl parted the curtains and entered the Adjutant's office. This was obviously Muriel, a tall, shy woman also in an ATS uniform. She had wavy brown hair and mournful eyes. Colonel Holmes followed her closely. Goodness, thought George, so *this* is the one, not Sergeant Sexy. Don't *they* look like a couple of cocker spaniels? And indeed the lovers dripped pathos from every pore. Muriel had obviously gone into the CO's office via the other door that opened directly onto the shaded veranda. The other woman looked scornfully from one to the other, completely unafraid of the CO and his exalted rank.

'Well, if you both are done with "work", I want to get some riding done before tea,' she remarked contemptuously and strode out.

'I'll meet up with you at the stables, then. Don't . . . er, forget the notes, Muriel.' The Colonel's attempt at covering up his entanglement was as pathetic as his situation. The two women left, followed shortly by the CO who disappeared as he had come, in a small cloud of dust.

'Didn't know there were any ATS here,' remarked George conversationally, wondering if Lewis would divulge some more information on the subject.

'Oh yes, those are the daughters of Colonel Bates—Signal's—and Brigadier Curtis, the Indian Army Brigade Commander. Muriel Bates and Barbara Curtis. Great friends, both of them. Stuck in India because of the war. Both joined the ATS when they could, and now they just, you know, help around the office with typing and all that.'

What a battalion this was! On his very first day, George had met an incompetent Adjutant, a literary-minded Company Commander, and now an imperious ATS and an adulterous Commanding Officer.

'Good heavens, look at the time!' Lewis exclaimed prissily and eased George out of his office.

Indeed, it was getting on to four o'clock and George could see the other dining members heading towards the mess for tea. In the dining room, the motley crowd gathered again and began cutting themselves slices from a large, soggy-looking fruit cake on the sideboard. Helping himself to tea and cake, George slid between Bacon and Barrington.

'Watch out for the ladies here, me boy,' said the irrepressible Bacon. 'You'll be over for tea at one of their places and then the wives get to eat you for the meal. Real burra-mems, the lot of them. There's no escape from the memsahibs, my friend, no escape at all. War in Europe's over and the wives are trickling back. Although the CO's sister-in-law is quite fetching. Lives with the CO and his wife. Any more cake left?'

George told him about his afternoon at the Adjutant's office, biting into his cake. The cake tasted stale, heavy and soggy. The cook here was really bad, George thought, concentrating on the weak tea instead. Bacon frowned at the news.

'Damn fool, why couldn't he catch C Company or B for the Delhi job?' he said bitterly. 'Anyway, the CO will put up with anything from Lewis, you might as well know that. He's a bit scatterbrained after the beating he took in Burma, but he saved his entire company by digging in and covering the retreat back into India. Only three men, and old Lewis, and a battered machine gun between them, but they managed to make the enemy think there was a whole company. Kept moving around and firing till they ran out of ammo. He took three shots in the head and about seven in the leg. So, the CO will do anything for him, even if Lewis muddles things up sometimes. Everyone will do a lot to cover up for him, actually.' That explained why Lewis was allowed to stay on as Adjutant, George reflected, finding that all his resentment against Lewis had vanished in the light of this information. It was the protective cover of the unit thrown over the man, a regimental spirit of watching out for one's own that would last the disabled man's entire active duty career and that would extend into his retirement.

His ruminations were interrupted at this point by the expostulations of the other old Major in the unit, Hugh Shelton, who had bitten into something hard in Rajinder Singh's cake.

Later, over evening drinks, Bacon and Barrington explained to George that there was trouble brewing in the battalion. Although the 33rd King's Own and the 23rd East Yorks had been married into one organization, there had not yet been a meeting of hearts between the officers of the two regiments. The 33rd officers were particularly cut up because Holmes, the new CO, was originally from the 23rd; so there were dark rumblings about favouritism and so on.

To make matters particularly intolerable, the quality of the mess food was absolutely execrable. 'I wouldn't give the crap that Rajinder Singh here turns out to a sick and starving pye-dog,' said John Bacon, sipping his chilled beer. It turned out that

Rajinder Singh loved the bottle as dearly as did the senior dining member, Maj. Brassey. Dinner that night descended into the depths of the inedible—tinned chicken in a brown gravy that ran thinly around the plate. Tinned peas and tinned carrots rounded off a particularly bleak meal. George was utterly dismayed.

After dinner, Brassey and Shelton hovered in the lounge, while the captains and lieutenants and subalterns hung around gloomily near the bar, waiting for the two senior officers to go away. The 23rd occupied one end of the anteroom and the 33rd settled at the other end. After a while when the two senior majors wandered out, everyone ordered drinks and settled down to talk. George was introduced to the other officers, who mostly said nothing to him by way of welcome, each returning to his unit's end of the lounge. For lack of knowing anyone from the 33rd camp, George remained with Bacon and Barrington in the 23rd area.

As it turned out, George found himself calling on the Commanding Officer's wife, Mrs Holmes, sooner than he had imagined. She organized a tea at her house for all the A Company officers leaving for Delhi. And so, on Friday, on a blistering hot afternoon, George found himself walking up the straight, wide road to No. 16 Peterson Road, thinking uneasily about the afternoon ahead.

In the event, Ellen Holmes turned out to be quite startling. For one thing, unlike a typical CO's wife, and despite what Bacon had said earlier about memsahibs, she was quite warm and welcoming. 'How are you?' she smiled at him, when the servant showed him in to her cool, white-and-green drawing room. For another, Mrs Holmes was American. George never quite recovered from the surprise.

George had not met any American women before but from

his brief interaction with American troops in Ranchi en route to Burma in 1942, he had the distinct impression that Americans in general were quite different than the English. Many of the American rankers he had seen had been quite hostile to the British, although that didn't stop them from being rather cruel to their own black troops, who were firmly separated from the whites by barbed wire and space, both in Ranchi and in Calcutta.

But Ellen Holmes seemed just a normal Commanding Officer's wife, chatting with everyone seated around her, pointedly ignoring the uneasy ties that existed between the 33rd King's Own and the 23rd East Yorks, as well as the fact that the officers had divided into two distinct camps right here in her drawing room.

'Why, John, won't you pass some of that cake over to Dennis here?' John Bacon who had been loitering sulkily by George's elbow stirred himself reluctantly and handed a plate of cake to George who then relayed it over to Dennis Middles, the stern captain who had reprimanded him at lunch earlier in the week. Two other captains from A Company reclined stiffly on flowered upholstery, occasionally shooting glances of pure dislike at John and slightly less hostile ones at George. Clearly, the 33rd outnumbered the 23rd in A Company.

'Now, Andy, John and George have been looking at those sandwiches for a while. *Would* you, please?' Ellen would intervene with periodic social requests. And so it went on.

Halfway through the tea, there was a collective excitement as the sheer curtains separating the drawing room from the dining room parted. A slender young woman walked in, throwing smiles all around and causing the atmosphere to lighten up noticeably.

'I say, Anna,' piped up Dennis Middles, his nose almost quivering in excitement, 'how was the photo shoot?'

His wife, Jill, frowned at him from across the room.

'Fine,' replied the newcomer, filling up a tiny tea plate with indelicately large helpings of cake and sandwiches. 'The light's almost faded, so I had to come home.'

'My sister, Anna Benson,' said Ellen Holmes, by way of a general introduction. Anna smiled at George, raising an inquiring eyebrow at the new face.

'Just joined up?'

'Yes, been here only a few days, Miss Benson,' George said shyly.

'It's Anna. Well, welcome to Bajapur, gateway to dust and damnation.'

'Really, Anna,' scolded her sister. 'Bajapur's really a very nice station, Mr Clark,' she assured him hastily.

'What brought you here?' asked George, slightly distracted by Anna's auburn hair that fell in attractive, natural waves on to the shoulders of her green cotton dress.

'Oh goodness, everybody's already heard about that,' Ellen Holmes said. 'Why don't you sit here, Anna, and catch Mr Clark up with your news.' The CO's wife had taken a liking to George. What a relief to have someone over who did not carry the weight of these mystifying regimental feuds.

'Do you like photography?' Anna asked George.

'I've never really done any,' he confessed, wondering if she would now lose interest in talking to him. 'What sort of photographs do you like to take?'

'People,' she said, emphatically. 'I have taken some very good pictures of people both in Jamshedpur—where I was before this—and also here in Bajapur. But my dear sister and brother-in-law are trying to keep me from doing that kind of stuff these days.'

'That's because she goes to where trouble's brewing,' said Ellen, who had been half-listening, trying to keep a conversation going with the vinegar-faced Jill Middles, Dennis's wife.

'Well, actually I take the pictures before the trouble starts,' said Anna, munching on a sandwich. 'It's when the cops arrive that all hell breaks loose.'

'So, what's interesting about these people?'

Anna turned to look at him, with interest. 'You know, you're the first person in the last four years who's asked me that. Most people just harangue me about how dirty and unsafe the whole business is. But, honestly, it's fascinating. You know, there's so much energy in these meetings. And I like to capture it before they get underway, when the speakers are still thinking about their talk, before their faces start getting all purple with rage and emotion. My sister here thinks I'm crazy; Richard probably thinks I'm disloyal but disloyal to whom, I say? I'm American, aren't I? I can say this stuff without being hauled off to London to get my head chopped off.' She sounded defiant.

'Encouraging troublemakers, that's all!' snorted Col Holmes, who had walked in halfway through Anna's declamation. 'I really do wish you would stay away from the bazaar, Anna.'

Ellen came up to George, concerned and twittering. 'I hope Anna's not been boring you with all her talk of those . . . all that politics. She's not easy these days.' George smiled and, changing the obviously difficult subject, asked her what she thought of A Company's upcoming trip to Delhi.

'Oh, it's a great honour, I'm sure you recognize that! And I am sure that you will do the 126th East Yorks proud, all of you.' She sounded very much the CO's wife at that moment, beaming at him like a benevolent martinet. Beneath her smile, though, George could sense a brittle tension. He felt sorry for her at that moment. It could not be easy, having to play gracious matriarch to a group of mutually hostile and bickering people.

In fact, every day Ellen Holmes negotiated the mined path of social intercourse in the battalion with her heart in her mouth. Snide comments from the 33rd wives would abruptly stop when she entered the room; they expected her to favour the 23rd officers and their wives. As the war in Europe drew to a close, a steady trickle of battalion wives had descended on Bajapur, to further aggravate matters.

Small actions could cause a social catastrophe. Once she had praised Ruth Betford's brownies–they *had* been delicious–and before she knew it, a major row had broken out between Ruth Betford and Jill Middles. Mrs Middles had waspishly asked for recipes that might contain the secret to one's husband's career. That had brought Ruth to Ellen, in tears and outrage. As the matter grew like a cancer, Ellen could no longer skirt the wretched business of the brownies. So she asked Jill for the recipe of that seed cake she had eaten at her place for tea one day. She loathed seedcake, but now in the interests of battalion harmony she felt compelled to add the damned recipe to her collection for the sake of at least quiet, if not peace. Her feeble little gesture backfired however, for then the 33rd wives spitefully spread the word that 'Her Ladyship' demanded tribute by way of baked goods.

Then there had been the matter of the play. The ladies of the 126th East Yorkshire Regiment were to put up a play for the annual flower show in Bajapur. The flower show was a feeble affair at the best of times. And the general sense of dislocation and wartime upheaval had left very few women with the desire for any serious gardening. The flower show had dwindled to a variety of roses, gerberas and pinks in tepid colours, produced in the Brigade Commander's gardens by the remaining malis in the cantonment. The black metal tags embedded in the soil carried names painted in military-neat white strokes: one red bloom claimed to be 'Qeen Victria', another called itself simply 'Ros', while a yellow blossom struck the gallant pose of 'Goldan Buty'. The flowers asserted their misnamed presence all over the fabulous grounds of the Brigade Commander's house, mocking the correct order of things with their brazen claim to recognition and reward.

The row with the play had brought things to a dismal conclusion. The 126th East Yorks women had been rehearsing for six weeks, some sort of silly spoof of *The Merry Wives of Windsor*. The stage was set, the chairs were set out in neat rows, with name signs for the distinguished senior officers and their wives. And then a vicious quarrel broke out in the dressing room. The wives of a 33rd King's Own captain and a 23rd East Yorks major began to hiss and spit at each other—an eyewitness later recalled that it was about the first use of a mirror. The whole affair came to a head when the 23rd wife snapped, 'Don't talk to me like that, you're just a captain's wife!' Whereupon the 33rd woman, who was in a leading role, flounced out of the room and out of the play and the show had to be cancelled. The Brigade Commander's wife was furious and blamed Ellen for not keeping her flock in order (as if she could) and the 126th East Yorks had become the laughing stock of the whole cantonment.

Sometimes, Ellen thought that she should just leave it all and return to America. After all, travel was possible now. But then, she thought, Richard was working so hard to create something here. And, at least this afternoon had gone off well. At least this young man, Clark, was nice. At least *he* wasn't sulking around her drawing room and being rude to her other guests.

'I like that young Clark,' she told her husband later that evening as they got into bed.

Richard Holmes grunted and turned over, away from her. He was asleep in two minutes. Ellen looked at him and sighed. She had married him just as the war began and had then lost him for six years. In a sense she and Richard were discovering each other; they had begun the life of newly-weds six years after the wedding. And it had to be in goddamn Bajapur, she thought with some bitterness, that she had to build a home with her old-new husband.

Poor Richard, trying so hard to keep this nasty fighting bunch in some sort of order. And she, Ellen, had awful 33rd women like that Jill Middles informing her smugly that Muriel Bates and Richard were up to hanky-panky. As if he would ever go for that horse-faced girl who hardly knew how to dress herself for an official party. Not that the 23rd women were any better, always quarrelling loudly, like that Rita Rudolph who had pulled Jill Middles's hair out by the roots during an altercation at the club, all under the eyes of the *servants* (which added to the cantonment's sense of collective horror). No wonder poor Major Rudolph spent so much time in his office. He had that dreamy, vacant look that came with having to put up with a shamelessly domineering wife. He was also very literary-minded, so one heard, but what could you possibly write about, being stuck here in dreary old Bajapur? Oh well, Rita was away in the hills for the summer as were most of the other battalion wives. George really was such a nice young man . . . Ellen was asleep before she knew it. She had forgotten to tell Richard the news, yet again.

George ran into Anna again a few days before he was to leave for Delhi. For nine days, Major Rudolph had made the various platoons drill before dawn and just after sundown. Uniforms were examined in anxious and minute detail. Polish was applied and reapplied to belt buckles and Sam Browne belts. The Saturday before their departure, there was a dance at the club and, wanting some company other than the fractious 126th East Yorks, George decided to check out the local attractions for himself. Ratan Singh laid out a crisply starched shirt and dark trousers, while Lal Ram set a flawlessly polished pair of shoes in front of him.

The tonga set him down in front of the low, red-brick building. From the gates he could hear a band playing indifferently in a corner. As always, there were more men than women, but now in the summer, the disparity was even more acute as most of the women had gone up to the hills, some to nearby Mussoorie, others to Nainital farther away. A few Indian officers and their wives were chattering amongst themselves in a corner of the club; the British officers of the old school shunned them, so the Indian couples were amusing themselves as best as they could. George felt sorry but beyond a general sympathy, didn't know what to do. He noticed that in the Indian corner there was also an older, civilian-looking Indian speaking to a brunette in a pink dress who had her back to him.

George walked over to the bar and ordered a gin and tonic. He didn't know anybody in this crowd—there was not one familiar face. He wished that Bacon would hurry up and arrive.

'Why, hello there, it's the new kid on the block!' Anna looked stunning in a pink dress, her hair brushed to a shining mass, pinned behind her head.

'I've been talking to Judge Bharadwaj here,' she said, walking George over to the older man. 'His brother is the local Congress organizer, and since Judge Bharadwaj escorted me, I was allowed to take pictures of their meeting.'

'As long as you understand, Anna, that I cannot be responsible for what action the police might or might not take against the meetings,' Judge Bharadwaj looked rueful. 'Also, the organizers would have driven you out as a spy. Besides, I feel responsible for your safety,' he ended simply.

'This is so unfair,' Anna joked. 'I sympathize with them and they think I am a spy. Mr Bharadwaj arrests them and tries them, and he is still acceptable at their meetings.'

'Anyway, under the new ordinances passed last week, all such meetings are banned till further notice.' Mr Bharadwaj smiled and then moved on to interact with the Indian officers and their wives.

'I heard there's another American here tonight,' Anna said as she looked around. 'But I don't see him. Have you seen one?'

'You're the only one I've seen today.'

Then the shadows moved and a familiar-looking man moved towards him, smiling in recognition. Behind him, a taller, more reticent figure advanced less eagerly.

'Why, I know you!' It was the Intelligence-branch officer, Captain James Ruffington, still pink-faced and cheerful, a cunning little ball of energy even in the wilting heat. 'Remember me from Pithampur?'

'Oh yes, of course!' They exchanged greetings and Ruffington introduced the other man.

'This is Captain Dennis Porter, US Army,' he emphasized this with a wink, so George understood that Porter was also a part of the international Intelligence fraternity.

'Oh, you're the American,' said Anna who had been silent all this while. 'I'm Anna Benson.' She began to chatter delightedly to him, in the manner of all expatriates who always find things in common when they meet in a foreign country. George couldn't help noticing though that Captain Porter was a bit aloof and that Anna rapidly cooled off, then went away to join a nearby group of women, all fanning themselves with little paper fans.

'Clark here did us a good turn in Pithampur,' Ruffington told Porter in a confidential way when Anna was safely out of earshot. Porter nodded and although he glanced at George in an assessing way, did not become noticeably friendlier.

'Did anything come of it?' asked George, feeling a pang of guilt at his role in the downfall of Deborah Sunderland Silonia.

'No,' said Ruffington and for a moment his face clouded over, then brightened again. 'But we did send a message to everyone in the opposition, Congress or communists, that we could fix them whenever we wanted. Disrupting their activities helps out the British Resident there and the Raja.'

'Communists are dogs,' said Captain Porter suddenly, succinctly. 'I hate' em.'

Ruffington laughed heartily.

'Captain Porter was a very useful addition to our little team in Pithampur and is doing good work in Bajapur too,' he said. 'But he does tend to see a lot of communists everywhere.'

'So what brings you to Bajapur, sir?' asked George, not really expecting an answer.

'Oh, we're stationed here now, following some more leads,' Ruffington sounded both evasive and sly. 'We find that . . .' He gave George an appraising look and then nodded his head. 'In fact . . . you would be ideal for the job.'

'Well, I don't know,' said George uneasily, then saw a way out. 'In any case, I'm leaving for Delhi on Thursday, so I won't be here.'

'Delhi? Oh super, super.' Ruffington dismissed his plans. 'I'll talk to your CO and you can also let him know.'

'Really, I don't know at all, sir,' said George, now worried. 'I've only just joined and . . . I really don't know.'

'We'll talk tomorrow,' said Ruffington firmly.

George left the party feeling irritated beyond description. Why had that idiot Ruffington and his American partner showed up in Bajapur? He wanted to go to Delhi with Bacon and Ruffington and Alpha Company, not get involved in some silly Intelligence caper.

The next day was a Sunday and in the morning when George walked over to the mess he found the dining room in an uproar. The cook, Rajinder Singh, had gone a step too far—he had not come into work at all in the morning and having been roused from his alcohol-induced slumber had flown into a rage and had attacked the British mess sergeant and pushed him into a bush. He was fired on the spot, but now there was no cook, and the mess sergeant and a team of unwilling, press-ganged soldiers were turning out an indifferent sort of meal.

Capt. Andy Ross, who George remembered from the CO's tea, was the Mess Secretary. Also an A Company officer, Ross was beside himself with rage. He kept leaving the table to check on things in the pantry and the kitchen.

'We are leaving for Delhi in four days! Who the bloody hell is going to run the mess now, without a cook? I had it all worked out. Maj. Betford of C Company was going to take over from me while we were gone. But now with this chaos here, he wants none of it.'

It was then that George had the brainwave. He had been feeling extremely guilty about Indumati and Ramu, still living somewhere in town with Lal Ram. This job vacancy was a heaven-sent opportunity.

'Er . . . I think, sir . . . if I may . . . there may be someone who can cook, at least while we are gone.' He was hesitant, wondering if he would be scolded and put in his place as the juniormost subaltern in the place. But Ross was desperate and grasped eagerly at his suggestion. So that very morning, Indumati and Ramu were sent for and inspected and interviewed. They were both hired on the spot. Indumati would cook, and Ramu would tend to the unit vegetable gardens at the back of the mess. There was the small problem of Indumati's gender but wartime emergencies allowed for the bending of regulations, and as for the problem of language—for, unlike Rajinder Singh, Indumati spoke not even broken pidgin English—well that was solved beautifully by the availability of Lal Ram, the orphan boy who spoke some English.

'Well done, Clark,' Capt. Ross beamed, no longer the stern and serious 33rd camp-walla. 'You've really got us all out of a very sticky situation. Anyway, I hope this woman will be a better cook than that damned scoundrel Rajinder Singh. I say, why don't *you* order the meals till we leave for Delhi?' And just like that, George had made a new friend in the battalion. And, it was a fellow from the 33rd, no less. Perhaps there was hope for the future.

He went into the kitchen to find Indumati already at work, with a huge bowl of chopped onions to one side, grinding pastes of ginger and garlic on a giant stone. She greeted George happily, recognizing his sponsorship of her employment, her dark eyes following him shyly as he moved around the large, stone-floored space. She was grateful to this young British officer and she meant to demonstrate her gratitude in the manner she knew best—by turning out meal after delicious meal.

SIX

Monday morning brought Indumati and Lal Ram very early to George's quarters. George was awakened at five o'clock, even before the bugler had sounded the reveille, with the smell of tea brewed in spices and rich milk. He drank it with deep appreciation, thankful that the era of Rajinder Singh's dishwater brews was over. The previous evening, as George had sat on his bed, holding the jewel-like booklet of recipes on his knees, he thought that it might be enjoyable to try some of the local vegetables mentioned. He gazed appreciatively at the stylized representations of vegetables on the page, curlicues of gourd stalks and vines, a border of aubergine and green alpana motifs, women and men with one arm raised to steady the baskets on their heads, the other arm poised to strike the elongated dholak strung impossibly lightly around their necks.

Handing Lal Ram his cup and saucer, George took the portfolio out into the veranda where the soft light of the morning made the colours on the pages glow. Indumati was amazed at the beauty in front of her eyes, as George pointed out the vegetables in the pictures to her. Lal Ram joined them, the unlikely trio bending their heads over the burnished pages, translating from one language into another, using mime and images to transmit their information and questions to each other. Then, George went off to change, after instructing Lal Ram to fetch him breakfast from the mess.

The feeling of relative calm was shattered a scant half-hour later. George was summoned to the CO's office at half-past six; he arrived at the Adjutant's office unsure of the reason behind the summons. He was ushered in by Adjutant Lewis who wagged his finger at him in barely-suppressed glee.

'What *have* you been up to, Clark? The Old Man's livid.'

Col. Holmes glared at George when he entered, did not acknowledge his salute, and launched into a tirade.

'I don't know what sort of company you kept before you came here, Clark,' he bit off the words, his face looking even more strained in the shadowed light that filtered through the blinds. 'But I absolutely will not permit such tomfoolery here!' George was totally flummoxed.

'Sir?'

'Oh, don't try to be clever now. Captain Ruffington has spoken to me. If you wanted yourself out of the unit, you should have been man enough to tell me beforehand. I can't stand all this string-pulling!'

George's anger rose in his throat, almost choking him. The blood rushing to his ears made his words sound thick and blurred. 'I can explain, sir,' he began. But Holmes would not be stopped just then.

'Look, I know that things are not that great in the battalion right now. You've probably noticed it in the mess yourself. But they are getting better, I'm trying, we're *all* trying.'

'I just want to say, sir, that I don't know what Ruffington—Captain Ruffington—has said to you, sir. But if he implied that I wanted to leave the unit, that's simply not true. He made me . . . I had done some work for him in Pithampur earlier. It was terrible. And now he has some madcap operations going on here and he wants me to join in. If you could tell him, sir, that I really don't want to . . .' George's face was pale with the strain of his emotions. He hesitatingly explained to the CO what had transpired during his brief stopover in Pithampur. Col. Holmes began to look somewhat placated.

'Look here, Clark,' he said, lighting a pipe. '*You* tell this Ruffington that you don't want anything to do with him. And I will tell him, as my wife says, to beat it from Bajapur. And that idiot Yank who's always with him. Who does he think *he* is? Clark bloody Gable, that's who. Bloody idiots, they think they can come here and overturn a whole unit just for their damn fool adventures! This Ruffington,' Col Holmes concluded as he shuffled some papers wearily, 'is going to end up as a lying, thieving murderer one day. Of course, he'll say that's it's all right because he did it for King and Country, as if that ever makes rascality all right. No, Clark, if you want to go around killing people for a living, be a regular soldier. There's honour in that. We're fighting openly, following whatever orders we are given. All right, you can go now. I'll take care of this at my end. But for Chrissake, can you stop going through life like Alice in bloody Wonderland, meeting up with March hares and Mad Hatters?' Holmes ended abruptly. He seemed embarrassed at having been so outspoken and emotional.

Still too dazed to consider breakfast, George made his way over to his Company Headquarters, where Major Rudolph, the Company Commander, was going over lists with the CSM, Sergeant Billings. A novel lay overturned on a box close by. He nodded as George entered and saluted. 'Heard you were in trouble with the CO, Clark. What the hell is going on?'

George explained and Rudolph added to the CO's warning.

'These Special Ops chaps in Bajapur are a bunch of lying, deceiving prats. Problem is there's no real work for those two here so they are always up to no good. The men tell me that they've seen that Porter sneaking around the unit buildings.'

'Sir.'

'Now, go and get your platoon in order. We leave in three days, you know.'

George went first to the mess, to supervise the preparation of the afternoon meal. His stomach was growling from his missed breakfast, but first, the mess needed to be taken care of and the meals for the day looked into. George sent for Lal Ram to accompany him and as the lad loped beside him silently, he reflected how grateful he was for this small moment of routine in the face of all the disconcerting developments of the morning.

The cookhouse was separated from the main body of the mess building by a long, covered walkway. It was its own little unit with a courtyard onto which opened larders and pantries. As he passed one, he noticed that there were some small mesh-covered cupboards whose legs were placed in bowls of water, to ward off ants and cockroaches. Indumati greeted George with a namaste, her head covered firmly with her sari because of all the strange men she had to work with now. A mess corporal and some other ranks moved around a table in the pantry next door, polishing regimental silver carefully to a dull gleam. All of this was an endearingly domestic circus and yet, with the exception of Indumati's presence as the ringmaster in a faded sari, a deeply masculine one. There was the smell that gave it away—no roses and lemon fragrances here, just an odour of harsh tobacco and polish.

Indumati sat on the kitchen floor with a big blade set in a wooden footboard. George had never seen anything like it. Indumati's foot kept the board in place, while with both hands she chopped vegetables and placed the pieces in a giant brass bowl of water. There were already bowls full of chopped squashes—bottle gourds, snake gourds and ridged gourds. Also, the unavoidable mass of potatoes—or so it seemed to Indumati—that made it easier for rations to slide down British throats. She had already ground the ginger and garlic, and these too sat awaiting their culinary fate in little, round bowls. There was to be pot-roasted chicken with potatoes, with Worcestershire sauce and parsley from Ramu's garden of potted plants forming the marinade for the meat. Around this centrepiece would be arranged several kinds of sautéed vegetables, with simple seasonings. From Deborah Sunderland's cookbook, George had copied out a recipe that involved some *hing* and a dash of cumin in the vegetables instead of onion and garlic. There was also a recipe that called for the *tori*, or ridged gourd, to be baked in the oven with oil and garlic.

As George consulted with Indumati through Lal Ram, he wondered how anyone could work in the hellhole of this room. It was hot almost beyond endurance. The room had been whitewashed in regulation orange and white, but the walls were black with soot. There was a large oven with a black earthen top set in a corner with its own chimney, and now shimmering with heat. There were also two or three wood-fired chulhas. A kitchen helper was busy kneading dough for the chapattis that would be served at lunch. As George left, he noticed a young mess servant scurrying over to mop the floor clean with a wet cloth.

Walking back to the main building, George noticed an Other Rank, a lance corporal, in one of the rooms off the kitchen's courtyard. The OR, his hair clipped short behind his rather large ears, was carving a huge joint of beef. This was one meat that Indumati refused to touch. She was prepared to starve rather than cook what she called '*bade ka* meat'. She would gladly cook fish and poultry and even mutton and goat, but absolutely no beef. It was vexing, but given the shortage of cooking talent available at the moment, the battalion agreed to let a soldier perform the task of preparing and cooking the weekly beef allowance for the mess.

George asked the young man how things were going. The soldier was dripping sweat, his apron was bloodstained, while flies buzzed around the whole room. He looked like he had just murdered someone. But he managed to muster a quick smile and replied that he would soon be done. The unit had also had to commission a special, separate oven for the beef, as otherwise Indumati refused to use the appliance for the daily cooking. But this was easy enough. A man had come the very morning that Indumati had been hired and had crafted an earthen oven with a chimney in the corner of the courtyard farthest away from her area of work. And in this way, through mutual adjustment, disgust and vexation, a working compromise was reached by all concerned. It would suffice till it was time for the battalion to leave on its next posting.

George moved on indoors. Here, he found Capt. Ross scowling at a vast array of bills and receipts presented to him by the duty corporal in the mess. It was a tedious task, George thought, and he now understood why Mess Secretaries were always a harassed lot. Trying not to attract attention to himself, George slid past Ross, and returned to his room to get his things ready for the trip.

But George's journey to Delhi was not to be. Later that afternoon, he was summoned to the Adjutant's office.

'There was a phone call from Simla,' Lewis said, half-impressed. 'You are to go with Ruffington's unit, after all.' Then George was called into the CO's office.

'Well, young Clark, looks like I couldn't save you after all.' Holmes looked glum. 'I really don't know what to believe. Although I wouldn't put it past Ruffington to have one of his friends phone me, pretending to be someone important in Simla.' The CO's voice was caustic.

'Can I refuse, sir?' George was miserable and furious.

'Oh, I suppose you can. Do you want to stay on in the army after the war?'

'No, sir.'

'What are you planning to do?'

'I want to . . .' George realized that he had absolutely no idea about what he wanted to do afterwards. The dream of becoming a veterinarian had died somewhere in Burma. Did he want to become a salesman for a company? Try for university? Go back to farming? With a new shock, he realized that Alice figured nowhere in his future plans anymore. In fact, ever since he had set eyes on Anna Benson, Alice had not been much on his mind. Col. Holmes was looking at him, waiting for an answer.

'I don't know, sir.' It sounded terribly lame. Maybe I am bloody Alice in Wonderland, he thought bitterly.

'In that case, Clark, here is my advice, for whatever it's worth,' said the CO. 'Take the assignment with these wretched chaps and try to do a good job of it. If you catch their attention then you can get ahead in the army afterwards, should you decide to stay on. If you decide to leave, well, it's just another wartime experience.'

'Can I stay on in the unit, sir?'

'We'll see. I'll try to arrange something.'

It turned out that Col. Holmes was able to arrange matters so that George remained on the battalion's roster while being farmed out to Ruffington and Porter. But to add to George's distress, Captain Ross handed over all the mess duties to him before leaving. The day before A Company left town, he called George to the Company office and told him that with effect on Thursday, he, George Clark, would be taking over as temporary Mess Secretary, responsible for the daily menus and the feeding and care of twenty dining members, including two curmudgeonly majors.

'Nobody wants to do it, Clark, and after all you're practically running the show as you know these two from your OTS days, and Major Betford will do the job of Mess President. Everybody will pitch in and do their best.' In this manner, Capt. Ross half-wheedled, half-threatened poor George into accepting the position. George felt very gloomy. The job of Mess Secretary was a tedious, thankless task which involved dealing with complaints from ungrateful dining members and the inspection of all sorts of odious bills and receipts. And this on top of his other loathsome assignment—working on that damn fool Military Intelligence caper with Capt. James Ruffington. Really, his career as an officer was starting off on an astonishingly bad wicket.

On Thursday morning, George helped load A Company men onto ten 15 cwt. trucks, and tried hard to look cheerful as the vehicles snaked away in a convoy out of the cantonment gates. Bacon waved happily while the CSM eyed his men grimly as they sat in the backs of the trucks. George went back to the mess with a heavy heart, and busied himself with looking at menus and purchase orders with Lal Ram, Indumati and Mess Sergeant Dixon. After that, it was back to his room to await fresh orders. They came about mid-morning in the shape of a bearer with a note. Second Lieutenant George Clark was to report to Captain Ruffington's office at 3 Rotherford Square at the opposite end of the cantonment. George borrowed a cycle from Barrington, nodded at an unfriendly 33rd face and rode off towards Rotherford Square.

Sweat streamed down his face, making his chin itch. When did it get cool in Bajapur? Would the monsoon never come this year? He pedalled wearily through the neat, freshly painted cantonment. Everywhere there was a deep, heat-heavy sense of stillness. No shouts from the parade ground or the barracks interrupted his slow journey. Alpha Company had gone to Delhi, and George felt a deep, aching sense of regret that his regimental life had started off so badly.

Rotherford Square was indeed a square—a small parade ground around which were set red-brick buildings with deep, shady verandas whose arched openings led into inner offices. The colourful flags of the Indian Army Brigade, the British Army and other units lay limp in the still morning. One of the buildings was for the local Brigade Commander; its entrance was embellished with pennants and ceremonial guards. Staff officers occupied the other buildings. Rotherford Square had beautifully tended gardens and tightly disciplined bushes that managed to look green even under the hot summer sun. Clearly, Ruffington did not believe in roughing it out. No tents in the wilderness for this bloke or compo tea or eating Spam sandwiches at NAAFI canteens.

George peeked into his new office and a corporal sprang up immediately from his chair. Ruffington was not in yet but he had left instructions and a thick file for Mr Clark. George was shown into a small office next to Ruffington's room and he settled back to read, thankful that the office was so wonderfully cool.

The file contained about seventy typed pages. There was a

simple heading on the first page: 'Communication between Communists and Congress in Bajapur and neighbouring Pithampur'. The first page carried a brief history of Congress and communist activity in Pithampur and Bajapur. The report suggested that the communists were the primary threat to the Raja of Pithampur's stability and they needed to be stamped out, even if the Soviet Union was currently an ally.

The second section was about the local Bajapur Tanzeem, the Bajapur Swabhiman Samaj and the Pithampur College Students' Association. These organizations had been set up in the 1920s as a way to divert high-born Muslim, Hindu and Sikh youth from joining the Communist Party; the organizations sought to strengthen the bonds of religion, encourage loyalty to the Raja of Pithampur next door and discourage sedition. But this was no longer the case since all these groups now tended towards criminal activity. About the only programme on which there was consensus had to do with punitive action against the communists.

Among other acts of lawlessness, the Pithampur College Students' Association, so the reports stated, was actively involved in forcing young Pithampur Sikh men to grow their hair and beards. Members of the PCSA had also disrupted some long-standing local traditions such as the intermarriage of Hindu men and Sikh women of some families of the landholding community. In Bajapur, the belligerence of the Tanzeem and the Swabhiman Samaj against dissenters had raised fears among the people. A Tanzeem member had attacked an old Congress supporter (a Muslim) and had cut him into pieces in front of his family, and a feudal member of the Swabhiman Samaj had kicked one of his tenants to death for participating in the 1942 agitation.

The report turned next to the broader problem of the war and to the trials, shortly to commence, of the Japanese Independent

Forces or the Indian National Army troops. George had barely started on this section, when the plush, dark curtains of the office parted and James Ruffington entered, looking cool and freshly bathed, having stopped by his rooms for a quick change.

'Good to see you, Clark,' he grinned. 'I had a tough time getting your CO to let you go. You know these regular johnnies. Luckily, I have some good friends up in Simla who were willing to listen to me. Ah good, good, I see you've been reading the field report on Pithampur and Bajapur. What do you think?'

George said that he hadn't read the whole thing as it was too large. Ruffington began to gather some papers when the office Sergeant announced the arrival of Dennis Porter. Porter entered, nodding curtly at George. He was only slightly more unbending towards Ruffington, remarking, 'Nice little place you have here, this Rotherford Square. Any news yet from Simla on the project?'

'Ah yes, *Ruther*-ford Square is the prized address in town,' replied Ruffington, gently correcting the American's pronunciation, and ignoring the second question.

'Well, *Rother*-ford Square is . . .' began Porter.

'It's *Ruther*-ford,' said Ruffington, tetchily. Porter was clearly getting on his nerves.

'Well,' remarked Porter insolently. 'While it's our money that pays for this little operation you've got set up here, it's going to be whatever I want it to be. And I say *Rother*-ford. I'll be in my office if you guys need help. That's half a mile down the road in Stimson Lines. Not as nice as this swell joint, but the food's a darned sight better.' He walked out of the room without any further statement. Ruffington looked glum and drummed his fingers on the polished wooden table.

'These Americans,' he sighed exasperatedly. 'I tell you, Clark, we teach them how to *be* Special Ops, we practically invented the damn thing, and then they turn on us.' This unfortunate remark was overheard by the exiting Porter who was still in Ruffington's outer, adjoining office. He stormed back, looking menacing.

'Teach *us* Special Ops?' he snarled. 'You guys couldn't even win the war without us. Fuckin' useless Andy Gumps, the lot of you. You had to have us and the Reds beat Jerry for you. I've seen how you guys ran the war over in London, I've seen how you ran your affairs in Pithampur and it's the biggest mess. And besides, you wouldn't *have* any Special Ops without our money. Problem is, you guys just want our money but can't stand to be told how to spend it. I intend to spend *our* money the right way in this town to get this job done.' This time Porter left for good.

Ruffington had turned a bright shade of red and his snout-like nose was fairly twitching in suppressed rage.

'You mustn't mind this, Clark,' he said when he had recovered his composure. 'We'll soon sort this chap out, with all his big talk of money, vulgar American that he is. You'll see. Let's meet for a drink in the club this evening and we'll have a talk about what's going on here.'

'Yes, sir. Er . . . what's an Andy Gump, sir?'

'Oh, that I believe is our dear Porter's way of saying that we are all a bunch of snivelling sissies. Andy Gump is a comic character of that sort, I believe.' Ruffington retired to his own office where he spent the rest of a very short afternoon, making telephone calls to arrange a game of tennis.

George returned to studying the Bajapur file, while the annoying drone of the tailor-bird chipped away monotonously outside. He learned that the Congress had been dramatically successful in Bajapur during the 1937 elections when limited franchise had led to Congress-led governments in vast parts of

British India. Prominent among the local winners was Dr Pratap Kumar Bharadwaj, from a well-known Punjabi family settled in Bajapur for several generations. His older brother, Radhey Lal, was the local judge and a reliable loyalist. Dr Pratap Bharadwaj's only daughter, Mira Chaturvedi, was also very active in the women's wing of the Congress and had organized several demonstrations when the men had been imprisoned. Pratap Bharadwaj's younger brother, Shyam, belonged to the Communist Party. When the Communist Party had been banned, Shyam had been arrested and, under a draconian measure, had been sent to neighbouring Pithampur to serve his sentence. He had survived the rigorous prison regimen in force in that state. Not only that, but to the great annoyance of the British Political Adviser, he had befriended a local, well-connected agitator, Satinder Singh Silonia. George's interest leapt at the sight of the familiar name. Silonia's connections had finagled a release for Shyam Bharadwaj on grounds of ill-health. He had been repatriated to Bajapur, where he was currently busy organizing peasants and railway workers against the authorities.

'As the family connection makes clear,' the report said, 'the Communists and the Congress are part of the same problem in Bajapur. We need to mobilise international opinion more broadly regarding India. Unfortunately, as is well-known, the American mission, led by Col. Louis Johnson in 1942, was not in sympathy with our views and was very much taken up with Mr. Nehru. The current envoy, Mr. William Phillips, appears just as unenthusiastic towards our views. Everything must be done to encourage American sympathies with our effort.'

George was now mesmerized. What a cast of characters! And he knew some of them, too—Deborah Sunderland, Satinder Silonia. He continued reading.

'At the local level, our efforts to counter the growing menace of the Congress and the Communists involve supporting—in every manner—two local organizations: the Bajapur Tanzeem and the Swabhiman Samaj. They are led by Mir Ali Sharif and Amar Mani Chaturvedi respectively. Deep religious beliefs have made the organisations hostile to each other. Family linkages, moreover, complicate Bajapur politics. The Congress second-in-command is Syed Ali Sharif, Mir Ali Sharif's cousin, a very popular young Muslim leader, educated at the Aligarh School and deeply devoted to Mr. Gandhi. Further, Amar Mani Chaturvedi's nephew is the son-in-law of Pratap Kumar Bharadwaj. Rajendra Chaturvedi has business interests in Bajapur, Simla and Mussoorie. In Pithampur the Congress is weaker but the Communists are active. All measures have been taken to oust the Communists by bolstering the courage of the Pithampur College Students' Association (PCSA).'

However, scribbled notes in the margins and at the end dismissed the entire report. One said:

'This is clearly something for the police and the civil administration to take up. There is absolutely no role here for the army. File should be considered closed.' So, why had James Ruffington decided to open a closed file? Especially when it was clearly stated that nothing in these developments had any military connection at all.

When George looked up, he saw that beyond the latticed veranda, the sun had mellowed to a warm and steady glow, a hot honey. Almost too late for tea. Back to the little world of the 126th East Yorks, full of the battles between the 33rd and 23rd men and their squabbling wives. It was almost tempting to stay back in the office than face what he knew would be the hostile jostling at the mess.

The cycle ride back to the mess was hot, but already the promise of a cooler evening hung in the air. A squad of men trotted past him and stiffened their shoulders in a salute. He nodded at them, happily. Not too long ago, he was on the other side, running past officers and looking at them out of the corner of his eye, waiting for an acknowledgment. As an officer now, George was very careful to return every salute he noticed.

The sideboard in the dining room was once again full of dishes of food, but this time there were no dry sandwiches or a heavy cake. Instead, as per his instructions, light puffy scones, with tinned jam were served along with a delicious chocolate cake made of flour and tinned milk. Indumati was not a good baker but even her mediocre effort—shaped more out of a will to learn and to please the young subaltern who had given her family fresh hope, than out of any real talent at baking—was far better than anything Rajinder Singh had ever produced. Waiters were handing out cups of tea and the usual intimidating clusters of the 23rd and 33rd men were eating their meal amidst muted mutters of conversation. George helped himself and nodded to everyone.

The padre came over to let him know that the cow that was troubling people in the cantonment had been released back to its owner who had promised corrective measures. As he chatted, George was startled to see Maj. Hugh Shelton actually greet him with a smile, almost a friendly smile if a grimace and a flash of yellow teeth could be called that. As he pulled up his chair, he noticed another 33rd man, the pugnacious Capt. Duncan whom George had met at the CO's house the previous week, give him a half-wave of acknowledgment. Something had happened in just a day whereby the 33rd no longer saw him as part of the enemy 23rd camp.

Ralph Barrington, who was going to Delhi later over the

weekend, came in smiling, but as he seated himself next to George, he muttered, 'So, how did you manage to swing that, my boy?'

'What?'

'Oh, don't pretend. You got yourself out of this whole bloody mess of a unit and without getting anyone all huffy about it. You're a clever one, you are.' Well, that explained the sudden warmth coming from the 33rd men.

In the evening, George changed into the long-sleeved white shirt and black trousers that Lal Ram had hung up on the almirah. After sundown, all officers and men had to wear long sleeves and long pants, part of anti-malaria discipline. Then he climbed into the tonga whose little starveling horse stamped its foot, and went off to meet James Ruffington for the promised drink and the briefing on the muddied international politics of the Special Operations clan. It seemed everyone everywhere was feuding with everyone else. In the battalion it was the 23rd versus the 33rd. Outside it, the regular army and the Special Ops 'adventurers' despised each other. In the Special Ops, it was the Yanks versus the British. In Bajapur, it was the Congress against the Bajapur Tanzeem and the Swabhiman Samaj. In Pithampur, it was the PCSA against the communists. Muslim, Hindu and Sikh groups against each other. Was there no peace anywhere?

At the club, it was very quiet, being a weekday. There were only a few officers and their wives, talking among themselves. Ruffington was sipping a gin and tonic in a languid, leisured way. He spotted George and waved him over.

'What'll you have? This one's on me. Your first drink as a Force 136 man.' Force 136 was the cover name for the India Mission of the Special Operations Executive of the British Army, George learned. But he seemed to recall that the whole establishment had been shifted to Ceylon the previous year. What was Ruffington still doing here? Was he trying to avoid a transfer to the south? Or was he just pretending to be a member of the SOE?

After the waiter brought over George's gin and tonic, Ruffington became serious.

'You must be wondering about that little scene we had in the office this morning, Clark?' He leaned forward and looked earnest. 'Well, the truth is that we—you and I—have a bunch of things to do. Porter is all right, but he thinks too much of himself and if we follow his way of doing things, it's going to be a right royal mess in Bajapur and in the rest of India, that's for sure.'

Dennis Porter had come into the Bajapur case by way of the OSS, the American Office of Strategic Services. A native of New York, the nephew of a prominent Republican politician, Porter had studied law at Yale University before the war took over his life. Like the OSS in general, Porter had started off as an apprentice to the British Intelligence Services, training first at Portsmouth in England, and then heading a special team that landed behind the Japanese lines to help the nationalist Chinese forces. It was here that he had first displayed a fanatical hostility to the Chinese communists despite their better ability to fight the Imperial Japanese Army. He had fought bitterly with his Commanding Officer who supported Gen. 'Vinegar Joe' Stilwell's tirades against the forces of Chiang Kai-Shek, the leader of the Chinese nationalist party, the Kuomintang. Finally, Porter had been transferred to Pithampur, seconded to the British detachment there.

'If it's communists you want to fight,' his CO had said to him acidly, 'go do it where you can't do any harm. I have a war to fight here and I would like to win it.'

'And so Porter's here, now,' said Ruffington, gloomily. 'Came to Pithampur first and then tagged along with me to Bajapur. Damn fool, won't listen to a word we say and just wants to take over. You have to keep an eye on him, Clark, is that clear?'

George made a noncommittal sound. Porter seemed horrible but Ruffington was an absolute ass.

'Truth is, Clark,' Ruffington continued, 'we *do* need to win this war against the Reds here. But our problem is more than that. If you had any idea what's going on in this country, Clark, you would see that India is going . . . Well, it's gone. Heading towards bloody independence and the most god-awful chaos. I doubt for all the noise they make that Gandhi and Nehru and this whole Congress bunch could rule a single week after we leave. In fact, I guarantee it, one month after we leave, Congress will break up, and there will be no government worth the name in India. The only strong ones in the whole picture are the Rajas and the Maharajas. So we have to keep chaps like Pithampur happy, although their personal, er, virtues are not . . . well, never mind. In any case, we have to make sure that we have a say in this part of the world and we simply *cannot* afford to have Moscow spreading its influence here; think about what's happening in China already. And if Moscow gets a foothold near Iraq, why, that would be just—just a disaster! That's the big picture.

'Now about Bajapur, this is what we can do. The way I— *we*—see it, we need to work on those in the Congress here who are less hardline and wean them away from the more incorrigible chappies like Pratap Bharadwaj and his daughter Mira and that odious communist brother of Pratap's—whatshisname?—Shyam. Now if that doesn't happen, and frankly I don't think it will, then we have to strengthen the hands of the Tanzeem and the

Swabhiman Samaj. They are a nasty bunch of blokes, both lots, but right now as Congress looks very strong, we need to keep it in check with these Tanzeem and Swabhiman Samaj chaps. Now, Porter is very obsessed with the communists. That's good, we can keep pointing out the links between the communists and Congress, and that keeps Porter more or less on our side. Anyway, once we have Congress under control, we'll see about the rest.'

It all seemed hopelessly confusing to George. He began cautiously. 'The file you gave me, sir, did say that this was for the civilians to deal with.'

'Ah, yes, there's the other matter.' Ruffington sighed. 'The biggest obstacle in this whole operation, Clark, has been the army itself. General Headquarters just wants to fight the war, but the war has to be fought in quite a different manner than before. It's about more than the Jap or Jerry, but in Simla and Delhi they all suffer from tunnel vision. So, in a sense, Clark, we have to modify whatever opinions Simla sends down to us.'

'Sir, the note said that as far as the army was concerned, the file was closed.' Clark was troubled at what he perceived was Ruffington's overreaching of his authority. Ruffington frowned.

'Don't worry about that, Clark,' Ruffington reassured him. 'I've managed to get that, er, overridden, shall we say? How did you think I got you attached to my set-up here, if I didn't have some influence in Simla? No, the army *is* taking up this particular case again, Clark, but under my—*our*—direction. It's covert now. Oh, and next time you see any notations in the files, run them by me, will you?"

So, first we have to work with the Congress here?'

'Well, we have to move the more sensible ones away from the main body of Congress. That's *part* of the plan, only a part of it.'

'And if that doesn't work, we make sure that Tanzeem and this Samajthingy are with us?'

'No, no!' Ruffington waved his plump, pink hands in exasperation. 'We have to work with all of them at the same time—of course, without letting on to each of them that we are also engaging the others. It's all so difficult and, and . . . *delicate*! And I can't get that ass, Porter, to cooperate at all.'

'And he wants?' George tried to understand the situation better. It made no sense whatsoever to him.

'He wants?!' Rufffington was almost beside himself with rage. 'He just wants the whole damn operation to himself. Damn fool! He hates the communists—which is good —but he wants to also get rid of the Congress. Anyone who even suggests that a communist is a human being is an agent of the devil, according to Porter. Therefore, the Congress is a traitor, according to him, no better than the communists. What *he* wants is to throw all our strength and resources behind the Tanzeem and the Swabhiman Samaj and use them to crush everyone else, especially the communists and the Congress. And *we* want to get them to work together for our purposes, preferably without knowing that they are all working for *us*.'

A little silence followed this explosion. Clark wondered if the other man had any idea how absurd the whole thing sounded. Was he absolutely mad? Col. Holmes was right: he, George, was Alice in Wonderland stuck with a sly, devious Mad Hatter at a crazy tea party. Ruffington pulled deeply on his cigarette, and coughed. The sound of busy conversation from the bar drifted out to them.

'The problem is, Clark, this operation is being financed mainly by Porter and his crowd. We don't have the money to spread around as thickly as the Americans do. But Porter's so . . . he absolutely will have it no other way but his own. And so now, we really have another problem. Communists, Congress, Tanzeem, Swabhiman Samaj, and now our damned American allies.'

It certainly was a complex situation, thought George, and a highly unattractive one.

'I'm trying to understand Capt. Porter here, sir,' said George. 'So bear with my next question, please. What is wrong with our supporting the Tanzeem and the Samaj Council outright? And also the PCSA in Pithampur? They seem to be the only ones supporting our policy right now which is to get rid of the communists and the Congress.'

'But don't you *see*?' Ruffington almost screeched, causing the conversation in the anteroom to hush a little. He lowered his voice a little and carried on. 'Tanzeem and Swabhiman Samaj would be nowhere without support from the administration. They really have no strength of their own. *We* built them up, meeting their leaders, inviting them for tea at the Bajapur DM's house, getting the old Raja of Pithampur to support them and invite them to his garden parties—you have no idea how *ghastly* those garden parties are—and all that. In fact, the funds for all the three—the PCSA, the Bajapur Tanzeem and the Bajapur Swabhiman Samaj are raised in Pithampur by our friend, the Raja of Pithampur. That way, no one can say that we're involved.

'But they are all such damn fools, these Tanzeems and the Swabhiman Samaj and the PCSA; they still have a credibility problem. Neither the Tanzeem nor the Swabhiman Samaj nor the PCSA are ready to fill the space of the Congress just yet. Oh, they did well these past few years while the Congress was banned, but really their strength doesn't go much beyond breaking up strikes and flexing raw muscle power to settle differences. They are all just a bunch of lumpens with some religious mumbo-jumbo thrown in to make it all seem respectable. Most of them think that going about bashing unveiled women or beating striking workers is very manly and all that, and that's all right as long as we don't let it get out of hand.

'And that's precisely the problem with Porter. *He* thinks we should use their goons as *part* of our covert ops. *We* believe that we should just nudge them in the right direction when we need to, but Porter wants to actually build close ties with them. He had the most awful idea, of getting some church-run group in the North-East to help train them here. He has gone and got some awful old American lady from the North-East to head the mission school here. That's the first step. Can you imagine the mess it will be now? Getting Christian groups from the North-East to train Hindu, Sikh and Muslim agitators? Basically, that's the plan, according to Porter—no prisoners of war, just get the PCSA and Tanzeem bullies and the Swabhiman Samaj thugs to kick the remains of Congressmen and the Bolshies into the nearest river.'

'And how does he plan to infiltrate?' George was curious.

'Well, that's the saving grace here. He doesn't quite know how.' Ruffington smiled, his curly red hair glistening in the evening light. 'He just beats up whatever is in his path, just steamrollers right over it. He has some vague idea that the Congress cadres have developed some secret communication code to liaise between people in jail and those outside, and he's determined to get hold of it. That, he thinks, is the key to bringing the whole Congress house down. And he's been using the Tanzeem and the Samaj boys for the job. They've done some digging but all they've achieved so far is to beat up a fair number of Congress workers—they have recovered no information at all.'

'So is there a secret communication code?' George was intrigued.

'Oh, I'm quite sure there is,' Ruffington sipped his drink and his podgy face took on a wistful hue. 'I mean, how do they communicate otherwise? Most of their leaders are still in jail and hopefully will stay there a long time, but Congress is still active. So, there must be a secret code by which the leaders get the message to their workers outside and the workers also pass on news from outside to those who are inside. So, we have to get to the bottom of it all.'

'How?' George asked the inevitable. His heart sank at Ruffington's beaming smile.

'That, my friend, Clark, is where you come in.'

'Me, sir?'

'Yes, yes, *you*. You, Clark, are the secret weapon of our operations here. You're just perfect for the job—you're friendly, you're pleasant, and you *listen*. You seem to get on well with Indians, and you will meet all sorts of Indians in Bajapur and extract all sorts of information from them, without their even being aware of it.'

'But I don't know any Indians here, sir,' George said firmly.

'Of course, you do,' Ruffington squelched him firmly. 'What's come over you? Don't you remember Silonia and Miss Sunderland? I suppose she's Mrs Silonia now.'

'Well, they are in Pithampur, sir,' George began, but Ruffington stopped him.

'But, my dear chap, Pithampur is right next door. The Silonias visit here very often. You read in the report, didn't you, that Satinder Silonia became friends with Shyam Bharadwaj, the communist brother of Congressman Pratap Bharadwaj when the two of them were in the Raja's prison in Pithampur? And through Shyam, the Silonias have become very good friends with Pratap, and they visit here very often. I bet you didn't know this, but Pratap Bharadwaj is also some sort of writer and his daughter Mira trained as an artist at Santiniketan, the university near Calcutta. Anyway, you, Clark, have to renew your friendship with the Silonias. We'll arrange to have you bump into them accidentally, maybe in the bazaar or something and then you can get to know the Bharadwajs, get the secret code and then, shucks to the bloody fool Porter.' Rufffington was particularly pleased at the last resolution to the problem. 'It won't last forever, Clark,' he continued, noticing the dismayed look on George's face. 'And then you can get back to your unit. I know you're new and are rather keen on it. Who knows, maybe you'll enjoy the operation so much that you'll opt to stay with us.' He cut George a sharp look as he said this. George kept his face deadpan, giving nothing away.

'I don't think I'm cut out for work like this,' he said candidly but politely, restraining himself. 'When are the Silonias coming next, sir?'

'My informers tell me that they are due in a week's time. Or thereabouts.'

'What happens if the Congress is broken? What then?' George asked, trying to visualize himself in the role yet again of an affable, unwilling spy, getting Deborah and Satinder Silonia to spill the beans and let him into their world of supposed intrigue and secret languages.

'Well, we can't have them cave in too soon,' Ruffington said crisply, as if by sheer force of will he could keep his scheme going. 'Not until the Tanzeem and the Swabhiman Samaj have been properly trained by us to run things. Ideally, we wouldn't need the Tanzeem and the Samaj at all; they are absolutely ineffective and villainous to boot, but they are the only ones who understand that *we* have a role and will let *us* run the show. If the communists look like they are going to take over Bajapur, I would quietly encourage Pithampur to take over this place. The Raja can always claim some ancient right over the area, or something. And we can use the Raja against Porter too. You know, tell the Raja how Yanks hate royalty and all that. Although God knows Porter thinks the monarchy is the best thing in the world; I've seen him reading up about the King and he talks a lot about his English aristocratic ancestors. Wonder why his lot rebelled at all, don't you? And wonder why that doesn't make him a bit friendlier to us, but there you are. That's the Americans for you.' George was getting a little irritated now. So far, Ruffington had met each one of his questions with evasion and a full-blown lecture. He decided to concentrate on practicalities.

'Who's our source for the Silonias?'

'It's the Bharadwajs' neighbour. They share a maid and she tells them about the comings and goings at the Bharadwajs. The neighbour passes on the information to us. They don't even know they are doing it, poor things. I just happen to arrange social encounters and we chat about this and that—isn't Judge Bharadwaj wonderful, etc. Of course, your CO's sister-in-law, Anna Benson, is mentioned very often—too often for my liking. But there you are again—a damned American meddling away for all she's worth and we can't even stop her, as she isn't our subject. On both sides of this matter, with us or against us, the Americans are nothing but trouble.' Ruffington frowned, reflecting momentarily on the perfidious ways of Americans.

'I don't think I want to be in a position where I have to deceive anyone, sir,' said George. 'But about the other matters, well, I don't know a lot about the Bharadwajs. You'll have to fill me in and tell me a little bit more than there is in the files.'

'Glad to.'

Pratap Bharadwaj, Ruffington told George, was the middle son of the well-established Bharadwaj clan in Bajapur. A well-known doctor, he also had a flair for writing Hindi fiction. Sometime in the 1920s, after returning from a trip to England, he became involved with the local Congress organization. To his father—himself a well-to-do doctor in the Railways, winner of a Rai Bahadur medal for service to the Raj—this step into political activism by his generally quiet son was puzzling. Dr Pratap Bharadwaj had spent much of the last three years in various jails around the region and was only released in January 1945 to return to the family home in Bajapur. In the interim, it had been the youngest brother, the professed communist Shyam Lal, who had been the thorn in the side of the local administration. He had been very ill in Pithampur jail where his jailors had been eager to follow Bajapur's suggestion to be 'very vigilant' with him. He had suffered pneumonia and had been nursed back to health by Satinder and Deborah Silonia, an odd Anglo-Sikh couple ('Your friends,' beamed Ruffington) who had petitioned the Raja for his release by working old contacts until Shyam Lal had been released into their custody.

Shyam Lal's return to Bajapur had begun a series of reciprocal visits between the Bharadwajs and the Silonias. A surprisingly strong bond of friendship had then developed between the Silonias and Pratap Bharadwaj, the Congress leader, and Pratap's thirty-two year old daughter, Mira. In fact, it was Mira who often visited the Silonias in Pithampur. She was also friendly with Anna Benson, and the two women, a few years apart in age, spent a lot of time together, usually Anna taking a lot of pictures of Congress gatherings.

The eldest Bharadwaj son, now de facto pater familias, was

the local district judge. Radhey Lal Bharadwaj, the upright keeper of Bajapur's order, sentenced Congress workers to varying terms of jail and detention with an air of resigned equanimity. As the brother of the local Congress big shot, though, he was allowed into party meetings and often worked as the liaison between the police and potential troublemakers.

'So, given the family ties, all parties are tangled with each other,' Ruffington ended. 'The main thing is that Congressmen are often in jail these days, and the communists are mostly out. How the Congress and the communists communicate, is what we need to know. How do they get all these people together for meetings and so on. So you need to get to know the Bharadwajs, Clark, and then find out for us.'

They talked for a while and then headed to the club's dining room. The waiters seated them and then served them a cutlet-and-salad dinner. Over this tasteless meal, they decided the best course would be for George to renew his contacts with Satinder Silonia and Deborah Sunderland. That way, he might meet Pratap Bharadwaj and Mira Chaturvedi socially and get to know the whole Congress network in Pithampur. As he ate, George reflected on the snake of a man that sat across the table from him. Was there a creature in the British Army more loathsome than James Ruffington? Immediately after dinner, George took leave, pleading his responsibilities as Mess Secretary, and returned as quickly as he could to his quarters.

Taking out the portfolio of recipes again, George took some comfort from such images of joyful creation. On the border of the sheets, glowing wood fires lit beautifully decorated clay pots full of golden morsels of food; women in gorgeous raw colours pounded spices, and danced as they harvested rice. Most of the food represented in the pictures was, he realized, the hungry dreams of imprisoned artists who could only imagine the rich dishes they illustrated. Not for them the braised fish, the seared vegetables, the delicious caramelized curries with sprinklings of scraped coconut as garnish. And so they had poured their hearts into this imagined richness of produce, these groaning vessels of plenty. George finished planning the menu for the next few days and got into bed. As he drifted off to sleep, he began to devise a plan to work his way through the bad hand that fate had dealt him recently. His last thought before his mind went blank was of a girl with burnished hair, a camera slung around her neck, her body delicate yet strong, her lips drawn back in a smile to reveal her hallmark American feature—strong, impossibly white teeth.

SEVEN

Another June day dawned, overheated and suffocating even before sunrise. As Lal Ram put his polished shoes in front of him, George thought about his plans yet again. The young boy dusted off a last little speck of dust and then shuffled backward, silent as always. They never smiled in India, George thought. The servants hovered, sullen and watchful; the Indian bureaucrats (like that Judge Bharadwaj at the party), too, were watchful, polite and unsmiling. And the British in India were a pompous, heavy-handed lot, sensitive to every perceived slight to their status. Or else, their humour became a tight, overstretched caricature of the smart set at home, the only amusement coming from ridiculing someone or making people look foolish.

He had already eaten, a slice of toast and marmalade, and drank Indumati's rather strong coffee which Lal Ram had brought to his room early in the morning. He did not want to face the heavy and tense atmosphere in the mess. Then he went out and walked through the still barracks and crossed the painted squares towards Col. Holmes's office. He had requested an interview and Holmes had made him wait several days before granting him this brief moment before his morning ride. George had spent the days formulating menus and meeting with Major Betford, the temporary Mess President, the two of them trying to keep costs down. It had been a special pleasure to go over

Deborah and Satinder Silonia's cookbook in the evenings. The contemplation of the beautiful pages had a calming effect on him; his nerves were often frayed to breaking point after a day's interaction with James Ruffington and Dennis Porter. Lal Ram had become so used to George's routine that he would put the portfolio on the desk after dinner so that it was ready for George's attention each evening. George liked the way the boy treated the book with reverence, holding it carefully and wrapping it up in a piece of old, gauzy cotton. The beauty of the images touched the boy, the raw talent on the pages a testimony to the skills that neither the poor boy from the Himalayan foothills nor the young man from England possessed.

Early in the morning, Indumati would appear in George's veranda, awaiting instructions, and to negotiate with the young Mess Secretary the culinary possibilities that might emerge from the mess kitchen that day. Every day she gestured at the portfolio that Lal Ram brought out—the boy treating it like a sacred book—in order to show George what might be feasible given the summer and the war-induced paucity of rations and of produce. She liked having George open the cookbook; she too looked forward to feasting her eyes on the brilliant pages of the portfolio, the depictions of village life and especially the birds on the trees, their necks bent in impossible angles to peck at the luscious fruits hanging from emerald trees.

It was a fine way to start a day, as energizing to Indumati's mind as the prayer she hastily muttered before she left her tenement in the old part of town. She, Lal Ram and Ramu, her husband, walked a mile every day to get to their jobs. Her sons, Shambhu and Hari, often accompanied them to help their father in the little patch of garden behind the messs kitchen, where the three tried to prepare the ground for the season of planting that was to come. There were seedlings that Ramu was eager to transplant, but the weather was too hot and the tender plants would perish if he was too hasty with them.

As he walked to the CO's office, George could see no sign of the Adjutant, Capt. Lewis. Either he had forgotten as usual, or else the CO had asked him not to be present for the meeting. George suspected it was the latter.

'Well, Clark?' asked the CO, after George had saluted. It was awkward, standing in the rather hot veranda, but it was clear that they were not going inside the office. So, standing there, stiff and ill at ease, George told him about his meeting with Ruffington, including his directive to cultivate the Silonias and the fact that Anna had been mentioned in the dossier.

'I don't know if it's right to tell you, sir,' he ended, 'but this is the battalion and I thought you should know what was going on, especially since Miss Benson . . .'

'. . . is my sister-in-law,' Holmes finished for him. He looked thoughtfully away in the distance. 'Well, let me think about it for a while. How about you come to the office after lunch? I should have thought of something by then.' He turned away and went towards his waiting car.

George fetched his bicycle and trundled over slowly to Rotherford Square. Chances were Ruffington wouldn't be in this early. The podgy Captain led a leisurely existence, almost as if there weren't a war on, strolling in at about ten o'clock, always looking freshly bathed. George really disliked the man. Thanks to Ruffington, here he was, stuck in a rotten unit full of quarrelling officers and their beastly wives (well, technically, that wasn't Ruffington's fault, but well . . .), playing cloak-and-dagger stuff with Americans, communists and Congresswallas. It just wasn't bloody fair that the war was ending like this, when he could have been a good regimental officer, working his way up perhaps to a captain's rank before demobilization began. But then, in his life, nothing had quite worked out the way he had imagined. No veterinary training in Edinburgh, no Alice (although he had got over the hurt), no seamless passage from parents' house to his own, no calm continuity to his life in the countryside with its rolling hills and winding lanes. Just this restless buffeting by the war into remote parts of the world full of all sorts of politics and intrigue.

At the office, there was only the waiter, who poured him a cup of tea (Ruffington always managed to pinch a waiter off the mess detail, God knows how he managed that). Then, George returned to the matter of reading the remaining bits of the file. At nine-thirty, Ruffington put in an unexpectedly early entry.

'Well, good morning!' he chorused cheerfully. 'We have visitors today, you know.' Of course, he hadn't told George about any visitors, he never did, always keeping close to himself whatever information he had, just in case. The ass! 'I wanted to let you know a bit about them before you actually meet them. Useful sort of chaps to know, but you've got to be careful not to let them in on our matters too much.'

Oh dear, the eternal turf wars again. The visitors with whom they were to have coffee were District Superintendent of Police, Charles Mack, and his deputy, Assistant Superintendent Ramakant Batra, one of the new Indian officers.

'IPS, you know,' said Ruffington, referring to the Indian Police Service. 'Think they know everything about Bajapur, and will probably try to boss you around and keep you out of stuff. So, just remember that this is between us and GHQ and Whitehall, ultimately. None of the bloody IPS's business, anyway.' Self-important idiot, George thought as he hid his face behind the teacup. Whitehall, indeed!

The two IPS officers arrived at ten and Ruffington welcomed them warmly, introducing George as his junior colleague. The older man, Mack, was a quiet man, an old India hand by the looks of him. His deputy, Ramakant Batra, was watchful and asked a few questions about the cantonment. He then asked George what his experience was in political matters.

'Well,' George felt himself begin to redden. Then Ruffington stepped in smoothly.

'Mr Clark is personally known to Deborah and Satinder Silonia and that should make his entry into their circles easier.'

'Why is the army so interested in Indian Congress and communist politics?' the question, unexpected and direct, came out as barely above a whisper from the till-then silent Mack. Even Ruffington was surprised into a momentary silence, before recovering.

'We-ell,' he tried to affect a careless drawl. 'It's not really the Congress or the communists we are interested in, Inspector. That is of course your business to pursue. We are looking for connections between these and JIFs.'

'Ah, the Japanese Indian Forces,' said Mack, still looking unconvinced. 'But I doubt that you will find any here in Bajapur or even next door in Pithampur, Captain Ruffington. The ones who have been captured are safely either in prison camps in the east or are being interrogated in Delhi and Calcutta.'

'But we believe the Congress and the communists are mobilizing support for the INA. That very much concerns us in the army, especially since it relates to information they might try to conceal at the trials, if there are any,' Ruffington ended darkly.

'The communists are not aiding the INA at this time,' said Mack, firmly. 'It goes against their orders from Moscow. A few independent-minded underlings might be trying to give aid to their immediate friends and relatives involved, but I doubt that you will find those higher up the Communist Party hierarchy helping those caught fighting on the fascist side, as they put it.'

'All very well,' rejoined Ruffington and proceeded to lie brazenly, or so it seemed to George. 'But we have information that one of the Bharadwaj brothers, the communist Shyam, tried to get in touch with an officer in Bose's crowd. We really should find out what is going on, in order to gain an upper hand during the interrogation.' His words sounded like mere bluster and bluff.

'Hmm.' Mack was quite clearly sceptical, but he let it go. George decided to say as little as possible. He had no idea of the whole INA angle as Ruffington had not told him anything about it. He was also coldly angry: this ass Ruffington would have thrown him into the whole business without having told him the true reason. Probably, another of his devious ploys: get the information without telling your informer what you're really looking for.

At the end of the conversation, it was decided that George should go ahead with his plans, keeping Ruffington and Mack fully informed, through the intermediary of Batra. 'I'll be in touch,' said ASP Batra in parting, waving his swagger stick threateningly. They saw them out to the veranda and watched them drive away in a dusty police car.

'Well, I'm glad that's over, aren't you, Clark?' said Ruffington, wiping his streaming forehead as they returned to the relative coolness of the office. 'I thought for a while that Mr Mack was going to throw a spanner in the works of this little operation.'

'Do I need to know anything about the INA angle, sir?' George was businesslike, concealing the anger he could feel welling up inside him.

'Oh goodness, you don't know, do you? Ha ha! Well, there's nothing much at all. But, we have to tell the IPS that *we* are looking for INA types, so that we can keep the police's nose out of our operation here. That's the big picture.' Ruffington was fond of using that expression along with 'damn fool'.

'It's a plausible story, you know, because the Congress does seem to be helping members of the INA, taking out donations to help the INA people in their trials and all that. Of course, there is tension too. Chaps like Pratap Bharadwaj here say that if the INA gets help from the Congress, then their folks bloody well will have to toe the Congress line. Anyway, what we are really, *really* looking for is the Congress–communist link. Damn it, Clark, if Porter needs his communists, why, then, we have to give him communists. What *we* are interested in is keeping control over the whole damn thing and making sure that nobody else barges in and tries to take over our show. But do be especially careful of the IPS lot, they're old hands at this sort of stuff, very sly bunch, the lot of them.' With these words of cunning wisdom, Ruffington left the office for an early and, in his eyes, well-deserved, lunch.

George decided to stay in the office and read a little bit more about the whole complicated affair. Since Ruffington had declared so openly that his only role was to ensure that he, Ruffington, and his set-up–whatever it was–could keep playing a leading role in the whole affair–whatever affair it really was–George now had only a passing interest in the business. As far as he could see, his job was to be the class monitor and to stay on top of things. Well, at least this way he could meet a lot of the local crowd, perhaps even run into Anna Benson as she ran around town, taking photographs. Now with his senses lifting at the thought of her, he realized that that was the only agreeable part of this whole foolish circus.

At one o'clock he headed back in the blistering sunshine for lunch at the mess. Now that he was no longer a potential faction member to be courted or slighted, he found that he was treated with an almost genial indifference by both the 23rd and the 33rdwallas. He quite liked this pleasant state of limbo, of being ignored by both sides. The food was superb. Indumati had produced fare that made even the sour-faced 33rdwallas more amiable. The 23rd's red-faced senior Major, Richard Brassey, actually deigned to converse with George over the tender chops and the flavourful Russian salad. Almost regretfully, George tore himself away to tread the scorching roads once again, to Col Holmes's office.

He found the CO looking cheerful, for a change. 'Sit down, Clark,' the Colonel said, lighting up a cigarette. 'I've been thinking over this matter that you brought to me this morning. And I've been thinking that it's probably a good idea to keep tabs on Anna, after all.'

George almost heard himself sucking in his breath sharply. What, the treacherous old man, casting his own sister-in-law to the wolves! He felt a sudden hot rage behind his eyes. Here he was—fool! fool!—trying to keep battalion honour above all else and now this humiliation, of having the ground removed from under his feet by Anna's own family, no less. Through a dim red mist he heard the CO continuing.

'Don't get me wrong, Clark. I know Anna isn't mixed up in anything. She's just American. Your Ruffington, on the other hand, seems like a first-class snake. From what you've told me, it seems he wants to use the Silonias and perhaps Anna to get to the communists or Congress or whoever—I don't really care who he wants to nab. Who knows what that idiot *really* wants, probably thinks he is in some detective novel, the bloody fool.

But, inadvertently, the ass has helped me. You know, my wife and I do worry when Anna wanders off into town without an armed escort or anything, trying to get her precious photographs. Anna does tend to go charging into situations without thinking, just to get her damned photographs. You can keep an eye on her as you get on with your own work. It would be a favour to us, actually. Ellen would be so relieved to know that someone from the battalion is with Anna, making sure that nobody sticks a knife into her or burns her alive.'

George exhaled his pent-up tension. This concern—for the safety of a relative—was a straightforward one, and a mission that he was happy to accept. He nodded and promised to do his best. He suddenly felt very warm, even inside the relatively cool office. He waited impatiently until the CO had finished his cigarette and then took his leave. At the Rotherford Square office, he told Ruffington that he might tag along with Anna to see a bit of the town, as she seemed to be more knowledgeable about it than most people in the cantonment. Ruffington beamed.

'Splendid, splendid, Clark. And this way you can keep an eye on who she . . . oh never mind,' he ended abruptly, noticing his subordinate's thunderous expression.

When George rang the Commanding Officer's house a couple of days later, Mrs Holmes came on the line. She sounded delighted when he said that he was calling to invite Anna to the club that Saturday. There was to be a movie at the club, followed by dinner and he wondered if she would like to go.

'Oh, she would like that very much,' said Ellen Holmes firmly, without having asked her sister at all. 'What time will you pick her up?'

'Er . . . whenever it's convenient for her. Shall I ring back?' George countered tactfully.

'She'll call you this afternoon,' said Mrs. Holmes decisively.

When Anna rang him just after lunch, as he was preparing to go back to his room and wait out the heat, there was laughter in her voice.

'Ellen said you called. She kept pestering me to call you. In fact, I've been practically ordered to telephone you. How *are* you?' She seemed delighted about the plans and invited George at six for a drink before they went to the club. He went to nap that afternoon with a happy glow inside him.

Saturday arrived as hot and miserable a day as the ones before. The humidity in the air was ferocious. In a few days the monsoons would break over Bajapur and then there would be brief periods of cool. Perhaps, George fantasized, the Congress and the communists would stop communicating for a few weeks, so that he could take some leave and travel up to Mussoorie?

George's sense of anticipation deflated when he walked into the Holmes's drawing room and found Dennis Porter making an exit. He growled a greeting at George and saw himself out. Ellen Holmes who was also in the room welcomed the young man warmly. She looked pale and tired, but was trying to be cheerful. Anna uncurled herself from an armchair and came forward smilingly.

'Well, hello, hello,' she said, fingering her chiffon dress, looking unfamiliarly glamorous in high heels and dark lipstick. 'Dennis [Dennis? Were they on such familiar terms?] was here for tea. Goodness, what a pleasant day it's been. You know, I could quite get used to this life: no work, no cooking, just a bunch of servants to order around, eat and drink all day.'

'Well, now, Anna, why don't you ring for Rati Ram? Let's

have some drinks. It's so-o warm, isn't it, Mr Clark?' Ellen tried hard to steer her sister away to safe, small talk. What a girl she was, this Anna. Couldn't she at least flirt with the man who had come to take her out?

George accepted a gin and tonic, Anna had a lemonade, and Ellen settled down with a small, fizzy drink.

'So, how do you find Bajapur so far?' Ellen asked sociably, trying to set an example for Anna in a sisterly way.

'Oh, it's very interesting,' said George, truthfully. It *had* been interesting, even if the matters he was involved in were not his cup of tea.

'Captain Porter said that you now work with him and Captain Ruffington. He said that Captain Ruffington really values your work.'

'That's right, ma'am. I mean, thank you.' George flushed.

'Be careful,' Anna joked. 'Dennis is going to turn you into one of his spying minions.' George nearly choked on his drink.

'His what?' he spluttered.

'Oh, you know. He was trying to get our Rati Ram to spy on one of the unit servants the other day. Really, he takes his Intelligence job too seriously. Someone should tell him the war is almost over.'

'Now, *An-na!*' Ellen almost screeched. This incorrigible girl would ruin everything.

'It was just a misunderstanding. He was trying to find a servant for himself.' Ellen was emphatic.

'Strange way of finding one. But oh well. Oh *all right*, Ell. What's the matter? You look a bit green. Are you feeling all right?'

Ellen's eyes had filled up with tears of embarrassment. Why could not Anna just learn to smile nicely and flutter her eyelashes, like that Barbara Curtis, daughter of the local Brigade Commander? Barbara had almost all the young officers in the cantonment eating out of her hand. She was always busy playing tennis, riding, going out for dinner, usually in the company of a gang of boisterous bachelors or laughing girls like herself.

'I'm fine, I think it's just the heat,' said Ellen, who was looking quite pale. She made some excuses and left the room.

George was feeling hugely relieved that Anna didn't know of his true mission. He was also disturbingly aware of how much he was enjoying looking at her, her clear skin and eyes, her wonderful hair that gleamed in the evening light, and her mouthful of white, even teeth. Now that Mrs Holmes was no longer there to put a strain on things, George prepared to enjoy himself thoroughly. Soon, they were talking happily of all sorts of things, the war, his experiences, her parents in faraway Minnesota. Guiltily, he remembered that Ruffington was encouraging this interaction, that he was expecting some Intelligence information on Anna's friends, the Bharadwajs. As it turned out, the links were established more easily than he had imagined.

There was a nice painting hanging on the Holmes's drawing room wall, boats in a harbour and people promenading on the shore. Ellen had put it up because it reminded her of the placid lakes of her Minnesota childhood, a time of unending (or so it seemed) peace, now removed from her by war and death and the remaking of the world as she knew it.

'That's a nice painting,' remarked George as they exited the drawing room, on their way to the club.

'Yes, that's by a family friend of ours. He now lives somewhere in New York, along the Hudson River. Very talented. He had a thing for Ellen a long time ago, probably still does. Anyway, that was his wedding present to her.'

'I've met some artists too,' he said, unthinkingly. 'Indians. In Pithampur, a whole bunch of them. One of them was married to an Englishwoman. Very nice paintings they did, too.'

Anna turned her clear, smooth face to him, mouth half-open in astonishment.

'Do you mean the Silonias?' she said. 'Deborah and Satinder?'

'Why, yes!' For a minute he thought she would withdraw into herself, say that she wanted to have nothing to do with those who persecuted her friends. But instead, what was this? Anna's eyes were shining with delight. She put her arm through his and said happily.

'What a great coincidence! I met them here through mutual friends. Do you know that they travel to Bajapur often? I must put you in touch with them.'

'That would be wonderful,' said George, truthfully. And then the whole plan just worked itself out like magic.

'They stay with the Bharadwajs when they come to Bajapur, did you know that? Remember the gentleman, the Judge at the club? Well, the Silonias are friends with him, or rather with his brother, Pratap, my friend Mira's father. I would say that Mira is my best friend by far in this town. Oh, this is just too great. Did you manage to get a car or shall we call for a tonga?' George had managed to finagle a car out of Ruffington, one of the perks of working with the ruffian that he was determined to enjoy.

Anna smiled the entire way to the club. The squat building's lawns were lit up with fairy lights, the driveway crunchy under their feet. She was warm and happy, laughing uproariously during the cinema. The sound tended to get a little foggy at times, at which point the audience's chatter would rise to a loud grumble, only to die down again as the mechanism righted itself. The movie featured some older actors too. Halfway through the feature, Richard Clarke, that old hero of so many flicks of the 1920s and 1930s, appeared in the role of a patriarch, exhorting his rather lazy children to work hard. George smiled, remembering how he had a connection to the film star through Alice and then through Deborah Sunderland. Beside him, Anna stirred.

'Did you know?' she said as the sound went off again momentarily. 'Did you know that Richard Clarke and Deborah Sunderland were in love, very briefly, many, many years ago?'

George was taken aback. Of course, Deborah had not told him of her romantic connection to the actor, just that she had known him briefly many years ago.

'She told me in Pithampur that she knew him, but she did not say how well,' he replied.

Later in the evening, after the cinema was over, someone put on some records and a few people began dancing in a desultory way in the gazebo of the club's garden. Anna and George went into the building first to get something to drink, she still smiling from the memory of the film and of the evening.

'How did the matter of Richard Clarke come up between you and Deborah?' Anna asked as she sipped her orange drink.

'Er . . . my . . . friend . . . in England, that is, she works for the Clarkes as a cook. She began there soon after Richard Clarke and his wife moved to England so that he could serve during the war.' How to describe Alice to Anna? His former love, his might-have been fiancé?

'Your girlfriend?'

'She is no longer my . . . er . . . girlfriend.' The unfamiliar Americanism tripped off his tongue clumsily. 'We . . . er . . . she decided to move to America to continue working with the Clarkes.' There. It was said, his history with Alice summarized as a change of locale, a displacement to another country.

'I see.' Anna was quiet. Then she got up and moved outdoors, looking at the people still dancing to the scratchy music emanating from the phonograph.

'Would you care to dance?' George asked cautiously.

'I would love to,' she replied simply, accepting his proffered hand and slipping easily into his arms and into the syncopated rhythm of the jazz music.

'This is just too neat,' she smiled up at him, his hand against her back as they danced. 'I can't believe that you know the same people I do here in Bajapur.'

'Well, I know the Silonias a bit. I don't really know all the others you visit.'

She told him about her friendship with Mira Chaturvedi, their meeting at a political-cum-social gathering, and her deepening acquaintance and friendship with the Bharadwaj family.

'Well, the next time you see the Silonias . . .' he advanced cautiously.

'Oh, I'll be sure to tell them about you. I bet they would love to see you when they come here. They arrive soon, I believe.'

Between dances, she sent him for a drink. She was a teetotaller, so he chose an orangeade for her. When he returned to her side, Dennis Porter had materialized, to his annoyance, along with the Brigade Commander's daughter, Barbara Curtis, the haughty ATS Sergeant he had seen in the CO's office. She was looking sexy in a sleeveless chiffon dress with some sort of a frill at the bottom. There was a noticeable coolness between Anna and Barbara though. The Brigade Commander's daughter alternated between hostile silences directed at Anna and adoring smiles bestowed on Porter.

'Oh, *thank* you,' she trilled when Porter whisked a drink off a bearer's tray and gave it to her.

Curiously, and to George's annoyance and to Barbara's silent, pouting fury, Porter directed his attention at Anna.

'How's the photography going these days?'

Anna was almost as surprised as George, then recovered her poise quickly.

'Very well, thanks. And how's the servant hunt going?' she asked mischievously.

Porter was not expecting this riposte. He flushed and stammered.

'Servants?'

'Yes, my sister said that you were asking our Rati Ram about servants.'

'Oh, oh, you know, just need someone who can polish shoes and that sort of stuff, nothing serious.' Barbara was now pulling on Porter's arm impatiently. He looked relieved and was led away agreeably enough to the dance floor. Barbara and Anna had not exchanged a word during this entire interlude.

'Gee, that sure made him run away really fast.' Anna laughed. 'Let's go back and dance.'

On the floor, she turned confidentially to George, her shining hair close to his face, her long-lashed eyes surveying the crowd as she murmured the words that turned his blood cold.

'He's so odd, that guy, Dennis Porter. Do you know that he's convinced that many servants in the officers' houses are communist agents? He was trying to get Rati Ram to spy on people from his native region? Of course, Dennis is so clueless, he wouldn't know that you just don't do that without sending people into a state of panic. Rati Ram complained that this sahib is asking all sorts of questions, that he's particularly interested in some poor orphan boy called Lal Ram who, it turns out, is from a village neighbouring Rati Ram's. Dennis wants to know what sort of gossip this Lal Ram engages in about his sahib, what the sahib sees, hears, and all that.'

She saw the slackening expression spreading down George's face, from top to bottom, his mouth tugged open in involuntary, astonished rage, and her own eyes opened wide in shocked comprehension. They stood there a moment, like two puppets, in each other's arms, dancing in spite of themselves, staring in dismay at each other.

'Oh no!' she said. 'Not your servant! Oh no, that scum, that— weasel!'

George had recovered sufficiently to steer Anna to the edge of the gazebo, away from the other, moving, shuffling couples. The music ebbed a little, then started again in a confused clatter and clash of instruments. He escorted her out, away from the shadow-dancing melée, to a quiet place under a tree. Another couple that had come out there to find some privacy, looked at them in annoyance and slipped away. He offered Anna a cigarette and when she declined it, he lit up and inhaled deeply, once, twice, thrice. Then he cursed loud and long, foul words that he hadn't used in the longest time poured out of him in a minute-long outburst, all the frustrations of the past few days, the past few months and all the bloody stupidity of the whole damn thing that was the war. Anna stood silently by his side, afraid of his anger but too miserable about her own part in bringing him to this state.

'This is just—just, awful,' he finally managed, after a weak apology for his appalling, foul-mouthed outburst in front of a woman, that too his CO's sister-in-law. His voice sounded very thin to his own ears, very prissy and totally inadequate. 'I just can't believe it! The chap works with me, or at least he's supposed to. How could he do this?'

'Are you some sort of a political agitator?' Anna asked in her usual direct manner.

'Of course, not!' George was shocked, then angry again. 'And even if I was, how dare he try to spy on *me*! And through my own servant, that too.'

'Of course, he could be trying to get information *on* the boy,' suggested Anna, but shook her head as soon as she spoke. 'No, Dennis Porter wants to play the major league, he isn't going after servants and other small fry, I don't think.'

'But, I'm *not* a big fry," George exploded. 'I'm *not*. I don't think there is *anybody* in the unit who is a big fry. Good Lord, all I ever asked was to be left alone to be a goddamn officer in my own goddamn unit. And instead, I'm stuck with a demented, too-clever-by-half spook, and a lunatic American. And if that isn't bad enough, the battalion's falling apart because of those fighting, bickering schoolboys who would as soon kill each other as the Japanese or the Germans, and both that fool of an Adjutant and that skirt-chasing CO just don't seem to . . .' his voice trailed off as he realized his unforgivable gaffe. Anna turned away from him.

'This evening hasn't turned out well at all, Anna, and I'm just so sorry,' he said at last to her back. 'Let me take you home.'

'I'd rather go somewhere where we could just talk,' she said, hesitantly. George dismissed his staff car and they hailed a tonga from among the many that stood outside the club gates.

They finally went to Chen's, a small, greasy Chinese restaurant just inside the circle of Bajapur permitted to officers without a pass. Its dim interior was a relief to George's tired eyes who in any case was trying to avoid his companion's clear-eyed looks. Chen, old and wizened, far from his family who lived in Calcutta, looked unblinkingly at them. His team of three Gurkhas—all of them young men who had failed to be recruited at the Gurkha Regimental Centre in Dehradun—flitted about in lacklustre fashion, bringing out poisonous-looking egg rolls and lukewarm beer. The usual nightly quarrel began in the kitchen between the cook and one of the Gurkha waiters. Chen disappeared inside to head it off. George lit a cigarette and reflected miserably on his immediate future. It looked pretty bleak, whichever way he looked at it. He had just informed his CO's sister-in-law that her sister's husband, the battalion's CO, was a womanizer and well . . . George tried to think if any other unit would have him, a subaltern of three weeks' standing, expelled in disgrace from his first battalion.

'You were speaking of Richard and Muriel Bates, weren't you?' Anna's voice was distant, but not angry.

George nodded shortly, it was too late for lies, too late for anything. Might as well just tell her everything and make a clean break.

'Everyone *always* thinks that they are up to something.' There was a quiet annoyance in Anna's voice but she was not directing her anger at George. It was an exasperation directed at the world in general. 'Don't they realize what Muriel is going through, has been through?' Chen emerged from a quietened kitchen, and a mutinous-looking Gurkha brought out their food and slammed it in front of them. Greasy noodles, some soggy fried rice and a stir-fried chicken with dubious-looking vegetables in a brown sauce.

'But, we'll talk about her later. Don't you want to know how I came to be here in Bajapur?'

EIGHT

I suppose I should really start with myself, my story, said Anna. How did I end up here in India when, apart from my brother-in-law being posted here, I have no direct connection with India at all? Everyone always says how nice it is that Ellen and I are here together, such good company for her when Richard was in Burma, and all that stuff. But in fact, I was in India much before Ell arrived. I don't think people realize that she's been here only about six months or so. She came over when the war in Europe was basically winding down. I've been here since November 1941. And Richard only arrived here in time for the mass slaughter in Burma in 1942. Were you in that too?

Anyway, I've been stuck here in India since 1941. When the United States joined the war, you know, after Pearl Harbor, things became pretty chaotic here. It was terribly worrying for Mom and Dad, but I was in Jamshedpur, where there was no real trouble apart from . . . well, I'll tell you about that.

I came to Jamshedpur to visit my friend, Mary Louise. Her husband, John Duncanson, is an engineer with the Tata Steel Company there. They hired a number of American engineers for their plants because there weren't enough Indian or British engineers well trained for their projects. And I was trying to get over an engagement that had gone wrong. Yes, I called the marriage off in January '41, and Ben went off to war later, to

Italy, I think. God knows how he is or even where he is. Nowadays, people call off engagements all the time—well, *you* know that. Sorry, I didn't mean to open old wounds. But you know, the war has done strange things to us. Life is too short and one does what one must do in order to gain a few short moments of happiness. But before the war, one just didn't do these things. At least not in Minnetonka, Minnesota, where everyone would always remind you of the ugly deed. The looks—always so reproachful, the words—carefully chosen censure. I suppose it is the same everywhere, isn't it?

So to get away from it all, at least for a few hours a day, I persuaded the editor of a local newspaper—I had taken a few classes in photography—to take me on as a reporter. *The Minneapolis Newsday*—it was a grand name for the pitiful rag that was trying to take on the *Star-Tribune*—that's the really big newspaper in Minneapolis. It was willing to try new faces demanding less pay. Anyway, at first all I got were silly little pieces like the Minneapolis Women's Knitting Society, the Ladies' Christian Reading Group, Rotary Club meetings and all that kind of stuff. I had to go and take pictures of their meetings and write short pieces about them. Of course, I didn't get any of the glamorous things like when the odd film star passed through on his or her way to New York or California. That was the editor's business and he would often take them to expensive lunches or dinners while they looked down their noses at him, wondering when they could request their car.

I found that although the speeches at the meetings I covered were quite boring, I enjoyed photographing the meetings, especially the period just before the sessions started. I took pictures of the people as they waited, of the audience as it trickled in, but especially of the speakers just before they put on their public faces and went to the podium or on to the stage. It was interesting to me, and my photographs were doing well. In fact, so many readers wrote to praise my work that they even promoted me to cover slightly more important meetings where I was actually working with the men. The men! Oh my! They were a real aggressive lot, those guys. Much worse than anybody you can find in the British Army, I can tell you. But I held my own by not talking about my work, by just taking my pictures and getting on with it. Since I didn't go out for drinks with them and turned down all invitations—some of them were really sleazy—they finally decided that I was too dumb—too *female*—to be much of a threat to any of them.

Anyway, my friend Mary Louise wrote to me inviting me to India. I suppose she thought I was heartbroken and fading away or something after my break-up with Ben. But I was actually doing really well. I was only nineteen when I had gotten engaged, and being with Ben had been so constricting—I thought that I would suffocate and die. Like my father, Ben was a lawyer, a son of a lawyer too, and our lives would have been boring as hell. Ben would never even have considered it possible for his wife to have a life separate from his own career. He had political ambitions too, and all the right credentials to support those goals. Yale Law School, good connections—he was a distant cousin of Harold Stassen, a Republican who became the Governor of Minnesota in '39 although I never did get to meet the big shot.

Ben was 'such a good catch' that I sort of went along with it for a while, swallowing my anger every time he said things about people I liked and admired like Eleanor Roosevelt. My parents didn't much care for him either, I can tell now, the way Dad was extra polite with him and Mom looked down when his name was mentioned. Yes, I might as well tell you now that we used to be very wealthy. Seriously wealthy. At least my grandfather was. He had a house on Summit Avenue in Saint Paul. A summer home in Maine, a winter home in Florida. He invested heavily in stocks and things and then—well, you know what happened in 1929. It all pretty much went up in smoke.

But we were luckier than most. Dad was a lawyer, so we went down in the world from being seriously wealthy to being just comfortable. Mom comes from less money than Dad, and so she was the one who was mentally the most prepared to make the changes that we had to make. I was only eight or nine at the time, so I don't remember much anyway, except that Grandpa never had huge birthday parties for Ellen and me anymore. For people like us, a marriage with one of the Stassens was supposed to be a ticket back to our rightful place in society; so everyone was shocked when I broke off my engagement to Ben. But each time I thought I'd made a mistake, I would remind myself that marrying Ben meant marrying sheer, tedious boredom, and then I'd be happy again. But still, I was longing for a change of scene, to get away from everybody reminding me of my Mistake.

India seemed exciting. Far away from Ben and Minnetonka and Mrs Ryan at the library with her knitting. I had never visited Asia before. We only went to Europe every other year for short visits. My boss at the *Newsday* encouraged me to go, telling me that I could supply the paper with photographs about British India at War and such stuff. So although he couldn't formally offer me a contract—the paper didn't have such deep pockets— he did offer me a steady trickle of money. And what could be better than that? A vacation that paid for itself.

My parents were beside themselves with anger and worry. They just did not want me to leave in the middle of a war, especially a war involving so many foreign countries. The United

States wasn't in the war yet, but my sister Ellen was home with them in Minnetonka and she too kept advising me not to go so far away. She spent most of the days driving around with her friends because she didn't want to think about her husband who was in England, waiting to be sent to the Far East somewhere.

Ellen's sudden marriage had been yet another in a series of shocks that began to rain down on my family from 1929 onwards. She had been in London in the late summer of 1939, under the benevolent protection of Aunt Germaine, Dad's older sister, and with a group of wide-eyed Minnesotan friends. At a London nightclub she had drifted away from her group of friends and had begun chatting with a tall, serious-faced man in his early thirties. He was an infantry officer on leave, a precious few days, before reporting back to duty with his regiment, the 23rd battalion of the East Yorkshire Regiment. Drawn to the seriousness he represented in contrast to the forced gaiety of her friends, Ellen had given her address to him impulsively. To her surprise he had landed up at her hotel with flowers, and despite the protests of Aunt Germaine, her chaperone, had carried Ellen off for lunch in a rather beat-up old car and had brought her back with cheeks flushed with delirious happiness.

To Aunt Germaine's wailing despair, Ellen decided to stay back in England after the vacation was over, and no amount of persuasion from my parents could convince her otherwise. My parents finally prevailed on Aunt Germaine to stay back with her and to take care of their daughter who had been seized, so it seemed, by a temporary and blinding madness. Ellen spent most of August in London while Richard burnt up precious leave visiting her at every opportunity. But things were to get worse from the Minnesota point of view.

The day Britain declared war on Germany, Ellen announced

that she was going to marry Richard Holmes, the unknown major from Plymouth. In fact, she told her shocked and weeping aunt that they were going to get married that very afternoon. Richard had proposed to her the first week they met, and they had kept it quiet because of all the complications with getting permission and all that. But the permission was finally there—Americans were not in the category of undesirable foreign spouses—and Ellen was off, to marry her soldier before he went off to war. She had also wired her parents to inform them of this happy occasion. More tears from Aunt Germaine, but finally she was persuaded to stay back for a bit and witness the union, also attended by Richard's rather bewildered parents. A four-day honeymoon followed and then Richard was off with his battalion.

In fact, do you know that the next time Ellen saw Richard was six months ago, here in India, in Bajapur? She came back to Minnesota glowing with health and happiness. And she wrote every three days to Richard, even though she heard only sporadically from him.

And so my parents, only just recovering from the shock of Ellen's wedding, were bowled over by my decision to travel to India in 1941. 'Please don't,' my Mom begged. I still remember her face all wrinkled with worry. 'There's a war going on and who knows what might happen.'

'But Mom, that's exactly why I need to go,' I said. 'Suppose places like India and Jamshedpur vanish because of the war?'

'Jam-shed-pour,' harrumphed Dad. 'What sort of names are those anyway? The world's better off without them.'

But I finally got my way after my editor spoke reassuring words to them. He also wrote to some friends of his friends who were in India; they wrote back to assure everybody that things were not as bad as all that in India. They would be happy to put me on the train from Bombay to Jamshedpur. So I packed a whole trunkful of film, took the long way around to India, bypassing London. I stopped at Paris, where my father knew somebody at the Embassy.

Oh Paris, Paris! How low my spirits were in that beautiful city. Crawling with creepy-looking Nazis and their creepier hangers-on. The people looked downcast, the autumn days were grey, although the women still managed to dress beautifully and looked wonderful. It rained the three days that I was there and I was glad. I remembered it from happier times and I didn't want to go out and see it all bathed in sunshine and mild weather. I was happy to leave.

Bombay was different from anything I had ever seen. India in general struck me as that—the most un-Minnesotan place I had ever seen. The people so poor, and so colourful, the British so British, and so many soldiers and troopships that it took us a whole day to dock. I was fascinated and horrified. Anyway, my editor's friends came to meet my ship at Bombay. I don't mind saying that I was thrilled to see Americans, my own kind, talking like me and still so friendly and open even after having been in India for so long. India does that to people, you know. The Americans here associate mainly with British businessmen—boxwallas, I think they call them. What can I say about the boxwallas that you don't already know? They live life with a desperate sort of enjoyment because they know that it will all be over when they go home and have to pick up their shabby little lives all over again. Anyway, that frantic live-in-the-moment stuff gets old after a while.

But this couple—the Raymonds—were still fresh and sweet. She was old and grey and he dealt with things with a quiet sense of good humour, not the mocking sort of humour that you British have but a genial American good-natured wit.

I don't mind telling you either that I've been desperately homesick these past three and a half years that I've been here. I miss my parents and my fresh, clean hometown, my nosy but kind neighbours. I miss the long drives up north to the Canadian border, the deep green, glowing summers. I even miss the long, hard winters. These days when I miss Minnesota too much, I remind myself that there are also scumbags like Dennis Porter stateside, and that makes me step back a little. But even with all those people like him, there's such a sense of freedom there, of wide, open horizons and good, good food.

I had always heard about this colonial society here, and I guess the war has only made things worse, but it was a shock to encounter it first-hand. I've had to put up with it for nearly four years now, you know. The only thing that makes it bearable for me is that I have made good Indian friends here, Mira Chaturvedi and her family. And meeting you has been great too. You and Richard remind me that not all the English in India are like that scumbag Ruffington or Ian MacGregor in Jamshedpur. But Ian MacGregor comes later . . .

My editor's friends, the Raymonds, lived in a wonderful apartment in Bombay that looked over the sea. Most of the rest of the building had been requisitioned for war purposes, but the Raymonds were allowed to stay. It was good to eat mashed potatoes and gravy again, after that bilge on the ship. Paula even came with me to Jamshedpur. She said that she had to go to Calcutta anyway, so it wasn't out of the way for her. But really, it was. She was just trying to be good to me. And, to be honest, I was happy to have a chaperone. The trains, the stations, everything was so different, and almost threatening. If a mob had decided to attack me, I had no language in which to tell them that I was American and not British. Not that that would have changed the minds of a bunch of rioters, I suppose.

We got off at the Tatanagar railway station in the evening. I must say I loved Jamshedpur right away. First, there was that glow, red-golden in the distance, like a fierce sun below the horizon. John, Mary Louise's husband, told me it was the pouring of the smelted iron at the foundry. It could be seen for miles around.

Jamshedpur was full of people but there was a serenity about it that was a refreshing change from Bombay. I would soon discover how shallow that serenity was, in only a few weeks. Mary Louise lived in a pretty little bungalow, full of mango trees and flowering bushes. It's strange that I barely remember the house although I remember the people so well. But I do recall that it was a nice little brick place with a tiled roof and a couple of chimneys for the fireplaces. Mary Louise's husband, John, would light fires every evening. 'Bloomin' hot,' he would bellow at me, being a little short of conversation with women. But a nice man, perfect for little Mary Louise with all her fusses over tablecloths and brownies and cookies.

And the servants. I had never been in a house with so many servants. Mary Louise herself was bewildered that she had to supervise so many people in one medium-sized household. And it was a good thing that Paula came with me, because she was able to give Mary Louise quite a few tips about things like that.

Jamshedpur was beautiful in those days. It was mid-November, the nights were cool and comfortable, and Mary Louise's servants served up large, hot mugs of coffee every day. Oh, I feel nostalgic for home every time I remember those mugs of coffee, rich and dark and creamy. I was so tired of the watery soup-like thing they served up everywhere east of France. Mary Louise had people travelling from the States bring over stocks of coffee beans for her. On one vacation home, she had had several barrels shipped back with her.

'I've got enough coffee to last me for two years here,' she had laughed. 'God forbid, if I can't go home for any reason, I can at least drink my three cups of good American coffee a day. I can't stand the stuff they sell in the stores in Calcutta.' Poor Mary Louise, little did she know that in a few weeks, dealing with shortages would be her reality.

But in the last few days before America entered the war, Jamshedpur seemed a wonderful retreat from real life. Mary Louise and I spent some enjoyable days visiting other American ladies, going to concerts and some rather awful theatre. One day, Mary Louise had about twenty local women over for lunch to meet me. The British women were worried about the war— tensions were building up in the Far East—and some of the British women had formed committees to discuss what to do if the Indians attacked them. I saw this as a great chance to continue my work. I was planning to leave India the second week of December and I hoped to get some pictures of these women and their meetings.

Anyway, Jemima Owens, the organizer of the committee, was quite happy to have me attend—in fact, she was thrilled that her little gang of gals was going to be in the papers, even if it was a sorry little paper like the *Minneapolis Newsday*.

They met at the Owens's bungalow every other evening, a worried, rather grey-faced group of women who chattered incessantly about servants and local scandals as they waited for the meeting to come to order. I took photographs of them in this mood; I'll show those to you some day. The horizon of worries spread far and wide for these women. Wizened Veronica Colby, wife of one of the senior engineers, dwelt on her pet theme: the problems of thieving servants. Sheila French, very religious, was obsessed with the philandering ways of the large numbers of single men in town, none of whom it appeared wanted to philander with any of her five daughters. There were others whose names I've forgotten but who also joined in these several, parallel discussions. But the whole point of the meeting, as Jemima Owens reminded us when she finally set the meeting on its true agenda, was the problem with the Indians.

The war had raised political tensions sky-high and the worry was that the steel workers in Jamshedpur would strike. The steel produced in Jamshedpur was used in the critical munitions industries. So, keeping the political temperature down was crucial to the authorities. There was an underlying tension in Jamshedpur which I, a happy, heedless tourist, had only too willingly ignored in my first few days in town, but here at the meeting the ugliness that lay under the orderliness came into full light.

'Well, if they attack us, we'll all have to move into a safe place. I propose my house as an ideal spot. We are in the centre of the road, far away from both the bazaar and the mill,' Sheila French said firmly.

The others looked at her in disgust. They all knew that she wanted her house chosen so that the authorities would spend money reinforcing it against attacks. Predictably, this proposal was voted down, with a barely disguised show of hostility from all present. They finally decided that the American Chapel was the best place, especially since the Americans might be spared as neutrals in the conflict. As the only American present, I almost protested at this harnessing of the American community without any representations from it, but then thought better of it. I wanted to get those photos and these women would be moving on to other things when their plans would be found unnecessary by the authorities.

It was at this meeting that I realized there was something stirring deep inside the political belly of the British Empire. Oh, I had read things like everybody else had, about Gandhi this and that, Nehru Somebody, but now they became real, as did the tension that I had only read about in the papers during breakfast. From this point on, I noticed that Mary Louise's servants often talked in low voices, and sometimes I heard the words Gandhiji and Panditji. From their whispered conversations I first guessed that there was dark talk of a strike at the mill.

Mary Louise's husband, John, often brought the gossip home. He was interested in the Indians' views in a good-natured sort of way. But he sometimes ribbed the Indian workers about their forthcoming independence and what they would do with it. I think it made the British engineers quite uncomfortable to hear him talking so freely to the Indians; it even made some of them angry. It was through Mary Louise's ayah that I got to know that there were small meetings held in the bazaar every night—even though they were illegal now that war was declared—where local leaders discussed their tactics and their plans for the future. I couldn't very well ask the ayah to take me for the meetings, but I really wanted to photograph them and send them to my editor in Minnetonka who was still probably dreaming about Mary Pickford or Greta Garbo stopping in Minneapolis on their way to Hollywood.

But it was very difficult to meet Indians at all. You know, I saw hundreds of Indians every day. They rode past Mary Louise's house on bicycles, or walked past it in bare feet. Some drove little Austin cars; John worked with several in the factory; but socially they were a world apart from us. The British women in Jamshedpur kept themselves very aloof from the Indians and only dealt with a few Parsi women who were connected to the Tata business in some way. I had come to India for purely personal reasons of adventure, but now I wanted to know what Indians thought about the British; I wanted to find out if they were aware that there were committees of horse-faced Englishwomen who were planning fortifications against Indians. I wanted all of this, I must admit, for purely selfish reasons: I wanted a story, a scoop, something that gave meaning to the photographs I took, the photographs that would land me awards. I was generous in my dreams. I imagined not just winning an armful of awards, but my editor, the garrulous old has-been, ending his career in a blaze of glory, dripping with Pulitzers.

After much badgering, Mary Louise gave in and asked John to invite some Indians home.

'I don't know, dear, whoever you know. The only Indians I know are ayahs and bearers and all those gardeners and their boys,' she replied absently when John asked which Indians he was to invite home.

So that was how I met Prabal Mitra Sarkar, a young, recent recruit to the steel mills of Jamshedpur. He had studied in the United States and in England and had been preparing to work for a company in Sheffield, when the war cut him off in Calcutta. Luckily for him, the Tatas snapped him up immediately. He lived in a small establishment in Bistupur, a bustling market centre just near the outer perimeter of the company's steel works. His widowed older sister and her ten-year-old son lived with him. Prabal worked under John, who liked him as a colleague but had never been interested in seeing him away from work. John had no real interest in associating socially with anyone; he was a very self-content individual. But his little Mary Louise had asked him to bring home an Indian and so he invited Prabal to dinner one evening, an invitation that the guy was happy to accept.

From the minute Prabal opened his mouth to wish me good evening, I knew I had struck gold. He was only a few years older than me, but he had an air of assurance and a composure that I liked. Over drinks I asked him his views on the ongoing political situation. At first he hesitated, looking at John, then he decided that this American household was probably a safe place.

'The truth is,' said Prabal, quaffing down a glass of Scotch, 'that British rule has become intolerable. Before, it was irritating, now, it is suffocating. The war has made it stifling here for all of us. Can you imagine that in our own country we are feeling stifled?' He became more and more impassioned as he spoke. Several of his friends and two cousins from school in Calcutta were in jail.

'I completely share their views. The only reason I am free is because I work for Mr Tata, and the police would not dream of embarrassing him by arresting one of his employees. But the day I leave or the day I am sacked, I will join my associates in some dank prison cell somewhere in rural Bengal.'

'Well, but the British system has been good for you, Prabal,' John reproved him mildly.

'Yes, for me but what about the thousands of people who are kept out of the system, Mr Duncanson? The problem is that those of us who manage to make our way up through the system are so drained by our own difficult climb up the ladder that we become the most slavish kind of people imaginable. We don't dare challenge anything or anybody because we are afraid that our own hard-won and very precarious status will be taken away. That is why,' Prabal looked bitterly at his own reflection in his amber-coloured glass, 'I don't have the courage to give up everything and join my friends in this struggle. My parents worked too hard to put me through school and university in England and then later in the United States. I have a sister and a nephew who are quite dependent on me and besides,' he smiled a little, 'working for the Tatas gives me the illusion that at least I am serving an Indian concern and not a British one.'

'Now come along, dinner's served,' Mary Louise said in her usual practical way. The inner workings of British India were only very mildly interesting to her; on the other hand, there was a nice pork roast that had just been cooked to perfection and was drying itself out in the kitchen. Prabal had particularly asked for pork when John had inquired about dietary restrictions. He was delighted to see the glorious American spread on the dining table.

'It reminds me of my days in New York,' he said, launching into the peas and mashed potatoes and the apple sauce. 'I love good American food, but alas I don't get to eat too much of it anymore.' As Mary Louise also loved good American food, she warmed to Prabal instantly and made sure he had second helpings of everything.

'Are you still in touch with your friends?' I asked him tentatively over coffee in the living room as we sat around chatting.

'No, I don't meet them anymore,' he replied. 'It's too dangerous for me. The police are probably watching my every movement as well, since my close relatives are involved in the agitation.'

'Well, that's a pity.' I decided to be bold and frank. 'I'm interested in photographing the meetings of these activists for my newspaper back in the United States. Would you by any chance know people here who could put me in touch with local Congress workers?'

He hesitated, then promised to try and use some of his contacts. We bid each other a pleasant good night. A few days later, he sent a note to me through John.

'Dear Miss Benson,' he wrote in a rounded, well-formed handwriting, 'I recommend that you contact Mr Shanta Kumar Sinha who lives in Sakchi Bazaar. He is a local journalist who knows a lot about political matters and is fairly influential. You can contact him at home or at the offices of *Jaihind Samachar* at 10 Muttarah Gali. Tel: 349076. Tell him that you spoke to me. I hope this helps you in your work.'

Excited, I set to work the very next day itself. I called *Jaihind Samachar* and caught Sinha right away. When I introduced myself, he sounded wary but agreed to meet with me and discuss matters. Mary Louise and John were, understandably, less than happy about the whole thing.

'You never know what's going on in the bazaar,' John muttered while his wife nodded in agreement. 'S'pose there's a riot, or something? How will we ever get you back alive?'

'I'll be fine, you two,' I reassured them. Truth was, I was a little nervous myself. But I had started the ball rolling and so I couldn't back down. So it was agreed that I would go forth into the unknown world of the bazaar escorted by Ayah and Ram Charan, the gardener.

We drove into Sakchi Bazaar and absolutely no untoward incident took place. But, finding Muttarah Gali proved an uphill task. We finally saw it, a narrow little street, absolutely teeming with people and I realized that I would have to leave my tonga and walk through the jostling, restless crowds to find Number

10. Some people turned to stare, but no one seemed overtly hostile. Ayah and Ram Charan followed me quietly. I suppose they were perfectly indifferent to my mission. Number 10 turned out to be an old-fashioned Indian building, with overhanging balconies and shuttered windows. High steps lifted the entrance off the rather dirty street. As I knocked on the door, I gave instructions to my two escorts to return to the building in a couple of hours. Ayah's face brightened. Ram Charan told me, in his broken English, that Mary—that was the first time I heard the woman's name, I had thought Ayah was her name— was going to go buy some bangles in anticipation of the Monday Shiva puja in the servants' quarters back home. She was a Christian tribal woman but in accordance with local tradition, observed faithfully the Monday fast for Lord Shiva.

A tiny, old peon let me in. I entered an absolutely beautiful room with polished tile floor and lots of gleaming dark-wood furniture. It was difficult to believe that this wonderful, shaded room existed just some feet away from a world of teeming crowds and dusty chaos. There were a few pictures on the walls, some images in alcoves over the doors and a couple of photographs of older, rather sombre-looking men and women. When I mentioned Sinha's name, the peon led me to the back of the building and to a flight of stairs.

Shanta Kumar Sinha met me at the top of the staircase. He folded his hands in a namaste, then, in order to not embarrass me, shook my outstretched hand politely and led me to his desk, a chaotic jumble of papers and a typewriter. His secretary, a portly middle-aged guy with round spectacles looked at me shyly, then applied himself once again to his work. This floor had been given over entirely to its function as a newspaper office. Copies of the newspaper were piled on the floor. The main landing functioned as Shanta Sinha's office and off this there were several rooms in all of which there were people typing and making typesets.

'We are a very small paper,' Sinha said apologetically, wiping his glasses. 'But we try and carry on as best as we can. Paper restrictions are in force, but of course sometimes that is just an excuse for the authorities to restrict newspapers that they don't like.'

I explained the purpose of my visit and asked if I could take some pictures of his office for the *Newsday*, back in Minneapolis.

'You can certainly take as many pictures as you wish of us and our work, Miss Benson. But regarding your other request, I don't know if I can oblige. You see, the Congress here is now de facto banned because so many members are being imprisoned everywhere. I think that situation will last as long as the war is on.'

'So, are their meetings illegal?' I was disappointed.

A small gleam appeared in Sinha's eyes.

'There are no longer any official party meetings. But we would love to have you over for an informal dinner at my house. There is nothing illegal in having social gatherings, and you may report freely on that.'

And so it was that on Saturday, December 6, 1941, I arrived at Shanta Kumar Sinha's house for a dinner party. 'Bring your camera,' his note had advised. The dinner was to be held in the same building that housed the newspaper office. It turned out that the second floor of the building was also the Sinha home. I arrived at 8 o'clock, again escorted by Mary and Ram Charan.

Sinha was at the door with a graceful woman in a green sari, whom he introduced as his wife, Kanta. 'Shanta and Kanta,' he quipped. 'We are quite a couple.' There were several people already there when I arrived, mostly men, but there were a few women too who were busy nattering away with each other in one corner. There were also some children, two boys and three girls who were darting in and out of the room and handing around glasses of drinks. A fat, rather jolly-looking servant kept putting in an appearance from time to time, urging fried foods on everybody. Everybody was interested when I first walked in, but soon they began to ignore me as their own conversations became of absorbing interest.

I was introduced to several people who eyed my equipment warily but when I explained my mission—the *Minneapolis Newsday*, etc.—everyone relaxed. I found myself drifting over to the women's corner. All were talking in Hindustani which I could not understand, but when I came over they switched over to English effortlessly. Except for one older woman with a stunning pearl necklace who explained through an interpreter, a young woman in a blue sari, that she spoke no English at all. They introduced themselves and in light of what happened later, I am amazed that I've forgotten all their names. I only remember their dresses and their jewellery. There was a woman in her thirties, wearing a printed sari in deep-maroon silk. She kept her head covered as did Lady Pearl Necklace. Another was constantly being harassed by her children who would come begging her to settle their endless disputes.

What did I think of the situation in India, they all asked.

'Confusing,' I answered truthfully. 'I really don't understand it at all. Over there—in the engineers' bungalows—there is a nameless dread that hangs over everything though on the surface everything is normal. Here, it almost seems normal except that all of you are asking me what I think about the situation, which I guess is not normal.'

'That's because you have not been here long,' communicated old Pearl Necklace through Blue Sari. 'Stay a few more weeks and you will see what problems there are under the surface. The price of rice and wheat, for example, is getting out of control here. People from the countryside are flooding the towns looking for work and for food. People are starving, the situation in the villages is desperate.'

I felt increasingly disoriented as the conversation continued. I thought of Sheila French and of her little committee of valiant defenders. Were they preparing a last stand against these people? I couldn't visualize it. But the steel workers? Well, they were probably a different breed, more experienced in wielding weapons and heavy instruments, probably maddened by the heat and the exhausting nature of their work, only too ready to strike out and slash everyone's throats.

I gingerly mentioned these fears to these women. They didn't deny outright my assertion.

'It is true,' said Harassed Mom. 'The steel workers feel that they are being exploited in this war. They feel that their needs are being overlooked, while they work long hours in the mills. It's equally true that the steel workers are a privileged lot in our country, where such jobs are very hard to come by. But everyone feels oppressed, no matter who he is. The constant feeling of being watched, whether you're a worker or a malik—an employer, I mean—it wears you down sometimes.'

'But, more than us it is Shantaji who is particularly targeted as he is also a newspaper editor,' said Maroon Sari. I took some pictures of these women, all of them in their neatly draped saris, some with their heads covered demurely, some not. All were talking about politics. In fact, if there was a theme to this party, it was politics. There was such a great interest in the affairs not only of India but also of the world. These people were thirsty for information and news. They lapped up whatever I could tell them of the American scene.

It was then that I realized the true meaning of Shanta Kumar's cryptic remark in the office when I had first met him. This dinner party was a political meeting. And through these political discussions, Indians like these were remaking their society. Men and women were mixing freely, or at least they were talking in the same room, if not always to each other. The women with their silver key rings attached to their saris or tucked into their waists, and the men in simple western or Indian clothing, all chattering like cheerful sparrows, discussing India, Jamshedpur and the world.

The gathering had a measured mix of formality and informality. Shanta Sinha and his wife were warm and attentive hosts, but there was none of the strict etiquette of European social events. There were no silent, white-gloved bearers here, only some rather harum-scarum servants who talked just as loudly as the guests. Dinner was a traditional Indian meal served on bronze platters set out on long tables. For my convenience, they had placed a spoon, knife and fork by my plate; everybody else ate with their fingers. Both Shanta and Kanta darted around serving their guests and, in a break with social norms, men and women dined together although for the most part they sat separately. Except for Blue Sari. I noticed that she sat between two men. She introduced one as her husband and the other as her brother-in-law, visiting from Calcutta. No one seemed taken aback by her brazen gesture, sitting between two men.

I took some pictures of Blue Sari and her family as they ate: rice and rotis, served with a number of courses. Dry vegetables, lentils fragrant with ghee, fish steamed in a mustard paste, and a meat dish they all insisted that I try. I realized that it was a special meal, put together painstakingly for the visiting foreign guest—luxurious eating in war conditions. That's when I decided that I really liked these Indians better than the starchy Englishwomen I had met. I think Mary Louise too would have liked them more than her circle of committee-forming women, if they could have ever met. Mind you, I would meet other, less likeable Indians in Bajapur. But interacting with this lot of people lifted my gloomy spirits a lot. No one examined my dress, no one made smart, snide remarks about anybody else's appearance, and there was little of the vicious social climbing that seems to characterize so much of social life among the British in India. I discovered later that Indians snipe at each other too but their mockery centres on other things. In fact, the people in the room that day reminded me very much of Prabal Sarkar. All of them, men and women, possessed in varying degrees, the same quiet self-assurance that was deep-rooted but not abrasive or confrontational.

I commented on this to Shanta Sinha. He smiled and replied, 'It really is all because of Gandhiji. He showed us how to be happy with ourselves, just as we were. And to worry about more important things, like freedom and reform.'

The talk immediately swung around to Gandhi. Gandhiji—where was he right now? What was he doing? What guidelines were coming from him?

'You see,' said Blue Sari eagerly, following up from my earlier comment. 'Before Gandhiji set an example for us, we spent our days foolishly, anxiously trying to keep our British overseers happy, but now we don't. I can't explain it, but it's as if a big stone has been lifted off our chests . . .' Her voice trailed off, but several people around our table nodded. That was how they experienced nationalism too.

'But it is still not perfect,' chipped in Maroon Sari. 'See, although I tell my sisters and cousins to come forward—I am Muslim—most hesitate. It is almost too much for them to give up their purdah, although I hope that they see me and take some courage that the sky will not fall on their heads if they embrace the world. But I am fortunate, my father,' she gestured towards a grey-bearded man talking animatedly at another table, 'and my mother'—she patted Pearl Necklace—'have allowed me much freedom and the power to choose my own path in life. But, take my uncle over there,' she pointed to a grey-haired man sitting beside her father, 'he loves coming out with us, but he cannot yet take the next step of allowing his daughters to come out with me.' She translated this for her mother, whereupon Pearl Necklace laughed and said something.

'She wants me to tell you that families will always gossip,' Blue Sari conveyed. 'But that one must live one's own life to the extent that it is possible.' Thinking about the life I had left behind in Minnetonka, the broken engagement, the disapproving gossip, I nodded, warmed by her empathy.

'It is hard for most orthodox families,' said the Harassed Mom who had not really spoken much all evening, on account of keeping busy with her children. 'In order to really become free, whether Hindu or Muslim or Sikh or Christian, we have had to confront our own families, walk away from our own inherited prejudices. And it is far from over yet, but at least among ourselves here, we have made a beginning, in our little circle of friends and like-minded acquaintances. It is better than the alternative.'

After dinner, we all went back to the living room, where tea was served. Then, after a while someone brought out a tanpura— it was the first time I had seen one actually being played—and

Kanta Sinha and Pearl Necklace sang. They were joined by Blue Sari's husband and brother-in-law. I took pictures of them in this happy mood, and it is only because I did so that I remember their faces so vividly. They sang some plaintive songs, some merry tunes. I didn't know what they were singing about but I do still remember that crisp, early December evening so full of music and the happiness of camaraderie in a warm house, full of good food and good people. Which is why what followed was so hard.

After dinner, Shanta and his wife dropped me back to the Duncansons. They wouldn't hear of my travelling back unescorted on a tonga. In fact, they were surprised that Mary Louise and John could have permitted such a thing. I told them that my friends had offered to drive me there and pick me up, but that I had refused the offer, fearing to draw too much attention to myself in the Sinhas' neighbourhood. Mary and Ram Charan were instructed to ride the tonga home by themselves. Thanking them for their hospitality on the dark road in front of Mary Louise's bungalow, I told Shanta and Kanta Sinha that I hoped to see them again soon. I wish I never had said that. I would hear about them again but under very different circumstances.

I was soon distracted by other things. The next few days brought in horrifying news about Pearl Harbour and the incredible number of casualties there. Mary Louise, John and I sat huddled miserably around the wireless—as you call the radio here—trying to get news about the United States. We cursed the Japanese, I with particular venom because with the entry of the United States into the war, there was no way I could return home for the foreseeable future. As a civilian and as a tourist, my repatriation was now the last priority for everybody—airlines, shipping companies, the government. Letters, always slow, took even longer. I received several letters from my mother written before December 7, wondering when I was coming home. She felt glad that I was with fellow Minnesotans, and to be honest, I did too.

A few days after America joined the war, I was sitting with Mary Louise in the living room. We were drinking coffee and munching on chocolate-chip cookies. Our gloomy conversation about the war was in total contrast to the beauty outside. The air was fragrant with flowers from the garden; there was a golden glow everywhere. Don't you just love the winter in India? I absolutely fell in love with it, even the dust seems to hang like a mist, rather than like a choking cloud. Suddenly, the telephone rang. It was John, asking if he could bring over a visitor for dinner that evening.

'Nothing fancy, he just wants to visit,' John told his wife. Of course, Mary Louise being Mary Louise, 'nothing fancy' meant four courses instead of three, with dessert and coffee to follow. The cook was roused from his mid-afternoon stupor and was given instructions about the dinner. The bearer was admonished about some tarnished silver pieces and Mary, the ayah, was told to change into a fresh sari for the evening.

There was a mystery about the visitor as John hadn't identified him except to say that he was British. We were all taken up with the excitement of the thing, even Mary seemed to go about her chores with less of a leaden foot than usual. John came back a little earlier than usual from work. He seemed a little bemused by the whole thing. He said that this man, Ian MacGregor, was a local police officer, part of a specially delegated team taking care of wartime security problems at the steel mills. There had been some unrest, nothing spectacular, but ever since America joined the war, MacGregor had been particularly solicitous towards John, even favouring him over the handful of other Americans in the office.

'He keeps on asking if we are safe in our home,' said John. 'In fact, he's been at it so often that I just invited him over on an impulse so that he can take a look for himself and give me some room at work. He seems all right, but I just don't like him hanging around at my elbow all day.'

Dinner, although arranged on short notice, was a relatively grand affair. Mary Louise had ordered a saddle of mutton, roasted, with mint sauce, made with fresh mint leaves, a cheese soufflé, wilted spinach and stuffed tomatoes, to be followed with a chocolate-layer cake and coffee. As the three of us sipped cocktails and waited for Ian MacGregor to arrive, we talked gloomily of home and the things that might be happening there. Of course, Minnesota was far from any potential action, but as we were speaking, my hometown was seeing off young men by the dozens. The thought that so many of Mary Louise's and my acquaintances from school would be embarking soon on battleships made us both look nervously at John, who was young enough to be called up for duty. As it turned out, John's work at a steel mill was considered essential war work, as Tata Steel's products were invaluable for the military. John was unhappy when the decision came down, but he bore the disappointment well enough. Men always long for the company of their peers, don't they, even when that means the unknown risks of war and battle?

MacGregor arrived punctually at seven-thirty, a large, burly man in long-sleeved white shirt and dark trousers—the regulation evening dress of official India—and accepted a drink straightaway, a large whisky and soda. John, conscious of his duties as a host, drank his cocktail slowly. MacGregor greeted both Mary Louise and me with great politeness and courtesy. His conversation was easy and drew us into chatter almost effortlessly. Only now have I come to recognize it as the style of a professional interrogator.

'I hope that you are not too troubled by all the unrest that has occurred in Jamshedpur these past few months?' he asked solicitously. 'It's been an unfortunate time for mill owners and the war has only aggravated things.'

'Oh not at all,' said Mary Louise artlessly. 'Except some of your lot—I mean, the English ladies—have started organizing committees for defence and all that. But I don't know much about that. Anna here is the one who has been keeping in touch with them. She takes photographs, you know.'

And with that innocent remark began the catastrophe that will always cloud my memories of that pretty little town with its spacious bungalows and its dusty markets. MacGregor leaned toward me, smiling, his body unfolding out of the flowered armchair. Now when I remember that movement, I think of it as predatory, a snake moving in for the kill. But at the time, I knew very little about the games that officials play and I, too, leaned forward, smiling.

'What sort of pictures do you take, Miss Benson?'

'I'm afraid you will think it all very dull, Mr MacGregor. I photograph meetings and the people who speak at meetings.'

'Well, have you found any meetings of interest in our little outpost here?'

'Oh, a few. I thought I could send some photos to my editor in Minneapolis about British India at war. So I took some at Mrs Owens's defence committee meeting.'

'How interesting! I wonder if I may have a look at your work? It's thrilling to think of our Jamshedpur in an American newspaper.'

'And she also took some great pictures of a party she was invited to by some Indians. Those are really neat!' Poor Mary Louise dug the hole of disaster deeper with her guileless talk. I went to my room and returned with the prints of the photographs. I couldn't set up my own dark room in Mary Louise's room as I didn't have the equipment, but Jagdish Studio, in the bazaar, had done a good job and I felt proud of the prints that I handed out like so much candy to MacGregor. He looked appreciatively, remarking on Sheila French's solemn demeanour and Jemima Owens's impressive pose. When he looked at the pictures of Shanta Sinha's party, his eyes glistened in appreciation.

'Oh, it was Mr Sinha who was your host. I know him quite well, the newspaperman. What a lot of friends he has. How was the food? And look, the women are all there too. That's so different from what we normally expect of Indians. You know, many orthodox Indian men simply leave their wives at home when they interact with us. But then these are not very orthodox Indians, are they? A different breed, this new generation of Indians.'

Warning bells should have gone off in my head when he went over the prints of the party twice, as if he wanted to memorize each face. He asked me some questions about some of the people in the pictures, smiling at them as if they were old friends. 'Of course, I know them,' he said, when John commented on his familiarity with the people I had met. 'Jamshedpur is a very small place.' And he closed the box of prints with a look of genuine appreciation directed at me.

'Splendid! No doubt your American readers will love the sight of such exotic stuff like Indian women in saris, Miss Benson.'

Dinner was served at eight-thirty, late by John's routine. But MacGregor was so relaxed and so charming throughout the meal that he won all of us over. He praised the food, wishing that he could eat like this every night—'but you know what sorry food we bachelors must be content with'; he asked intelligent questions about America and was generally very pleasant and jovial. After dinner, he and John discussed the war at great length, while Mary Louise and I drank our coffee quietly. MacGregor left with an invitation to return and in parting had a nice word for each of us. To me, he said, 'Your work is remarkably good, Miss Benson. I think you will be a very successful photographer.'

We never saw MacGregor socially again, except for brief encounters at the club. The week after the dinner, John said that he had stopped shadowing him at work. 'See, I told you once we had the guy over, he could see for himself how safe things are at home and he would stop worrying.'

But the truth emerged ten days later when I tried to contact Shanta Sinha again to invite them to Mary Louise's place for dinner. Sinha greeted me very courteously, but declined the invitation.

'I am very sorry, Miss Benson. We have had a series of rather upsetting encounters with the local police and I am busy with that. The police raided my premises, accusing me of violating the paper rationing limits. But what is more upsetting is that they have arrested several of my friends,' he mentioned the names of Maroon Sari's father and uncle.

I was shocked of course, but given that their political affiliations were no secret, I wondered if this was altogether unexpected.

'Oh, they didn't arrest them only because they were members of the Congress,' Sinha said wearily. 'They were betrayed by somebody who probably knew that we meet nowadays in these informal ways rather than in formal political sessions. You see, when DSP MacGregor told them the charges, he said rather smugly that he had absolute positive evidence that women too were assisting in these sessions. In fact, that was how he got all these men. He threatened to have their womenfolk arrested. I think for S-,' he mentioned Maroon Sari's uncle, the more orthodox Muslim, 'that was too much pressure. He has agreed to cooperate with the police in every respect as long as his women are kept out of the public view. You know, we never discuss anything at our gatherings that we wouldn't discuss anywhere else. In fact, I told you that you could report freely about the dinner you attended here. So, these arrests are only to harass us into ending our political and even our social networks.'

As Sinha was talking, I could feel the blood slowly draining from my head. I sat down on the chair next to the phone table and tried to collect my wits. From where had MacGregor got his evidence? From me, of course, stupid, half-witted, gullible dupe that I was, so taken in by his easy, spirited banter and his praise of my 'work' and his false encouragement. And all the while he had been looking at my pictures of the dinner party and had been thinking of how he could close the whole group down, had been noting which ones in the group would wilt under pressure.

I was only twenty-one in 1941, too young to become so cynical. But ever since that incident in Jamshedpur, I hate the British in India, all of them. They represent the ugliest possible face of Britain. I can't stand the calculated deception that's built into the whole system here, it is unbelievable. Can a system be *any* good, which is based on deviousness and hypocrisy, all directed at maintaining a hierarchical society and a total servility among the ruled? I guess it becomes a sort of addiction, doesn't it, this empire business? Some people justify the addiction by saying that we are humane and it's all for the good of the natives.

Sort of like spaying and declawing your cat and saying that's because you love it. Of course, you love the damned animal— but only as a helpless pet completely at your mercy. No, on the whole I prefer the kind like Dennis Porter, jerk that he is. At least, Dennis is quite straightforward about his ultimate aim and doesn't talk hogwash about 'humanity' and 'service' like that MacGregor creep.

After Jamshedpur, I have never been able to work as a journalist again. I wrote to my editor in Minneapolis and told him that I couldn't get any good pictures. He never replied, I doubt he cares about a bunch of unknown Indians in an unknown town. But that whole incident made me think about things. I had only looked at those meetings, at Shanta Sinha and his family and his friends, as a story, something with which I could make my mark in the world. Now, I take pictures for myself, my own education and to improve my technique. I take lots of pictures, but I'm not going to chase a story again, ever. The price is too high.

Actually, what's really killing me is that the whole incident in Jamshedpur showed me what a coward I am. I talked to Shanta Sinha for nearly twenty minutes that day but I couldn't bring myself to confess my own role in the matter; I couldn't apologize, and I couldn't beg his forgiveness. I'm just a goddamned coward.

And that's why I am here. I could have left anytime I wanted in later months—there were always passengers and ships leaving even during the worst of it. But this was the only way I knew of making amends, just staying and suffering through the war like everybody else here. I stay here because I do so want to repent.

Anna leaned across the table towards George and wept.

NINE

'Do you think your sister's still up?' George asked as he walked Anna up the dark street to the Holmes's bungalow. The tonga had dropped them off at the crossroads and the tired little pony had shuffled off into the darkness. George fervently hoped Ellen Holmes would be tactful enough to stay inside while he said his goodbye. It had been too emotionally draining an evening and he was feeling too tired to make small talk with his Commanding Officer's wife at this late hour. He was also uneasy about running into the CO himself; he remembered that throughout the evening Anna had not mentioned the CO's womanizing ways, in fact she had not explained at all beyond the initial exasperated rejoinder.

'You bet Ellen's still up,' Anna replied. She had recovered from her sadness during dinner. 'In fact, she'll be hoping for all sorts of exciting things to have happened to me. So maybe I should have something to tell her.'

She stopped under a honey-scented bahera tree and pulled George close to her, surprising him into kissing her. Her lips felt cool and then warm, and his arms began to tighten around her slim waist. Chiffon rustled under his hand, and then she pulled away, laughing.

'Well, at least the whole evening wasn't a complete waste. No, don't come to the door, the servants are already there, I can see them. Goodnight, George, do call me sometime.'

Then she was gone, a tall shadow moving towards a shadowed doorway. Other shadows emerged to welcome her, a sliver of yellow light, and then George was alone, facing a long walk home to his room. He could hear crickets and there was a slight breeze that turned the leaves on the trees into gently quivering shadows. He was happy, for the first time in months.

Lal Ram greeted him with his usual quietly intelligent visage. Remembering Porter's efforts with the lad, George tried to be extra careful and economical with his actions, but it was too late and he was too drained, emotionally and physically. It was a good thing that he had already decided on the next day's menu before he had gone out, so he did not need to make any selections this evening. Instead, his perusal of the Pithampur portfolio was purely therapeutic. The colours, rich and golden, sharply etched figures and softly blurred edges, all were soothing to his mind and his adrenaline-charged senses. At last, he lay down on the thin mattress, and tried to go over all the happenings of the evening, but the only thing that he could recall with any clarity was Anna's kiss and her smooth face in the shadowed lights.

At the mess on Monday morning, George was greeted with more smiles and even a gruff 'good morning' or two. There were fresh rolls on the sideboard, waiters handed out sausages and fried eggs and large platters of fried tomatoes and baked beans. Memories of Rajinder Singh and his appalling food were fading quickly, so it appeared. The 23rd and 33rd alike were busy feasting on the fresh, hot meal. The padre was expressive in his happiness; his delicate insides had suffered particular torture under Rajinder Singh's regimen. Watching the officers stuff their mouths, George felt slightly sickened. It was already very hot, even at seven o'clock in the morning. He had tea and toast, finishing up with some papaya. As he cycled away to his office, he reflected on the fact that had any of his fellow officers known about his dinner with Anna on Saturday night, he would have been back in the doghouse with the 33rd. Well, the gossip mills would spread the news soon but he was safe in the meantime.

On his way to Rotherford Square, George finally saw the cow that had attacked the padre. It was a brown cow, not as malnourished as some he had seen in the bazaar, and it stood quite still under a gulmohar tree. It had rather beautifully curving horns which it lowered at him menacingly, while shaking its head violently. Hadn't the padre said that he had complained about the belligerent animal and that the owner had promised to do something about the matter? Then, as he came closer, George saw that tied across the cow's horns was a small board that spelled out 'DANGER'. He shook with laughter as he raced away from the menacing animal. Bajapur was a mad, mad, mad place. He hoped the cow would get Ruffington in the rear with those horns, sometime.

When Capt. Ruffington came into the office, followed closely by a waiter with a tea tray, it was clear from his beaming face that he already knew about George and Anna's evening.

'Splendid job, Clark!' he almost clasped George to his round bosom. 'No better way to soften up a woman than to take her dancing. I heard that you two were quite the sight for sore eyes, as our friend Porter might say.'

'Well, Miss Benson—Anna—is a very nice person, sir,' said George, glaring at Ruffington who had already turned away and was pouring himself some tea from the silver teapot.

'Oh quite, quite, no doubt,' said Ruffington hastily. 'Oh I say, I have nothing against her at all! But you will be going to meet the Bharadwajs, won't you?' The expression on his round, pink face was a comic mix of anxiety and deep cunning.

'Sometime soon, I suppose.' George pretended to be deeply absorbed in the file that he had just opened. It was a relief when Capt. Porter came in and he could put the papers away. Ignoring George, Porter marched straight through to Ruffington's office and slapped something on the desk.

'This fellow in the 126th East Yorks is a communist,' George heard Porter declare.

'Ah, Clark, could you join us in here, please?' Ruffington called out pleasantly to George.

Inside the file that Porter—wearing an accusing expression—handed over to George, was a ten-page report titled, 'Activities of Arthur Rudolph, Major'.

'What proof do you have, Dennis?' asked Ruffington still pleasantly.

'He does commie things,' said Porter definitively, scowling at Ruffington's patronizing smile.

'Such as?'

'Well, my sources tell me that he spends a lot of time writing poetry,' said Porter belligerently. George took care not to meet Ruffington's eye. He was on the verge of laughing out aloud and he could see out of the corner of his eye that Ruffington's lips were also twitching.

'Do you know Major Rudolph, Clark?' asked Ruffington.

'Yes, sir, he is my Company Commander. He's presently away in Delhi with A Company, for ceremonial guard duty, sir.'

'Does he write poetry?'

George remembered the incident of the hastily put away novel from his first day.

'He might do so, sir. I really haven't heard him reciting any.' He again carefully looked at a point above Ruffington's head. He could feel his control wavering.

'You have to find it.' Porter was emphatic.

'Sir?'

'Find all those damned poems. That's where the code is.'

'The code?'

Porter looked at him as if he were retarded.

'The code—the code, didn't you read the file? That's what we've been hunting all along. The Congress and the communists probably share a code. Once we have something to go on with, we can then split them all apart and into smithereens. And I bet Rudolph has hidden his code in all this damned poetry. You goddamn amateurs don't know about poem codes, do you? You have to get your hands on this poetry, Clark!'

'Sir, firstly, it is inconceivable that Major Rudolph would be planning subversive activity against the authorities. It's absolutely poppycock, excuse me, it is nonse . . . it's unbelievable! In any case, sir, Major Rudolph is my Company Commander and a battalion officer. I cannot go around pinching his things. Wouldn't be quite the done thing, you know.'

'Well, I'll tell you what wouldn't be the done thing, Clark,' Porter sneered, looking menacing. 'It wouldn't be the done thing for me to tell Anna Benson that you're using her to get to the Congress and the communists in this little rathole of a town. *That* wouldn't be the done thing at all.' Blood rushed in and out of George's face. He turned so pale that Ruffington stepped away from his desk and towards him, sensing that George was about to hit Porter. That would end the recently commissioned subaltern's war quicker than anything else.

'Well, Dennis, we can talk about all this later, maybe over a drink at the club,' he said soothingly, drawing the American officer towards the door, safely out of George's reach.

Ruffington returned, apologetic and appeasing, seating himself behind his vast desk.

'Sorry, Clark, you know how pigheaded this Porter is. Sees Reds everywhere. I give you my word that Miss Benson will never get to know your role in this whole business, I will personally vouch for that.'

'Quite apart from Anna,' George said, hearing his words echo in his ears, and staring woodenly past Ruffington's piggy face at a spot on the wall. 'Major Rudolph is, as I told Captain Porter, a battalion officer, and I will not go around sneaking on him or stealing any of his things. Sir,' he added hastily.

'Oh dear, Clark.' Ruffington looked intensely bored. 'Battalion, regiment, unit. Very nice, very noble, old chap, but we are really not interested in things like that over here. If it's honour and loyalty you are after, you're in the wrong business.' He began to shift some papers about his desk.

'Well, sir.' George began to get really angry. 'I *didn't* want to be part of this whole operations. I still don't. I don't see how it's related to the war, to the army, to anything at all. In fact, shouldn't all this be a job for the police rather than for us? I don't know about you,' he went on, throwing all caution to the winds, 'but I just want to be a regimental officer till my number comes up for demobilization.' He turned quite red by the time he had finished. Ruffington eyed him coldly.

'Your battalion, Clark, shall we say, is not much of a unit. In fact, for you, stepping away from that snakepit of poisonous rivalry is probably the best thing that has happened in your, may I remind you, very short career.

As for this operation, the reason it is *not* with the Indian police is because,' Ruffington paused dramatically, 'the very highest circles in Simla wanted it kept *away* from any possible — ah, contact with anybody in the Indian circles. Naturally, the police with their large numbers of Indian officers and havaldars and all that, simply could not be trusted with such a sensitive task.'

'But what *is* the task?' George almost wailed.

Ruffington looked at him scornfully.

'My dear chap, weren't you paying any attention to what I said the other day in the club? The top brass in Simla haven't told me in so many words but from the periodic orders they give me, I can see quite clearly what they want us to do here in Bajapur, Clark. It's crystal clear. It has to do with the world situation.' George just stared at the man. Not only Porter, but Ruffington too was an utter lunatic. He had to be, none of this made any sense otherwise.

'Er . . . you mentioned a few days ago, sir, that the mission was about *us* maintaining the upper hand at all times,' he ventured, controlling his temper with great difficulty.

'Yes, yes, well that's what I believe too, in a bigger picture kind of way.' Ruffington dismissed his earlier misrepresentations with an airy wave of his hand. 'But more importantly, Clark, can't you see what's happening all over the world?' Ruffington became impatient, noticing George's incredulousness. 'The Americans are taking over one part of the world and the Soviets are taking over the other. We can't deal with the Reds at all, Clark, they are too busy trying to take the Empire for themselves. Though, personally, I think it's really Eastern Europe they are after. So, for the last time, Clark, our job—as I see it—is to guide as many Americans as we can towards our views, our way of thinking, if you like, on certain vital issues—like India, like the Empire. The only point where Americans have any contact with British policy is here, in the Services. So we just have to make sure that the better sort of American comes to see things our way. With Porter and people like him, that's not too difficult.

He already wants the same things that we do, except he lacks, ah, our subtlety, shall we say? He does rather like to bash people on the head and get whatever it is that he wants. But *we* can teach him subtlety, Clark, we are really good at that. Look how we got along beautifully with all sides in Spain before the war. Of course, we wanted Franco to win all along . . . Anyway, that's why Porter's presence in Bajapur is *very* important. He's frightfully cussed and a real bloody nuisance, I can tell you—I've worked with him in Pithampur. But now, I have it all planned. This little communist code business that Porter has his heart set on—well, Clark, it's the only chance we have to—to *educate* him so that when he leaves the army and enters civilian life—which for him is going to be politics undoubtedly, he will be already familiar with us and with *our* methods.'

Ruffington looked into the distance, recalling Porter's tactless outburst, then sighed in gentle exasperation. His eyes looked thoughtful and his expression firm. Suddenly, George realized what Ruffington was doing. He was practising a future speech. This pig-faced idiot, George thought, is going to stand for elections when the war was over. He was seeing the future Rt. Honourable James Ruffington, MP.

'You have no idea, really, do you, how much of a problem it is working with Americans?' Ruffington continued, not really talking to George anymore, just airing his own thoughts. 'You really have no idea, my dear chap. And it's not just the officials at the top either. There are the others, those who simply *can't* be brought around. Those damned American Other Ranks, for example, who sympathize with the Indian mobs on the streets. But at least we can ignore them for the most part. I mean, really, what difference does it make to us what a farmer's hand from Iowa thinks or does, isn't it? But it's the other sort that has us worried, frankly, the better sort, people with breeding and status who are in positions of power and can do serious damage to our interests. Have you seen the bunch they have in Delhi and in Simla? Always clucking their tongues about our security operations in India. Even Pearl Harbour didn't help change their minds.

'So, that's why we—you and I, Clark—have to keep a close eye on Yanks like Porter. People like him, ambitious, quite unpleasant personally, but otherwise already agreeable to a common project. We have to, you know, nudge the Porters of America into line, get them trained in our methods. Think of yourself as a housemaster in a public school, Clark—oh, never mind, you wouldn't know about all that.' George decided to let this condescending insult pass unchallenged, so Ruffington continued blithely.

'Anyway, the important thing is to let Porter lead—it's his outfit's money after all—but not ever take over. That part is hard because he does tend to want to stamp his own style on the whole operation, doesn't he? Still, he will do better than others. The Anna Bensons of the world are more difficult.' George began to stiffen, but Ruffington waved a placatory hand.

'But she too is manageable; she's not really very important, in a way she's as irrelevant as an American farmhand. We'll just get Porter's sort to bludgeon her aside, metaphorically speaking, of course, of *course,* don't look so put out, Clark. Don't worry, I don't see her as a security threat at all; she's quite useful actually, a sort of unwitting agent. Oh dear, you don't like that either, do you? I know that you wouldn't want her to find out about your work; women are very odd about things like that, aren't they? She'll never find out from me, or from Porter, I guarantee that, so don't worry.'

Ruffington added casually, 'And is there no way you could find some damned poems for our Porter? We really do need his outfit to continue to be involved in the Bajapur case,' he ended cunningly, leaving George to wonder whether Ruffington had finally told him the whole story for the sake of truth or for the immediate purpose of getting George to agree to steal Rudolph's writings. Or was this the truth at all? These chaps were all stark raving mad, George thought, cuckoo, the bunch of them. What a cock-and-bull story it all was. The world situation, indeed! Just a bunch of bounders let loose, that's what this operation was.

'I really would not like to poke around in Major Rudolph's private things, sir, if you don't mind.' George was quite firm. Ruffington nodded and left a little early for his three-hour lunch.

George waited a bit to make sure that Ruffington was safely out of the way and then phoned Col. Holmes's office. The CO was just leaving but agreed to meet George after lunch at his office. As he cycled over to the mess for lunch, he wondered what tempting feast Indumati had cooked up today.

To his surprise, there was a lot of activity at the mess. Waiters ran around, a mess corporal was directing a bevy of Indian waiters and a battalion working party with whirling gestures, broken Hindustani and a lot of curses. 'CO's having lunch today, sir,' was his brief explanation to George. 'You were at the other office and I didn't have time to telephone you. Maj. Shelton invited the CO.' He returned to alternately cajoling and threatening his workers' team.

Inside, the atmosphere was tight and frosty. The 23rd men were strutting around looking self-important and smug, while the 33rd officers sulked in a corner of the lounge. The CO arrived just as the last of the bearers was being whisked away into the kitchen where his frayed trousers would not offend anyone. Col. Holmes was immediately surrounded by the 23rd officers, who smiled and welcomed him loudly, with one eye on the 33rd wallas, gloating over their reaction. Col. Holmes greeted them all courteously, especially the senior dining member Maj. Richard Brassey, and then to everyone's amazement, walked over to the 33rd side. He engaged the senior Major from the 33rd, Hugh Shelton, who had invited him over to lunch, and then before anyone knew it, Brassey had joined them and the three were soon chatting away—like a bunch of jolly parrots, thought George. The whole situation had been defused from a potential social disaster to one of mere uncertainty.

Lunch proved to be a further tonic for everyone's agitated nerves. Indumati had come up with cold cucumber soup, succulent chops—lightly flavoured with lime and cumin—mashed potatoes flecked with cilantro, and a creamy caramel custard. Coffee was served in the lounge and even the portraits of long-dead or long-retired battalion patriarchs from the 23rd East Yorks and the 33rd King's Own seemed to look down benevolently on the gathering. Maj. Shelton's position by the CO's side seemed to have lessened some of the resentment on the 33rd side, and George found himself at the receiving end of some actually pleasant banter from Capt. James Duncan, of B Company. Duncan asked about George's new job, and then stunned him into silence by inviting him to tea that week. 'Tess is down from Mussoorie, it was too dull there, she said, so she'll deal with the heat here in Bajapur. She has been looking forward to meeting you; she hears that you're quite a hit with the ladies, ha, ha.' George thanked Captain Duncan and promised to show up at their residence at four-thirty on Thursday.

Then he was cornered by the padre who urged him to come

for a polo game and horse show in the cantonment in two days' time.

'I've been working with Miss Williams in the American Mission School here,' the reverend beamed. 'And she has introduced me to several nice Indian families here. We must reach out, you know, Mr Clark. So, the children of these families will be coming as my guests to the horse show on Wednesday. You will be there, I hope?' George agreed to come for the show and then told the chaplain about the cow situation.

'I should have known it,' said the padre gloomily. 'This place, I tell you. One step forward, two steps back. I explicitly warned Brigade Headquarters and the owner promised he would correct the problem. Ah well, that's the army for you, Mr Clark, that's the army for you.' He went away, grumbling, to the other side of the anteroom.

After about a half-hour of chatting about battalion activities, Col Holmes left for his office and George set out on his bicycle to keep his appointment with him. As he parked his cycle outside, he reflected ruefully that he had visited this office far too often, given his lowly rank. The three cement steps leading up to the porticoed veranda were slightly pockmarked with use.

The CO acknowledged his salute and looked at him meaningfully with his sad, dark eyes.

'Yes, Clark, what trouble have you brought me today?'

George reddened and then gave as brief and direct a report as he could before he lost his nerve. He told Holmes about Porter's suspicions of Rudolph, his insistence on prying into the Company Commander's writings in order to indict him. He also informed the CO that Ruffington was being quite sly and deceitful and that Ruffington saw no harm in stealing Rudolph's papers and giving them to Porter in order to keep the operation going. He told Holmes about James Ruffington's explanation about the whole operation really being a training mission specially commissioned from Simla to make sure that Porter would return to America fully tuned to the British view.

'In fact, sir,' he ended, 'I don't know who the worse snake is, Porter or Ruffington. Ruffington—Capt. Ruffington, sir—seems to be operating at multiple levels of deceit and I never know when he's telling me the truth and whether it's the whole truth or only part of it.'

Holmes had been listening intently to the story. At the end of it, he turned a bright red and George thought there was going to be a terrible explosion of anger. Instead, the CO began to laugh, at first quietly and then uproariously. He slapped the desk until it shook and then finally had to fish out his handkerchief and apologize while he wiped his eyes. The office orderly peeked in through the curtains.

'Bloody clowns!' Col Holmes finally exclaimed, weak with mirth. 'Bloody, bloody, *bloody* clowns, the lot of them! Oh Clark, you poor lad, how did you end up with chumps like Ruffington and Porter?' Then, the Colonel became more sombre.

'Of course, the problem is that the two of them aren't just clowns, they're absolutely cunning swine on top of it. Well, Clark, they're not going to mess around with this unit, you can be sure of that. We have quite enough problems as it is, without Porter and Ruffington prowling around our offices. Honestly, the war has seen all sorts of unspeakable rubbish entering the services. Training Porter, indeed! Both those bloody idiots should have been trained against the Japanese which is really what Special Ops are for, now that Hitler is gone. Anyway, I'll look into this matter with Rudolph right away. Thanks, Clark.' And then the CO was off again, in the ripe late-afternoon heat, hurrying towards his beloved horses. George returned to Rotherford Square, a huge weight lifted off his shoulders.

It was therefore a shock to him when Ruffington bounced in to see him just before he left office at four o' clock. His pink face glowing with a sweaty cheerfulness, Ruffington slapped a slim box on his desk. A piece of paper tumbled from his hands. It had a handwritten message on it. He picked it up hastily and stuffed it in his pocket, glancing quickly at George to make sure that he had not read the note.

'Here, Clark, now you don't have to worry about your precious battalion honour. Our chum, Porter, has gone and done the dirty work for you. He's raided Rudolph's desk during tea, I believe, the clever chap, and has come up with his writings. Now, you and I have to go over all this together as I'm afraid I have no eye for literature, ha, ha.'

George was appalled. 'Sir, there is no way I could help in this matter. I barely know Maj. Rudolph myself as I've only been in the unit a few weeks, not even a month.' Then, as the magnitude of Porter's deed struck him, he felt the anger rise again.

'May I ask how Porter—Capt. Porter—managed to get these papers, sir?'

'Think, Clark, think,' Ruffington said mockingly, but without any malice. 'How could he have pulled it off?'

Of course, it all made sense now. Rudolph was away with 'A' Company in Delhi. It was the perfect opportunity to order one of the unquestioningly obedient office orderlies or a sweeper to hand over the contents of Rudolph's desk to Porter. But the sheer audacity of Ruffington's and Porter's enterprise took George's breath away. In spite of his, George's, clearly stated objections to the scheme, Porter had gone ahead anyway and had pinched whatever the hell it was that Ruffington was writing—probably harmless, moony stuff about love in the moonlight or something like that. And Ruffington, the devious jackal, was willing to bless Porter's thievery, all in the name of his so-called international skulduggery.

It was almost as if the two of them were a different species than George or anybody else in Bajapur. Even though Ruffington and Porter wore more or less the same uniform as George, fought for the same side or claimed to do so, and claimed to share the same ideals and values, under all the superficial similarities there lurked strange, murky points of view, warped and rebellious instincts. Work, indeed life itself, was a sport to both Porter and Ruffington, hence the exploitative opportunism that both men displayed. Underneath it all, there was a strange bubbling activity, a repulsive restlessness, a perverse mix of lies and adventurism bordering on criminality. By this time, George was dimly aware that such perhaps were the ways of the Intelligence game itself. But now he began to wonder if these were not in fact the true values of men like Porter and Ruffington, adventurers who gravitated deliberately to the secret services during the war, faux aristocrats, displaying an insouciant, deliberately unintellectual attitude towards work.

These chaps had been drawn to Intelligence work not because they were more intelligent than the average regimental soldier, but because service in the Special Operations Executive and the Political Warfare Executive, and in the American counterpart, the Office of Strategic Services, allowed some men like Porter and Ruffington to give free rein to their inborn devious qualities, including that of latent criminality. That's part of what this whole war has been about for these people, George thought— it's been a giant opportunity for the toffs, chaps like Dennis Porter, and for socially ambitious opportunists like Ruffington, to refine their talent for duplicity and deviousness and to practise it on a worldwide stage.

All this farcical charade about communists in Bajapur was just another orchestrated accomplishment designed to solidify Ruffington's postwar career, his future elevation to the status of Member of Parliament, and then win him even more renown in the distant future as Peer of the Realm, a wise elder, someone who had kept the cowboy American cousins under check and had advanced Britain's interests in the bargain. As for Dennis Porter, he too would probably run for election in the United States on the strength of his strong anti-communist policy (no doubt the 'Bajapur Case' would find some mention in his campaign). He would marry some rich heiress and they would raise several unpleasant brats in a colonial mansion in Virginia, the kind that George had seen often in flicks, with majestic pillars and columns, and staircases running down onto sweeping driveways.

And he, George, where would he be twenty years from now? Frankly, he didn't know. He didn't see himself back on the farm at home. He just didn't. But what did he have going for him right now? All he had was a good war record, a certain eagerness in his new career as an officer, and this . . . this mix-up in a farcical Intelligence caper involving two international cads and some political hotheads, and, oh, yes, an attractive amateur photographer—his CO's American sister-in-law, auburn-haired, comfortable with herself, but uncomfortable in British India.

I wonder what Ruffington saw in me, George wondered, when he asked me to call on Deborah Sunderland in Pithampur. Even as the thought entered his head, he knew the answer. He saw that I was a dupe, of course. The dull, plodding, recently commissioned regular who could be put to useful work without his even realizing it. The modus operandi was to get the work done by reliable dupes and through informal networks and personal recommendations. Nothing left for future Commissions of Inquiry to explore or to indict. George now understood, and as the fog began to lift, he heard Ruffington speaking through it.

'So I'm going to take these papers to my room, Clark, and then tomorrow we can all go over it together and see what we can make of all of this.' Ruffington was pleasant but his tone brooked no argument. George said nothing. He pulled out one of the files on the Bharadwajs and began to read again the police views on the family's activities.

After dinner, he went to see Anna to take her out for a walk. As they strolled back in the still, hot night, he asked hesitantly, 'Do you think the CO might agree to see me for just ten minutes?' George's heart fluttered as he waited in the neat drawing room, the servants hovering outside. Finally the CO walked in, his face grim and rather unwelcoming, no doubt pushed into meeting the subaltern on his sister-in-law's appeals. Without much preamble, George informed Col Holmes about Porter's burglarizing of Maj. Rudolph's papers. The CO, cracking his knuckles, smiled enigmatically.

'Well, I don't know why I'm telling you this—you've been quite enough trouble as it is, Clark—but here's a little secret for *you* to keep from Ruffington. I had Maj. Rudolph's office desk cleared this afternoon immediately after our meeting. I took the liberty of replacing his writing—a whole bunch of rubbish it is too, but that doesn't mean that Porter or anyone else has the bloody right to take off with it—with the poetry written by a young officer of my original regiment—the 23rd East Yorks— who died in Burma. His personal effects were scattered in the retreat of '42 and I've been receiving his papers in dribs and drabs ever since. I just received a new batch a few days ago. Whenever a new piece shows up, I hand them over to his wife. Technically speaking, it's out of line. Sam Bates had no business keeping any personal papers on his mission. The poems are all about India mostly; he was born here and grew up here, and most of his scribbles are all about some cantonment town or the other. They seem quite boring—I don't understand all this modern stuff, anyway.

'Still, his wife is so comforted by his writings that I haven't the heart to refuse her, although it gets a bit much sometimes because she insists on reading out some of the damn things to me. And then she cries which makes it dashed awkward. You might have seen her around the cantonment—Muriel Bates, she's the daughter of the local Signals Commandant. Very sad, the whole thing. They were only married three months. Anyway, I'm sure Muriel won't miss this particular bunch of poems; she has quite a collection with her already. In any case, since we are supposed to confiscate any unauthorized papers, this helps me to cover my tracks too.

'So there you go, Clark, we've solved three things at one go— the matter of Rudolph's privacy, your regimental loyalty, and my duty to GHQ. And Sam Bates is still doing his duty by the unit. He was a good lad. Anna will see you to the door.' The CO nodded his head in dismissal and left the room. The meeting was over.

George was staggered by the CO's command over the situation. He blushed and stammered and then beat a quick retreat to his own quarters, overwhelmed by all the new information he had received. How different were the facts from his perception of them! Sam *Bates*, that's why Muriel was Muriel *Bates*. She was widowed, not the unmarried daughter of the local Signals

Commandant. Hence Anna's vexed exclamation, 'Don't they know what Muriel is going through, has gone through?' And the CO was *not* having an affair with Muriel—he was just handing over her dead husband's stuff as discreetly as he could. What a good plan—as an ATS sergeant, Muriel Bates had legitimate work in Col Holmes's office. The half-hour or so she spent there was not to exchange kisses but to collect things and to weep, perhaps on the CO's shoulders. It was all all right, George thought happily, the 126th East Yorks was a marvellous, fantastic unit, and the battalion had a super CO. No wonder Anna had not been upset when he blurted out the bit about the CO's womanizing. She knew the right story. Now if only he could get the news to the 23rd and the 33rdwallas. George almost didn't notice the heat as he cycled back to his rooms.

The next day George went to work in better spirits, if not exactly joyously. He even took the stolen papers enthusiastically from Ruffington's desk. It was a good thing that Ruffington was not in yet; he would have suspected something was up as soon as he saw George's face.

Later in the evening, after seeing Anna home after their drink at the club, George ate his dinner at the mess. The food was wonderful—a first course of clear soup, followed by vegetable rissoles in a white sauce, then a main course of braised chicken with puréed pumpkin on the side, scented with cinnamon and cloves. Indumati was not quite an accomplished baker, although she was learning fast. The rolls were softer than they had been the first week. The woman was rapidly becoming a legend in the mess. It was doubtful whether any of the unit's officers had eaten as well as they had begun to under George's watch. Everybody was in a stupor of contentment after the meal and the evening might even have been prolonged if not for the heat bearing down like a visible weight.

After the senior dining members had left the mess, George retreated to his room with strict instructions to Lal Ram that he not be disturbed. As he sat down to read Bates's papers, he could hear the boy moving around on the veranda, sometimes coughing, always listening. He smoothed out the rough, already yellowing papers, covered with small handwriting, blotted badly here and there as if Bates had had to leave off writing in a hurry. A deep sigh escaped George as he remembered the bleak days in the Burma jungle, meals abandoned in a hurry as weapons were gathered, and the long retreat back into India. Thank God I escaped that, he said silently as he began to read. An hour later, after taking many notes, he could read nothing more than innocent nonsense into the verses. This was clearly just poetry, most of which George did not much care for. It would be interesting, though, to see Porter extract secret communist communication from verses like the following:

This is Zin,
all body, all madness
with no voice.
Shehe remembers moonlit nights
and hiser lover walking
in silvery light.
The flowers and the stars.
A lifetime of togetherness.

Must love be always so sweet,
so overpoweringly pure?
Must it always end with sleepless nights
and restless affairs?
Forgetting begins before remembrance
in the beginning
of the end.

Emotional words spring
to lips.
Oh, Zin! If only you knew
How much I think and brood
Can't seem to forget those
dusty days and mad obsession.
That long walk from home,
you at my side,
asking me if it was true that
we were the talk of town,
that small town.
There was a man, men, you said.
How could you!
I?
It was so easy, jumping through
space and time.

At length, Lal Ram knocked on the door. He reminded George that there was still the menu for the following day to be decided. In his absorption in the poetry, his mess duties had completely slipped George's mind. He opened the cookbook and began to peruse the lustrous portfolio of recipes.

As it turned out, Porter not only *could* see communist propaganda when he read it, he could also recognize secret communist codes in the strange, disjointed verses of Capt. Sam Bates. The next day, he barged into the office again, with his usual lack of deference to the rank or the status of his British colleagues. Ruffington sighed painfully and said nothing, waiting for Porter to speak.

'This poetry business shows that Rudolph is running a bigger ring than I thought.'

'Anything particular you had in mind?' Ruffington dripped

with sarcasm that Porter either did not get or, more likely, ignored.

'It's all there, dammit, you guys either just don't get it, or you just don't care. This is huge. If we can just nail this guy, we can blow this whole operation apart.'

As they rustled through the sheets full of Bates's handwriting, Porter stopped with a triumphant sound at a particular piece:

> There was once
> a dance hall,
> long ago, beautiful,
> already defunct
> when we saw it.
> A starry evening
> and Zin, bored and restless,
> watched the woman dance.
> Those eyes, pitch black
> and smouldering,
> braided hair
> swinging off hips.
> This woman will die,
> said Zin and I cried
> because she danced lightly
> like a flower.
> The ghosts of courtesans
> seemed to gather
> around her then.

'So, we have to look for a dancer,' said Porter triumphantly. 'That's the clue. The commies probably use her to pass on secret messages to each other and to the Congress.'

'All rubbish, Dennis,' said Ruffington, briskly. 'Do you want to go and interview every single nautch girl in Bajapur, then? Or maybe that's your plan, eh? Have a good dekko yourself?' He added slyly, leering and winking in the horrible, crude way that grated on George's nerves.

'Well, that's our first clue,' repeated Porter, taking not the slightest notice of Ruffington. 'I'll find more in these pages before I'm done.' He left soon after, clutching the file to his chest tightly as if the pages were about to blow away in a strong wind.

'He's just mad, absolutely bloody mad,' Ruffington laughed. 'Ah well, he must have his little game, I suppose. What do you think, Clark?'

George busied himself with some files, shaking his head at the utter foolishness of his new colleagues. That afternoon there was a polo match and show jumping organized by some of the Indian units. Since the padre had asked George to be there, he decided to show his face at the event. At least there would be tea and halfway decent cakes, and while Indumati was a terrific cook, he fancied a change of scenery from the usual grouchiness at the mess. If George was honest though, he would have to admit that he was going to the horseshow because he knew Anna would be there too. He got ready and had Lal Ram hail him a tonga. It was far too hot to walk even that short distance.

At half-past five, the ground was still shimmering with heat when the show jumping got under way. The VIPs—the Brigade Commander and his wife, assorted colonels and their wives, a few prominent civilians—were seated under a white canopy in the centre. The Other Ranks—British and Indian—were seated across the polo ground, the races segregated firmly, British ORs on chairs, Indian ORs seated cross-legged and at attention on the tarpaulin-covered ground.

From his perch on the edge of the seated area, George could see some Indians sitting in the VIP enclosure, clustered around Judge Bharadwaj. They were being offered sandwiches and drinks. Anna was a faint patch of blue chiffon, talking to and smiling at Muriel Bates. Barbara Curtis, the local Brigade Commander's daughter, was dressed in riding gear, so clearly she was going to participate in the events of the afternoon. On George's right, a tarpaulin covered the ground, and presently the battalion chaplain came by, fussing over some children. He seated them on the ground near George.

'I'm sure you won't mind, Mr Clark, if these children sit by you. You remember, I told you about them? I thought that bringing them to some army functions might show them a little of our lives. These are Mr Bharadwaj's grand-nephew and grand-niece—you know *Judge* Bharadwaj [the padre was a bit of a social snob]—and these other children are their houseguests, and these are the children of the Bharadwajs' neighbour, Dr Matthew, who works in the local hospital. The Bharadwajs are over in the white tent there, but I thought it might be nice for the children to sit by us. What do you think, Mr. Clark? Do settle down, children. I'm sure the show will start soon.' The children settled themselves on the tarpaulin near George and soon began quarrelling. They used Hindi and English interchangeably and with equal vehemence.

'Now, now, children.' The padre tried to calm everyone down and after a while there was an uneasy peace in the disgruntled little camp. This was the first time that George was having any extended conversation with the battalion's minister, apart from the matter of the cow which had not yet been fully resolved. The padre was a busy man, who rarely put in an appearance at the mess, pleading ministerial duties when pressed. He was always on a mission of mercy or of social work, typically something that kept him away for long hours from the unit. Sometimes his religious duties took him out of the cantonment into the town for days at a stretch. But everyone also knew that he was simply avoiding the mess at mealtimes. Inspecting the padre's charges, George saw that there were four girls and three boys, all between eight and twelve. Two of the girls were craning their necks trying to see the horses as they pranced in the field away from the competition area, their riders patting, coaxing and whispering, whips not being used for now. There would be tent-pegging, dressage, showjumping, and after tea there would be a few chukkers of polo.

'Why is there so much horse riding happening over there?' one little girl asked, pointing to the hustle and bustle off to the side as the horses and riders practised.

'And when are they going to actually start the show?' her friend complained.

'Hai, it's so hot,' sighed one of the boys, cupping his face in his hand as he picked at some grass on the edge of the tarpaulin.

'Don't say "hai", Ram,' admonished another girl, who was clearly his sister. 'You're a Christian, not a Hindu. Christians don't say "hai".'

'Why not, Renuka?' asked another boy, clearly fascinated by these restrictions on free speech.

'Because "hai" is a Hindu word,' said the girl emphatically. 'Christians don't say "hai".'

'Hai,' murmured Ram defiantly, looking at his friend. Both boys burst into fits of giggles.

Renuka tossed her head and looked away. The padre glared at all of them.

'It really has been so difficult with these children,' he

complained to George, who was unable to slip away because all the other seats had been taken by this time.

'The girl there,' the padre pointed to Renuka 'is rather overbearing, as you can see. But still, I feel it is my duty to reach out and guide them spiritually. The war has been so disruptive of any religious influence on these young minds. It's especially important these days as the communist influence seems to be growing in India among young people. Captain Porter—you know him—and I had a long chat about it a few weeks ago. It is so very difficult to convince any of the grown-ups about this menace. So I am focusing on the children. They might be more receptive. Although with these here,' he indicated his unruly charges again, 'I don't know, I really don't know . . .'

His further ramblings on the subject were interrupted by a thundering of hooves as the first event in the programme got under way. A rider in full ceremonial regalia, white jodhpurs, turban and polished, black riding boots, galloped past, swooped low and triumphantly held up a peg at the end of his lance. Everyone applauded. The children were instantly quiet, captivated by the sight. George leaned forward to look at the horses and their riders. They were superb. He had treated many horses in his days assisting old Dr Farthers and he had always liked them. But these cavalry horses, utterly magnificent creatures, were very different from their plodding, farming cousins in faraway England. The riders here were mainly Indian sawars with some English officers, in simple and striking dress: dark-blue-and-white striped turbans, blue jackets with white cummerbunds, white jodhpurs and black riding boots. George didn't know it at the time, but this was the last few times the 21st Lancers sawars would ride their horses. This was the last mounted squadron left in the unit. In a few months, it too would be mechanized, like the other squadrons in the regiment and like all cavalry units had been over the course of the war. Sawars and steeds would be let go, distributed, shuffled around and disposed of, the regiment itself divided between India and Pakistan. But that was still a few years into the future. Now, George just gazed as did the others in silent appreciation of the beauty of the horses and the riders, the riders' perfect control over their animals and over themselves, the horses' ears twitching back and forth, responding to their riders' imperceptible commands through the reins.

After this thunderous opening, the horse show became rather tepid. First, there was dressage. While the judges were no doubt impressed at the discipline and intelligence of the horses on show, and the perfect control their riders had over them, the children sitting next to George became bored rapidly. Renuka bullied her brother Ram about some other minor theological matter, while the other two boys scuffled with each other.

Suddenly, one turned to George.

'Uncle, he is biting me.' His English was clear, his complaint undeniable. There was a ring of teeth-marks on his little forearm. This was a tricky situation.

'You are not allowed to bite him,' George said firmly to the smaller chap.

'But he's bigger than me, why can't I bite him?' said the offender calmly.

'No, that's cheating,' said George, hiding a grin. 'You're not allowed to bite him, see?'

'Now, children,' said the padre. 'In a few minutes, the showjumping will start. That will be something, I can tell you.'

Renuka was picking grass moodily because the three other girls were ignoring her. Two of them were writing something on a piece of paper. They laughed and giggled, while the third girl shushed them from time to time.

'Now, what is your name, dear?' the padre asked the shush-er in a kind voice, hoping to win at least one of these children over.

'Paripurnasahasrachandravati,' she replied smoothly.

That silenced the padre. 'Er . . . do you call her that at home?' asked George, finally.

'No, we call her Munni,' answered one of the other girls, looking up from her writing game. 'She's my didi, my older sister.'

'And what's your name?'

'My name is Lokajanini.'

'But everyone calls her Chinu,' said the third girl. 'Both Munni and Chinu live with us now. And their brother is Satyakarman, the one who bit my brother. We call him Totu. Their father and mother are in jail. I'm Snehala,' she added.

The sisters Munni and Chinu looked glum, reminded that they were guests in another's house while their family situation was uncertain.

'Oh dear,' said the padre.

'Inquilab Zindabad!' shouted the boy who had been bitten by Totu.

'That's my brother, Tarun Kumar Chaturvedi,' said Snehala. 'We call him Bittu. And I'm Choti. And our mother is Mira Chaturvedi, and she is very good at music and painting and dance, and our father is Rajendra Kumar Chaturvedi. And my grandfather is Nana.'

It was all very confusing to George and the padre.

'Hai, I'm just Ram,' said the Christian boy who was not allowed to say "Hai".'

'I've told you not to say "hai", Ram.' His sister Renuka glared at him.

'I'm glad you are so mindful of the Gospel, my dear,' said the padre. 'But really, you mustn't be so zealous. Are your parents very good Christians then?'

'Yes!' Renuka screwed up her face in displeasure, though. 'But although Appa goes to church, at home, he is always sitting and reading Hindu books.'

Then, Snehala, aka Choti, said something rapidly to Renuka in Hindi, clearly telling her to stop tattling.

'What books?' George was intrigued in spite of himself.

'Oh, the Ramayana, the Mahabharata, all those stories. And he tells us the stories too. But ever since Miss Williams from school told us that those books are sinful for Christians, I have stopped listening to them.'

'I was named Ram because Appa loves the Ramayana,' said Renuka's brother shyly. 'Appa says that Ram was a hero for the ages.'

'Miss Williams says that only Jesus is the real hero,' said his sister, angrily. The three other girls laughed and pulled her away from the argument. They resumed their interrupted game, putting pencil to paper again as the dressage continued. George tried to remember their names and keep their identities clear in his head. Bittu and Choti were the children of Mira Chaturvedi (Anna's friend) and the grandchildren of Pratap Kumar Bharadwaj. The three children with the long names, Munni, Chinu and Totu were the kids of jailed friends. Ram and Renuka were children of the Chaturvedis' neighbour, the physician Dr Matthew.

'Er . . . Miss Williams is the American missionary who teaches at the local school,' the padre explained. 'I believe Capt. Porter invited her to Bajapur to further the work of her mission. She used to teach near Aizawl, in the North-East Frontier earlier. I try to help with her work in the community, especially with the children.'

So that was Porter's plan that Ruffington had mentioned—import Christian missionaries from the North-East to bolster anti-communism in Bajapur. The ass, the benighted ass, George thought. Not ass, rogue, he reminded himself.

'Miss Williams seems, rather . . . er, ardent,' he told the padre. 'Doesn't that create any problems with the local people?'

'Yes,' the padre agreed glumly. 'She is quite vehement in her declarations of piety. Recently, there was a political meeting attended by some fairly important people. She created quite a lot of discord by telling them they were all going to burn in hell.'

'That was at my Amar dada's meeting, he's my father's uncle,' piped up Snehala Chaturvedi, or Choti, who had been listening to the grown-ups' chatter. 'Miss Williams said that he was going to hell and that the devil would snatch him up and he would suffer the torture and agonies of eternal fire.' She quoted from memory, enjoying recalling the moment when the meeting broke up in fractious theological dispute. 'My father's chacha said that anybody who ate beef like she did had no business talking about hell and that our Deepavali lamps would light up the sky for thousands of years to come. Then his servants beat Miss Williams's ekka driver and threw all her books into the river.'

'Yes, and remember what Mir Ali Mianji said after that?' her brother Bittu piped in excitedly. 'He said that the British ate beef *and* pork and so did the Americans and that they would wander in pain and misery through jehannum just like the Hindus would and in the end the world would be saved by Islam. And then all the Muslims shouted Allah-ho-Akbar! And then everyone fought everyone else. Allah-ho-Akbar!' Bittu shouted. The nearby spectators, lowly lieutenants and captains, corralled off to the side with the children, frowned at him. One raised his finger to his lips and pointed at the horses, now about to start the showjumping.

The showjumping part of the programme went off mostly uneventfully. Brig. Curtis's daughter, Barbara, rode well and made it through all the twelve hurdles, knocking down only one log on the fifth hurdle. But the star of the show was a woman whom George had never seen before in the cantonment. She wore a boxy jacket, jodhpurs and an engaging smile, her short hair peeking out from under her riding hat in a cut that was both fashionable and practical. It was almost as if she and her horse were one, so effortlessly did they sail over all the hurdles in less than the allotted time, dropping no logs or bricks. There was no question of her horse refusing any jump. She received a long and sustained round of applause. This was talent that clearly stood above and beyond the equestrian standard of the present gathering. The rest of the showjumping proceeded with the usual litany of missed jumps, refused hurdles, and a couple of ejections of riders by their stubborn steeds. At the end of the round, it was clear that it was the unknown woman who was going to win the prize for showjumping. Soon, there was a break for tea.

George went to the refreshment tent as soon as the top brass had been fed and nourished and had returned to their seats. There was the usual melée of junior officers scrounging for cake, sandwiches and tea. Some of them escorted laughing women into the area. The end of hostilities in Europe had lifted at least some of the tension; the lighter mood was palpable under the shaded canvas, even as the heat pressed down on all of them. A slight stir set amongst the lot and the crowd parted respectfully as the winning showjumper, the woman in the boxy jacket, entered. She spotted Anna standing in the corner and went over to chat with her. George drifted there, intrigued by the talented stranger.

'Oh, George!' Anna smilingly beckoned him over. 'Meet my fellow American in Bajapur, Carol Hagerman.'

Carol Hagerman smiled her acknowledgement.

'Your riding was just superb!' George could hear himself gushing, but couldn't hold back.

'Thank you,' Miss Hagerman smiled modestly. The crowds swirled around them. 'He has real heart, that Snowflake. Strange to call a horse Snowflake in India, isn't it? He isn't even white or anything.'

'How long have you been here in Bajapur?' George was curious why he hadn't seen her before.

'Actually, I'm on my way to Delhi. I stopped on the way to do some work with the local Red Cross Committee. They told me that there was a horse show being held. And, well, luckily for me, Brig. Curtis very kindly agreed to have me compete even at such short notice.' A bunch of people crowded around Carol Hagerman enthusiastically. George stood close to Anna and put his arm around her waist discreetly, then withdrew it as someone called out to her.

'I have to go to Richard and Ellen,' she said. 'Can you meet me later? The Silonias are in town and I would love to have you meet them.'

He nodded, excited and also apprehensive, and made his way back to his seat, next to the padre and his gaggle of children. To his surprise, Porter was also there, chatting with the priest and glaring from time to time at the children who were being noisy and clamorous again. Porter nodded curtly to George—his usual form of acknowledgement—and continued to mutter in a low tone to the padre. George looked at the children who had suddenly become quiet. One of the girls, Munni, was writing something on a piece of paper while the other girls were giggling and the boys were scowling at them. After she finished, the boys took the paper and began to read it. They seemed puzzled by it. This amused the girls even more.

'They don't understand!' Snehala, or Choti, was almost prostrate with laughter. 'It's so easy, but they don't know!'

'Here, Uncle, you tell us what this is.' Ram gave the paper to George. He looked down at the letters on the page and it made no sense to him too.

ABBG

TPOG

PKIG

UPOG

'That's their code!' An excited bark from Porter who had silently crept up behind George. His outburst startled George who dropped the paper. The girls picked it up, giggling. Porter bent down and snatched it out of their hands.

'Give me that!' he snarled. The youngest girl Chinu began to cry and Snehala Chaturvedi's chin also began to quiver.

'Captain Porter!' the padre exclaimed in outrage. 'Whatever do you think you are doing? You are frightening these children!'

'That's the code,' repeated Dennis Porter smugly. He folded the paper in half, tucked it into his trouser pocket and walked away rapidly. 'Report to the office early tomorrow,' he called over his shoulder to George. 'I want to see you at eight o'clock.'

'Well, fuck you!' thought George sourly. He and the padre calmed the girls down as best as they could. Luckily, one of the other officers, a subaltern from one of the Indian regiments, had some boiled sweets with him and these helped to tide over the crisis. The children settled back again to watch a fast and furious game of polo. George was hot and seething at Dennis Porter's outrageous behaviour. He resolved to confront the man as soon as he saw him in the office the next day.

TEN

The morning after the polo match, Dennis Porter called a meeting of the three members of the Bajapur Special Executive Group, a pompous flight of fancy that Ruffington had come up with in the previous week. When George walked in, he caught Ruffington quickly stuffing something into the waste-paper basket. Again! This was the second time he had discarded something as soon as George entered. Whatever was the sly rascal up to?

Outside, a stifling oven of a June day was starting its course. When would the rains come? George felt almost faint, the scratchiness of his uniform did not help, neither did the electric fans swirling the sluggish air around the room. While Ruffington poured himself another cup of tea, Dennis Porter set out the scrap of paper that he had snatched from the little girls the afternoon before. The crumples in the paper along with the uneven scribbles made the whole thing seem even more pathetic in George's eyes.

'Here it is, guys!' Porter crowed. 'The code.'

'How do you know it is the one, Porter?' Ruffington sipped his tea and stared impassively at the American.

'You know how the Congress uses kids to run messages to and from jail?' Porter asked. 'I've heard that in Allahabad they had quite a racket going, oh about ten years ago. They were called the Monkey Brigades. Well, these kids here in Bajapur also pass messages from the inside to the outside. Their parents—who are a bunch of communists—probably just asked them to pass it along to the Congress and the commies still inside jail. The kids were playing a game with the code; they didn't know what the letters meant, but we will find that out.'

'Does that mean, sir, that Major Rudolph's . . . er, writings, are no longer suspect?' George tried to intervene on behalf of his unit officer.

'Of course not, Clark,' Porter snapped at him. 'Anyone who writes poetry in his spare time, is most likely a communist. So, no, you must continue with the analysis there.' George subsided.

'Just look at this thing,' Porter continued, holding up the children's paper. 'These letters are clearly *code*!'

'Well, it certainly looks like some sort of secret language,' Ruffington agreed, still not wholly persuaded. 'But how do we not exclude the possibility that the children were just practising their English? After all, they all take English lessons. The padre over at George's unit, the 126th East Yorks, helps them out with weekly lessons too.'

'Does this look like English to you?' Porter was emphatic. 'Does it make any sense? It seems to be nonsense for a reason. It's code.'

It was true. The four acronyms or whatever they were certainly did not look like any English lesson.

ABBG TPOG PKIG UPOG

'Now the question is, how does one crack the code? Do you have any codebreakers here?' Porter asked Ruffington.

'The nearest one is in Delhi, several hundred miles away. I don't think they want us wasting time on the wires with this stuff. Er . . . you know, they may not take it too seriously, being children's writing and all that.'

'That's the problem with the whole set-up here!' Porter growled. 'Full of fucking amateurs who don't know how to go after the real thing.'

George was quiet and coldly angry, remembering the truckloads of soldiers who were leaving for the east daily. The war with Japan was still on, whether Ruffington or Porter realized it or not. He cleared his throat and made a move to leave. As he exited he saw Porter still waving the scrap of paper about and Ruffington looking expressionless.

'Between his poems and his children's codes, this idiot will be the ruin of the whole army here in Bajapur,' George thought as he cycled through the muggy heat back to his room. The only good thing was that, as part of his deputation to Ruffington's and Porter's madcap scheme, he was free of the drills and routines of regimental life. He lay on his hard bed in the room, the shades drawn against the glare, stripped down to his vest and pants. Lal Ram hovered around outside. The sounds began of the donkeys congregating outside the cantonment walls. The donkey fair would be held the next day and the animals and their owners were busy, judging by the clamour. There were also hoarse orders and crashing boots, noises that reminded George that somewhere there were still soldiers going through the tedious but necessary routines of military training. Against this familiar background of commands and shouts, George fell asleep.

He awoke drenched in sweat, tired despite the rest. Looking at the round face of his alarm clock on the small table next to his cot, he saw that it was already one o'clock. Too late for lunch, which would already have started. Not that he cared. The heat had put him off his appetite. Lal Ram brought him some tea and he considered his day's schedule. He was due to have tea with the Duncans that afternoon and later, he was to drive Anna over to the Bharadwajs' place to meet Deborah and Satinder Silonia. They had come to visit their friend, Pratap Kumar Bharadwaj, and were staying a few days in Bajapur. George smiled. He was looking forward to reconnecting with Deborah. This time he felt more in control of the situation, not so fearful, and not carrying the guilt of being a traitor to their friendship.

He knew why he felt so calm this time: he was in concord with and had the strong support of his Commanding Officer, Col. Holmes, and that steadied him against the malicious deviousness of the Porters and the Ruffingtons of the world. George decided to make his lunch off Marie biscuits and some tinned fruit. After he ate, he took out the big album of pictures from his trunk and gazed at the beautiful pages, appreciating the colours, the masterful strokes of the brush, the glowing images . . . At the centre of each page, there was Deborah's rounded Edwardian writing, specifying the amount of this and that, oil and flour, fish and vegetables, grains and salt. No wonder the officers of the 126th East Yorks were eating so well, he thought—these recipes, read out by him, translated by Lal Ram, rendered by Indumati, were absolutely first class. The woman on folio 23 smiled up at him from over her cooking pot, her sari drawn over her head, vivid red against black hair and brown skin, liquid eyes shimmering. So many hands had made this book, so many people whose only outlet to freedom had been their art. He sighed.

His light lunch ensured that by teatime, George was ravenous despite the heat. He dressed carefully in his regulation uniform, eschewing the more elaborate rituals of evening dress. It was still wartime after all, nobody could complain. He called for the tonga and in about ten minutes was deposited outside a small house. Like all cantonment bungalows, it stood at the centre of a moderate-sized lot, a rambling lawn to the front and the back. Capt. Duncan opened the door to him personally (none of the usual stuffiness with the servants) and his wife, Tess, came out to greet him. She was plump like her husband but had the hardness around the mouth that six years of war had etched on many faces. Her eyes were large and grey, and in happier, less troubled times, George could imagine her smiling and jolly. Now, though, the bitterness was palpable. The future was uncertain, especially the immediate future, and Tess Duncan had let her fears sublimate into anger, usually directed at other army wives. Tess's rage was her way of expressing her terrible disappointment that all that awaited the Duncans at the end of Empire was demobilization, some boring job and then a dull retirement in some damp little house in the Home Counties.

They sat and chatted about this and that, how terrible the heat was, how Tess had written to Capt. Andy Ross's wife to stay away a while longer so that she would escape the worst of the heat before she came out to India.

'Though I've heard that the rationing is something awful back home,' Tess Duncan sighed as she rang her little bell to usher in the bearer with the tea tray. Clearly, rationing was not a problem here in Bajapur. The tray groaned with cake, buttered bread, freshly baked biscuits, everything dripping with butter and cream.

'I had to be really firm with the dudhwalla, you know,' said Mrs Duncan as she poured the tea. 'He said that in the summer the cows don't give as much milk. Have you heard of anything so absurd? So I told him that I would not pay him for last month's supply if he did not give me at least another bowl of milk. He was ever so grumpy about it.'

Having spent a great deal of time listening to Anna criticizing the British methods of requisitioning during the war, George felt guilty as he ate the buttery biscuits and allowed Tess to lighten his tea with creamy milk. James Duncan, too, was an attentive host, taking care of George in a way that obscured temporarily the gaps in rank and in outlook. Duncan was clearly a career-army type. He would stay in the service till they booted him out and forced him to go home.

'I've heard that you are working with that American officer, Captain Porter,' said Tess, raising her large, grey eyes at him. 'How do you like that?' She was quite unsubtle in her quest for information.

'Well, Capt. Porter certainly works very hard,' George said carefully.

'Ah come now, Clark,' Duncan chuckled. 'We all know that he is a complete git! He was skulking around near your Company offices recently, did you know?'

'Yes, sir, I had heard. What did he want?'

'He was looking for your papers, my boy.'

'My papers!' George spluttered. 'But I don't have any *papers*! I never got to have an office with the Company!'

'Precisely, my dear chap. That's what we told him, but he insisted that you wanted your papers sent down to the new set-up in Rotherford Square. So, he sent a corporal to look inside the A Company offices.'

'Why did no one ever tell me?'

'Oh we did!' Duncan was indignant. 'I had one of the B Company corporals go over with a chitty. Several times. Didn't you get them?'

George remembered the bit of paper that Ruffington had quickly stuffed into the waste-paper basket. That arsehat! Then he sighed. He was beyond anger now. Remembering Anna, he stood up and made the usual polite noises and expressed thanks. He had to bathe and leave for the Bharadwajs' house soon.

At about seven o'clock, George bathed and wore the clean white shirt and trousers that Lal Ram had set out on the bed for him. He carefully put the little girls' scrap of paper into his pocket to return to its rightful owners. It occurred to him that he had no idea how to dress to go call on an Indian home. He had never been inside an Indian home, had only seen huts and houses from railway coaches as they swept by in a blur. Or else, he had encountered the little villages of eastern India, which emptied in a flash as soon as anybody in uniform appeared. It had been hard to persuade the villagers to return, so terrified had they been of sudden, unreasoned military rage descending on their heads for unknown transgressions. George felt a sense of anticipation as he finished dressing. He was lucky, he knew, that he was going with Anna who already knew the Chaturvedis and Bharadwajs very well and so there would be less awkwardness all around.

He picked up Anna at seven-thirty and they drove Col. Holmes's car—generously loaned, considering that George was a lowly subaltern—out through the cantonment gates and into the town. As always, Anna looked striking. She glowed in her pale-pink dress, knee length, her hair, unpermed and not bobbed in the usual fashion, tied back neatly with a ribbon. Small pearl drops gleamed in her ears. George kissed her enthusiastically. She made the hot June night bearable.

Outside the cantonment gates, there was a small road that led first past a bank of trees, followed by the cremation grounds. Then there were more trees, and at last the first of the civilian settlements began.

'Are you nervous?' Anna smiled at him, squeezing his thigh. He patted her hand and shook his head.

'I wouldn't say nervous, exactly. I'm looking forward to seeing Miss Sunderland, again, I mean Mrs Silonia, but I don't know what I expect for the rest of it.'

'They are all nice people, you'll see. There is no alcohol, though. They'll serve you a number of sherbets and some pretty heavy titbits to eat.'

The Bharadwaj house was in the middle of a lane full of old, porticoed houses off the main road. The neighbourhood could not have been more than two miles from the cantonment, George calculated, but it was a different world entirely. He eased up on the accelerator and carefully made his way down the little street. As he opened the car door, some dogs took up barking. A thin man in a lungi approached him, two scrawny dogs at his heels, both of whom snarled at George while keeping a safe distance.

'I am looking for Judge Bharadwaj's house,' George said in the best Hindustani he could muster.

The man nodded, he was the watchman for the street. George helped Anna out and the man nodded his recognition at her. They all walked to a gate, another gravelled drive. The man gestured to George to bring the car inside the compound.

'I'll meet you by the door,' Anna said and began walking up the drive. A tumult of children fell upon Anna, and swept up in the general melée, they all went inside. George recognized some of the children from the horse show. They recognized him too, and smiled at him.

'Hello, Uncle,' said Snehala, aka Choti, when they were all seated. 'You have come to see my nana, my grandfather, yes?'

Her brother Bittu, and Dr Matthew's son, Ram, hung back

more watchfully. The very zealous child Renuka stood at the top of the stairs inside the house; she, too, smiled at him. She clutched a large book in her arms.

'Yes, and also Mr and Mrs Silonia. I hear they are staying here?'

'Yes, they arrived today from Pithampur. It was very hot and the drive was very long, that was what Deborah nani said.'

George and Anna were seated on art deco style chairs in the large living room. There was a striking contrast between the outside and the inside. Outside, the fading evening was full of the sounds of barking dogs and perhaps of other animals. Inside, there was soft illumination. Electric lights glowed on the walls, painted a fresh, crisp cream. Above the doors and windows were framed photographs of family members, hung high. Lower on the walls, at about eye level, hung some paintings, canvases full of colour, simple brush strokes depicting women in saris, working, bending over children, reading from pages, dancing. That woman there in the blue sari might be Indumati with her two boys in tow, walking on the dusty road from the civilian quarters to the cantonment at the crack of dawn.

He had just taken all this in, when more of the family swept in. A woman in a printed cotton sari greeted him with a namaste.

'Welcome, welcome, Mr Clark,' she smiled. She appeared to be in her mid-thirties, with a calm face and large, brown eyes. She was very attractive, something about the smoothness of her skin and her high forehead with a red bindi. Her expression was fearless—she was clearly used to being in charge of situations, social or political.

'I'm Mira Chaturvedi,' she said 'My uncle is Judge Bharadwaj, if that makes the connection easier. This is my husband, Rajendra Chaturvedi.' She introduced her husband, who was balding early and wore black-rimmed spectacles. Rajendra shook George's hand and then settled down in a chair. He was clearly a man of few words.

'I told this uncle about our family already,' said her daughter Choti shyly, peeking out from behind Mira's sari.

'Oh?' Mira was surprised.

'Yes, at the horse show—remember when the military padre uncle took us to the other side to sit by the army people? You know, where the other uncle took away our game.' Choti frowned at the memory.

'I've brought it back to you.' George took out the crumpled paper and smoothed it out for the child. She was delighted. George looked at Mira's face for some sign of discomfort but she showed no sign of terrified recognition at the mysterious anagrams. She was either a very good actor or she knew nothing about these strange letters.

At this point, Deborah Silonia and her husband Satinder entered the room. In the ensuing exclamations of welcome and greeting, the paper and its code were forgotten, and soon everybody was chatting about this and that. Deborah asked George about his recent travels and expressed pleasure that the war in Europe was now over.

'I hope it ends soon in the East too and then you can go home. You must be longing to go home, aren't you?'

Well, was he? George couldn't be sure. He knew he was heartily sick of the war; he was tired of living and fighting in India; he was weary with the heat and the clammy sweat that drenched him as soon as he stepped out of his room. He wanted to go home and yet . . . he was not sure. Where was home? Just a few months ago, he had imagined going back to England and perhaps training to be a veterinarian and joining old Mr Farthers in his practice. But that life was gone forever, never to return again. That was what the war had wrought. Instead, he now thought of a new life with a tall, American girl. He knew that he wanted this life to go forward with Anna now, but where that life together was to unfold, he did not know.

He responded to Deborah in a noncommittal fashion.

'How are things in Pithampur?'

'They are terrible, Mr Clark,' she sighed. 'If you had any idea, oh dear, just how bad things are there.'

'Is it the politics again?'

'Oh, yes, but there is now a virulent enmity between the Sikhs and the Muslims in Pithampur which has us all in despair,' Satinder joined the conversation. 'There is great violence brewing, I am afraid.'

Confirming the reports that George had read in his Intelligence files, Satinder and Silonia described the raised political temperature in the princely state across the border from Bajapur. The Pithampur College Students' Association had been engaged in a programme of systematic harassment of the local Muslims. There was also sheer banditry going on in the name of settling religious scores. For example, only the previous week, there had been a sensational kidnapping of a rich Muslim merchant and his entire family who had been on their way to a wedding in Patiala. The family had only been set free after an enormous ransom had been paid. After this incident, the local PCSA leader, Mohinder Singh Lalpuria, had been seen to have become very prosperous, overnight so to speak. There were also rumours that the merchant's kidnapped daughter was now housed in Lalpuria's residence in the bazaar area.

'I am an active member of the Pithampur People's Movement, Mr Clark,' said Satinder Silonia, stroking his beard sorrowfully, 'and I also attend the meetings of the Punjab Riyasti Praja Mandal—the Punjab States Peoples' Conference, is what you would call it, I suppose. These days we notice that the Pithampur College Students' Association is working very closely with the Raja Sahib of Pithampur and his courtiers. The future does not look good if these are the kind of people leading the state. It's just shameful.' Satinder Silonia shook his head sorrowfully.

George nodded, but it was all too complicated for him. There were too many organizations, all fighting with each other and grappling for power. It was all about power, finally, all the scheming, the agitating, the kidnapping, the killing.

'And how about the communists?' he probed. 'Are they also involved in all of this?'

'Ah, the communists,' Satinder smiled. 'It would be better to ask him. He knows all about it.' He indicated a tall man who had entered the room. In his late forties, he had the Bharadwaj nose, hair slicked back with a lot of pomade, and was dressed in handspun cotton shirt and rather well-tailored pants.

'How do you do?' he greeted George in a clipped, well-bred tone. 'I'm Shyam Bharadwaj, younger brother of Judge Bharadwaj and Mira's other uncle. And,' he continued smoothly, 'as I am the only legal political activist here, I can proudly declare that I am a member of the Communist Party of India.' He offered George an expensive-looking imported cigarette.

'Those don't look Soviet to me,' George took one, twinkling.

'Of course not, Mr Clark!' Shyam Bharadwaj smiled back. 'Have you ever tried a Russian cigarette? Execrable!'

Despite himself, George took a liking to Shyam. Here was Porter's enemy—clearly educated at great expense in both India and England, and very much a gentleman of taste and cultivation. As Shyam bent forward with the light, George noticed with a shock that the fingers of his left hand were bent and twisted into—no, the fingers were not bent and twisted, rather the tips of his fingers were bent and twisted flesh. The man had no fingernails on his left hand.

Shyam noticed his look and smiled again.

'It's the hospitality I endured in his master's guesthouse,' he indicated Satinder Silonia who nodded grimly.

'That's where we met Shyam,' Satinder said. 'We were both in the Pithampur Jail. Shyam fell very ill with pneumonia and we persuaded the warden to release him into Deborah's care. Then after he recovered, he went right back to organizing the peasants of Pithampur and was expelled from the territory. Thanks to his brother, the Judge Sahib, he has been able to wriggle out of other sticky situations, especially here in Bajapur.'

George noticed that Judge Bharadwaj was not present in the room. Mira saw his expression and smiled.

'He will be here soon. He allows us to finish all our political talk before we all gather for a perfectly pleasant evening.' She and Anna giggled like schoolgirls.

'Those are beautiful paintings, Mrs Chaturvedi,' George pointed to the canvases on the walls.

'Please call me Mira. Thank you. Those are from the two years that I spent in Santiniketan—Rabindranath Tagore's university in Bengal.' She sighed. 'Siloniaji and I often get together and talk about how much we miss the place.' Mira was wistful.

'They were really the best years of my life in many ways.' Satinder Silonia reflected. 'I was there for a few years in my late thirties. It was magical.'

'It was so peaceful there,' Mira reminisced. 'The trees, the flowers.'

'And the silence that Gurudeb insisted we start our mornings with. Do you remember that?'

'And our training under Roymoshai and Baijmoshai.' Mira added. 'Oh, it was divine!'

Deborah explained to George that Jamini Roy and Ramkinkar Baij were among the foremost artists of the Bengal school who drew heavily upon traditional motifs in their work. They were also teachers at Santiniketan.

'Satinder was also heavily influenced by their approach. He tries to apply it to the Punjabi setting.' She smiled at her husband.

'Yes, the mustard fields, the women churning butter in their pots. Truly, they were masters—Jaminibabu and Baijbabu, for they drew upon those familiar daily rituals without making kitsch. I try to keep that approach in my work too. But it is a harder struggle in Pithampur, I must admit. In Gurudeb's Santiniketan, one never felt alone or marginal for art, music and dance were celebrated as grand achievements and accomplishments to be applauded, not derided.' Satinder frowned.

'That is why I visit Siloniaji so often in Pithampur,' Mira Chaturvedi sighed. 'At least, there is one person here who knows how glorious things can be and also understands how truly alone we artists are here in Bajapur and in Pithampur. He at least understands and supports me in my efforts.'

'Yes, dear,' Deborah acknowledged Mira's anguish. 'Come, Anna, let us go and see some of Mira's new work,' she said. The three women disappeared, the children trailing behind them. George was left with the men.

'But do tell us a little about your life, Mr Clark.' They listened interestedly about life in the cantonment. He carefully mentioned his work with Ruffington and Porter, without giving away the gist of his mission there. They were most interested in the daily life of the military, the drills, the regimented routine, the lunches and the dinners served punctually at one o'clock and eight thirty.

'Your life is so far removed from our own, you understand,' Satinder said. 'In my youth, I did the things you mention—ride horses, drink fine wines, eat with knives and forks. It all seems so far away now, like a distant mirage.'

'Well, it isn't always glamorous,' George replied. He recounted his days in the battlefields of Burma, the endless waiting, the dogged jungle warfare, waiting for the enemy to show his head, the sudden furious bursts of gunfire, and the blood and the piteous state of the wounded.

'Those days, all I ever wanted was a dry pair of boots, a tin of bully beef and a dry patch of ground to sleep on. That would have been heaven to me. But I only ever managed to get one of them at a time.'

And that was how a rapport was struck, over the telling and retelling of wartime stories. The Indian National Army fighters were mentioned and all stuck to their own points of view: George that he would happily punch one in the face if he ever came across him; Satinder that all members of the Indian National Army were patriots; and Shyam Bharadwaj that as a card-carrying anti-fascist communist, he would let them be but would keep a strict watch on them. And yet, there was no discomfort in the room, no shuffling of feet, or shifting in chairs, as the three men expressed their respective strongly held views. George remarked on this ease of political discussion, when a servant broke the intensity of the conversation by entering the room with a tray piled high with eats and drinks. He was followed by Judge Bharadwaj, the patriarch of the family, wearing his usual noncommittal expression and a well-stitched shirt with oxford collars.

'Oh, Mr Clark, in another household, you would have been shown the door,' said Satinder Silonia, rising to his feet to greet Judge Bharadwaj. 'But here, regard this gathering—it represents four different political opinions present in this country—the businessman, Rajendra Chaturvedi, the communist, Shyam Bharadwaj, the upholder of British order, Judge Sahib, and the Congressman, myself. We discuss, we dissect, we attack. But at the end of the day, we all sit down to dinner together.'

'As long as it's a vegetarian dinner,' smiled the usually dour Judge Bharadwaj. George took a glass of a violently red drink from the tray offered. It was ghastly sweet to the taste and he put it down hastily after one swallow. As they began to eat the samosas, the kachoris and the chaat, the as-yet-silent Rajendra Chaturvedi, Mira's husband, said to George.

'And don't forget my uncle, Shri Amar Mani Chaturvedi. Through him we are also connected to the Hindu politics of Bajapur. We are only missing the Bajapur Tanzeem here. But that can't be helped.'

The children entered noisily again and were seated at a small table in the corner. They all gaped at George unblinkingly between bites and swallows.

'The children find you fascinating,' said Shyam. 'This is the first time that they have had a British officer in our house.'

'Not the first, Shyam Chacha,' Rajendra Chaturvedi corrected his wife's uncle. 'Don't forget that the padre sahib visits the Matthews at least once a week and we had a visit from that American officer only a few days ago. Remember, he came with the padreji when Mira and I were here.'

Porter again! What was the man up to?

'What drew Capt. Porter here?' George tried to sound casual.

'Oh, he was trying to set up something with the padre and our neighbour, Dr Matthew, who works at the local hospital. They were trying, I think, to set up a local Christian medical charity with the help of Miss Williams who teaches at the mission school.'

'Yes, he wanted to know if we could refer some domestic help to the new charity.' Judge Bharadwaj looked sceptical but not entirely dismissive.

'You don't think that it will work?'

'Oh, I daresay a clinic of the kind he is proposing might work, Mr Clark. But, hospitals and schools, I believe, are too important to be left to the whims of private charity. They need to be supported by the government in order to have a beneficial impact on society. Otherwise, charities come, charities go.'

There was a knock on the door and a couple was shown in by a servant. 'This is our neighbour, Dr Thomas Matthew and his wife, Vani.' Judge Bharadwaj did the introductions. The Matthews were a pleasant and lively couple. Their children, Renuka and Ram, ran to them for hugs and beamed. They were clearly proud of their parents.

'Ah, another military visitor,' said Dr Matthew. 'I have had so many this week. The padre sahib is always visiting us and recently Capt. Porter has also taken to dropping in every few days.'

'I hope that makes you feel very protected,' George joked, not feeling half as jolly as he hoped he looked.

'Oh, Mr Clark, I don't know if we are protected. You do know, don't you, how the communal temperature is rising constantly in Bajapur and across the state border in Pithampur?' Dr Matthew was suddenly serious. 'It is very distressing for me, as a doctor, to treat the kind of horrific injuries I see every day. But let us not speak of all that now, in front of the children.'

'This uncle was there at the horse show that padre uncle took us to see,' Renuka said to her mother.

'And the other uncle took away our game,' said Snehala calmly, no longer hurt.

'Can you believe Ram and Bittu and Totu have not discovered what the answer is, yet?' Renuka burst into giggles.

'Where are your other friends . . . er . . . the ones with the very long names?' asked George.

'Oh you mean Munni, Chinu and Totu?' asked Snehala. 'They are away in Mithapur, visiting their parents in jail. They will be back in a few days.'

Deborah, Mira and Anna came back into the drawing room. Anna had a big camera with her.

'I keep it here with Mira and Rajendrabhaisahib,' she smiled. 'That makes it easier to take photographs. I don't have to lug the darned thing all the way from the cantonment.'

As the others chitchatted, she moved around the room, taking photos, adjusting a lamp, lighting a paraffin lamp for more illumination. Her movements were quick and professional, the clicking and snapping, biting reminders of urgency on a fluid evening. With a shock George realized that the social gathering taking place around him was in fact a political meeting. All of a sudden, although he was aware that Porter and Ruffington were fools, his sense of alertness heightened. Would someone now let slip something about the code that Porter was so obsessed with?

'Do you find yourself a little bit out of place, Mr Clark?' Deborah Silonia stationed herself next to George. 'I don't blame you. Sometimes I too feel like an outsider, although I have spent so many years in India.'

'Are you going to go home when the war ends, Miss Sunderl . . . ma'am?' For some reason, it was still hellishly awkward for George to call her Mrs Silonia.

'Home?' She looked puzzled, then laughed. 'Oh, you mean England. No, Mr Clark. Home for me is right here, with Satinder, unless the Raja of Pithampur drives us away.'

'Don't you feel afraid, though? It seems as though a collective madness is taking hold of this country.'

'Yes, but there is madness everywhere in the world. Every day we receive news on the wireless of the many death camps in Poland and Eastern Europe that have been uncovered. We all have to live with the mad frenzy of our age and I have chosen to live through the nightmare here in Pithampur.'

George's attention was taken up by Mira Chaturvedi who pressed some food and drink on him.

'Do eat something, Mr Clark, otherwise what will people think—that we didn't take care of our chhotejijaji?' She smiled mischievously. George accepted another glass of the red, sweet drink and took a very tiny sip.

'What did she call me—chho—?'

'Chhotejijaji—younger brother-in-law—she's just teasing you,' Deborah said.

George's eyes softened as they alighted on Anna, still clicking away. Her delicate, pink dress was getting slightly smudged as she kneeled on the floor to get some shots.

'You do look very happy. And Anna is outstanding,' Deborah told him. 'It is so rare that I get to meet somebody with whom I can be in sympathy. Most of the English visitors to Pithampur are just taken up with the Raja Sahib and his wretched palace and all his hunting expeditions and parties. Really shallow and quite impossible, the whole lot of them.' They both gazed at Anna, her richly coloured hair glinting in the dim glow of the electric bulbs overhead, her dress a softly gleaming splash against the mahogany of the furniture and the dark stone floor.

'I look at your recipes every day, ma'am. The portfolio is stunning—the colours on the pages are fantastic! Wish I could draw like that but I was never any good at painting.' George explained to Deborah how he ordered from the pages every day and how Indumati and Lal Ram had come into his life.

'She is an exceptional cook, Indumati. She does great justice to your recipes.'

'I would love to meet her one day,' said Deborah. 'I can give her some more recipes. Why don't you give her Judge Sahib's address and have her come over here? Satinder and I visit often.'

George promised to send her over sometime.

'Now, Mr Clark, my children tell me that they had a wonderful time at your army function.' Dr Matthew entered the conversation. 'Renuka loved the horses and the showjumping.'

'Yes, it was a bit of all right, the horseshow.' George took another sip of his very sweet drink and then put it down on the table. Both Deborah and Dr Matthew roared with laughter when they saw him do so.

'You do not like the Rooh Afza? Is that so? Don't worry, it is nothing to be ashamed of. I cannot abide it myself.' Dr Matthew turned to Judge Bharadwaj. 'Judge Sahib, another casualty of your foul drink here. Won't you order him a nimbupani instead? He is far too polite to criticize your hospitality with any negative remarks.'

'I know the perfect remedy for that wretched drink,' said Shyam Bharadwaj, taking the glass and winking at George. 'It involves lemon juice and some other—er, secret ingredient.'

When he returned, the drink looked just as foul as ever. But when George took a sip, he found that the sweetness had been diluted with lemon juice and the whole concoction spiked with a liberal splash of gin. He smiled and raised his glass to Shyam.

'Cheers!' Shyam nodded, winked again, and moved on to another little group around his niece, Mira Chaturvedi. Anna was listening intently while Mira spoke passionately about something. Vani Matthew nodded from time to time.

'They are discussing women's rights issues,' Deborah said. 'I should go and put in my opinion. After all, once British rule ceases to operate, the new laws are going to affect me as well.'

'Do you think that British rule is going to end, Miss Sun . . . ma'am.'

'Oh, for heaven's sake, Mr Clark, call me Deborah. Everyone calls me either Deborah, or Deborah didi or Deborah nani or Deborah-something or the other. And I shall call you George.' The brusque no-nonsense Englishwoman in her rose to the surface.

And that was how Miss Sunderland became Deborah to George Clark.

The talk in Mira Chaturvedi's little group was about the steady stream of Muslim refugees streaming into Bajapur from neighbouring Pithampur. The plight of the womenfolk in the refugee population was particularly dire as Pithampur's Muslim women were in general urban dwellers, used to seclusion, unlike their farming Muslim sisters in Bajapur who went about unveiled and worked alongside their menfolk in the fields.

'We have to protect them as far as possible,' Mira insisted, in disagreement with her communist uncle, Shyam. 'And gradually educate them in taking on more responsibility for themselves and their children. We cannot, Shyamchacha, just throw them into the fields and tell them to take care of themselves. They simply do not know how to do it.'

'These women from the petty bourgeoisie!' snorted Shyam. 'They should be forced to discard their false, class-imposed sense of modesty and get down to some productive work like their proletarian sisters. Do you see the honest peasant women shrinking from hard toil in the fields?'

'Typical communist,' sighed Deborah Silonia. 'Won't put in a hard day's labour himself, in either farm or factory. But, has all the Theories of Labour at his fingertips.' George was mildly amused, unable to conjure up a vision of the rather elegant Shyam Bharadwaj with his refined clothes and his expensive cigarettes getting his hands soiled with engine grease or farm tools.

'Well, perhaps I will have Shabnamapa go and speak with these women. Where are they housed, these wives of tailors and carpenters?' Shyam Bharadwaj waved his hand exasperatedly.

The Muslim families fleeing the persecution of Pithampur were mostly established along the western edge of Bajapur. Many had set up shacks on the summer-parched fields just outside the town. Most of the settlements housed women and children, and they were terrified of the very real physical danger posed by wild animals and, even worse, predatory human beings. Peasants were quite ruthless plunderers when the opportunity arose. One family had already lost its mother to a kidnapping, suspected to be engineered by a powerful landlord of a nearby village who had claimed her for his own household. Her helpless children were being cared for by the others in the encampment but the situation was too precarious to endure much longer. Vani Matthew suggested that some families be shifted further east across the Yamuna River to Saharanpur or sent even further eastward to Rampur—the Muslim-majority Nawabate of Rampur—where the refugees might feel more secure among their co-religionists.

'No, no Vanididi, that would not be good,' said Rajendra

Chaturvedi, Mira's laconic husband, who had also joined the discussion.

'Why not, Rajendraji?' asked Vani. 'It would help them feel more secure, wouldn't it?'

'No, the best thing is to keep them here and to make sure that they feel safe amongst *us*, Hindus and Sikhs.' Rajendra was quite emphatic. 'They must feel protected *here*, not in resentful Muslim enclaves. That means that all of us—including myself—have a lot of work to do. I am willing to employ some of them in my business. They can help in the factory or can do some housekeeping work at the company guesthouse in Kamalpur. It is a peaceful little place on the Yamuna, and they will be safe from the marauders that harass them here.'

'Send them all to Ambala on the other side of Pithampur!' thundered Shyam Bharadwaj. 'There are lots of heavy industry there and they will be gainfully employed as wage-earning proletarians. My friends in Ambala will make sure that they are properly politicized.' His ideological announcement put an end to the practical solution being offered by his niece's husband.

'Shyamchacha!' Mira burst out in exasperation. 'Do you not understand? These are *very* sheltered Muslim women here. They have never held even a shovel in their hands and for them to enter a factory to work amongst strange men would be to die a thousand deaths! On top of that, they are severely traumatized. They are not in a state to think about such drastic politicization as you have planned for them. Even in our family, chacha, your mother was always secluded. Can you imagine dadi, my dadi, ever going to work in a factory? It's only in our generation that women go out without their faces covered. And you do remember, don't you, how much you and Baba had to fight to let Ma attend political meetings and to let me continue my studies in Santiniketan? Everybody was trying to get me married off from the day I turned fifteen!' Mira's eyes blazed at the memory.

As if on cue, a tall, thin man entered the room. He was Pratap Kumar Bharadwaj, Mira's father, the old doctor turned Congress activist. The children who had left the room after eating their food now entered in a rush of shouts and screams of laughter to greet Dr Bharadwaj, clearly much beloved by his grandchildren and the neighbours' children. He produced toffees and boiled sweets from his pockets for all of them which caused more joyous uproar. Anna moved between the two groups silently adjusting her camera and the lights, clicking every now and then, shaking her head sometimes. She was utterly concentrated on her work, to the point that when George went up to her, she was startled.

'I'm so sorry, you must think I am cruel to abandon you here amongst them all.' She began to put away her equipment. George protested, saying that he had had a very good evening, catching up with Deborah Silonia and with all her news from Pithampur. Anna looked relieved.

'Do bring Mr Clark over here, Anna.' Mira beckoned to her. 'Mr Clark, I am so sorry that you have had to bear the brunt of our social and political preoccupations today. You see, we cannot help it. The situation is so grim these days that even a pleasant social evening invariably turns into a Congress session.'

'Please call me George.' George smiled.

'Not just the Congress, Mira beti,' Shyam called out from the other end of the room. 'You're forgetting the hammer and the sickle here.'

'But most of us here are Congress people, chacha,' replied the feisty Mira. 'And until my husband's Amar chacha joins us and until Mir Ali Sharif mian is here, we cannot be overruled.'

'Well, but we can at least have the Christian voice here,' Shyam indicated Dr Thomas Matthew who was engaged in a deep conversation with Satinder Silonia.

'Oh no, no, Shyambabu. I am a Christian all right but for the point of view of Christendom, you will have to get Miss Williams from the mission school.'

'You know she has taken to visiting us several times a week,' announced his wife, Vani. 'She thinks that we are dreadfully lax in our religious education.'

'That is because I keep and read the Ramayana in my house,' Dr Matthews replied. His look became dreamy. 'For me, it is the culture of my ancestors. As long as I live, it will always be part of my heritage.'

'Coming to my house and trying to teach me about Christianity,' harrumphed Vani Matthew.

'You and Appa are very bad Christians,' shouted their daughter Renuka suddenly. To her anger, everyone burst into laughter.

'Miss Williams says if you don't stop reading the Ramayana, you will go to hell!' she yelled again, enraged.

'You tell your Miss Williams that your ancestors were converted by St Thomas the Apostle himself,' said Vani dismissively. 'When her ancestors were hanging from the trees like monkeys, we already had the Bible and knew about Jesus. So we don't need her lessons about religion.'

'Hai,' interjected Ram, Renuka's brother, mischievously, sending his sister into further paroxysms of rage.

'Do you not feel worried for the child, Dr Matthew?' Deborah asked gently. 'She seems quite influenced by Miss Williams. I have met the lady and she is rather—er . . . fanatical.'

'Oh no, Deborah didi. You see, Renuka will come across many people with warped religious views in the future. This country is headed in that direction, unfortunately. But it is better that we, her parents, are there to balance out the ugliness and to show her that one can be a good Christian without being a fanatic. Renuka will grow out of her childish opinions, she has to, she sees around her every day the incredible diversity of this country, in all its beauty and in all its ugliness.'

'Just as I too never keep my children from my Amar chacha's loud lessons on Hinduism,' said Rajendra Chaturvedi suddenly. 'I think that by our example, my wife and I can balance out the ugliness as Dr Matthew has put it so well.'

Suddenly, George was tired. His mind was full of the conflicting opinions that had been presented this evening and he needed to get away and make sense of them. He stood up, catching Anna's eye, and they made moves to leave. In the confusion of goodbyes, Snehala, Mira's daughter came up to him. She was waving a piece of paper.

'There are four more riddles now, Uncle.' She showed him a piece of paper with the same maddening little groups of letters.

ABBG

TPOG

PKIG

UPOG

TPAG?

QPAG?

QKAG

GGPG

'I made up the last four just now,' Renuka said smugly. 'And the boys still can't guess them.'

'What are these?' asked George, looking at Mira Chaturvedi. If these were indeed codes between the Congress and the Communists, then everyone was looking very relaxed about the whole thing. There was no look of alarm on everyone's face, no exchange of worried looks. The grown-ups all laughed at the girls' paper.

'Oh, you have to be fluent in Hindi as well as in English, Mr Clark, to understand the humour behind this,' said Pratap

Bharadwaj, Snehala's grandfather. 'You see, it's a children's joke. What it means in English-Hindi or Hindi-English is this:

ABBG: Hey, ma'am
TPOG: Drink some tea
PKIG: I had some already
UPOG: You drink it
'The others are new but they are also quite clever:
TPAG?: You drank tea?
QPAG?: Why did you drink it?
QKAG: Because, sir (or madam)
GGPG: Elder sister drank some'

'I knew that, I knew that!' shouted Ram Matthew, who clearly had not known it at all. Snehala's brother Bittu also joined in the noisy excitement of the cracking of the puzzle.

Everybody laughed at the bilingual joke. George flushed, thinking of Porter and how completely foolish his whole scheme would look now. The ass, the benighted ass, trust the blithering fool to pick a children's joke as some sort of dark, communist conspiracy. Still, he tested the theory one more time.

'Very funny. But honestly, if you hadn't told me what it was, I would think it was some horrible spy code.' He looked carefully for reactions. But everyone just laughed.

'Yes, yes, Mr Clark was fighting a war in Burma recently. Of course, everything looks like Morse code to him.' Pratap Bharadwaj was amused. 'Now run along, girls. Go and make up another puzzle with which to torment your brothers.' Everyone saw George and Anna off to the door. George promised to return and see the Silonias before they returned to Pithampur. They drove off in the gathering darkness to the club where they could have some dinner.

ELEVEN

'Wasn't that kids' game just so clever?' Anna was effusive in her enthusiasm. 'They are so smart and clever, these children, the way they can slip from English into Hindi and back again. I can barely speak any kind of language at all these days, it's so hot.' She sighed and fanned herself with a hand fan that lay on the front seat. She leaned over and fanned George a little. 'I feel like my brain is frying slowly.'

George nodded. He was miserable too, his clean white shirt already a sweaty mass on his back where it touched the seat. He shifted into third gear as they coasted the clear stretch of road back to the gates of the cantonment.

'Why don't the rains come?' Anna complained, fanning herself fast in a futile effort to get the torpid air moving.

'They say any day now.' He smiled at her, her company lifting his spirits in spite of the dull and heavy air. 'Let's go have a quick drink at the club and then we can go eat dinner. Feel like Chinese tonight?'

Anna shook her head, her hair sticking to her forehead in damp curls, her face glistening with moisture.

'It's way too hot for those damn fried noodles, my love. Why don't we have a drink in the lounge and then we can order dinner at the club itself. That way, we'll have fewer places to drive to.'

George agreed, relieved. He did not want to be running

242

around Bajapur in the sweltering weather either. The petrol fumes from the car were making him feel slightly sick. They drew up to the painted white gates of the club, presented their credentials to be checked by the sentry and then were waved through to the back where other cars were parked. Behind the row of assorted army vehicles and private cars were a bunch of tongas, with some ponies tossing their heads while others were greedily nuzzling inside their nosebags. The drivers sat around gossiping and smoking bidis, the strong smell of unfiltered tobacco drifting over to George and Anna as they went around to the main front door.

As usual, the hall smelt of old polish and old leather. There were some hats on the wooden tree by the door, but clearly not many had bothered with headgear in the humidity. The receptionist checked in their names, glancing at Anna and then at George, his face inscrutable. George took Anna's hand and guided her into the dimly lit interior where old portraits of past Bajapur administrators shared space on the yellowing walls with monocled generals frozen in sepia, the mandatory dead tiger at their feet, and Indian attendants gathered around like so many turbaned angels in spotless white robes.

'Sharp place, this, isn't it?' Anna joked as they made their way to the lounge. She was always less than impressed with the carefully cultivated shabbiness of British India, trying to evoke centuries of grandeur with scruffy rugs and scratched, faded cushions. While George often felt irritated by Anna's scorn, tonight he reflected that he shared her feelings. Enough with the contrived old and shabby, he thought. Let's wash this whole grimy place down with some soap and water. And let's have some nice, light furniture please. The kind one found in new, modern hotels.

'When this war is done,' George leaned over and whispered to Anna as their drinks arrived. 'I want to take you to . . . to London. We could stay in some really new, posh hotel with new furniture. With fancy soap and hot water and no bloody blackouts all the time.'

'Now, did you really think I was that type of a girl, mister?' Anna smiled coquettishly, her lips so pink and moist against her white teeth that he felt desire stir. At this point the assistant to the club secretary, a dusty looking man in his forties, came over with a message.

'Er . . . Col. Holmes called, Miss Benson. He wanted to know if you were here. There's been some trouble in the town.'

'Oh, whereabouts?'

'Oh, in the old bazaar. The usual. Apparently, some Pithampur refugees are crowding the tenements of the workers near the temple. And, well, you know . . .' His voice trailed off. 'Oh well, I will tell Col. Holmes that you are here. He will be so relieved.' He went off.

Damned Bajapur! Always intruding into everything. Just like the bloody war. George scowled.

'Not London.' Anna smiled, inviting him back to the future with an emphatic gesture of her hand that dismissed the shabby present. 'New York! Oh, yes, we will go and stay in some nice, new hotel in New York. With a view of Central Park! What do you say, George?' For the second time, a woman was making him an offer to change the course of his life, to take a chance with her, to travel as a pair. This time, George was ready.

'You bet!' he said, mimicking her American way of speaking. 'To New York—here we come.' Then he sealed his toast with a kiss. He had hardly embraced Anna, it seemed, when a creaking old waiter appeared at their side, telling them that a table was ready, and giving them disapproving looks all the way into the dining room. He placed himself conspicuously in their sight, so that the club's upright setting was not sullied further by the animal impulses of the members the institute was unfortunately obliged to enrol and entertain.

'Now wasn't it wonderful,' asked Anna, 'that you were able to visit with Deborah and Satinder right here in Bajapur?'

'Yes, Deborah was really very kind to me when I was posted in Pithampur last year. I used to go over to her house every week and she fed us and fed us till we thought we were going to burst our buttons.' George could almost taste her wonderful teatime snacks as he spoke. 'And she gave me this wonderful portfolio of recipes with paintings on them, done by Satinder and his artist friends. You should see this collection. It's quite amazing and wonderful. I use those recipes a lot these days, given that I'm the bloody Mess Secretary and all. And what an amazing job Indumati does with them.'

'Yes, I have heard from several people about the great food in the mess these days. Those recipes sound wonderful,' said Anna, forking another mouthful of pulao. 'Maybe, Richard can have Indumati over at the house to cook for an official dinner or something, for it doesn't look like they are going to start up with the Ladies' Nights at the mess anytime soon, or at least Ellen hasn't said anything yet, so I won't be going in there. Not that I want to sit and eat with a bunch of stuffed shirts anyway. By the way, what's Indumati going to do when the unit leaves for Europe or wherever?'

George had not thought of this.

'I suppose anyone will be happy to have her as a cook, she is so good at her job.' He tried not to think about Indumati, hunting for work, trying to feed her children. Everyone's position was so insecure, he thought—the British in India, the unit in Bajapur, Indumati's job with the mess, his future with Anna . . . he looked at her and smiled. Well, that might be the only thing that might last a little longer than a few months.

They ate their lamb chops and pulao with almonds and saffron, an interesting combination. Both George and Anna had declined the shrimp salad ('In this weather, who knows how sick that would make us,' Anna shuddered) and the rather tepid consommé.

'Deborah and Satinder are . . . different, that's why we get along so well,' Anna reflected on the evening, adding bitterly. 'I feel different too but it doesn't pay to be different in India, does it? You just have to blend in, or otherwise . . .'

'Please, Anna, no politics right now. It—it makes my head ache. As it is, I get enough of that in the office.'

'Really?' Now he'd let the cat out of the bag. George kicked himself mentally. You idiot, what did you do that for?

'Well, you know, Ruffington and Porter have quite strong political views about—India and stuff.'

'I see.' Anna's expression, to his relief, was one of amusement. 'So, while there is a war still going on in the East, Capt. Ruffington and Capt. Porter sit around letting off a whole lot of hot air about 'politics'.' Her sarcasm was both gently worded and biting.

'I guess that explains why Dennis is so fascinated with what the servants and other civilians do here in Bajapur cantonment. I did think he was taking his Intelligence work a bit too far. Porter's definitely got a bee in his bonnet about your man, Lal Ram. And you—but I told you that.'

'You did mention that . . . the other evening, in case you don't remember,' George pulled her leg gently. 'Funnily though, Porter never lets on that he has me under surveillance.' George tried to keep his tone casual, neutral even.

'Well, since I know that you aren't some sort of violent murderous gangster, darling, why don't we just have some fun with him?'

'Well, I do happen to work for the man, great big ass though he is,' George pointed out.

'Things aren't good in the town, are they?' Anna said. Whether they liked it or not, politics had infiltrated their conversation again.

'No, I think everyone is very worried about how things will shape up when we leave,' George replied carefully.

'I think,' Anna said, choosing her words carefully. 'Things will be fine as long as the innocent are protected and the process of self-government is allowed to run its course. The problem, as I see it, is that the government in Delhi is very angry with the Congress and will do anything to sabotage any transfer of power to Nehru and the others without some sort of petty revenge. But given what utter, utter slimeballs most of the government here is,' her anger was rising with every phrase, she was clearly remembering her experience in Jamshedpur, 'it's not going to be *petty* revenge, it's going to be *massive* revenge.'

'You mean, the government is going to set the Hindus and the Muslims against each other? But, darling, they don't need our help to start hating each other. They are already at each other's throats.' George couldn't hide his cynicism. The politics of religion in India seemed vicious to him.

'Well, the problem is,' Anna started carefully again, 'the administration mollycoddles the fanatics of all colours—the Muslims, the Hindus, the Sikhs—because they think that they can weaken the Congress in that way. And they think that that way, they can also get the communists. Although the commies are such a pitiful force here that they really don't count. But all of this does hurt the Congress.'

'Why would we want to weaken the Congress?'

'Oh, I don't know,' Anna sighed, waving away the tray of desserts that the waiter brought over. She waited while George chose a vanilla ice, then spoke again. 'I think it's a case of being a bad loser. Freedom is coming to India, the British and the French are finished, their empires are finished, only the Soviets and America count for anything these days. I mean, let's face it, it wasn't British soldiers who took Berlin last month, was it? What would you do if you thought that everything that was dear to you, that gave you status and prestige, was disappearing faster than a snowflake in Bajapur right now?' George was silent, so Anna continued.

'It would make perfect sense, wouldn't it, to encourage the splintering of this land into a million pieces if the only other choice was to leave? Leave the place so weak and bloody that they would cry to have me back in charge. Set it up so that I might actually return one day when I had recovered my strength.'

George finished his pudding and then signed the chit brought over by the old waiter, who glared at both of them till they disappeared from the dining room. In the dimly lit hallway, the club secretary's assistant showed them out politely, then went back to looking at the register behind the desk.

The braying of donkeys and the bleating of goats greeted them like a fanfare as they walked towards the car. The animals were being led to the fairground in the dark, in preparation for the next day's fair. Anna and George both burst out laughing. Despite everything, the spirit of Bajapur always prevailed, sneaking past officially sponsored horse shows and polo games, garden parties and tea dances.

'Very apt, don't you think?' said Anna as George opened the

door for her. 'The donkey—as a symbol of Bajapur. A very highly intelligent animal who deceives others by acting stupid. Also, a very stubborn animal. Hmmm . . . maybe we should tie Porter and Ruffington to one.'

Driving back in the dark, their desire hung almost like a visible cloud over them . . . desire destined to be frustrated in the short term at least. There was no way that the CO's sister-in-law could be smuggled into the bachelors' living quarters. Nor George accommodated at Col Holmes's house. When he kissed her goodnight, Anna clung to George, her breath warm, her eagerness palpable. He left her clinging body reluctantly, forcing himself away, forcing himself to think of other things—like how to break the news to Porter in the morning that his precious communist code was nothing more than a children's game.

A distant rumble of thunder greeted him when he awoke very early in the morning. His sheets were drenched in sweat, despite the fan whirring noisily overhead. His first thought was of Anna: she, too, must be awake in this heat; its surly heaviness must surely have awakened her. Lal Ram was already sitting outside his door, waiting for his orders for the day. George sent him for tea from the mess which soon arrived on a tray along with some tea biscuits and two slices of thick bread, buttered. He reflected on the previous night's events, the children, Anna, the Silonias, the Bharadwajs, Mira Chaturvedi. How was he going to tell Porter the truth about his stupid suspicions? Well, how did one tell an arsewipe that he was, well, an arsewipe?

Indumati was at her usual place in the veranda when he went out, Lal Ram bringing up the rear with the portfolio. Three heads again bent over the pictures and the recipes. Today, lunch was to consist of the depictions of folio 44—a pot-roast of partridge (the Mess Corporal was a good hunter, having been a poacher in civilian life), marinated in lime juice, cayenne pepper, cumin, coriander and cinnamon—and of folio 31—a pulao of summer vegetables. Paisleys decorated the borders and cunning parrots peeked out suddenly, eyeing the soft squashes and gourds. Indumati recommended a cucumber salad on the side. Lal Ram translated the meaning of 'braise' for her. Indumati smiled and nodded, her tiny frame wrapped in a printed cotton sari, her feet in cheap slippers, the toes and the heels cracked by lack of care. George noticed that she no longer wore her garment in the style that she used to earlier, where her sari had been pulled between her legs like a pair of loose pantaloons. Now she wore it in the style of the Bajapur peasant woman. No doubt, she did not want to stand out although the minute she opened her mouth, it was clear that she was as much an outsider here as was George. He felt a deep pity for her welling in his heart.

'Do you ever wish to go home, Indumati?' he asked her via Lal Ram. 'Are you happy here?'

She reflected and then nodded. There was work here and her two boys were getting enough to eat, so happiness to her was a relative thing.

'What about you, Lal Ram? Do you feel like going home someday?'

'My home, Clark sir, is here. I am an orphan and my taiji, my uncle's wife, used to beat me and abuse me. So, I will make my life here in Bajapur now. But the situation in the bazaar is getting worse from day to day. All of us—mataji, babuji, Hari and Shambhu—we say prayers all the way to the cantonment. We never know when someone might pounce on us and cut our throats for no reason at all.'

George nodded, upset with the information and feeling powerless to do anything concrete about the situation.

'Well, let's get back to dinner, shall we?' Fear receded as they decided on the evening meal.

~

At six thirty, a messenger arrived from Col. Holmes's residence with a chitty, asking George if he could make himself available for lunch that day at the District Magistrate's house. The DM had invited a number of local dignitaries and their families and had asked if the army could also be represented. Obviously, the CO had decided that, given George's current line of work, such a social occasion might be highly advantageous. George sent a message to Ruffington through Lal Ram, asking for permission, stressing the opportunities such a lunch might present. He then had a bath in water that, despite being unheated, felt warm to the touch. Lal Ram had set out his Service Dress and, as he wore his uniform, he thought ahead to breakfast. He could barely bear to face the groaning sideboard of food that Indumati would have got ready by now—the eggs, the bacon, the sausages, the racks of toast, the nimbupani with a hint of rock salt. And for those feeling the heat, Indumati had also set out slices of watermelon, papaya, melon, mangoes. There was a large glass dish full of yogurt with some saffron threads on top. There was cold cereal too, and puffed rice. And a pitcher of nice, cold milk.

The senior dining member, Maj. Richard Brassey, his eyes still bloodshot from the previous evening's indulgences, settled down to eat and began asking George some questions.

'So, Clark, how's the new posting going?'

'Sir?'

'Oh, you know, your little thingummyjig with whatshisname?'

'Going well, sir, not too much happening there.'

'Don't suppose you know where the unit's going next, do you?'

Brassey's tone was casual but his eyes displayed a keen interest. All eyes at the table turned to George. It dawned on him that everyone in the 126th East Yorks probably thought he was doing something terribly important, involving the Viceroy in Simla and the manipulation of unit postings during wartime. George almost laughed out loud, then cleared his throat to control himself.

'No, sir, I'm afraid it isn't that sort of work.'

'I suppose you're not at liberty to tell, eh? Top Secret, eh? Ha, ha! Well, make sure that we go somewhere better next time, will you, Clark? Don't want another one-horse town like this Bajapur. Be indebted to you and all that.' Maj. Brassey slurped down his tea and began chatting with the others. Some of the other officers looked speculatively at George, clearly wondering if it was worth buttering him up so that they might be posted somewhere pleasant in the near future.

The humidity was already killing when he biked over to the office. The cantonment was quiet except for a koel that called desperately from the trees, raising its pitch maddeningly with each shriek. It's just us, the bloody good-for-nothings, thought George, us and the senior officers here in the building. As he went up the three steps to his office, the Brigade Commander drove up in a great flurry of flag car, flustered staff officers and a number of Other Ranks crashing to attention and stiff salutes. George stopped in the veranda and saluted as Brig. Michael Curtis, a small, bald man with a hint of humour around his eyes, trotted up the central pathway. He noticed George and nodded curtly, as one might do to a very small dog. Such was the lot of subalterns—ignored by the higher-ups, and kicked around by their immediate superiors.

In about half an hour, the telephone rang in George's office. It was the staff officer to Brigadier Curtis.

'Maj. Burr here,' he said crisply. 'The Brigade Commander wants to meet you.' There was a note of satisfaction in the officer's voice, of having the pleasure of delivering bad news.

George walked over to the other side of the courtyard where two guards saluted him and let him into the Brigade Commander's office. George looked around appreciatively. This was the kind of office he thought of when he imagined higher office. Enormous desk, silver plates and trophies gleaming softly from the walls, framed maps and photographs of previous Commanders. Burr greeted him and then took him into the sanctum sanctorum—more brass, silver, red carpeting. George saluted and Brigadier Curtis, who was speaking to someone on the phone, motioned to him to sit. Really, he thought nervously, he was in close proximity to too many senior officers than was good for him, as a young subaltern.

After a number of yes's and no's and we-shall-see's, Brigadier Curtis put the phone back in its cradle and nodded to Maj. Burr who promptly saluted and left the room.

The Brigadier regarded George gravely.

'Some tea, Clark?'

'Er . . . no, thank you, sir. I mean, I would love some.' George was thoroughly flustered. At the ping of the bell, a waiter entered, took the order and disappeared. Brig. Curtis resumed his inspection of the young officer.

'Well, Clark, I don't have to tell you that Capt. Ruffington and Capt. Porter have been quite busy around Bajapur.'

'Er . . . yes, sir.' George didn't know where this was heading.

'Be a good chap, won't you, and have a talk with Maj. Burr outside before you leave?' The tea arrived in clinking tea cups and was sent to Burr's office. George was dismissed with a nod of the head. The staff officer was considerably less oblique than his boss.

'Tell that blasted Capt. Porter, won't you, to stay the hell away from the riding stables. He is scaring the syces with his endless questions. I understand that security is very important especially in wartime and 8 Infantry Brigade appreciates his efforts. But the syces are civilian staff and they are leaving the stables in fear of imminent imprisonment. The Commander's daughter, Barbara, is distraught because her favourite horse, Punch Bowl, has no one to take care of her. So be a good chap and steer Porter away from the stables. Sure you won't have another cup, Clark?'

Bloody Porter, George thought, as he walked back across the courtyard.

'We hear that you've been to the Brigade Commander's office for tea. Very impressive, Clark.' James Ruffington smiled patronizingly. Porter ignored him.

'Yes, I was told to let you know, sir, that all of 8 Infantry Brigade would like us to stop hassling the civilian stable staff, sir.' George was short.

'Well, well, Dennis, looks like you've been ruffling a few feathers, old chap.'

Dennis Porter looked unperturbed, still rifling through some reports in a file.

'Have a look at this, Clark,' he barked, completely ignoring George's previous comment. 'I think we may be close to cracking this little Bolshie code here.' He pushed over a piece of paper, typewritten on a foolscap paper. It seemed to be a list of something.

'This is a list that Amar Mani Chaturvedi, the local Swabhiman Samaj leader, has sent us. It lists all the illegal meetings that have been held in Bajapur in the last six months—at least twenty. The local Tanzeem guy, Mir Ali Sharif, confirmed these meetings when I showed him the list. He said that there were even more that had escaped notice. You've got to keep visiting the Bharadwajs, Clark, and keep getting more of those letter codes that the kids were using. Between that and the poem, I am sure that we'll crack it.' He snapped his fingers, his beetling eyebrows drawn low, giving him an angry rather than a jovial look.

'That, sir, was not a code.' George took great pleasure in demolishing the obnoxious Porter's self-satisfied demeanour. He proceeded to explain how the letters were a riddle in both English and Hindi, just harmless children's fun, absolutely in no way a threatening Communist or Congress code that was used to organize meetings, subversive or otherwise.

Porter scowled, still not convinced. 'I'll have to have someone else take a look at it before I buy that,' he grumbled before he left.

'And Maj. Rudolph is not a communist either, sir. Those poems are . . . just nothing.' The flapping of the curtain marked Porter's exit. Clearly, he was not interested in Rudolph's innocence.

'Ah, never mind, Clark,' Ruffington waved one pink hand and used the other podgy extremity to wipe the sweat from his face. 'Damned heat. How people tolerate it here for years on end, I don't know.'

'Well, shall we go over last night's events again?'

George recounted it, his distaste for Ruffington rising with every word he uttered. He kept the account neat, concise and dry. Ruffington continued to smile his ruffianly smile, curly hair peeking out from behind his ears, a tad too long for regulations. He listened intently to George, took some notes, and sighed.

'Clearly, there is nothing happening in Bajapur, Clark, nothing of any interest to us. But it keeps Porter busy and relatively happy. And in my mind, if we find a few Bolshies here and there, well, he will go back after the war is done with a feeling of satisfaction. And we will have earned a friend in America, one who might look back on his year in Bajapur as a useful training ground for his future role in the American government.'

'There *is* a lot going on in the town, sir,' George related everything he had learned about the refugees coming in from Pithampur, the rising religious tensions in the town, and the crowded and miserable housing conditions that were a huge burden on the civic administration.

'The law and order of Pithampur, Clark, is the business of the Raja and his ministers. It is none of my business at all, especially now that I am no longer attached to the Resident's office there. And as for Bajapur, it's up to the civil authorities to control the situation here. I suggest that you don't take it so much to heart. I must say, Clark, that you're quite belligerent this morning.' Ruffington's lips were pressed into a thin pink line of disapproval.

At noon, George left the office to head over to the District Magistrate's residence for lunch. He had asked for and had received permission to use a staff car, and proceeded to his quarters in unexpected luxury. He would wash and change into fresh clothes and then drive over to the DM's house, only a mile outside the cantonment. The bachelors' quarters were eerily quiet as everyone was either in the office or with the men somewhere, or, as in the case of A Company, away in Delhi. George thought how odd it was that he had no idea who his neighbour was. Perhaps it was that Capt. Andy Ross, who was now away in Delhi. He had never thought to ask Bacon or Barrington, such had been the superficial level of his interaction with the officers in the 126th East Yorks. He made a silent vow to himself that as soon as he was done with Porter's and

Ruffington's crazy operation, he would be a better battalion officer. He would get to know his fellow 126th East Yorkswallas, really get to know them, so that he could be a better fit in the unit.

As he moved around the room trying to find the cufflinks for his shirt, his eyes fell on more sheets of Bates's poetry. Poor, poor Bates, who never made it back from Burma to the arms of his wife, the sad-faced Muriel who wept on Col Holmes's shoulder. The war had undone so many lives, George thought. Please God, let me be able to move forward with my plans, my hopes, with Anna if possible.

> But Zin, shehe has now
> spent a lifetime away.
> Both of us are older.
> Two days ago another
> year was over and still
> we pass by each other
> on our erratic forays
> into romance.
> When will he come to me?
> I've changed, for the better
> I think.
> How much has he, I wonder.
> Will he know me or am
> I also a part of his
> future-in-the-past?
> I did so much with him
> in those joyless years of boyhood,
> snatched kisses in the middle
> of suffocating social events,
> asphyxiating parties,

laughed with him
at pompous military men
and their self-conscious
chivalry.
Zin will meet him this summer
but will shehe tell
him of my strange defeats
and my longing
for him in
the winter
deadliness that is
Arakan.

George was struck by this verse, the recognition of its meaning dawning slowly. He looked rapidly at another verse:

Some stories are never told,
are never meant to be.
But Zin wants
so desperately to hear it
that I have to struggle
to recover the words
which were almost erased
from mind as they
were being formed.
I had another dream
this morning,
just before dawn.
As usual, a man
whose face and figure
are hidden
by misted glass,

whose voice is muffled,
whose breath clouds the
already-clouded glass.
Tapping sounds, musical,
brittle.
Is he looking for me
or for a way out of
his prison cell?
I hope I will be a part
of that freedom,
if it is freedom he is
searching for.
Morning sounds and Zin
wake me
whenever I raise
that question.

And now, George understood the significance of Bates's poetry. Poor, tortured Bates, tormented by the knowledge that he was condemned to always look 'for a way out of his prison cell'. Had Muriel guessed any of this, George wondered, in the three short months that she had been married to Sam Bates? Did she know that somewhere in the world there was a man who had held the keys to her husband's happiness? Or perhaps that man too lay dead in the killing fields of Kohima or Arakan or Rangoon? When she wept in the CO's office, were they tears of grief or tears of regret for the place that she could never occupy in her husband's heart? Ah well, George sighed, it was all over and done with, this saga of poor Sam Bates. He put the papers away in a drawer and left the portfolio of recipes lying on his desk. He would need to go through it again in the evening for the following day's menu.

A short, dusty drive took him past the grounds of the donkey fair. George was fascinated. He had not ventured out to the scene of the fair before as he had always been busy with work during the day. The parched fields right outside the cantonment gates were a heaving sea of grey, braying animals. Men in white turbans and dhotis stood around in whatever shade they could find, chatting and negotiating. The donkeys were scrawny, but had determined expressions on their faces. Very donkey-like, thought George. He felt a sudden nostalgia for the farming life of his childhood. The donkeys reminded him of the calm routine of country life and farming, the ebbs and flows of seasons, the planting of seedlings, the harvest, the inevitability of life and death . . . then he saw a flash of OG uniform in the distance. Was that . . .? It looked like Porter out there in the distance, but that couldn't be of course. Just the heat playing tricks on his mind. He leaned back against the seat and closed his eyes for the rest of the journey to the DM's bungalow.

The District Magistrate's government bungalow was set back from the road. Bricks lined a circular lawn in the front, ringed by a driveway. Unlike a military home, where a formal lunch would showcase a number of mess waiters in their whites, running around with trays, civilians called on the resources of the club and their neighbours. George recognized the wizened old waiter from the dinner at the club the previous night. He was shuffling around behind a bar set up in the veranda, wiping glasses and setting them neatly on a tray. Inside, a cool room was full of the usual bric-a-brac of Indian officialdom, brass ashtrays and carved elephants. As his eyes got used to the interior, he noticed two men in traditional Indian outfits sitting in armchairs. In the room beyond, there were more people milling around, drinking cooldrinks out of tall glasses. The two men looked at George expressionlessly, nodding their heads when he said, 'Good afternoon.'

'I'm George Clark,' he introduced himself, leaving out his lowly rank. 'From the army.'

'I am Amar Mani Chaturvedi,' replied one of the men. His face was as round as his body—he looked like a couple of circles placed on top of each other, with some limbs attached.

'Oh, yes,' said George enthusiastically. 'I met your nephew Rajendra and his wife yesterday.'

'Accha? Oh, so you know them? Good, good,' Amar Mani Chaturvedi looked away into the distance. 'He is a good boy, Rajendra. His father is my elder brother.'

'And I am Mir Ali Sharif,' said the other man, who wore a fez and sported round glasses. 'How do you do?'

'Looks like they are having some eats back in there,' George gestured to the lively scene in the other room.

'Yes, but I cannot go into that room,' said Amar Mani Chaturvedi regretfully. 'They are serving alcohol there.'

'The bearer has gone to get us some nimbupani,' added Mir Ali Sharif. George left them, conscious of the deep irony that the practices of their respective faiths brought these two men together in their isolation at parties while their insistence on their own religious purities brought them to violence on the streets.

In the other room, he was pleasantly surprised to see Deborah Silonia and Satinder, both standing around with glasses of nimbupani. The District Magistrate, William Hastings, was rumoured to be a descendant of Warren Hastings, the first Governor General of Bengal, an incorrect assumption that he was in no hurry to repudiate. He was a pleasant man, worn out with the recent state of affairs—the rising communal temperature in the district, the influx of refugees from Pithampur. He greeted George affably, made sure that he got a nice, chilled beer and then resumed talking to the Silonias.

'How is the catching of the Indian National Army fugitives going?' a low voice startled George. It was ASP Ramakant Batra, the Indian IPS officer, who had come to see him and Ruffington in the office in his first week at work. Next to him was Joseph Mack, his superior. George greeted both of them respectfully.

'I've not seen any,' he told Batra, truthfully.

'That's because there aren't any in Bajapur,' said Batra decisively. 'I wonder why Capt. Ruffington is so insistent about them.' His face was a study in intelligence. He was not the kind that one could deceive by trying to lay red herrings. Mack too was an old hand.

'Most Indians sympathize with the INA,' Mack said. 'But I doubt that any fugitives have fled here to our district.'

'You know, the war has seen some absolutely revolting scum rise to the surface.' Batra's tone was pleasant, conversational. 'And scum has a way of taking over the whole pond unless it is controlled in time. You have to clean your pond from time to time, Mr Clark.'

'Hmmm . . . how many years have you been here in Bajapur, Mr Batra?' George tried to change the subject.

'Oh, a year or so. It's been very interesting, I must say. The problems one has to deal with—the communal conflicts, the land issues, the refugees trickling in every so often from Pithampur. Our days are busy, Mr Clark. This is the first time I've had lunch in many weeks. And the only reason I am here is because I heard that Mr Chaturvedi and Mr Sharif would be here. It's rare to get them together under one roof, much less in the same room. Of course, it's fantastic to see Mr and Mrs Silonia here, too. I would love to talk to them about Pithampur.' The prospect of killing so many birds with one stone made Batra positively drool. 'But I may have to leave early. Duty, alas. As you can see, I am still in uniform.'

'Well, now, George, won't you come and meet Mrs Hastings?' Deborah took George away from the police officers.

'Were they interrogating you, my boy?'

'Just fishing for information, nothing I can't handle,' George smiled as he walked with Deborah onto the back veranda where fans swirled the hot air around and where Mrs Hastings, a redoubtable figure in a dress printed with cabbage-patch roses, presided over a gaggle of women, some British, some Indian.

'Are those women there the wives of Mr Chaturvedi and Mr Sharif?' George indicated two ladies who sat in a corner, both in printed saris, chatting animatedly among themselves.

'Goodness, no, my boy.' Deborah made a disbelieving gesture with her hand. 'Rajendra's Amar chacha and Ali Sharif mian both keep their women in very tight seclusion. It would be unthinkable for them to take their women to attend a party of mixed company. Besides, what would they do for food?'

'Food?'

'Yes, in case you haven't noticed, Amar Chaturvedi has made a huge gesture of accommodation accepting even a drink in Mr Hastings' house. Food would be out of the question for him. He would be irredeemably contaminated, accepting anything else from the hands of a beef-eating *mleccha*. As it is, his family and relatives will probably demand some accounting for this party. And as for Ali Sharif, nothing would pass his standard for halal, so he too just drinks some nimbupani at the DM's house.'

'They have more in common than they think,' George said drily.

Deborah marched him over to the ladies and introduced him.

'This is George Clark,' she said. 'He is a bright young officer in one of the battalions posted here in Bajapur. I knew him when he was in Pithampur last year.'

'Good afternoon, ladies.'

He was introduced to the civilian ladies of the town. One of the Indian ladies was the wife of ASP Batra. The other woman was the wife of a local Indian businessman. While her husband was inside, catching up with Bajapur news, she was chatting with Seema Batra. They rarely got to meet these days because of the tensions in town. Going out was an unpredictable affair at best.

A waiter came by with drinks and some eats. George helped himself to some peanuts and listened to the women talk. It was mostly talk about the lack of availability of daily essentials. The tense communal situation in the bazaar meant that it was hard for the women to get to their tailors or grocers. Milkmen's rounds had become sketchy, while the man who brought them their weekly joint of mutton had disappeared mysteriously. Periodic scares cleared the town's little stores of jams, pickles, flour, rice and sugar. All the women had well-stocked pantries and storerooms but it was still nerve-racking, being held hostage to the whims of rioters and religious fanatics.

At last lunch was served. The long dining-room table glistened with china and glass, and the silverware looked polished and gleaming. George was happy to see that it was a buffet and not another tedious, sit-down affair. It was a veritable smorgasbord of Indian and English food. A macaroni bake sat next to a lamb curry, a roast chicken next to an aloo dum. There was no beef and no pork on the table, and plenty of vegetarian options, in deference to the Indians present. There were tables in an adjoining room, where guests could sit informally if they so wished. George found himself at a table with Amar Mani Chaturvedi and Mir Ali Sharif. They were still sipping their drinks and had no plates in front of them. George apologized for his gluttony in front of them. They nodded in acknowledgement.

'You may know my senior officer, Capt. James Ruffington,' George said carefully, waiting to see what sort of a reaction he might get out of them.

'Oh yes, Capt. Ruffington,' said Amar Mani. 'I speak with him a lot these days.'

'And your Capt. Porter too,' said Mir Ali. 'He gives me some useful tips now and then.'

'Useful, is it?'

'Oh, when you have to deal with communists, you need all the help you can get, ji. But unfortunately, Capt. Porter also seems to be very partial towards Miss Williams and her school. I told him that in Hindustan, you cannot have these aggressive missionaries. She will get into serious trouble if she is not careful.'

Deborah and Satinder joined the table and the talk became more general. As they were finishing up, George asked Deborah:

'You know, one day you really do have to tell me how you found yourself in Pithampur. I know that you were there for Satinder's sake but where did the two of you meet?'

'Come, I will tell you. Let us leave the gentlemen and their chatter. And let's go into the drawing room which is cool and empty now.'

Deborah led George into the other room; she had a slight stoop, and her steps were firm if no longer sprightly. He felt very affectionate towards her, no matter that her politics were probably subversive of the administration. They sat in the large, stone-floored room, the fan whirring above their heads, and at last Deborah told him of how she came to India, of her ill-fated shipboard love affair with Neville Shaw, of her deepening interest in cooking and the collection of recipes, of Kalimpong and the Misses Burton and of meeting the adventurous young Satinder, caretaker-cum-artist at the lodge.

After she had declared her love for Satinder, he went away suddenly. Ostensibly, he had gone to Darjeeling to meet his parents, but when he came back to Kalimpong he announced to his employers, the Burton sisters, that he would be moving in a few months to Calcutta, where he hoped to pursue art more seriously. As Deborah had just announced her own decision to her parents that she was staying in Kalimpong, it was particularly shattering to her. But it was the elder Miss Burton who had the best advice for her:

'My dear, stay awhile. You look very tired and you are far too young to be so distressed. Stay with us for some time, here in the mountains, help us in the lodge, read to the children and help them learn. In a few months you will be refreshed and then you can go back to your life in the plains.' And so Deborah had stayed.

She had just got to this point in her story, when the District Magistrate himself peeked into the room and called George.

'There's a phone call for you, Mr Clark. It's over that way, in the library.' The DM's library was a square room that looked over into the garden at the back of the house. George had an impression of a massive wooden desk, fountain pens with their pot of ink, writing paper and blotting sheets, and shelves full of tastefully bound books. He barely had said 'Hello!' when a squawking noise erupted from the other end.

'Hello?'

'Sir, sir!' He finally discerned that it was Lal Ram at the other end.

'Sir, sir, sir came and took it away!'

'Calm down, Lal Ram, who came?'

'Sir, Porter saab, sir.' George's heart grew cold. 'What did he take?'

Lal Ram was sobbing at the other end.

'The picture book, sir, the picture book. He snatched it from me, sir. It is gone.'

George made his excuses to the DM and the other guests, and sent for his staff car at once.

TWELVE

As he stood on the shaded veranda, waiting for the staff car to arrive, George felt slightly dazed. He did not know whether it was the muggy heat that shimmered off the gravelled driveway, or the shock of Porter's violation of his property. As he waited, he felt a movement near him. It was Deborah, in her plain poplin dress, her white hat placed firmly on her greying head, sensible shoes—outwardly the epitome of English womanhood, controlled and calm.

'I do hope everything is all right, George,' she said, looking concerned. 'You looked as if you had received some terrible news.'

George controlled his emotions.

'He took the pictures, Deborah. I mean, Porter did. He stole them from my servant.'

'Oh!' Deborah's mouth tightened in shock. Then, very quietly, she asked, 'May I please come with you, George? I may be able to persuade this person, this Porter, to return unharmed those beautiful works of art that my husband and his friends had spent so much time creating.' She went inside to tell Satinder about her change in plans and re-emerged to wait for the car.

George did not think that Porter could be persuaded, even by an elderly lady. But the black staff car was gliding to a stop now in the portico and he nodded and opened the rear door for

Deborah. They passed a line of cars and vehicles, some drivers sleeping on the front seats, others under a tree, playing cards and smoking their thin bidis. A gatekeeper in a khaki uniform opened the painted iron gates, and they turned left, starting the journey back to the cantonment.

The Bajapur donkey fair was even more crowded than it had been just a couple of hours ago. Grey, patient animals stood all over the fields; several were on the road and there were three or four that blocked the car itself. The driver honked his horn impatiently and after a minute the owner detached himself from a group of chatting men and sauntered over to steer his animals off the road. Deals were being struck, while some farmers were examining a fine, fat specimen. Another animal had dug his feet in, and was refusing to be led away. Still others stood quietly, ears twitching, the thick eyelashes giving their intelligent dark eyes a look of improbable beauty. These fellows were headed for a lifetime of hard labour, fetching water and stone in the quarries of the Mussoorie hills, or carrying bricks for the sugar mills being built so rapidly along the railway line.

Beside him, Deborah sat silently, looking out at the parched landscape that waited patiently for the rains.

'You know,' she said, 'poor Satinder thought that he had solved his problems by moving away to Calcutta. He was confused by my declaration of love; he wanted to dismiss it as just the emotional immaturity of a young girl. My poor put-upon parents—I drove my mother mad by making her uproot her life from one place to another. But she was a good mother, all said and done. She stayed with me, would not abandon her only child. She stayed with me in Kalimpong while my father went to work in Bhutan, then she moved back with me to Calcutta when Satinder moved there. Even in the rather more liberated days after the Great War, it must have been so difficult for her when I left Calcutta with Satinder in 1922 and moved to Bolpur, to Gurudeb Tagore's Santiniketan where Satinder wanted to study art from the great masters themselves. My mother tried hard to pretend that nothing untoward had happened, that her precious daughter had not run off like some kitchen maid with a footman.

'Those were such happy days in Santiniketan that I long for them now; there was so much peace there, even though life was simple to the point of being primitive. The art department was new, the university was still being constructed, and there were all these fantastic minds coming together to create something. Satinder and I spent six blissful years there. There were the chhatim trees under which the Patha Bhavan pupils in their buttercup yellow uniforms would sit for their lessons, just as Gurudeb had envisioned. We built a little house, I made it very English, all red brick and flowering creepers. We were the first ones to install indoor plumbing; I was too genteel for outhouses. There was always a crowd for tea, you know, many of whom would linger for dinner. I tell you, we never slept before midnight most nights. The conversation would start with some talk about somebody's work and then it would veer off into uncharted waters—politics, Gandhi, Nehru, whether Deshbandhu Chittaranjan Das was right to organize a Swarajya front within the Congress, whether Gandhiji's constructive work in the villages would bear fruit, whether we at Santiniketan could do anything for the tribal peoples who surrounded us in their colour, their vivacity and their stark, unrelenting poverty.

'And just as I had got used to this blissful, creative serenity, there came the call from Pithampur. One day, Satinder came to me and asked if I would move to Pithampur with him. There had been troubles there with the Raja, and Satinder wanted to be closer to his people, to be with them in their suffering. He could not offer me an easy life, he told me. And he would not marry me. As a single Englishwoman, he thought that I would be better protected from the wrath of the Raja than I would have been as his legally wedded wife. Having already dragged the Sunderland name through mud by now, I was past caring about such proprieties as marriage. So, I moved to Pithampur too, on the condition that I could recreate a little bit of Santiniketan there. In fact, it was I who persuaded many of our friends from Bolpur to move to the Punjab.

'It was so difficult, I can't describe to you just how hard it was for me to begin a new life in the Punjab. I bought a little house in the town from a wealthy farmer and began to live there. Somehow, I felt braver surrounded by the townspeople in the bazaar than I did out on Satinder's farm. The peasants are kind as individuals but there is something predatory about the village as a community, especially towards an outsider. Satinder was in and out of jail. His mother was kind to me, his father too bewildered by all the changes in his life, in his son, to take much notice of me. For fifteen years, we led this unusual life. First, Satinder's father, then his careworn mother passed away. My parents left for England in 1935. Mother died shortly before the war began. Father still writes to me. He is so old now, seventy-nine I believe next month. Now that the war is almost over, Satinder and I will go visit him.

'Then, one day—I believe it was in the summer of 1944—Satinder told me, "I don't think I'm going to survive, Deborah, you should go home to England." When I pressed him for a reason, he said that his long periods in jail, in confinement, were driving him insane. The only reason he wasn't finished off like many others was because his last name still carried weight in court circles, and his powerful relatives ensured that he would survive, even if in captivity. But, the tortured screams of his prison mates haunted his dreams, often waking him up at night. There were times when he was kept in complete darkness, for days at a time. Oh, George, I cannot describe to you the horror of that prison, hewn out of rock, damp with underground water, pitch dark at night. Satinder did not want me to be burdened with the care of an insane man.

'I cannot tell you how distressed I was. I was determined to save this man whom I loved so deeply, and yet I did not know how to rescue him from the depths of his agony. And then you, George, came into our lives. You, with your demands for recipes and food, your interest in its preparation and its presentation. And one day, talking to Satinder about you, we realized that you were the solution. So, that cookbook, those pictures, those recipes, are not just the work of artists, they are not just colours splashed on paper, they are also these men's collective escape from certain mental derangement. I shall not let this Porter, whoever he is, get away with stealing their deliverance.' She folded one hand over the other, both resting in her lap, trembling a little.

At length, the car drew into the white, painted gates of the officers' mess. George seated Deborah on the veranda—women were not allowed inside—and called for water and tea to be served to her. He sprinted towards his quarters at the rear of the mess compound. Lal Ram was crouching by the door, his head in his hands, stunned at what had transpired. His faded white shirt, already grimy with sweat and a hard morning's work under Ratan Singh's authoritarian supervision, hung on his frame. George got out of the boy that in the morning, soon after he had left for Rotherford Square, Captain Porter had stopped by his room to chat with Lal Ram. This had been the American officer's normal routine for the past few weeks; there was nothing untoward about it. Porter had made a few casual inquiries about where George saab was, whether he had eaten breakfast in the mess, etc. Then he had headed off elsewhere. Lal Ram had got busy himself. There were shoes and belts to be polished, uniforms to be delivered to the dhobi, clothes to be fetched and distributed to their owners.

Soon after, George had returned to change and leave for lunch at the District Magistrate's house. Then, Ratan Singh had come by, checking to make sure that Lal Ram's work was up to par. A cuff to his head sent Lal Ram scurrying into George's room to remake the already tidy bed and to dust the desk and chairs yet again. It was while he was dusting the table that he heard someone approach. He heard someone speak English and some basic Hindustani to Ratan Singh. Lal Ram was carefully wiping the cover of the portfolio of recipes when Ratan Singh summoned him outside. Unthinkingly, the lad went outside, still holding the book.

'Ah, Lal Ram.' Captain Porter's lips were drawn back from his teeth, in an insincere snarl of a smile. Ratan Singh stomped away in his worn-out shoes, clearly relieved not to have to go through the linguistic pantomime that involved any interaction with foreign officers.

'Well, Lal Ram, it's a good thing I found you here. Ah . . . your Clark saab has asked me to fetch something for him from his room and I need to be let in.'

This was most unusual and Lal Ram's expression must have showed it. Porter became more expansive.

'You see, he forgot his er . . . some important papers for the office, goddammit, the daftar, the daftar.'

'But, sahib, Clark sahib said that he will go out for lunch.'

'Oh!' Then, recovering quickly, Porter pressed on. 'Yes, but the daftar needs this stuff. Come on now, boy,' a more commanding tone crept in. 'Don't waste my time, I need to find those . . . *what's this*?' Porter deftly took the portfolio that Lal Ram had held loosely.

'Oh, sahib,' Lal Ram cried out, 'that is Clark sahib's book. It is for the mess, we need it for the dinner.'

But Porter wasn't listening any more. He was leafing through the gleaming pages, the jewel-like borders becoming a whirl of brilliant colour as he turned the pages. Dal Shepherd's Pie made him pause momentarily, and he considered the cleanly etched lines of an Englishwoman in a white summer dress supervising her colourfully attired maid's handling of the dish. There was the minced lamb, heavy rich kali dal, with a topping of mashed potatoes, coming out golden from the oven, with flecks of green coriander. The Englishwoman's dress swept one way, her maid's the other, a contrast of dark and pastel, of earth and sky. The Country Captain chicken absorbed Porter for a length of time. There was first of all the chicken itself, all golden brown and smothered in onions and spices and Worcestershire sauce. Then there was the silver of the platter on which it was set, fluted edges and gleaming polish. And finally there was the procession that took it in to the impatiently waiting diners. A conga line of men, probably waiters, the de rigueur black trousers of their formal wear subverted by the vivid red of their shirts, their hands curved over their heads in a tangle of exuberance, one hand holding a giant serving spoon, another a serving fork, one arm outstretched towards the dining room with a giant goblet of wine, another pouring more from a bottle.

Was Porter's mouth watering at the sight of such magnificent feasting? Was he thinking of summer days in Cape Cod or of Thanksgiving dinner with his father's family in upstate New York? And did Lal Ram hear Porter sigh as he turned the page to reveal the glories of a roasted whole fish, caught by fishermen on a wooden boat, then travelling the length of the page to land up at a boisterous marketplace where crows swooped down on the silvery scales. Its journey continued up the left margin of the page, in the bag of a shopper whose wife then coated it with oil and haldi, chilli and ginger before wrapping it in a banana leaf and cooking it over hot coals. At the top centre of the page, the fish ended up on the brass platter of the man of the house who cheerfully stuffed his face while pointing down to the recipe written below the picture.

'This is it!' Porter shouted and then he was off, charging away from George's quarters. Lal Ram chased after him, sobbing and begging.

'Sir, sir, do not take it! It is Clark sahib's cookery book. He needs it for the mess, for the cooking, sir.'

'Fuck off, boy!' Porter snarled at him, pounding through the afternoon heat towards his waiting jeep.

Lal Ram was beside himself with panic and shock. For a dazed minute, he could not believe that he had just witnessed the brazen theft of his employer's precious possession. He had never expected Dennis Porter to steal it so shamelessly. Crying, he ran towards the only other person who knew and appreciated the value of the cookbook. In the kitchen, Indumati was wearily rearranging bottles of freshly ground spices, in preparation for a short rest before teatime. Lal Ram burst into the kitchen, so distraught that he forgot to remove his shoes.

'Kai re, mulga,' Indumati began in Marathi, then turned to broken Hindustani. 'What is it, son? Why are you crying? Are you hungry? Who beat you?' She took Lal Ram into her arms and wiped his tearful face with the end of her sari. Ramu Chowkidar who had been surveying his beds from under a mango tree, heard the commotion and came running in, followed closely by the Mess Corporal who had been in the pantry, quietly polishing off the remnants of Indumati's delicious breakfast. Finally, the distressed lad was able to have them understand what Capt. Porter had done and that the cookbook was gone.

'Ah, the villain,' said the Mess Corporal, a weather-beaten man in his thirties, who didn't much care for officers, whether American or British. 'He be a right villain.'

Indumati was devastated. Not only was the recipe collection a valuable tool for her, but she loved the beauty of its pages. Each morning, when George opened the portfolio, she silently said a prayer of reverence, awed by its magnificence.

'Go and call Clark saab,' Indumati told Lal Ram authoritatively. 'Do you know where he went?'

'The staff car driver told me that they were going to the District Magistrate's house,' said the Mess Corporal through Lal Ram's translation.

'Then go and phone Clark saab,' Indumati told him firmly. 'You know how to use the telefoon. And,' pushing Lal Ram towards the Corporal, she said, 'take the boy with you, have him speak to the saab.' And so, using the mess phone, Lal Ram had placed perhaps the first phone call of his life. After that, he returned to George's room, squatting in the veranda, waiting for the officer.

George walked back with the boy to the mess where Deborah was sipping at her tea, waving away flies with one hand. Around the corner of the building appeared Indumati and Ramu

Chowkidar, hesitating at stepping into this hitherto forbidden part of the grounds. Leading them both was the cocky figure of the Mess Corporal who had decided, in the manner of all good NCOs, to take charge of the situation and to present the case on behalf of all the witnesses.

'Good afternoon, sir,' he greeted George, snapping off a careless salute, as befitted a well-fed and slightly indolent Mess Corporal. 'It was brought to my attention, sah, that an object of yours has been taken without your permission. By Capt. Porter, sir, of the Intelligence Wing.'

'At ease, Corporal,' George replied, ignoring the man's accusation. 'Er . . . do you know where Capt. Porter is?'

'I will find out right away, sah.' The corporal snapped off another salute, then went off to activate his network of informers to track down Dennis Porter's movements. Indumati, Lal Ram and Ramu Chowkidar waited in the shade of the giant bougainvillea that covered the porch with hot-pink colour.

'Soon, very soon,' Deborah pointed at the dark, threatening mass of clouds on the horizon, 'the rains will be here, thank God. I don't think I can survive much longer in this heat.' She took another sip of her drink. From a distance, the donkeys at the fair blasted out a cacophony of loud, harsh brays.

The idea occurred to everyone at the same time.

'Why, he's at the . . .' began George

'. . . donkey fair,' concluded Deborah and Lal Ram.

'We have to go, Deborah,' George said, moving towards the porch. 'Lal Ram, will you tell the Mess Corporal that Mrs Silonia and I are leaving?'

'I think, sir,' said Lal Ram hesitantly, 'you should ask for help from the other officers too.'

Deborah made a wry face.

'What an excellent idea! And what a clever young man! Why, here we were just about to rush off to a donkey fair when, really, the simplest thing to do would be to set the British Army on this Capt. Porter and his henchman, Capt. Ruffington.'

'I'll call Colonel Holmes,' said George, striding towards the interior of the mess.

But the CO was not in his office. Probably busy with Muriel Bates and those poems, thought George, vexed. Leaving instructions for Lal Ram to tell the Mess Corporal about their whereabouts, George and Deborah headed out to the donkey fair.

In five minutes, they could see the seething, grey mass of the donkey fair. George instructed the driver to pull over and park off the road and to wait for them. They staggered out of the car and towards the fairground, a frail Englishwoman and a slim subaltern, the hot air enveloping them like a horsehair blanket.

'He's here somewhere, Deborah,' George said. 'We'll ferret him out.' He walked over to the first group of men lounging in the shade of a tree. It was a gulmohar tree and its flowers were flame-red against the opaque sky in which a crowd of clouds grumbled, while the heat hung low and menacing over the dusty fields.

'What shall we say if we do find him?' Deborah's practical nature surfaced. And George realized that he had prepared nothing to tell Porter. He had nothing to hold over the man to make him return the portfolio—there were no threats he could make, no ominous promises of generations-long vendetta to force a penitent return of the stolen item. All he could feel at the moment was this deep anger building up inside him, joining the other pent-up frustrations, the disappointments, the sorrows of wartime loss—all festering inside like a giant, hot, pus-filled boil. Without replying to Deborah, he plunged into the crowd, searching for Dennis Porter, hell-bent on vengeance and retribution. Deborah followed him, pushing away furry donkeys as if she had been born and raised on a farm since childhood.

Left to ponder the swift-moving events of the day, Indumati, Lal Ram and Ramu Chowkidar watched as the black staff car pulled out of the gates and turned towards the Bajapur cantonment boundaries.

'What's going to happen now?' Ramu muttered as he shaded his eyes with his hands, the brim of his faded cap drooping. The Mess Corporal came out of the building and beckoned them all towards him.

'Cor!' he exclaimed and spat on the bushes nearby with deep satisfaction. 'This is a pretty pickle. Well, what are we to do now, me lads?' He included Indumati, too, in his expansive phrase.

'Clark sahib and the memsahib have gone to the donkey fair,' Indumati replied briskly in Marathi. She found British soldiers somewhat loutish, but this fellow was all right, quite tame really, always hanging around the kitchen, waiting for a bite. After Lal Ram translated, the man sighed.

'Ah well, there's nothing to be done, then. Well, I think this is it, then,' he yawned. 'Nothing to do now except sit around and wait. I always thought that Porter was a bit of a dodgy bastard, creeping around here in the mornings, thinking no one's paying any attention.'

'Sahib,' Lal Ram pulled on the Corporal's sleeve urgently, 'Clark sahib still needs our help.'

'Yes, but what are we to do, boy? Bugger could be anywhere in the town by now, he could. Prob'ly selling that bloomin' book by now.' The Mess Corporal finished on a note of gloom.

'Can you call the CO sahib?' Lal Ram persisted.

The Mess Corporal staggered back, scandalized.

'Call the CO? Don't be daft, lad! I'll get thrown in the quarterguard for a month if I do that.' He pulled a severe face at the boy.

Indumati asked Lal Ram impatiently for a quick translation of what had transpired. When she comprehended the information, she digested it for a couple of dismayed minutes; then she pulled the end of her sari over her head and took a decision.

'Tell this soldier bhai,' she instructed Lal Ram, 'that we shall go and help Clark sahib. But he must stay here and help make tea if any officer comes in wanting food and drink.' Lal Ram translated and the Mess Corporal became a picture of relief.

'O' course, o' course, you chappies can come and go, you probably have a pass, right? Well, hurry along, hurry along, then. Don't worry, I'll make sure that every bleedin' officer has whatever he needs till the woman here gets back. Maybe I'll have Fred up from the quarterguard, if the sarge allows it. We'll come up with some tea and toast and boiled eggs between us, we will.'

Taking turns to wash their hands and faces at the garden tap, Ramu, Indumati and Lal Ram set off on their quest to recover the portfolio.

As they exited the rear gate of the mess grounds, Indumati suddenly stopped.

'Lal,' she said, 'how are we going to get the CO sahib's help? You are just a boy, and Hari's father and I are strangers here.' There was an ominous rumble in the distance, all three turned hopefully to look at the clouds but the only thing that met their eyes was a thick haze of burning, sweltering heat.

'I know,' said Lal Ram, hesitantly again. 'There is the memsahib.'

'Arey, there are memsahibs and memsahibs only, in this cantonment,' said Indumati, annoyed. 'Which one will come here in this heat to help us?'

'I know, I know, Mataji!' Lal Ram said. 'The young memsahib!' He knew, of course, all servants always knew, the comings and the goings in the officers' houses. And the Holmes's servant, Rati Ram, was an acquaintance of his from the hills. So, Lal Ram knew about Anna.

'We will leave for the fair,' Indumati told the boy. 'If this young lady is not at home, then meet us near the big tree by the gates.' She and Ramu began their long, slow trudge through the murky heat towards the iron gates of the cantonment.

Lal Ram was off in a flash, his thin legs pumping as he raced towards No. 16 Peterson Road, the residence of Col. Richard Holmes, CO of the 126th East Yorkshire Regiment. His throat was as dry as a piece of old bark by the time he reached the CO's house. He knew better than to try and enter boldly by the front gate. He would be caught and turned out without any discussion. The lad went around to the back of the house where a small gate opened onto a dusty path that led to the servants' quarters, a set of rooms that had been converted from the original stables, reminder of an era when the residents of the bungalow had ridden to hounds and when syces and grooms had lived in the small, cell-like rooms.

Now, everybody had retired to their rooms and lay gasping on their mats, hoping, hoping for some relief, some break from the heat. Lal Ram was stuck. He could not enter without causing suspicion, and yet there was no one outside to whom he could turn for help. Luckily, one of the servants' dogs came out and snarled upon seeing the stranger. Lal Ram reached out a hand which led to a cacophony of barking. Irritated, one of the servants came out to investigate.

'Please send Rati Ram out, bhai,' Lal Ram implored. 'It is very important that I speak with him right away. He is from my village.' The boy hoped the small lie would work.

It did. The bearer had been about to send the boy on his way, but when he mentioned the village, he decided not to take a chance. Grumbling loudly about people who disturbed resting workers at very odd hours of the day, the bearer put on his white shirt and cap and went to fetch Rati Ram from the pantry, where the man was trying to while the hot afternoon away by polishing the cutlery under the electric fan.

Rati Ram was surprised to hear that someone from his village had come to deliver a message for him, and was even more surprised to see Lal Ram standing near the gate.

'What is it, boy?' he demanded. 'Is it news from home?'

'Ratibhaiyya,' Lal Ram folded his hands in a pleading gesture. 'I must meet the young memsahib. You know, Clark sahib . . .'

'Yes, yes,' Rati Ram cut all the indiscreet verbiage short. 'What is it?'

'Clark sahib needs the memsahib's help.' Lal Ram began to lie desperately. 'He has sent me to ask her for something. He is out of the cantonment but he needs a book.' That much at least was true, Lal Ram reasoned.

Rati Ram digested the information slowly.

'I don't know, lad,' he said. 'Is there a chitthi?'

'No, Clark sahib is at the District Magistrate's house for lunch,' Lal Ram lunged on, trying to make it sound important. 'And he needs the memsahib to look for a book. He phoned the Mess Corporal who asked me to come here and talk to the young memsahib and give her the message personally.' It all came out sounding rather odd but Rati Ram acquiesced. In fact, the man had been persuaded not by the reference to the District Magistrate but by that to the Mess Corporal. The indolent English soldier, thought Rati Ram, had probably been feeling too lazy in this heat to walk over, and therefore had sent the boy, without even a chitthi, to give Anna memsahib the message. Rati Ram sighed and told Lal Ram to unlatch the gate and come into the compound. He saw the obvious look of thirst on the boy's face and had him go over to the garden tap and slake his thirst. Lal Ram drank gratefully, and then drew some water on his face and head to help cool the heat that gripped him tightly.

During the short walk over to the bungalow, Rati Ram instructed the boy about how to behave in a big house full of important people—remain quiet until spoken to, only answer questions and offer no further comments, etc.—and walked him around the side to a screened veranda where the khus-khus mats had been lowered over the wire screens in a futile attempt to cool the air, now laden with both heat and dampness.

'Wait here,' Rati Ram commanded Lal and then went inside to inform Anna. She appeared, still sleep-dishevelled, her hair pulled back into a hasty ponytail, wearing khaki pants and a short-sleeved white blouse, her face flushed with the heat. She looked at Lal Ram without recognition. They had never seen each other before. Lal Ram began to speak slowly in English, the way that Miss Williams in the mission school had taught him. This annoyed Rati Ram hugely, for he could no longer eavesdrop on the conversation. In a huff, he took himself back to the kitchen and began once again to polish the cutlery with a cloth now blackened with Silvo.

'Miss-sahib,' Lal Ram said, after introducing himself. 'Clark sahib needs some help. The American sahib has taken the book.'

'What book?' Anna became alert.

'The book full of pictures, you know . . . sahib uses the book for Indumati's cooking.'

'Oh yes, the recipes!' Anna exclaimed. She had never seen the book, but George had spoken of it so much that she knew what Lal Ram was talking about. 'What happened to them?'

'The American sahib . . . Porter sahib,' Lal was babbling now, 'he came to the room in the afternoon when Clark sahib was out at lunch and he took the book from me. He snatched it from my hand and he went away. Then I telephoned Clark sahib and he came back; there was another English mem, and now they have gone to look for Porter sahib. They have gone to the donkey fair to look for him. Please miss-sahib, he needs your help to call the CO sahib to get the book back.'

Anna was far too sensible to question the events as presented.

'That goddamn swine!' Anna cursed. 'You wait here. No, go around the front of the house and wait under the porch, there's plenty of shade there. I will be right out.' She marched inside, calling for Ellen.

'Ell, I'm off to get Richard. We might need to go to the donkey fair,' she told her sister as she put on some sturdy sandals. Her sister, who had been resting in bed, sat up and groaned.

'Not again, Anna, must you go to these strange places? And it's so *hot*!' When she saw that Anna was determined, she gave in resignedly. 'Who knows what sort of people are there?'

'Oh, all sorts of swine, Ell, absolute pigs!' Anna spat out the words. She marched into the hall, picked up the telephone and demanded a connection to the CO. He wasn't there still. But Anna knew where he was, at the stables with Muriel Bates, listening to her weepy recital of her dead husband's poetry.

Anna sighed. Really, Muriel picked very inconvenient times. Ellen was holding on the door frame, watching her.

'We'll be back very soon. You look tired, Ell. You're getting enough sleep at night?'

Ellen covered her mouth with her hand, retched, and then sank into a little heap on the floor.

'Oh God! Rati Ram, Rati Ram!' Anna yelled for the servants. Rati Ram came running, then stopped aghast. He quickly turned around and ran for the ayah. This was one for the ladies. The ayah, Rani, who had been sleeping on a mat in the kitchen rushed in, then she and Anna half-carried, half-dragged Ellen over to the bed.

'I will go get some water, miss-sahib,' Rani said. 'You loosen her clothing. It is too hot, she cannot take it anymore.' Anna moved around, and quickly loosened first Ellen's dress, then her bra and underwear, pulling a cotton sheet over her legs for modesty's sake. Ellen moaned and came to in a struggling little sigh.

'Oh, my head hurts, Anna,' she whimpered.

'Yes, dear, you fainted. Now lie down. Oh, good, here's Rani with some nice, iced water. Drink up, there you go.' Talking calmly, Anna moved around the bed, helping her sister up, fluffing the pillows, adjusting the speed of the electric fan.

'Oh, Anna, I'm so sorry, you should go now,' Ellen apologized feebly.

'Don't worry, Ell, I'll set you up here, before I go.' Anna couldn't help looking at the old alarm clock on the dresser.

'It's the heat, Ell, the heat's got to you. You need to rest a lot and drink lots of water.' Ellen opened her eyes, retched again, and finally told Anna everything.

'Oh, my!' Anna exclaimed, looking at her sister in amazement.

'Ell, why, honey, that's wonderful! You silly idiot, you never told anyone yet. You have told Richard, haven't you?' It was at this point that Colonel Holmes walked in, just as Anna had folded her sister into a heartfelt embrace.

'Told me what?' He asked, looking dumbfounded at his wife, lying pale and wan on the pillows. Anna was about to start scolding him for neglecting his wife, then common sense got the better of her and she exited, saying, 'Well, I'll let you two discuss things. Richard, I'll wait for you in the drawing room.'

A further ten minutes elapsed before Col. Holmes entered the drawing room. He blushed and stammered when Anna offered congratulations, then said, 'Ellen is going to take a nap now. What *is* happening, Anna? Who is that strange boy skulking around the porch? And where are you going in this heat?'

Anna quickly filled him in on what had transpired and on the message brought over by Lal Ram.

The CO slapped his hand against his thigh in irritation.

'That Porter and Ruffington again! And damn that Clark! He's always up to something or the other that needs my intervention. Wait here, I need to telephone someone.'

From the drawing room, Anna heard him making a number of phone calls, then there was a final conversation that began with, 'Col. Holmes here. I'd like to speak with you regarding that damn fool, Dennis Porter' and ended with 'Be here in ten minutes sharp. I'm perfectly well aware that you are in a conference—at the *club*, I believe. No, it will *not* wait!' Slam went the phone.

When Col. Holmes returned, his face was thunderous. But he was also worried.

'Well, much as I would like to go and kick those two idiots personally, I cannot go nor can I have you going into donkey fairs, Anna. It just wouldn't be safe. Or proper. Can we send the servants, do you think? Or maybe you could ask your Indian friends if they can perhaps send their servants to hunt Porter down?'

'Oh, Richard! I should have thought of that! Why, of course, Mira and her family will help, for sure.' Anna rushed off to make phone calls. Ten minutes later, she returned, looking relieved.

'Mira will come. She'll bring some people too. But they need us to meet them at the cantonment gates as they don't have permission to enter and it will take too much time to get official clearance. Let's go, Richard!'

She also explained to him that Lal Ram was waiting in the porch. Col. Holmes groaned.

'I really have to draw the line at civilians piling into army vehicles, Anna,' he said, exasperatedly. 'The servants can go in our personal car. You can travel with me in the staff car. I'll leave a note for Ruffington to meet us at the cantonment gates.'

'Just a minute, Richard.' Anna ran back into her sister's room, hugged her gently and for a long minute, then ran to wear a hat and snatch her dark glasses off the hall bureau.

In the porch, the two cars, a civilian Morris 8 and a military Morris 10, drew up in a little convoy. Lal Ram got into the CO's ageing car, taking the seat next to the driver, and they were off. Anna could not help noticing with pity that he was so thin and emaciated that he barely took up any place at all.

'You're taking your camera with you? On this dangerous mission?' Richard asked archly when they were finally on their way, his upper lip showing the edges of a smile.

'It's the only weapon I have, sir,' Anna grinned, patting the long lens of her camera, the brown leather strap dangling from her neck.

In front of them the haze thickened and swirled. The car paused for the sentry to open the cantonment gates and then they were out, raising more powdery earth to join the already dust-thickened air. Anna coughed into her handkerchief. Oh George, she thought, couldn't you have picked a better day to call for me, a better season, a better place than Bajapur? I don't know if I can do this, I don't know if my weak Minnesota body can make it through the day. She closed her eyes, the heat pressing against the lids, she could hardly bear to open them again and face the glare. Her stomach churned, the smell of petrol adding to the unbearable-ness of it all.

Luckily, Mira Chaturvedi and her entourage were not too long in arriving. She looked as energetic as ever, in her crisp, starched cotton sari. She then hauled out a sheepish Shyam Bharadwaj, her uncle, who smiled at Anna and nodded at Richard Holmes.

'I had to really twist Shyamchacha's arm,' said Mira. 'He was a little reluctant to tear himself away from the local committee meeting, but I convinced him that the donkey fair had lots of proletarians who needed to be organized.'

'I don't know,' said Shyam, shaking his head ruefully. 'Who would have thought that family obligations would reduce me, a card-carrying member of the Communist Party of India, to helping out members of the unrepentantly imperialist bourgeoisie?' He grinned at his niece.

'Anna is my friend,' said Mira, firmly. 'So you have to help her. Now what is this book of paintings that has been stolen, Anna?'

'It's a book of recipes,' Anna explained. 'I've never seen it, but Deborah gave it to George as a present when he was in Pithampur. The borders have been painted by Satinder and his friends, while they were in prison. From what I gather, Porter seems to think it's yet another clue in his goddamn quest to dig out communists in Bajapur and in the army.'

'So . . .' said Shyam, 'he thinks these recipes are subversive?'

'Oh, I guess. He probably thinks it's a communist cookbook with lots of code hidden in it.'

'Splendid!' said Shyam. 'I will be delighted to track this down. Are you sure he went to the donkey fair, though?'

'That is what Clark sahib said,' interjected Lal Ram, who had been listening quietly so far.

Shyam turned to him, interestedly.

'Why do you think Capt. Porter would head to the donkey fair?'

'I think,' said Lal Ram slowly, 'if what Miss Anna is saying is true about Capt. Porter's desire to find communists, then there are many working-class people at the fair. Capt. Porter may have gone there to see if he could use the code on them.'

'What an intelligent boy!' Shyam was effusive in his praise. 'Well, Mira, looks like this old radical has to go and hunt down a communist cookery book. But I will need the help of genuine proletarians in this task. Col. Holmes, may I borrow your civilian staff to augment my own forces?' He gestured and out of the Bharadwaj family car emerged two large, rather menacing-looking men.

'And mataji and babuji are also waiting for us by the tree near the fair,' offered Lal Ram. 'There will be enough people.'

'Wait!' said Mira Chaturvedi, fiddling with her handbag. 'Here, Chachaji, when you find those paintings, please wrap them in this oilcloth. They need to be protected from heat, dust and damp. I cannot believe that this man, this Porter, has been so careless with paintings done by Romesh Gupta and the Pithampur group of artists!'

At this point, James Ruffington drew up next to the group in a black staff car that was considerably nicer than Col. Holmes's vehicle. Close behind came a police car, driven by ASP Ramakant Batra.

'Good afternoon, sir,' said Ruffington smoothly to Col. Holmes. 'I was having a meeting with ASP Batra here over some common threats to the military and the police, when your phone call came through.'

'It was more like an extended tea break,' said Batra, looking coldly at Ruffington. 'But your call, Col. Holmes, sounded urgent, so I followed Capt. Ruffington here in case my help was required.'

The CO explained through gritted teeth that Dennis Porter had stolen the personal property of a unit officer, 2/Lt George Clark. And that if the item was not returned immediately, then there would be calls made all the way up to Simla, if necessary. James Ruffington made placating noises.

'I'm sure it's all a mistake, Col. Holmes, sir,' he said. 'I'll make sure that Porter brings the book back at once.'

'George used the book to order meals at the mess,' said Anna. 'And I've heard that Indumati's cooking does full justice to those recipes.'

'In that case, the charge against Capt. Porter is even more serious,' said Richard Holmes, looking grimmer. 'He has stolen my battalion property and has disrupted battalion harmony.'

'It will be my pleasure to assist this investigation,' said Ramakant Batra, straightening his peak cap. 'I think Capt. Ruffington here could use some lessons in old-fashioned policing. Chalo, ladke.' He commanded Lal Ram to begin walking towards the donkey fair. Several plain-clothes policemen appeared out of Batra's vehicle and were quickly dispatched to search the fair grounds for two white men and an English lady.

'Super, splendid!' said Shyam Bharadwaj as he led the group away. 'An example of perfect cooperation between the armed apparatus of the state, the party of the workers, and genuine proletarians.'

'If you ever step into my unit barracks with your propaganda, I will arrest you,' said Col. Holmes, seriously.

'Oh, I have no doubt about that, Colonel, no doubt at all. Anna, are you coming too? Surely not.'

'Oh yes, I am,' said Anna, looking defiantly at her brother-in-law. 'Come *on*, Richard! When will I get another chance like this to photograph a donkey fair? And I have a police escort too.' Richard Holmes waved her away, resignedly.

'I'm going to get permission for you civilians to enter the cantonment,' he told Shyam Bharadwaj as the group vanished into the shimmering haze. 'We shall meet you in the battalion mess. Ruffington, you are to report back to the 126th East Yorks mess,' he barked, as he and Mira got into their cars to proceed to the cantonment.

It was easy to arrange for the drivers to be accommodated at the back of the mess, and then to place phone calls to Brigade Headquarters seeking permission for civilian visitors to the mess. It was even easier to curtly order James Ruffington to wait in the anteroom. Far more awkward for Col. Holmes was dealing with Mira Chaturvedi whom he finally installed in the covered veranda at one side of the mess building. It was that annoying time, right between lunch and tea, when one could not really distract a guest with lots of food and drink. Richard Holmes had never been a graceful one with the ladies, and he was now reduced to a series of clumsy 'er's' and 'umm's'. He longed for Ellen's pleasant social dispensation just then. She would have handled this situation without any problems. Thinking of Ellen and her news made him smile inwardly. All of a sudden, the future seemed hopeful again despite the clammy heat that bore down all around, despite the thick and angry clouds that threatened but did not deliver the longed-for driving rain, despite the exhausted grass that lay parched and matted all around the building.

'Do you have any children, Mrs Chaturvedi?'

'Two, a boy and a girl,' said Mira, so used to being in unexpected social situations, thanks to her political activities, that Richard's discomfiture had not registered at all with her. 'And I wish they would get to spend more time in school than they do. The situation in the town is very strained and tense, you understand, Col. Holmes?'

Richard was about to tell her of the flag marches his troops had conducted when Maj. Burr, the staff officer to the Brigade Commander, made an appearance, saluting the Colonel and acknowledging Mira's presence.

'Brig. Curtis's compliments, sir. He heard that you had some problems with Captains Ruffington and Porter. He's sent me over to assist you in any way I can.'

'Ah, thank you, Burr. Much obliged.' Richard Holmes explained again the case of the missing portfolio of recipes.

'Well, it's time to put an end to all this nonsense,' said Maj. Burr smoothly, the experienced staff officer in him taking over, picking up the burdens of senior officers with practised ease. 'I'll take care of it, sir. The Brigade Commander has been quite fed up and made some telephone calls to Simla this morning. Turns out that Ruffington has really no written authorization for this show he's running here in Bajapur.' He retreated into the anteroom to confront Ruffington.

Mira Chaturvedi had been fanning herself with the end of her sari during this interlude and examining the armour that hung as display on the veranda walls.

'These are quite impressive,' she said. "Did your unit ever serve in China, Col. Holmes?'

'Not recently. Those are what the 33rd King's Own—one of the constituent units of my battalion—er, picked up in the last century when they were in Shanghai during the Boxer rebellion.'

'Well, let us call it what it is—loot,' said Mira, crisply. 'But now that you have inherited it, it is your responsibility to take care of it. Do you know what you have here, Col. Holmes?'

'No.' The CO looked at her curiously.

'Here, hanging on your walls, exposed to the elements, is Ming-era lamellar armour. Do you see this scale-like construction, without any cloth or leather backing? It probably belonged to a cavalryman and helped protect him from arrows. Do you have more things like these?'

'Oh! Richard Holmes was staggered. 'Yes, we have a lot of Chinese bowls and stuff in our dining room and also shields, and things like that.'

'Well, you have to take care of these things, you know.' Mira was stern. 'Are they all catalogued?' Holmes shook his head.

'Well, I could take a look at it,' Mira offered. 'But when you finally return to England, you must have an expert in to examine them. In the meantime, please make sure that no one on your mess staff takes strong acid to this delicate metal. And please, no Silvo!' The mess staff was sent for and instructed right away on the proper care of early modern armour.

'Oh, I say,' said Richard Holmes, immensely pleased. 'I'm ever so grateful. Actually, the whole battalion is really obliged to you. Would love to have you and your husband over sometime, if that's all right.'

'Well, thank you, Colonel Holmes,' Mira accepted the invitation. 'Although I hope you understand that this in no way releases me from my political obligations in Bajapur?' Her large, brown eyes looked at him calmly, unafraid. In her gaze, Richard Holmes saw clearly the retreat of armies, ships moving away, uncelebrated, from shores on which they had arrived unheralded. He nodded.

'I too have certain responsibilities,' he replied. 'If that uncle of yours comes by my barracks, I shall arrest him.'

'That uncle of mine is perfectly capable of looking after himself,' Mira retorted. 'As is my husband's uncle, fighting on the other side of the barricades. It's we, the others, who somehow have to find a way to muddle through all the death, destruction and chaos.'

Before Richard Holmes could reply, the monsoon burst all around them with a crash, like an exploding boiler. Fat, heavy raindrops came down like bullets, and lightning crackled on the horizon. Claps of thunder burst everywhere in quick succession, out of engorged, enraged, purple clouds.

'The rains,' whispered Mira, joyfully. 'At last, they are here.' She leaned out of the veranda, letting the plump drops of water run down her arm. The water beaded on the dust-covered bushes and dripped onto the grass that had been dried almost into straw over the summer.

'I think this calls for a relaxation of the rules against ladies in the mess,' Col. Holmes said and ushered Mira Chaturvedi into the anteroom where Ruffington sat sulkily next to a victorious-looking Maj. Burr.

Just as the Mess Corporal was getting into a bustle about drinks and refreshments, switching on lights, closing the windows against the rain that now lashed the walls, the party that had set out for the donkey fair began to trickle into the mess. A scandalized Guard Commander led Shyam Bharadwaj, Deborah Silonia and Anna into the anteroom. They were followed closely by George and a thunderous-looking Dennis Porter. All were dripping wet and the Mess Corporal was sent away for hot tea and napkins.

'All them servants is gone around the back, sah,' the Guard Commander told the CO before returning to his duties at the gate.

Deborah and Anna retreated to the Ladies' Room to dry themselves, followed by Mira who asked excited questions all the way.

'I believe this belongs to you,' said Shyam, handing over to Col. Holmes a bundle wrapped in oilcloth. Richard opened it gingerly. In the yellow light of the electric bulb, the colours on the pages looked golden and rich, shadows falling at angles across patterns and words. Here was the recipe for that delicious cucumber soup he had eaten the other day at lunch, all light and dark greens, from the fat cucumber on the vine, to the sari of the woman in her little vegetable patch.

'Amazing!' he exclaimed.

Dennis Porter stepped forward, breaking protocol and military etiquette, brushing past Richard Holmes.

'It was you all the time!' He snarled at James Ruffington who stood looking bewildered and crestfallen. 'You're the communist! This is your codebook!'

'What on earth are you *talking* about?' screeched Ruffington.

'He told me that you were in cahoots with him in Pithampur!' Porter gestured at Shyam Bharadwaj. 'You and he were the two communist spies there. While he was in jail, you were helping him communicate with the other prisoners. No wonder we never got anywhere in Pithampur.'

Ruffington looked at Bharadwaj, stunned. Shyam bowed slightly.

'That's just absurd,' Ruffington finally got something out.

'Now, you two,' said Maj. Burr, of Brigade Headquarters. 'That's enough! Ruffington, Porter, report to my office right now.' He led the two men away into the gloam-like afternoon, lashed with rain and thunder. The Mess Corporal arrived with a bearer and soon cups of hot tea were being distributed. It was followed by piping hot pakoras and toast and jam. Clearly, Indumati had wasted no time in getting back to work.

'I don't believe I understood that,' said Col. Holmes as the women came back into the room.

'Ah, Capt. Ruffington had it coming,' said Shyam, biting into a pakora. 'But to be honest, it was also the only way we could get Porter back to the cantonment without murdering Indumati. And far more than me, it was those three, Lal Ram, Indumati and Ramu Chowkidar, who saved the day.'

When the little group had set out for the donkey fair, there hadn't been much chatter in the crushing heat. The police contingent led by ASP Batra walked ahead, authoritatively. A five-minute silent walk had brought them suddenly to the scene, astonishing to Anna, interesting to the others. There were donkeys everywhere, mostly grey, here and there an occasional fleck of black, fading into the horizon that was hazy and the colour of gunmetal. The two concave halves of the field met in a gulley, a dusty line right now which no doubt was a roaring stream in the rainy season. Oh, the rain, the rain, why did it not come, thought Indumati. The clouds were so thick, the rumbles of thunder so regular, but it was a rainless, red heat that bounced off the backs of an undulating field of grey that moved and brayed and sometimes kicked.

Indumati stopped and spoke rapidly to Lal Ram.

'Sahib,' Lal Ram conveyed the message to Shyam Bharadwaj. 'Mataji says that we should split up into two groups to search the fair.'

'Perhaps, meet in the middle? That is a good idea,' said Shyam. 'Anna, you stay with me since you don't speak the language. Lal Ram, why don't you, Ramu and Indumati take the other side of the field? Let's meet in twenty minutes and see what happens.' ASP Batra, who was not used to being ordered around by either communists or servants, grunted and took off with his own posse. Surveillance was a policeman's forte and the cops were not about to be directed by a bunch of amateurs.

Given the oddness of a white woman in khaki trousers at the fair, it was only a matter of minutes before Shyam's group acquired a trail of followers, mostly little boys and girls. Like the Pied Piper of Hamelin, thought Anna. They were joined by several pye-dogs and a small boy leading a goat.

Anna's mind wandered into random thoughts as she ploughed through the fair in the blistering heat. It was a good thing I grabbed my wide-brimmed hat on the way out of the door. How privileged I have been, I was busy taking photographs of political meetings but I never dared set foot in places like this fair. Poor Ellen, oh lucky Ellen, how pleased Mom and Pop will be to hear the news. I bet Mom starts knitting little hats right away. Oh, this heat, this heat! Oh, I wish I were back in the cool stillness of Minnesota. Chilled watermelon slices, iced lemonade, walking around Lyndale Park, the cool breeze off Lake Calhoun. Once I am done with this, she resolved, I am going back to the States, to Duluth to rest a while in Grandpa's old summer home with its porch catching the cool breezes blowing off Lake Superior. It would be cool there, so cool and so green and so calm that one could rest forever. Then, she tried to get a grip on her thoughts. Concentrate now, girl, she told herself, you have to find George and help him find Porter and get the book back.

Despite the grimness of the mission, Anna found time to stop and take some pictures. She would never get this opportunity again, she knew. There was one particularly nice one of a group of owners leaning on their animals, in the pitiful shade of a thorn tree, gossiping and smoking bidis. There were some women too, in bright saris, one of them bargaining with customers. The heat made the woman's face shine and down her armpits ran rivulets of sweat that drenched her blouse down the side. I wonder if she would mind if I took her photograph, Anna considered her options. That thought startled her. Only a few years ago, she had been a hard-boiled, self-absorbed photographer who rarely noticed the objects of her interest except in terms of lighting and frames. Boy, have I changed, she thought as she took the pictures (without asking for permission) and scanned the horizon over the backs of the animals, looking for a dark, slim young man, her love.

On their side of the fair, Lal Ram, Indumati and Ramu Chowkidar pushed donkeys out of their way effortlessly, clucking, shouting, tweaking tails, so much so that the group made very good time, first going up the slope of the field, then down again towards the gulley. Like beating for tigers, theirs was a methodical sweep through the grey jungle of donkeys. The smell, not surprisingly, was overwhelming when combined with the heat. Here in the Bajapur donkey fair, it was of animal dung, cheap bidis, urine, sweat, some strong flowery odour, and dust, dust, dust.

The three of them could see Shyam, Anna and the two burly guards walking down the other side of the gulley, almost at the bottom of the slope, when Lal Ram spotted Porter. He stood with two other people, neither one of them a farmer or a peasant, under a parched tree, conferring. A book-like object was clamped under the officer's arm. Some men, clearly their servants, waited around them.

Like a leopard, ASP Batra emerged at Lal Ram's side.

'What do you see, lad?' Lal Ram pointed wordlessly to Porter and his companions.

'That is the book he took from my hands, sahib.'

The plain-clothes policemen emerged from the crowd at a sign from their boss.

On the other side of the gulley, they joined Anna and Shyam Bharadwaj. All of them looked at Porter and his friends, who had their backs to the group.

'Well, I can certainly question Capt. Porter,' said ASP Batra. 'But I can't arrest him, you know, without military permission. And as for the others, do you really want a relative in prison?' He pointed to one of Porter's companions, the portly Amar Mani Chaturvedi. 'The other gentleman is Mir Ali Sharif, again not a personage I could arrest for the sake of a book.'

'Why is the bourgeoisie at a donkey fair?' murmured Shyam.

'Well, it's the safest place to meet. Of course, that explains it. Porter isn't here to harangue the proletarians. He wouldn't know how. He's meeting with his local collaborators to try and figure out this so-called code. Ha! Well, now we know where they meet.' ASP Batra drummed his fingers on his thigh triumphantly.

'I will get the book back, sahib!' Lal Ram asserted. 'I have an idea.'

'Be sure that your idea doesn't earn you a beating, lad,' said Shyam. 'Those servants of Sharif mian and Amar bhaisahib look quite bad-tempered.'

But Lal Ram was already leading Indumati and Ramu towards the confabulating trio.

'I'm going along too,' said Shyam. He followed the three discreetly.

ASP Batra signalled one of his men to stay with Anna, while he began to assess the potential for a riot in case of a confrontation between Shyam Bharadwaj and the others.

Lal Ram walked up boldly to Dennis Porter, trailed a little cautiously by Indumati and Ramu Chowkidar.

'Ram-Ram, sahib,' he greeted Porter. Mir Ali Sharif and Amar Mani Chaturvedi looked at him scornfully, a mere servant walking up so impertinently to the rich and powerful. Their attendants looked at him even more menacingly. Trying to quell his nerves, Lal Ram began to speak slowly in English, just as he had been taught.

'That book, sahib, is very important,' he said.

'I bet it is!' Porter barked a laugh. 'What sort of things does your master cook up with this, is what I'd like to know.'

'I'm the one who knows the secret that you're looking for. You see, that book is meant for me. The pictures carry the commands. Each time Clark sahib reads out the recipes, he is actually reading from . . .'

'A communist cookbook,' finished Porter. 'But you hardly look like a senior member of the Communist Party.' Mir Ali Sharif and Amar Mani Chaturvedi laughed derisively.

'Pranam, bhaisahib.' Shyam Bharadwaj emerged from the crowd.

'Arey, Shyam. *Tum yahan?*' Mr Chaturvedi was perplexed. 'What are you doing here?'

'Oh, just organizing the toiling masses here in Bajapur. For some unfathomable reason, the masses do not wish to be organized by me.'

'I think,' said Mir Ali Sharif, eyeing Shyam and assessing him. 'I think, Capt. Porter, that you are mistaken this time. This is just a collection of paintings and recipes, more to do with housewives than communists. Shyam, is this from your people?' Mir Ali Sharif handed over the portfolio to Shyam to examine.

'Very amusing, gentlemen, that you think that this bunch of pretty pictures has anything to do with my party. Despite what the boy here says, do you really think we communists would be doing something as bourgeois as cooking? And that too out of a book?' Shyam's tone was dry, masking the nervousness he felt.

Mir Ali Sharif's servant landed a blow on Lal Ram's back that almost doubled the boy over.

'How dare you say this book is yours, you thief!' He began to yell. The Chaturvedi retainers looked ready to join in, and the situation was quickly made worse when Indumati came up and pushed Mr Sharif's servant hard, scooping Lal Ram close to her. Ramu Chowkidar ran up to defend his wife from the blow that was certain to land on her.

Before he could stop her, Indumati took the portfolio from Shyam's hand and ran off into the crowd. Ramu followed and the situation looked like it was going to get out of control—with the Sharif and Chaturvedi lathiyals making menacing moves— when ASP Batra and his policemen appeared. Everybody sobered up immediately. Suddenly, Lal Ram spoke up.

'Why don't you tell Porter sahib who the actual ringleader is?' he made a desperate overture to Shyam, silently imploring him to take up the lie and run with it, and give Indumati and Ramu time to get away. And Shyam obliged, struck with sudden, manic inspiration that made the words flow with powerful persuasive force.

'You have gone to such trouble, Capt. Porter, to find a code that we communists are supposed to be using. That cookery book is nothing, just a harmless collection of recipes from some artists residing in Pithampur. But in your pursuit of all this silliness, you've neglected to investigate the most obvious ringleader of all these subversive activities in Bajapur. How do you think we can operate with such impunity if we were not connected to someone powerful and, more importantly, agreeable to our ideology? He has you in his grip, Capt. Porter, and you dance willy-nilly to his tune. Excuse the mixed metaphors and all that. He works with you, dines with you, goes out to parties with you and yet he is also our biggest patron.'

'Ruffington . . .' breathed Porter.

'And to show you just how closely we work together, I will return immediately to Mr Clark's battalion mess where I have arranged for Capt. Ruffington to be there, waiting for me. See, he can even arrange a pass for me, the radical communist that I am, to visit him inside the cantonment. If you don't believe me, come with me and see for yourself.' The rains broke just then and everybody scattered, Porter accompanying Shyam with an angry glare in his eye.

'They found us walking back to the car, sir,' said George, picking up the story. 'Deborah and I were unable to find Porter. But of course we thought he was involved with buying and selling donkeys, and interrogating the farmers. Didn't imagine he would hold his political meetings in that place. Then we found Indumati and the others scampering back to the cantonment, as fast as they could. Mr Bharadwaj had to hurry and wrap the paintings in oilcloth before they got all soaked.'

'You picked Ruffington for a reason, didn't you?' asked Col. Holmes, looking at Shyam Bharadwaj.

'Oh, actually five very good reasons, Colonel Holmes,' said Shyam, holding up his deformed fingers. 'You see, Capt. Ruffington was a frequent visitor to Pithampur prison during my time there, although of course he doesn't recognize me. He could have put a stop to the torture and the beatings anytime he wished to. But he let many innocent people die. And while I am entirely willing to stand up for my beliefs, backed as I am by a powerful and well-connected family, there were very many people there, innocent of all ideological affiliations, who confessed to all sorts of crimes just to stop the inflicted pain, but who died nonetheless. And so, although I was just babbling when I blurted out Ruffington's name, I feel, in an odd, irrational way, that all those suffering people were speaking through me to ruin Ruffington's relationship with his chief patron. It will never be the same again, you know, even if the misunderstanding is cleared up. Porter will never again trust Capt. Ruffington completely, or at least not enough to fund his activities. But enough about me, Col. Holmes, you must be relieved at how this has ended?'

'My first duty,' Richard Holmes said evenly, 'is to my country— even if it sounds trite to you. And my second duty is to my battalion. That collection of recipes is used to make the most delicious meals for my battalion's officers who dine at the mess. It is not just Clark's book, it is unit property and it is back where it belongs rightfully. I thank you for your efforts but as far as I'm concerned, you, Ruffington and Porter are all, in your different ways, against what I believe in. So, if you ever disrupt my battalion's routine and harmony, I will come all the way to your Politburo if necessary, to arrest you.'

'And I shall spend the rest of my week, writing pamphlets against the organized economic extortion that is the British Army in India,' said Shyam, rising wearily to his feet. 'But I admire your devotion to your battalion. Anna, will you make sure that Mira and Deborah bhabhi reach home safely? I need the car to go somewhere else. Oh, and when your unit leaves the station, Col. Holmes, could you send Indumati and her husband over to our Bharadwaj family house? Mira's husband may be able to employ them in his expanding hotel and guest house business. George, don't be surprised if you see Lal Ram disappear from your employ. I think he has a bright future ahead of him, but I need to train him for that. Good afternoon, Col. Holmes. It's been a pleasure.'

He walked out into the downpour, a slim figure in well-cut clothes, whose mangled left hand clutched an unlit French cigarette. In a matter of seconds, he was lost to view, vanishing behind the sheets of rain that pierced the dry, cracked soil of Bajapur.

AUTHOR'S NOTE

Pithampur is a fictional princely state in the present-day Yamunanagar district of Haryana (what used to be eastern Punjab in British times). Bajapur, a fictional army cantonment, is close by, on the banks of the Yamuna. The 126th East Yorkshire Regiment is a fictional battalion, as are the 33rd battalion of the King's Own Regiment, and the 23rd East Yorkshire Regiment. The fort of Ahirabad is also fictional. But German prisoners of war were indeed imprisoned in the fort of Purandar near Pune. The detachment of the Seaforth Highlanders with whom George went on patrol in Burma did actually undertake similar missions in 1943.

Historical personalities apart—such as Carol Hagerman Durand, the first woman to qualify for the US Olympic equestrian team—the characters, places and political organizations mentioned in this book are fictional. Some, like Ramu Chowkidar, are inspired, though, by real-life personalities. While Captain Dennis Porter is a fictional caricature, his extreme ideology has real-life echoes. Major General Edwin Walker of the United States Army was dismissed from service in 1961 for his extreme anti-communist views in the 1950s and 1960s. At the other end of the spectrum, Americans like Anna Benson too existed, many of whom would eventually end up as targets of Senator Joseph McCarthy's anti-communist witch-hunts in the 1950s.

ACKNOWLEDGEMENTS

To my parents, Shankar and Krishna Roychowdhury—for giving me a unique childhood in places that helped me imagine Pithampur and Bajapur.

To the Indian Army—for little cantonment towns, and libraries full of dusty old books. That's where my love of reading and writing began.

To Bharati Jagannathan—more thanks than words can ever acknowledge. Our email interchanges kept the drafts of this novel focused, and gave an old friendship unexpected editorial dimensions.

To Wendy Batteau, for guiding me through the technicalities of the publishing world.

To all my editors at Penguin Books India—thank you! Mekhala Moorthy, Somak Ghoshal, Ambar Sahil Chatterjee and Shanuj V.C.—in particular. And to the larger team at PBI, many thanks.